Timel

The Law of

Timeless:
The Law of the Coven

Jessa Lynn Pease Garrett

Cover by Justine Dahl

Edited by Grace Keller Scotch

Jessa Lynn Pease Garrett
2020

First Printing: 2020

ISBN 9780578708034

Jessa Lynn Pease Garrett
Birmingham, AL

www.jessagarrett.com

Ordering Information:

Special discounts are available on quantity purchases by corporations, associations, educators, and others. For details, contact the publisher at the above listed address.

U.S. trade bookstores and wholesalers: Please contact Jessa Lynn Pease Garrett at TEL: 678-794-6356 or email authorjessagarrett@gmail.com.

For Joe, my Quincy
and
For Jessica, my Emily

Acknowledgments

They say during troublesome times you find out who your genuine friends are. The people who love and support you will show up in times of need, ready to help you through any mess or obstacle. I have found this to be 100% true.

I published my first book last year in February 2019. That was a massive high-point for me. I never expected to reach the amount of people I did, and I never expected *Timeless: The Becoming of a Teenage Witch* to become a favorite for students at a small middle school in Augusta, Ga. (Thank you buy the way!)

Despite the incredible excitement surrounding my first novel, 2019 was also one of the most tough years of my life. There was much loss—loss of loved ones and normalcy. I won't get into the details, but it was a tough year. We also found out how lucky and loved we are. Every person mentioned in my previous acknowledgements was there to prop us up, cry with us, face the battles with us, and stand beside up. You offered words of support, physical labor, and shoulders to lean on.

I think of Emlyn's journey. Didn't Emily, Marjorie, Jeb, and Quinn get Emlyn through everything she experienced in the last book? If *Timeless: The Becoming of a Teenage Witch* was about the strength you find in yourself after a significant loss, what must this book be about? How much support will Emlyn need as she faces even more adversity?

It was obvious from the start that this list of important characters would continue to grow to encompass and mirror what my husband and I have in our authentic life. There's a bit of everyone I love in this book—some are more clearly placed than others. Thank you to everyone who has been there for Joe and I, lending bits of your magic to improve our lives. Without your support and love, this second book wouldn't be reaching you this quickly.

Joe Garrett, my husband, who allowed me to bounce ideas off him all the time. He knew the story before I ever wrote it, and he was very patient during my ramblings.

Jenanne Hillman, my mother, who has always been my biggest fan.

Jeff Pease, my father, who literally bought a case of books to give to his clients' teenage children.

Justine Dahl, my sister, who designed the most amazing cover for my book and is responsible for the great following the first book has in Augusta.

Jillian Pease, my other sister, who has always encouraged me and who inspired me all the time with her originality.

The Skenders, my bonus family. You've always been there for me through everything, and it's always meant so much to me. Daniel included!

The Frands (Andrew, Derek, Erica, Keith, and Madison), my chosen family. The people who framed my first novel after it released and presented it to me like I was a big time author. No one could ask for better friends.

Grace E Keller Scotch, my editor extraordinaire, who took on more projects than I ever expected and has help shape this book into something I cherish. Thank you.

The Garretts/Tidewells, my in-laws, who inspired the safe house in Alabama with the very real dogs who live there.

Jeb and Zoe, my sweet pups. You may have passed, but you'll live on forever in these pages. I cherish the chapters you're in.

There are many more people who've been there for us. Even if you I didn't mention you by name, you know who you are. You're greatly appreciated.

Chapter One

I took a deep breath, absorbing the atmosphere of the crisp autumn evening. An altar, built on an orange silk cloth, sat in front of me as I knelt in the grass. Freshly carved pumpkin mixed with the scents of apple candles and burning cinnamon incense in the air. I'd carefully placed my silver chalice on the top left corner of the cloth with the face of the wolf gazing at me. The moonlight from above reflected in the dark red wine inside and shined brightly off the amethyst gemstones circling the rim of the cup. I'd gathered a selection of harvest crops—acorns, pomegranates, apples, and a brown gourd—and placed them around a stone-faced jack-o'-lantern to my right.

My eyes watched as the flickering light from the carved pumpkin's face danced across the ivy vines of my athame, my ceremonial knife. I'd placed it delicately in the center of my display. Three black candles, representing the Triple Goddess, were inches from my knee. The candles stood for the maiden, the mother, and the crone—the stages in a female life cycle. Among my many items, I'd also decorated the space in front of me with black gemstones positioned at five points around my incense-burning cauldron and my deck of tarot cards.

Sharing the center of my altar was a photograph of my mother, Rhiannon Finnerty-Perry, in a golden frame. The picture was taken when she was about 35, still youthful and untouched by age. Her wild, fire-red hair practically matched the orange tapestry beneath the altar, and her all-gums grin was the same one I thought of every time I pictured her face. She died a little more than a year ago when I was 17. But somehow? I felt closer to her than I ever had before.

"How long is this going to take? We have a party to get to!" a harsh whisper broke the silence of my concentration.

"Be quiet," an angry voice scolded. "I won't have you distract Emlyn. Wait in the car if you can't hush up."

The bickering voices belonged to my best friend, Emily, and my grandmother, Marjorie. I'd known Emily since kindergarten—we bonded over our similar names—but I'd only known Marjorie for about a year. After finding out I was a witch, I discovered Marjorie and her magic shop. That Halloween, Marjorie revealed she was my grandmother on my mother's side when she presented me with the family Book of Shadows. My parents decided when I was born not to raise me with magic, but my mother had second thoughts on my 15th birthday. She left me a copy of our Book of Shadows hidden on a flash drive under the floorboards of the house, leaving it up to fate to decide if I should inherit my powers. Fate also brought Marjorie and me together after 17 years of being estranged.

"Ugh... this is taking sooo long," Emily groaned.

"Hush!" Marjorie spat at Emily before sucking in a mouthful of night air to calm herself. Despite the loudness of their bickering behind me, I tuned them out. This was an important day for me, so I let all the distractions fade into emptiness. Tonight was Halloween, which meant it was Samhain for Celtic witches. This day welcomed the harvest and embraced the beginning of winter. Samhain was also a time to celebrate people who died, which was why I was sitting in a cemetery.

Bonaventure Cemetery dated back to the 1800s when the site was Bonaventure Plantation. Still, it was most famously known for the book and movie *Midnight in the Garden of Good and Evil*. It was a beautiful setting with rows of old oak trees, crypts, and elaborate tombstones. The grave of little Gracie Watson was a famous landmark, and tourists would come from all over to leave toys and dolls for the stone replica of Gracie. The cute six-year-old was the daughter of a hotel owner 125 years ago. She, unfortunately, died of pneumonia, but her memory lived on as the face of Bonaventure through postcards and paintings.

I was there for a more recent resident, though, on the opposite side of the cemetery from Gracie. I was there for Mom.

There are 78 cards in a tarot deck, each with its own interpretations and meanings. The question was imperative as well because one card could mean something different for a query about love versus one about a career path. My inquiry, the one I had come to the cemetery to ask, focused on my life's trajectory. I wanted guidance, and I wanted it from the person I trusted most: my mother.

I took my deck and shuffled thoroughly, focusing intently as I mixed the yellows and greys of the cards together. The tarot design I used was probably the most common one: the Rider-Waite deck. It utilized simple drawings and primary colors to illustrate meaning. The cards belonged to Marjorie first, which I felt cultivated a stronger bond. They were worn around the edges a bit, and the vibrant yellow colors had dulled into a pale cream now, but they had personality.

I cut the deck into five equal piles and set them face down on the cloth in front of me. A little more than a year ago, my journey as a witch began. Since then, I'd worked to cultivate one life to combine two seemingly separate identities. I started school at the Savannah College of Art and Design with two majors—art history and visual effects. Art was always part of my life, even before I was a witch. So, my goal was to work for a museum, because being a curator seemed like a good fit for my new identity in magic. Still, there was this nagging feeling I couldn't fight off, urging me to pick up where my mother left off. I felt compelled to continue her fight to protect light magic from dark witches.

"Tonight, the night of the Feast of the Dead, I invite the spirits of my ancestors to join me here. This night, when the veil between our worlds is thin, I call on thee with gratitude to grant me wisdom," I began. "I, Emlyn Finnerty-Perry, call deliberately on the spirit of my mother, Rhiannon Finnerty-Perry, to join me under this full moon."

I pulled a loaf of soda bread from my green robe and placed it on the orange cloth in front of the photograph of my mother. "I offer this meal for all who would join me in our feast, with the promise of good health and happiness," I continued.

"I light three candles for Badb, the Crone aspect of the Triple Goddess, the Goddess of death, destruction, and battle. Aid me as I contact the spirit of Rhiannon Finnerty-Perry on this night of ancestors. I light these candles also for you, the Cailleach, for the knowledge you carry from your many cycles of birth and rebirth. I ask you to grant me the understanding to perceive any messages from the ancestors on this night."

My fingers found the brown satin ribbon on both ends of a harvest mask, and I gracefully fitted the cover to my face. I'd spent hours embellishing the mask with golden autumn leaves and fresh rooster feathers, creating a symbol of the fall days passing.

After the mask was securely tied to my face, I continued. "The veil has been lifted; the wheel of the year has turned. The harvest comes again. Let the good be harvested, and let those who would harm me be cast aside. Triple Goddess, I ask you to allow Rhiannon Finnerty-Perry to cover me with her gentle hands, guide my steps, and lead me to greater knowledge."

I brought the five piles of tarot cards together and gave them one last shuffle before setting the full deck face down in front of me. After breaking the deck twice, I pulled the top five cards from the pile and laid them in front of me. Each card would represent an aspect of my question.

I took a deep breath and flipped over the left-most card to reveal the image of a shining knight riding an orange-colored horse and carrying a thin staff adorned with green leaves. This first card symbolized my present concern with myself. Because the knights represented sudden change and new opportunities, I felt in sync with the placement. It fit.

"The Knight of Wands," I said aloud. This moment felt like a test. It was the first ceremony I'd conducted by myself, and I felt pressured by my insecurity to prove I could do this. "This knight expresses points of uncertainty in figuring out who I am and what my passions are. It asks me to embrace the fire within this period of growth. There are moments of positive change worth seizing."

I flipped the second card, instantly feeling connected to the melancholy image of a broken man leaning against his staff. I'd always imagined him as a wary soldier, defending his people to the tune of "Carry on My Wayward Son." This card, this man in need of peaceful resolution, represented my drive and motivation for asking this question.

"The Nine of Wands reveals my feelings of frustration with the past. I've grown impatient to see the payoff of my efforts. Events from the past also leave me eager to move forward. The picture of the man illustrated his weary demeanor as a reminder that challenges shouldn't keep me from following my path or diminish my passions."

I moved on to the third position, which would show my fears, or the things blocking my journey. When I turned over the card, I recognized the skeleton instantly. He was riding a white horse, carrying a flowered flag.

"Death," I paused. "Frequently misunderstood as literal death, we know that Death is more a symbol of the phoenix rising from the ashes. I think here, Death represents my uncertainty toward the future. I fear the ending that will come if I choose one path instead of the other, but I can only grow and move forward with that choice."

I was halfway through the ceremony, and, although I thought I was doing okay, I broke focus to meet Marjorie's gaze. She had the gift of foresight, and I wanted to see her reaction to the reading. She, of course, quickly motioned for me to continue. Seeming to know I needed encouragement, Emily gave me a big smile and a thumbs up. I took a deep breath and returned to my reading.

"The fourth card shows what perspective I must take to see things more clearly," I flipped the second to last card. It was a bright, sunny card—one of my favorite cards in the deck. The illustration was of the yellow sun gazing over a child who was carrying a red banner from the back of a white horse.

"The Sun indicates happy days ahead, illumination, and the ability to celebrate the fruits of labor. Like the child, I should take a risk without fear and try to see myself truly and honestly. I've started a new journey in life, and I need to recognize that I can shape my destiny."

I'd never felt so connected to a reading before. This felt almost electric, as if every card was revealing a truth about me. I could practically feel my mother's presence.

"The final card is my course of action. It's The Hanged Man," I announced as I turned the card face up. It wasn't my favorite card, depicting a man strung upside-down on a pole from his foot. The man didn't look upset, though. He seemed at peace, as though he was happy to let himself hang. Life could take what it wanted, and the man would simply accept it.

"Here, the message is surrender. It's telling me to let go and trust the universe. My course of action is to remain open to the guidance of divine inspiration. I should allow room for a new direction and follow the Higher Powers as they lead me toward the best path."

After a moment of silence, allowing me to absorb the full meaning of the reading, I grabbed the goblet of wine, tilted it up, and offered a toast to an unseen force. "May I always be strong of mind, will, and body. To the Goddesses: Be we merry as we part, until we meet again."

I took a drink from the chalice and set it back down on the cloth. This time, I made sure the wolf faced away from me so it could watch over my mother's grave. "For this, I give thee love and honor. Blessed be forever."

With that, I blew out the candles and waited silently under the light of the moon.

"Blessed be," Marjorie's voice echoed as she joined me next to Mom's grave. "Well done, my darling." She reached down to take my hands and helped pull me up from the altar.

"Mom was here," I smiled. "I could feel her here."

Emily appeared behind Marjorie, attended by Jeb, my 100-pound, happy-go-lucky Labrador. Jeb was my familiar, which meant we had a special connection. Besides an extended lifespan, Jeb understood more than most dogs did, and his presence had a calming effect on me. He was my protector, as well as a guide and trusted friend.

"I didn't see her," Emily blurted. "Wasn't she supposed to appear or something?"

"Not really. It was more Mom's essence," I told her.

"Oh, I imagined her all covered in white lights, like an angel or something."

Marjorie rolled her eyes. "Tonight was about renewing the Wheel of the Year. We focus on growth and rebirth while celebrating life. Rhiannon was here. She wouldn't have missed it."

"Except...," I started, wondering if I should finish my thought.

"What?" Marjorie looked at me, eyebrows raised.

"She didn't show me my path. I'm still just as confused as I was before."

"But you did the whole tarot thing, right? Did it not work?" Emily asked.

"Yeah, but the cards basically just told me to let go. I'll figure everything out, eventually."

"Did you expect more from your mother? Rhiannon was far too clever to reveal too much," Marjorie chortled to herself. She pulled her wild grey hair out of a messy braid and shook it out. She closed her eyes, allowing light from the full moon to bathe her face. "The Goddesses wouldn't want that."

"So that was pointless? Why are we even here?" Emily groaned.

Marjorie glared at her. "You didn't need to be here. You weren't formally invited."

"Jeez, it was just a question," Emily scoffed back.

"Young people always want instant gratification. Who cares about where you came from—your ancestors, the very people who created you," Marjorie mumbled as she leaned down to grab the jack-o'-lantern from my altar. She took a deep breath as she gazed over the carved face of the pumpkin and then silently walked to Mom's grave. "Mother Goddess Dana, watch over my Rhiannon until we meet again." She placed the jack-o'-lantern in front of the headstone. "Blessed Be."

I motioned to Emily, illustrating that she should follow my example as I grabbed a pomegranate from the altar to balance on the headstone. Emily picked an apple and set it next to the pumpkin.

"Love you, Mom," I told her.

"We miss you, Mrs. P," Emily added.

After a moment of silence, Marjorie was ready to go. "Come on, girls. Gather your things," she said as she turned to head back to her black SUV parked on the gravel cemetery road a few yards away. Jeb was close on her heels, ready to get out of the cemetery. He hated graveyards.

"Finally! Okay, it's only 10 p.m., so it's prime party time!" Emily mused. "You think we could make it in 30 minutes? This party is supposed to be legit!"

"Sounds like a blast," I told her less than enthusiastically.

"Um, are you sure you don't want to wear a different costume?"

Emily had gone with the traditional college costume route—a skimpy Greek goddess toga. Her Shirley Temple curls were pinned up on her head with four long strands framing her face. She'd expertly applied golden shimmery eyeshadow, and she sparkled from head to toe with glitter. Even though she was already tall at 5'8," she now towered over me in her four-inch heeled sandals that laced up to her knees. Emily was ready to take on the party.

I, on the other hand, was just along for the ride. My costume was actually my ritual cloak, a floor-length, emerald wool fabric with golden Celtic knots embroidered up both sides. The tree of life, a large oak tree with deep roots, was stitched into the back of the cloak in beautiful gold and silver thread. If I wore my hood, it concealed everything except my harvest mask. The wool specialty paper, rooster feathers, acorn accents, satin ribbon, and golden autumn leaves weren't "hot" by young adult standards, but it was original.

"What's wrong with my costume?" I asked her, pretending not to understand her concerns.

"Maybe do a little something with your hair? Or put on some makeup?" she offered.

I pushed the hood off my head and pulled my frizzy, strawberry-blonde hair out of the bun it had been contained in, trying to tame it by tucking it behind my ears. I'd done the minimum with makeup for the ceremony, using only a thin layer of powered foundation and a single coat of mascara. It would have to do.

"Better?" I asked her.

"Eh."

"It's fine. I'm not there to impress anyone."

After falling for an evil psychopath last year, I had been taking a significant break from dating. Blaine Corwin, a handsome and horrible witch, had turned me against my boyfriend last year. That was before he tried to kill me to be initiated into the Ainbertach Coven. The coven's main objective was to eliminate all light magic from the world, starting with Irish descendants. My ex-boyfriend, Quinn, was used against me as part of Blaine's manipulative warfare. Luckily, Blaine was now trapped in an unescapable tomb, and I didn't have to focus on him anymore. Unfortunately, I hadn't seen or heard from Quinn since graduation last year. I told myself it was a good thing, though. I had a lot more time to train with Marjorie without a boyfriend.

"You need to cut it with that attitude, boo. Take some advice from me. I'm practically dating three guys, and it's great," Emily laughed as we made our way to the SUV. I saw Marjorie roll her eyes.

"Shall I take Jeb to the shop tonight then?" Marjorie's voice seemed to scold me.

"Would you mind?" I asked her.

"He need not be alone all night. Come get him in the morning."

"Thank you. I'll see you first thing," I grinned at Marjorie.

"You did very well tonight, Emlyn," Marjorie replied with a smile. She squeezed my shoulder.

"Oh yes, very well, Emlyn," a sarcastic female voice fluttered out from behind us. We all spun around, and Jeb immediately uttered a low grunt as the hair on the back of his neck perked up. A ghostly pale pixie of a girl faced us, who was leaning against a tombstone. She stared at us with two pale green eyes, accentuated by thick cat-eye liner and long, carbon-black lashes. Her hair was charcoal that faded to grey as it cascaded in big waves past her pointed chin to her shoulders. The girl's lips were stained a deep eggplant color and pressed together in a smirk. I found her clothing unusual. A brown, woolen cape, resembling the elvish cloaks of Lothlórien in *The Lord of the Rings*, hung over her shoulders with an attached scarf draped loosely around her neck.

"It's almost like you're a real witch now," the girl scoffed, pushing her body off the gravestone. "Interesting reading, though. It's cute that you still use tarot cards in your ceremonies. Still, it seems like you're harboring a lot of fear and self-doubt. You should work on that."

The fabric of her cloak flowed dramatically with each step she took toward us. My gut told me this girl was dangerous, even if she didn't look it. Marjorie must have felt it too. She placed herself between the girl and our group, ready for a fight if it came to it.

"Who are you?" Marjorie demanded. I stood firmly behind her, preparing to freeze the girl where she stood. The adrenaline in my chest started pumping quickly, causing my hands to tremble. I ignored it, though.

The girl laughed, and I felt Emily grab the back of my cloak. Instead of responding, the girl just looked at us with a smirk on her face. Even though she was only five feet tall, I could tell she didn't have any issues with self-doubt or fear.

"Don't worry, Múireann," she jeered. "I'm not here to fight. I'm here because you have something that belongs to me, and I want it back."

My heart stopped for a moment, and I was sure Marjorie felt similarly. There were very few people who knew we were witches in this part of town. Fewer people knew Marjorie's given Irish name, Múireann. Marjorie had been cloaked from magical beings for decades, since before she opened the magic shop. It was a trick we used again after the Ainbertach Coven targeted me last year. We magically separated pieces of my essence from my body—the ones connected to my powers—and scattered them all over the country. Marjorie described them as little beacons that could trace my location. They were signals in the universe saying my magic existed, so we diverted them. Marjorie and I were also disguised magically. To certain auras and beings—ones with negative or evil energies—we both had black hair, brown eyes, and rich olive skin tones. This girl shouldn't have been able to see us unless she'd broken our spell.

"Who are you?" I demanded again, attempting to replicate this girl's confidence.

"Maeve." She smiled. "Maeve Corwin."

Chapter Two

"Corwin? As in Blaine Corwin?" Emily blurted out seconds before I could ask the same question.

"My brother," Maeve told us, tossing her charcoal hair behind her head. Her brow furrowed as she narrowed her eyes on me. "He came here a year ago to kill you."

Blaine never mentioned having a sister. I knew Blaine had a father who might come looking for us. Mr. Corwin murdered my mother with a nasty trick. He was a coward, so Marjorie and I were confident we could deal with him. Maeve might be a different story, though. I glanced at Marjorie, whose face was stone cold and firm. She was keeping her cards close to her chest.

"He did, and he failed," I told her, matter-of-factly.

"Obviously," Maeve snarked. "I came to bring him home."

"Why do you think we know where he is?" I asked.

"Or that we left him alive?" Marjorie inserted more aggressively.

Maeve laughed. She paused and locked eyes with me, almost oblivious to Marjorie and Emily. "You practice white magic," she ridiculed, emphasizing the word "white." "You're all so concerned with the Rule of Three and Harm None. You didn't kill him, and you didn't let him go either." Her voice drifted off like she was caught in a moment. She touched her lips with her fingertips, and then slowly closed them into fists. "I can feel him. He's alive. And he's close."

"He's gone," Marjorie snapped. "He's been stripped of his powers and his memories. You know that's our specialty as 'white' witches. Now, unless the coven assigned you to take his place and you're here for a fight, your business here is done. Your brother failed his mission. Accept it." Marjorie kept her eyes on Maeve. "Girls, get to the car. We're leaving."

"No! You leave when I say so!" Maeve growled. Jeb reacted by jumping in front of us and baring his teeth. She ignored him, unfazed by the large, angry dog in front of her. "Blaine and I are connected. If he were dead, I would know. If he were lost, I would find him. Something draws me here, which means he's here. You will tell me where he is."

She lunged past Marjorie, fingers stretched toward my throat. I instinctively moved to freeze her. Instead of sticking in place, she stopped herself mid-lunge. Her plum-stained lips spread wide with amusement. She gave herself a once over, then met my gaze, shrugging her shoulders sarcastically. She was putting on a show for me.

"One perk of being me," Maeve gloated.

"We're going to wipe that smile off your witch face. Freeze her, Emlyn!" Emily shouted.

"I can't." It dumbfounded me. Over the past year, I'd honed my ability to freeze people and time. It was second nature, but it didn't work on Maeve.

"What? Try again!" Emily sounded terrified. Marjorie looked concerned.

"I'm immune to abilities like yours," Maeve jeered. "Blaine can't affect my emotions, you can't freeze me, and I can't be thrown across a room with telekinesis, among other things."

My heartbeat was deafening in my ears, and a metallic taste formed in the back of my throat. I wasn't a stranger to feeling helpless. My first fight with Blaine, I felt weak, but that was before I started training. I was at the top of my game. I was more prepared than I'd ever been before, and I couldn't touch Maeve.

"You're all shaking like little bunnies. Calm down," Maeve smiled, grabbing the apple from Mom's grave. "I'm not here to fight." She bit through the red skin. "I'm here to make a deal with you."

"What deal?" Marjorie glowered.

"Not with you, Múireann," Maeve hissed at Marjorie before returning her pale eyes to mine. "My deal is with you, Emlyn, and only you."

I cleared my throat as silently as I could, hoping I could mirror Maeve's strength. "I don't make deals with dark witches."

"You'll want to hear this one; believe me."

I paused and thought it over. "What are you proposing?"

"It's simple. Give me my brother, and I'll get you off our list."

"What list?" Emily blurted out.

"The list. The one with initiation targets for new inductees. Every known light witch of Irish descent is on that list."

"Why would I take that deal?" I rebuked.

"Think about it. You were a novice witch with less than a week's training. You bested a witch with far greater experience than you. What do you think that does to the bounty on your head? For a witch looking to make an impression, you'd be an enticing challenge."

I didn't respond, which must have signaled that Maeve was getting to me. So she took a step closer. "The cloaking trick was cute, Emlyn. Hey, it worked for Múireann all those years. We only found her when she tried to help you. The appearance glamour you two pulled was smart but far too easy to break. You could keep up this charade a while, sure, but wouldn't it be great if you never had to worry about being a target again? Gee, you might even get your life back—complete freedom."

"You couldn't possibly guarantee that," Marjorie interjected. "No one but Fionn Ainbertach himself could make a promise that big. Even then, we couldn't trust it."

"You're right. I'm not the leader of the coven, but this deal is real. I negotiated the terms myself, and by the wrath and wisdom of Mong Finn, the White-Haired One, you have my word," she insisted.

"Who are you to make this kind of promise?" Marjorie demanded. "Blaine is a failure, and your father is a coward. It's hard to think the coven would give anyone in the Corwin family any kind of real power."

"I'm the one with the real power in the family. Look at you. You can't even touch me." The pitch in her voice sank, and the anger seemed to seep into her mind. "Do you think an opportunity like this comes around often? Think again. And it won't be around for long."

Jeb growled, and I took a protective step in front of Marjorie and Emily.

"It's Samhain," I stated, hoping to calm her down and gain more time. "Don't you think we should decide this at a later date?"

Maeve paused, her anger fading into calm as the wheels turned in her head. Then she smirked. "Of course." She glanced from me to Marjorie to Emily, then back to me again. "How rude of me to interrupt Ancestor Day. Enjoy your celebration. I'll give you more time to think this all over. You'll be hearing from me soon."

She spun around on her heel and seemed to glide toward the center of the cemetery. I watched her pull the hood of her forest green cloak over her head, but instead of fading into the darkness, she turned back to me. "And Emlyn?"

"What Maeve?"

"If you choose not to take the deal, you may not live through our next meeting," she mused in a sing-song voice. "Until next time."

"We'll be ready," I tried to mimic her confidence, but it felt like my attempt fell short.

Maeve disappeared, and the four of us practically ran back to Marjorie's black SUV. Once we were inside and had locked all the doors, we sat in silence as Marjorie revved out of Bonaventure towards her shop. We were processing what happened.

It was Emily who finally broke the silence.

"Well, that was pleasant," she blurted out sarcastically. "Was it just me, or did she seem kind of cray?"

"Crazy or not, we've got a decision to make," I looked towards Marjorie for guidance. She looked deep in thought.

"… Indeed," Marjorie nodded.

"A decision, yes, but tomorrow, right? This is totally a decision we can make tomorrow—after the party." Emily seemed determined to act like our evening hadn't been totally disrupted.

"You still want to go to the party? Didn't you hear what Maeve said? She's prepared to kill us, Emily."

"Um, no. Maeve said she'd give you time to think it all over, which means we're safe for the night. I'll bet it's a couple days before she even shows up again. She's a crazy chick, so she probably wants you to obsess over this for a while before she makes her next move. Smart, really. Like its own form of torture."

"Emily!"

"Emlyn! It's a sacred night, right? It's time to celebrate your ancestors, so you should party with your friends. Take your mind off the drama of the night, ya know?"

"No way."

"You should go, Emlyn," Marjorie met my eyes in the rear-view mirror.

"What?" I was shocked.

"While her intentions are selfish, Emily's right. We have time to figure this out, and we won't get anything accomplished tonight. You should relax and try to enjoy yourself for the evening. You've earned it."

Emily smiled. "Marjorie," she mused. "I'm even going to forgive the selfish intentions comment."

"Oh goody," Marjorie muttered.

"It's a good thing too because Johnny will be there. I already told him I'd meet up with him. It wouldn't be safe for me to go alone." Emily blasted me with a big toothy grin.

"No, you can't go alone," I admitted. "I just feel like we should be in research mode tonight."

"Well, I don't have a party to go to, so I'll start our research. We can reconvene tomorrow," Marjorie suggested.

"Now, where have I heard that before?" I reminded her. She had offered to help me by doing some research on Blaine's family last year, but before she could find anything, Blaine attacked her and she ended up in a coma. I was the one who found her unconscious in her shop.

"Hush," Marjorie scolded. The fight against Blaine made her feel weak and naïve, even though it wasn't her fault he caught her by surprise. "I'm prepared this time. I've better protected the shop. Crazy or not, Maeve sounded true to her word. I'd say we have a day or two to sort everything out."

"Take the night off," Emily agreed. "Our lives will still be in danger tomorrow."

By the time we made it to Janice's house, I was kicking myself for going along with them. I couldn't stop thinking about what had happened, even as everyone else seemed like they couldn't care less about the world around them. I posted up against the wall of Janice's living room, watching the dozens of other college students dancing and gulping various beverages out of Solo cups. While they twerked and gossiped, I went over every detail of the night, searching for a sign of Maeve's weakness and contemplating the deal she offered. The more I thought about it, the more appealing the deal sounded. Sure, Blaine would be released from the women's track trophy I trapped him in last year, but I'd get my life back. If Maeve's deal was legit, I'd have a clean slate. On the other hand, I wouldn't be able to follow in Mom's footsteps. Battling dark magic would be off the docket for my life's trajectory. My tarot reading told me to surrender. Maybe this was it. Perhaps it meant not fighting. After all, if battling the forces of darkness was my calling, why was I being given an out?

"It's a lot, isn't it," a soft voice interrupted my thoughts, pulling me back into the party. She was a petite, thin-framed girl at about 5'4", and at the moment, she was dressed as Rosie the Riveter. Her dark blonde hair was pulled into a bun under a red polka-dot handkerchief. She wore black yoga pants with a midriff button-up jean blouse, black combat boots, and bright red lipstick.

"Hey Marnie, sorry. I didn't notice you walk up," I told her.

"No worries. You looked deep in thought. I figured you were plotting your escape." She leaned against the wall next to me and scanned the room.

"I wish. Emily would kill me if I left, but you're right. It's a lot. I'm guessing she's the reason you're here as well?"

"My duty as a new roommate."

Marnie had moved in with Emily and me before we started school this year. After my run-in with Blaine, Marjorie suggested I move out of my father's house if I was going to continue using magic. The Ainbertach Coven could locate me too quickly if I stayed in my childhood home. We rented a three-bedroom townhouse off of Broughton Street—two blocks away from Marjorie's shop. Marjorie stayed with me a few months to make sure I was safe. We weren't sure if the coven would send another agent.

When the school year ended, Marjorie eased up, though. I was better with my magic, and I could protect myself if the worst happened. So Emily moved in with me. She started at Savannah State College in August, working toward an education degree for the middle school grades. For as long as I could remember, Emily's dream was to be a teacher. The school being so close to home, we were worried Emily's parents would want her to live at home to save money. It turned out they were thrilled at the idea of her being more independent. My theory was they just wanted to be empty-nesters. They hadn't spent a full month in their home since Emily moved out. They were currently in Mexico.

Marnie was the niece of Marjorie's former coven member. She also practiced Wicca, but not the active magic that Marjorie and I used. She didn't have any specific magical abilities, and she didn't know that I did. Marnie's aunt had asked us not to use active magic around Marnie, so I kept my stories of demon hunting and dark covens to myself. Despite growing up in Birmingham, Alabama, she'd always wanted to go to SCAD. She was studying graphic design. The three of us had grown close over the past few months.

Emily would always be my best friend, but it was nice having another witch around—especially one who was a fellow artist.

"I love the costumes, though," she smiled, pointing to a group of people dancing in the middle of the living room. Four people were dressed like professors from Hogwarts—Hagrid, Snape, Trelawney, and a werewolf version of Lupin. A couple was dressed as Mermaid Man and Barnacle Boy from "SpongeBob SquarePants." The costumes were admittedly good, which was to be expected when so many of the guests were SCAD students. It was a weird mix of people. There were people from high school that Emily and I knew, like Janice, and then there were college people too. It was almost like a senior party, but with a bunch of new faces thrown in.

Emily joined the Harry Potter crew on the dance floor with her new guy, Johnny, who was dressed up as a character I didn't recognize from "The Simpsons." Some other costumes were more generic too, like Danny and Sandy from *Grease*, a half-devil-half-angel, Fred Flintstone, and an alien-looking thing.

"There are some good ones. Course, maybe I should have dressed more like Glinda the Good Witch over there," I joked. Another witch was wearing a shimmering green tutu under a purple corset, complemented by striped, knee-high socks and a pointy hat. It was all covered in a layer of glitter. "She asked about my costume. I told her I was a witch, and she asked where my hat was."

Marnie smirked at me, "Halloween is great for emphasizing cultural biases. Oh, how did the ancestral celebration go at the cemetery?"

"It was interesting. My cards gave me a bizarre reading," I paused, wanting to tell her about Maeve. I figured it'd be better not to get her involved, though. Not just because I was afraid of her aunt, but also because I didn't know who Maeve was willing to hurt to get what she wanted. "There's just a lot to think about."

"Understood."

She let it go at that, without asking for more information. One of the best things about Marnie was the un-awkward silence. She had a non-invasive attitude. There was never a moment you felt pushed for something to say; it was calm and comfortable. Maybe that was her magic.

A few minutes passed before Emily's boisterous laughter cut through the room to Marnie and me. She seemed to be having a grand time with a card game in the kitchen. Marnie and I both gave each other a look, knowing one of us should check in with Emily.

"I'll do it," I told her.

"Sounds good. I'm gonna take a break and step outside."

I made my way into the kitchen where Johnny and Emily were playing a card game called "What Do You Meme" with half a dozen other people. Thunderous laughter arose from the group every time they pulled a new card. Some responses even earned applause from other rooms in the house—or at least from those who could hear over the loud dance music. I made eye contact with Emily after a few minutes, and she signaled she was okay.

Had Maeve not showed up an hour ago, I probably would've been there with her, laughing and having a good time. I pushed thoughts of Maeve from my mind and grabbed a drink from the fridge, deciding I'd find Marnie outside. On my way out, however, I nearly bulldozed over some guy who was standing behind me. I scrambled to catch myself before I fell on top of him, but he still hit the floor.

I turned bright red. "Oh my gosh, I'm so sorry! Let me help you up," I held out my hand to him, and then I saw his face.

"Quinn?!?" I shouted his name in surprise.

"Emlyn… hi," Quinn stammered over his words. He didn't grab my hand, choosing to pull himself up rather than touching me. "I should have known you'd be here. Emily was always close with Janice."

I barely heard his words because I was busy taking in the scene. Quinn looked different. He was bulkier than the last time I'd seen him. Not taller, but broader and more muscular. I had heard he walked onto the football team at Georgia Southern, a smaller university about an hour away from Savannah. One of his friends told me he turned down an academic scholarship from the University of Georgia to pursue playing ball at Georgia Southern. The University of Georgia's team was crazy competitive and talented, so Quinn had small chances of making it, especially because our high school didn't have a football team. Georgia Southern seemed like a better fit for him.

"Hi," I mumbled dumbly. For the second time that night, I was speechless. The last real conversation Quinn and I had was around Halloween last year after Blaine tried to kill us both. Even though we

18

ended up saving each other, Quinn told me he needed time apart. That time apart turned into a full-on breakup, but I couldn't blame him. I wrongfully accused Quinn of trying to kill me, and I kissed Blaine a few times while dating Quinn.

I imagined the things I'd say to Quinn if I bumped into him again, but "hi" was all I could think of. I was just standing there, bright red, with a shocked look on my face.

"Who's your friend, babe?" a female voice stretched out from behind Quinn. I hadn't noticed her before, but I should have. She was dressed in a skintight Wonder Woman suit, complete with perfectly postured hair and awesome go-go boots. Quinn didn't match her—he was dressed like a lumberjack—but they were together. And she called him "Babe."

"Quincy!" Emily yelled from behind me, acting as my savior. "Long time, no see! How are you, doll?" She slammed into Quinn with an overly enthusiastic embrace, practically dividing Wonder Woman from his side. When Emily was satisfied, she turned to the girl. "I'm Emily, and this is Emlyn."

"Paige," the girl said politely. "So, you know these two from high school, babe?" She chose not to address us directly. I couldn't tell if she was being passive-aggressive or shy. Had Quinn mentioned me before?

"Heck yeah! We all went to school together," Emily responded before Quinn could. "In fact, these two were quite the couple back in the day. Or you know, last year."

I shoved my elbow into Emily's ribcage and noticed Paige pull Quinn closer. It was time to flee.

"It was so nice to see you both," I smiled at Quinn and Paige, and then quickly darted into the other room, pulling Emily along with me.

"How dare he come here with a date. He had to know you'd be here," Emily hissed. "That's disrespectful."

"What did I miss?" Marnie met us in the middle of the room, immediately noticing Emily's irritation.

"Emlyn's ex is here… with a hot date," Emily blurted out. A few of the girls from high school glanced from me to the kitchen. They wanted to catch the gossip.

"Yikes," Marnie said, before taking a gulp from her Solo cup. She gave me a sympathetic look, and I instinctively put my mask back on.

"I think since my ex made an appearance, I'm gonna pull a disappearing act," I told them both.

Emily frown and signaled me with two thumbs down. "Don't let him chase you off!"

"Yeah, you shouldn't have to leave just because he's here," Marnie nodded in agreement.

"You're a hella powerful woman, Em. Stay!" Emily was in full protective friend mode, which I loved about her, but I just felt anxious. There was a hint of jealously thrown in, too, but I was choosing to ignore it.

"I mean, but don't feel like you have to stay either. We'll be okay if you want to take off. It's totally understandable." Marnie averted her eyes from Emily's gaze.

I was sure my eyes were bugging out of my head. "It'd just be easier if I left."

"Coward," Emily accused.

I ignored her. "Take care of each other? Don't walk home alone?"

Marnie nodded. "We'll be safe."

"See you at home." I threw the hood of my cloak over my head and walked out to the patio to take my leave. A small group of students was gathered around a fire pit, exchanging new college stories over the crackling logs. Part of me wanted to stay, but I exited through the garden gate onto West Charlton Street near Pulaski Square. While it was one of the less ornate squares in Savannah, it was still beautifully packed with large oak trees and Spanish moss. I'd walk from square to square until hitting Broughton, near the townhouse.

It was a chilly night, and quiet, which made it very easy to hear the footsteps following me. I thought nothing of it at first. It was Halloween—people were bound to be out. But then, they seemed to be right behind me. I spun around quickly and froze my assailant, only to find Quinn standing there with his pale blue eyes locked on me.

"Quinn!" I exclaimed after unfreezing him. "Don't sneak up on me like that."

"I didn't mean to sneak," he told me, running his hand through his hair and avoiding direct eye contact. "I was trying to catch up to you."

"Shouldn't you be with the new girlfriend? Paige, wasn't it?" I was letting my insecurities get the better of me, and the words were coming out meaner than I'd intended.

"Yes, and no. I mean—Paige isn't my girlfriend. She's my date, but we aren't really serious." He paused. "I just wanted to make sure you were okay."

"I'm fine."

Then we stood there silently for a minute or so. We both seemed unwilling to speak, but also reluctant to leave.

"It's not a costume, is it?" he finally, and awkwardly, blurted out. "You're still a witch?"

"It's not really something that goes away." His question hurt for some reason. It was more like an accusation that I wasn't a human anymore.

"I figured. I hope that's going well for you."

"Can I do something for you, Quinn? Did you want something?"

"No. Just, I'm sorry for bringing Paige tonight. I should've known you'd be at the party, and we shouldn't have come."

"You can do what you want, Quinn. I'm not your girlfriend, and I'm not leaving because of you. It's a big night for us witches. We should party with our own kind."

"I'm still sorry…" he trailed off.

"Thanks. Anyway, I hope you and Paige have a great night." I turned to leave in one dramatic swoop with my cloak, hoping not to trip over my own feet as I made my exit.

"I'm glad you ran into me tonight," he called after me.

I didn't dare ruin my "angry" exit by turning back for a last look at Quinn. Surprisingly, though—despite the tension in my chest and the knots in my stomach—I couldn't help but smile to myself. Quinn still cared.

Chapter Three

"It was horrible. I basically rammed into him, and then I was just standing there with this stupid look on my face. Not to mention how weird I looked. Emily told me to put makeup on, but did I listen? No." I ranted to Marjorie as she brewed us a pot of tea.

She was at her mini stove in the back room of her shop, which served as a living room of sorts. Detailed maps of various historic cities in the southeast plastered the walls, illustrating the places she had traveled with her old coven fighting dark magic. Shelves lined the walls, filled with books and artifacts of historical magic.

"His mega-hot date was there, wearing this sleek Wonder Woman outfit. I'm standing there in ceremonial robes, with a mask dangling around my neck," I groaned and plopped myself down into a brown armchair.

"What an interesting time for him to make an appearance, though," Marjorie commented, ignoring the more dramatic "teenage sorrow" portion of my story. She set a tea tray down on a small side table between us and took a seat in the armchair opposite mine. Immediately, her grey cat, Tephi, jumped into her lap. Tephi was a spunky, fluffy tabby who I'd called "Kitty" before I knew her official name. She was named after the legendary protector of Tara, the mythical center of Ireland. I thought the name fit Tephi's personality. The cat was also Marjorie's familiar; she'd aided Marjorie for dozens of years.

"What do you mean? It was a terrible time."

"Emlyn, you're smarter than that. The timing makes perfect sense."

Marjorie sipped her tea and stroked Tephi behind the ears.

"What am I not getting?"

"Last night, you asked for answers—for a guiding light to your path—and already you've been shown the fork in the road."

"Come again?"

"Maeve is a complicated representation of what your future as a witch could involve. If you follow the path of a witch, she won't be the last evil you'll come up against. You could spend your entire life pushing back dark magic, battling for good. Then there's the other path—your human path. Quinn is an emotional reminder of the past, an illustration of what your life could be without witchcraft: stable, consistent, comfortable."

I slumped down into the chair.

"It's still two choices, though. There was no answer. It's just a deadline. It's not really the guiding light I was searching for."

"Is it ever?" Marjorie laughed.

"I just wanted to know what's best for me."

"It seems the underlying theme is you must make this decision for yourself. Neither the Goddesses nor I can make it for you."

I sighed, feeling sorry for myself, but Marjorie wouldn't have it. She got up and motioned for me to follow her over to the round table she used for Tarot readings.

"Our friend Maeve appears just as difficult to read," she announced.

"What were you able to find out?"

"Nothing."

"Nothing? How is that possible?" I scanned the table, trying to assess which spells Marjorie had used to research Maeve. Several books were piled up on one side of the table, and a group of crystals was placed on a map of downtown Savannah. Across from the map was a round, black, 8-inch crystal disc. The disc was an obsidian scrying mirror, a tool for prophecy and fortune-telling. For a witch like Marjorie, whose gift was foresight, the mirror was a powerful instrument. If it revealed nothing, it meant we were in a worse position than I feared.

"I've exhausted everything I can think of. I enchanted the essence of a rose to divulge Maeve's secrets. Its spirit seemed to evaporate before I could see anything. The crystals on the map won't reveal her position, and my scrying mirror might as well have been a dinner plate." She pinched the bridge of her nose, looking defeated.

"Maybe there's a spell protecting her? Last year, Blaine enchanted a medallion to block my freezing abilities."

"It could be a spell. Perhaps something blocks us from reaching Maeve magically."

"If it's a spell, she might not have protected herself from everything. Maybe she only thought about the things experienced witches would use against her. There's a chance something simpler would work."

"I'm afraid not. I used one of those crystal balls we display up front for tourists. Nothing. I opened a new off-brand pack of tarot cards. Nothing. She's immune to my foresight."

"Maybe it's because you're a Finnerty? Maybe she's blocked our powers. We could have Marnie try. She practices Wicca, so she could probably pull it off."

"I hesitate to get another person involved in this," Marjorie argued. "Emily and Quinn were both attacked last year. Maeve saw Emily last night, so Emily is no longer safe. I don't want another person trapped by this. Marnie's aunt would also curse me if she found out."

"So, what options are left?" I asked.

"I had one thought,"

Marjorie narrowed her eyes at me.

"You could try again."

I felt heat rush to my face. I turned away from the table, returning to my brown armchair.

"No," I told her flatly. "We've tried it before, and it doesn't work."

"If you focused harder, you could fight through it. We could figure it out," Marjorie pushed.

"I'll go back to the dark place, and we don't know how long I'll get stuck there."

"I'll be with you the whole time to pull you back."

"The scrying mirror didn't work. What makes you think this will?"

"You can go back in time, Emlyn. We wouldn't be casting a spell on Maeve. You'd be traveling back in time. The magic wouldn't be affecting her. Go back. You can find the spell she's using to protect herself, or you can learn what magic she is susceptible to."

Part of me knew she might be right. Over the past year, I'd successfully replayed moments. I typically couldn't go back more than a few minutes, but my magic worked a little differently in my dreams. I saw the day my mother died. I also traveled forward in time to the day Blaine planned to kill me. I couldn't control it when I was asleep, though. My subconscious created the magic, and I was only along for the ride, watching the moment happen.

During our training, Marjorie and I had been working on my time-traveling abilities. I wanted to relive memories from the past like

I did when I was asleep, but be able to control it while I was awake. The problem was that I could never get back far enough. There was a roadblock in my mind, and it always stopped me in the middle of the night when Blaine tried to kill me. I'd find myself stuck in a loop, chained to the ground in a courtyard at the Savannah School of the Arts. Quinn was always there with me, trapped across the yard. Blaine would stand over me in black robes, wielding a ceremonial knife. Marjorie guessed the trauma from that night had built a wall, and nothing we tried could penetrate it. The last time we tried was about two months ago, and I was stuck in that courtyard for hours—an endless loop of fear and adrenaline with Blaine.

"We can find another way. Maeve is just a witch. So she's immune to our special abilities—she can't be immune to every spell."

"One would hope," Marjorie agreed.

"What about binding her powers? That was the ultimate plan with Blaine until I... you know," I suddenly felt paranoid about what I said out loud.

"She can't hear inside the shop. I've protected it with at least a dozen charms and enchantments. Our words should be safe."

"Okay," I said, still feeling cautious. "Stripping Maeve's powers—could that work? We use the essence of poppy just like we planned with Blaine. We invite her to the shop—bring her into our space so we have the upper hand. We tell her we're ready to give her Blaine in exchange for our promised safety from Ainbertach attacks. We use the poppies to make her fall asleep, and then we strip her powers. Once she's no longer a threat, we could question her about who else knows about us."

"Emlyn, I don't think that will work on Maeve. She's too smart. We can try, but we'd better be prepared with a Plan B."

She was right, but it was the only plan of attack I had. I wasn't sure I could pull off trapping another person in a trophy.

"Hold that thought," I told Marjorie, as I felt my phone buzz in my back pocket. She groaned at me, muttering something about young people.

Quinn: *Hey. I'm not leaving town until tomorrow morning. Would you want to meet up for dinner or something tonight?*

"Quinn just asked me out to dinner!" A light-heard sensation filled my stomach, like the warmth of sunshine filling my body. I practically leaped with joy. I couldn't contain my excitement. "I shouldn't text back right away, though, right? That would seem way too eager."

Marjorie glared at me.

"A date? When?"

"Tonight!" I squeaked.

"Emlyn… I'm happy for you, but don't you think we have work to do?"

"Oh, come on! Last night, you were all for me going out and having a good time. Now it's no fun for Emlyn?"

"That was before we knew we wouldn't be able to find anything out about our enemy. We're about to go into this fight blind, and we need a plan. Not to mention, we also need to create potions and spells to prepare. I can't do it all myself."

I knew it was stupid and selfish, but I needed to see Quinn. This was the first time since the incidents last year that he wanted to see me. If I waited too long, he might make things official with Paige. I could lose my opportunity. Or worse, he could come to his senses and realize he was better off not being around me.

"If we get everything done now, could I go meet Quinn for dinner at like 7:30 p.m.?" I smiled big, knowing there was little chance it would affect her response.

"Do you really think this is the right time?"

"You said yourself, Quinn is the human part of my fork in the road. I can't just ignore the signs the Goddesses send me. This could be important."

"Using the Goddesses against me, huh? Fine, but we have much to do."

—

"We're meeting tonight at Spenkie's. I figured we should keep it casual. Plus, it's a familiar place with good memories," I told Emily. We were on the phone while Marjorie was picking up lunch, and I was taking a well-deserved break from mixing potions.

I spent the better part of the morning brewing "Perplexity & Puzzlement," a potion described as disorienting and hallucination-causing by the Book of Shadows. The mixture combined ague weed, poppy seeds, balmony, bdellium, and black mustard seeds with vinegar and red wine. While the mix of ingredients was effective against enemies, I wasn't enjoying brewing it either. The solution smelled terrible, sending Jeb and Tephi running from the room.

Marjorie created a few potions of her own. One was called "Fire Power" and produced a minor explosion. I was told it's more distracting than anything. The other potion she named "Flu-Like Symptoms," which did precisely what it sounded like. Everything we brewed was meant to slow down an attacker. The potions would allow us to execute Plan C, which was running.

Plan B consisted of shifting Maeve into an alternate dimension, a plan trickier than it sounded. I'd spent the second half of my morning researching the magic required for something so strenuous. Best-case scenario, Marjorie and I would peel a segment of reality apart for long enough to push Maeve into a parallel universe. She might or might not be able to escape after that, but it would take a lot for her to break back into our world.

Either way, our plans were moving forward, and while I knew I should be more focused on the upcoming fight with Maeve, I couldn't help thinking about my date with Quinn. He didn't technically call it a date, but it counted.

"Spenkie's is perfect. Plus, you can walk. That gives you the opportunity for some alone time on the way back if he wanted to walk you home," Emily told me.

"Fingers crossed that it goes well."

"I'll be cheering you on from the comfort of the couch. Last night was a bit too much. Marnie and I are binge-watching Golden Girls all day."

"Did anything fun happen after I left?" I asked her.

"Nothing really. Johnny got kind of extra, though. He started talking about us making things more official, so I shut that down. I do not need that drama!" She laughed.

"No relationships still?"

"No, ma'am. Wait, speaking of that, what about Wonder Woman? Quinn was just with her last night. What's their deal?"

"I asked that question too. Quinn took her home after the party. Her parents live in Georgetown, 30 minutes away. He was vague about it, but he acted like it wasn't a big deal."

"She was fuming when Quinn went after you last night," Emily snickered. "They left about an hour after he came back, but she looked miserable the entire time they were there. I wonder if someone told her about you two." I could feel Emily smirk through the phone.

"You didn't!"

"I might have vaguely mentioned the intense traumatic experience you shared last year. I briefly added that despite being totally in love with each other, circumstances out of your control forced the two of you apart."

"That's not hyperbolic at all."

"That's all I said, I promise. Marnie and I left her alone for the rest of the night."

"I'm sure you did."

"Speaking of those evil forces keeping you apart, did you find anything about Maeve in those books of yours?"

"Not really, unfortunately."

"You will. I'm sure it'll be fine."

"Yeah. We've got Plan A through Plan C, with Plan C meaning we leave town. I'm just hoping this all blows over in the next couple of days."

"Especially with finals coming up. We've basically got a month left. Can you believe it?"

"I know. I definitely don't have time for this to drag out," I groaned, knowing the amount of information I needed to memorize for art history.

"Can I help?" she asked. "I'm always here for backup. I could hold an ax or something in the background—be your muscle."

"Help by keeping a low profile the next couple days. I don't want you or Marnie getting involved in this if you don't have to."

"Lame. But okay. Just keep me updated."

"I will. Be safe."

Marjorie walked in a few minutes after my call with Emily. She had a paper fast food bag in one hand and a couple cardboard boxes folded under her arm. Jeb and Tephi greeted her quickly, smelling the aroma of Mexican food.

"Moving boxes?" I asked Marjorie, grabbing a burrito from her.

"If we're inviting Maeve into the shop, there are a few things I'd like to keep safe. I won't have her stealing anything. There are several irreplaceable items here."

It was a good excuse, but I knew stealing wasn't Marjorie's concern. She wasn't afraid things would disappear. She feared things being destroyed. The last time there was an attack at the shop, many of her displays and artifacts went up in flames. The real reason she was packing up was to protect the Finnerty legacy.

We sat in silence, taking only minutes to gobble up our lunches. Then we got to work pulling the rarer items from shelves. Marjorie carefully scanned the spines of her books, selecting many of the oldest-looking ones.

"Some of these are first editions, you know," she said with a sigh. "This particular book can't be found anywhere else in the world. It's a complete history of the original Irish witches. The families can be traced for generations. You used this one to study the Ainbertachs, and the Finnertys are in here as well."

She turned her attention to the drawers of her desk and the trunk sitting next to it. She pulled out a few small charms and crystals, making sure to also collect her obsidian mirror, which had been in our family for centuries. There were other items, too, like a statue of the Goddess Morrigan, the Celtic Goddess of fate and war. Marjorie added her personal witch bottle, a protection tool meant to capture negatively charged energy, to the box, along with a 12-inch Wheel of the Year wall mount depicting the eight Pagan Sabbaths. The latter was a wedding gift she'd received when she married my grandfather.

Marjorie seemed in low spirits after we loaded the boxes into her car. "I'll drop these off at your house tonight after you leave for your date. We can store them in the attic until Maeve is no longer a threat. Tephi will stay with you as well."

"We'll take good care of her." I looked over at Tephi, who was currently staring at us from her perch above Marjorie's desk. Her tail flicked from side-to-side, but her eyes remained focused on the door. She seemed on guard. She must have known we were preparing for a fight.

"You've prepared the 'Perplexity & Puzzlement'?" Marjorie asked.

I nodded.

"And the protection sachets?"

I handed her a pouch. "I've already attached one to Tephi's collar. I have one for everyone at the house too."

"Good." She held the charm bag to her nose and inhaled. "The cinnamon is strong. How much sage did you use?"

"Five to six leaves each."

"Good. Now tell me about the dimension spell. What did you find out?"

I motioned for her to follow me to the front counter in the main room. I'd collected a combination of crystals: danburite, apophyllite, and rose quartz. The variation of danburite we kept in the shop was a yellowish crystal of a rectangular shape. It came to a point at one end. Apophyllite looked like milky-white rock salt, all balled together to form a crystal. The quartz was a light pink color. It was the biggest, with long, pointed prisms poking out in all directions. All three stones were representations of the spiritual element, which was powerfully connected to transcendent and transformative magic.

"We use the energy from these crystals to open a portal. We know Maeve's strong, but according to the book, if Maeve is disoriented enough from our other potions, her mind will be susceptible to a transference of energy like this. I've written the incantation here." I handed Marjorie a notecard with the spell scribbled on it. "We form a line with the crystals, keeping one piece of quartz each, and then we say the spell together, combining our magic."

"Even then, it may not be enough. Messing with dimensions takes a lot of power, which we may not have enough of. Even with the right magic, the logistics are tricky. We may end up sending her to China or Alaska instead of another dimension. We may only be able to transport her to Atlanta."

"You think this is going to be bad, don't you?" I finally probed her.

"We just need to be prepared for anything. We don't know the extent of Maeve's abilities. We know nothing about her."

"What else can we do?"

"Nothing. We're prepared, and we both know the plan."

"Then I guess there's just one last thing to take care of," I told her.

She nodded and then walked to the front door of the shop. Marjorie placed a closed sign in the front window. The shop wasn't frequented by many, but it was better to avoid interruptions in our circle. I grabbed a sizeable purple tapestry from a drawer and laid it on the floor in the middle of the shop. Then I selected two black, two silver, and two white candles from the display up front. We kept spell candles of every color arranged on a glass tabletop, set delicately on the backs of two ornately carved, wooden griffins.

I organized the candles in a circle with each color positioned opposite its mate. In the center of the ring, we placed a small cauldron and a medium-sized bundle of dry white sage. Marjorie poured two chalices of cider and handed me one before we entered the circle together with the caldron and sage between us. Marjorie set her goblet of cider to her right, and I mirrored her. We both took a deep breath, locked eyes, and then began. Marjorie started by lighting a stick of dragon's blood incense inside the cauldron. She wafted the stream of smoke between us with her hand as Jeb and Tephi watched from outside the circle.

"Great mother Brid, Goddess of Ireland, the warrior and protector," Marjorie began. She took a handful of dried blackberries, a representation of Brid, and let them spill into the cauldron in front of us around the incense stand.

"Uathach, Goddess, and warrior who taught us to fight," I grabbed the sage and lit one end on fire, allowing the flames to engulf a quarter of the herb before blowing it out. The musky scent filled the room, drifting between Marjorie and me in the circle. We took in the smell for a moment, and then I placed the bundle of sage in the caldron with the blackberries.

"And Scathach, the shadowed one. The one who strikes fear," Marjorie said as she removed her ceremonial knife from her robes and set it in the center of tapestry between us. We were using a single garnet as the representation of Scathach, and I dropped it into the cauldron with the rest of the offerings.

"Goddesses—great warriors and teachers—we ask for protection as we weave our magic," we said together. We raised the chalices of cider to the center of the altar and clinked them.

"We provide this humble offering as we ask you to impart your divine essence now in us, acting as our shields. Help us deflect the ill-will of our approaching enemy and find strength when all courage would otherwise retreat," Marjorie said.

In synch, we each lit our three candles in order.

"Black for protection, followed by white, and then silver for the destruction of negative energy," I recited. "We thank you for joining our circle and graciously ask for your continued protection and strength as we depart from this sacred space. Blessed be."

Chapter Four

My heart was racing, beating so hard I could feel it in my brain—a constant, anxious reminder of my fears. Only an hour ago, Emily reassured me I could handle this. It was just a date—a date with a guy I had previously dated for a full year.

"You've done this a million times before with Quinn," Emily had said. Still, I didn't feel prepared. This was completely different.

"Can I help you?" a girlish voice asked, and I suddenly realized I was blocking the front door of the restaurant. I'd been standing there for the better part of five minutes—so long that the hostess finally decided to talk to me. She was younger than me, probably 15, and she was wearing a black Spenkie's T-shirt with a pair of skinny jeans. Her sandy blonde hair was braided to one side, and her impressively contoured face looked puzzled.

"Oh, I'm sorry," I jumped to the right of the door.

"Are you coming inside?" the girl asked.

"Maybe," I told her, which only intensified the confusion on her face.

"Um?"

"I'm meeting my ex here, and I'm nervous," I admitted as my face flushed bright red. I could've kicked myself for saying it out loud. I should've just walked through the door.

"Gotcha. Well… good luck." She let the front door drift closed, abandoning me to contemplate entering by myself.

"Pull it together, Emlyn," I instructed myself quietly.

A family of four was approaching. I told myself I should walk in with them instead of standing at the door like a coward. I was as prepared as I could have been. Emily and Marnie picked my dress—a knee-length, burgundy tunic number with long sleeves and a pair of brown ankle booties.

"It's the perfect outfit. It says, 'I'm super-hot. Look what you're missing.' At the same time, it expresses, 'I'm not trying too hard,'" Emily told me.

Marnie had been the voice of reason, assuring me it didn't matter what I wore. "You've already got through the hard part," Marnie said. "He knows you practice witchcraft, so just be yourself. He wouldn't have asked you to dinner if he couldn't deal with the Wicca thing."

"Plus, you guys are still in love. I can feel it," Emily added.

I took a deep breath, willing my heartbeat to slow down to a normal rate, and opened the door. I was officially inside the restaurant. It took me a minute or so to locate Quinn, and the moment I saw him, the nervous feeling returned. Suddenly, I was obsessing over the right greeting. I wondered if "hi" was too impersonal? A hug sounded overly friendly.

"Emlyn, hey," he said, and the anxiety melted away. Thank goodness he spoke first. His blue eyes invited me to the table, and he motioned to the seat across from him. "Is a booth okay?"

"Perfect," I nodded. I slid in, set my purse and jacket down next to me, and turned to face Quinn. I smiled at him, hoping he'd talk first.

"I know this is super random," Quinn grinned, "but seeing you last night, I realized how much I've missed you since graduation."

"Graduation?" I asked. My tone expressed the inaccuracy of his statement.

"Well, since… you know."

"Yeah, I know."

We were cut off by the waitress seconds later, which I was thankful for. Having eaten at Spenkie's about a hundred times, Quinn and I already knew our order. I could have ordered his meal for him. Quinn always wanted the wings, I got chicken fingers, and we both ordered a side of Spenkie Spuds. They were the best thing on the menu.

With our order out of the way, awkward silence followed. We knew what needed to be said, but neither of us wanted to be the first to address it. Another few silent moments passed, and I felt a little courage bubbling up in me. Maybe I was channeling my inner warrior Goddess.

"What happened last year—," I felt my eyes water. I held it together, though. "What I involved you in, and the lies I told you…"

"Also, thinking I wanted to kill you," Quinn added. I studied his face. It was severe at first, but seconds later, he started laughing. I tried to smile, but I didn't have his ability to chuckle at the painful memory.

"I thought that," I bit my bottom lip. "There's no excuse I can use. I can blame the magic Blaine used to manipulate my emotions or the shock of becoming a witch, but the truth is I fell for a lie. It's my fault, 100 percent."

He reached out and grabbed my hand with his, sending a warm sensation up my arm.

"We've done this already," he grinned. "You've explained and apologized and explained more. How about we don't?" I felt the tension leave my body, suddenly replaced by a feeling of hopefulness. "How about you and I just have dinner?" Quinn asked.

I quickly wiped the moisture from my eyes. "I'd like that very much," I beamed back.

He let go of my hand and sat back in his seat. "So, what have you been doing for the past four months?"

"How much time do you have?"

Two hours passed, filled with catching up and reminiscing about the "good-ole-days." It was so easy falling back into our intimate friendship. Quinn happily announced he'd walked onto the football team at Georgia Southern. I let him brag, even though I already knew it. He told me he'd been worried at first about keeping up with the other guys on the team, but the practices were getting more natural for him. The dorm room situation was his biggest hurdle. Quinn had procrastinated on roommate selection and was stuck with three guys he didn't know. Apparently, hygiene was an issue, but he refused to get too specific.

As expected, Quinn asked me about magic, but I kept my answers brief. I focused on school instead, describing the artsy group of students I shared classes with. It hadn't been a massive change from high school for me, but people were freer to express themselves now. Quinn was most surprised by my new living arrangement.

"Seriously? Your dad got you a townhouse?"

"Technically, Marjorie did. It's actually Marjorie's house. She bought it. It's just better for everyone I live there now," I explained, being vague about why.

"And Emily's parents are okay paying hundreds of dollars in rent when Emily could just live at home? How far away is your house from the old one? A few blocks?"

"Emily's parents are so happy to have her out of the house! They love being empty-nesters. They're in Mexico this week, and they have a cruise planned for the week after Thanksgiving."

"I can't wait to retire, so I can travel all the time."

"It's quite the life," I laughed.

"What about magic?"

A small twinge of fear emerged in my chest. I'd done so well to keep magical talk to a minimum. Now Quinn was getting straight to the point. "What about it?" I asked him.

"How's it going? I'm sure you're pretty good by now, right?"

I stared blankly at him, wondering what his angle was. "Yeah. I'm improving. I mean, I'm still very much a novice."

"I bet you're being modest," he chuckled. "What's the latest project?"

It felt like a test, but it also seemed like Quinn genuinely wanted to know about that side of my life. Was it possible he could live with me being a witch? Or, better yet, be supportive of it?

"Well, last night was Samhain, which is the Night of Ancestors," I paused to gauge his interest. "And I conducted my first solo ceremony."

"Ceremony? That sounds intense."

"It was a rush, honestly. It involves an invocation of the Goddess, which is always terrifying to me for some reason. There's no reason for it to be, though. Marjorie says I overthink it, but it feels so pushy or needy. It's like seeking approval from some high power you've never seen. I always wonder how I stack up to other witches. And... and I'm rambling." I felt my face flush red.

"It's not a bad thing to be passionate about it. It's part of who you are, right?"

The tarot card reading flashed into my brain. Quinn had unknowingly touched on the very core of my concerns right now. "It is."

"And Marjorie—she's your grandma?"

"Weird, huh?"

"It's all kind of weird, Emlyn." Quinn half-smiled at the end of his sentence, maybe to let me know it was okay to be odd.

"Too weird?" I asked him. My pulse rose with every passing second.

He shook his head. "I'll—."

"I hate to interrupt this super sweet moment," a female voice pierced Quinn's words, cutting him off before he could speak.

Immediately, the positive feeling in my chest turned to a cinder block. I recognized the voice, but Quinn didn't. There was no reason he should.

"I think we're okay for now, ma'am," Quinn beamed at Maeve, mistaking her for the waitress. It was only when he returned his gaze to my face that he realized the panic in my eyes. For a moment, I thought I could hear both our hearts drumming in the silence.

"I'm not here to help you, cutie," Maeve told him. "I'm here to help me."

"Emlyn, who is this?" Quinn asked cautiously.

"I'm here to collect a debt your girlfriend owes me," Maeve locked eyes with Quinn as if to threaten us both. "Isn't that rude? Shouldn't she give back what doesn't belong to her?"

I tried to signal Quinn with my eyes, warning him to remain silent. When Quinn had come face-to-face with Blaine, he didn't have the sense to back down.

"I don't have what you're looking for," I assured Maeve. "This isn't the place to discuss this either."

"Now, now, Emlyn. Lying isn't nice," Maeve scolded me, ignoring my plea to move locations. She placed her hand on Quinn's shoulder, and he recoiled, scooting backward in the booth away from where she was standing.

Quinn's rejection seemed to make her mad. "Where's Blaine?" Maeve demanded of me.

The moment Blaine's name was mentioned, a look of pain shot across Quinn's face. He suddenly realized what was happening. I'd got him involved in my magical mess yet again. Quinn was in danger because he had dinner with me.

"Maeve, this is between you and me. Leave him out of this," I ordered.

Maeve sat down next to Quinn, who turned to position himself flat against the wall. His eyes danced around the table, looking for something pointy to defend himself with. The waitress had already taken all the extra utensils, though.

"I think it is about him. See, you have someone I love. Now, I have someone you love." A cruel, twisted smile formed over her face. She lifted her hand to eye level, threatening some kind of magic. I hadn't seen what she could do yet, and she wanted to show me. "No more games Emlyn."

"I don't know where Blaine is!" I lied.

"Cute boy, tell your girlfriend to talk, or you won't like what happens," Maeve cackled.

"She's not my girlfriend," Quinn interjected. "I want nothing to do with this magic bullshit."

The words hit me hard. I knew immediately it was over. Any chance I had with Quinn was gone, and any feelings I just let myself feel were twisted into pain. My only goal now was to keep him alive.

"That makes it a lot less fun," Maeve puckered her plum-colored lips into a pouty face. "Still, I bet she wouldn't like it if I did this." She snapped her fingers, and I waited for something to catch fire or for Quinn to roll over in pain. I didn't notice anything, though. I looked from Quinn to myself and then back to Quinn again. Nothing seemed different, but Maeve seemed pleased with herself. Then fear spread over Quinn's face when he tried to breathe. He couldn't. Panic washed over him as he gasped for air with no success.

"Drowning someone is so easy when you don't need water," Maeve smirked. Her pale green eyes were locked on me, untroubled by the pain she was causing. Quinn's face was turning purple, and there was only one thought going through my mind: Give her Blaine.

"Stop!" I yelled, but Maeve continued. She was amused at my despair.

"Are you sure? Should I stop? Or should we punish Emlyn for her lies?"

"I'll give you Blaine!" I screamed, suddenly aware of a few unwanted stares from around the restaurant. I lowered my voice, "Let him go, and I'll give you Blaine."

Quinn immediately gasped for his first breath of air in what seemed like hours. The color started returning to his face, and a brief sense of relief eased the panic attack in my chest. Maeve patted Quinn on the head as he sat panting next to her, unable to escape with Maeve blocking the booth's exit.

"Where is he?" Maeve turned to me.

"It's more complicated than that," I paused, evaluating Maeve's anger level. Her eyes crossed in annoyance, and her jaw locked in a tight position. "I can't produce him right this second, but I will. There's a small magic shop on Broad Street next to The Pirate's Pub. Can you meet me there at 3 p.m. tomorrow?"

"You'll have Blaine? No tricks?"

"Yes, I'll give you Blaine. You have my word."

Maeve ran her fingers through Quinn's hair, and he recoiled from her. His face was red, but he seemed smart enough to stay quiet.

"How do I know you aren't lying?" Maeve wanted to know. "How do I know you'll really bring Blaine?"

"I'm the good one here, remember?"

"Good. Bad. That's antiquated. It's about who has the power and who doesn't." She shot me an amused smile and flipped her silver hair over her shoulder. She pressed her slender body up against Quinn, caressed the side of his face, and kissed him hard on the cheek, leaving a purple imprint of her lips on his skin.

She got up and grabbed me by both shoulders. "Cross me, and I'll kill every person in this city you care about." She pivoted on her heel toward the exit and disappeared out the front door without another word. I watched her leave, and it took me a few seconds to realize I'd been holding my breath.

I slumped back down into the booth and started to ask Quinn if he was okay, but Quinn wasn't sitting across from me anymore. He was up, heading toward the same exit.

"Quinn, wait!" I called after him. I grabbed my debit card from my purse, quickly leaving it on the table so I could chase after Quinn. It was hard to ignore the people looking at me. They saw the drama at the table, even if they didn't understand it. They probably thought Maeve and I were fighting over Quinn in a jealous rage. I ran through the door, catching a sympathetic gaze from the blonde waitress I met earlier. She didn't know what had happened, but she could tell things didn't end well.

I made it outside the restaurant and froze everything within a two-block radius. I wasn't supposed to do this; Marjorie said it could be dangerous to freeze that much at one time. All I could think about was catching up with Quinn, though. I nudged my way through a group of teenage boys huddled around a metal bench and darted around a happy couple holding hands. I got up right behind Quinn and unfroze everything. When everything around me began moving again, I grabbed Quinn's hand. He pulled away.

"Go away, Emlyn," he demanded.

"Quinn, please. Just talk to me." He turned and kept walking, so I followed him. We passed several shops and groups of people, but I waited to beg until we were in a quieter area. When we finally made it to the Waving Girl statue at the end of the street, I ran up in front of him to make him stop.

"Look, let me explain," I pled. "Can't you just do that?" The tears were already rolling down my cheeks.

"Why? What could you possibly say? Sorry I almost got you killed again?"

"You're right, but I didn't know Maeve would show up here. She appeared out of nowhere last night, and I really thought I had more time before she came looking for me."

"You knew this girl was out there, and yet you agreed to dinner? What the hell?"

"The timing sucked, yes, but when you asked me out to dinner, I couldn't say no. I had to see you. I thought if I let the moment pass, you might change your mind. And I really didn't think Maeve would come here."

"Emlyn, I can't do this." He shook his head at me. "We can't do this."

The tears rolled faster now. "Quinn, you can't say you didn't feel it. You saw it—what happened in there before she showed up. It was the old us. Didn't you feel it too? Don't tell me it meant nothing."

"It meant something, Emlyn, but I don't know if that matters anymore."

"Of course it matters! We still spark."

He sighed and ran his hand through his hair. I could see emotion building on his face. "So, what if we do? Does that change anything?"

"You know who I am. You know I'm a witch."

"I know."

"Then why did you invite me here tonight if you can't deal with that?"

"Because I still love you despite everything."

A little piece of my heart soared in my chest at Quinn's declaration, but it was quickly silenced. "I still love you too. So, shouldn't that be a great thing?"

"No, Emlyn. This can't be my life. It's dangerous and crazy. If it's not Maeve or Blaine, it'll be some other monster, and I can't do it."

"I can undo it," I told him, grabbing his hand. "What if I turn back time, so none of this happened? We'll leave the restaurant before Maeve ever shows up and end tonight better. It doesn't have to play out like this."

"Don't you understand? It'll always play out this way."

I looked at him. His face was resolved. "As long as you're a witch, these things will always happen."

"That's not true."

"It is." Quinn took a deep breath. He grabbed my hand, pulled it to his mouth, and softly kissed it. I watched a tear roll down his cheek as he met my eyes. His beautiful blue eyes were filled with sadness. "As long as you're a witch, we can't be together."

Chapter Five

"You're up early this morning," Marnie's soft voice broke the silence of our kitchen. She caught me staring out the wall-length window that overlooked the courtyard outside. My focus was on a couple birds who were transferring twigs and debris into a wooden house fastened on a tree. Jeb was positioned by my side with his head in my lap. I'd been absentmindedly stroking his ears when Marnie walked in.

"I didn't sleep well," I admitted. "Or really at all."

"That's understandable," Marnie told me. "It's a nice view, at least."

She was right. The previous owner did a lot of work on the small courtyard outside the window. They cultivated large flower arrangements and added a plethora of greenery to act as a natural decoration. Sitting at the faux wood kitchen table had become my calming place. The sitting space was my contribution to the kitchen, costing an astounding $150, including the four chairs. The dollar store placemats and fake fruit bowl gave our kitchen nook a touch of class.

"Need a pick-me-up?" Marnie asked as she headed to the pantry. She pulled out a box of blueberry Pop-Tarts and lifted her eyebrows at me.

"That'd be awesome. Thanks," I told Marnie, grateful she didn't want to talk about last night. I had been vague about it when I got home from dinner. I kept it simple and announced that Quinn and I were over for real. Then I retreated to my bedroom, leaving Emily and Marnie to finish their Netflix movie.

Marnie pulled two plates from the cherry-stained kitchen cabinet, placed a Pop-Tart on each one, smothered them both with butter, and placed them in the microwave for 10 seconds. Marnie placed my breakfast on the table in front of me and then returned to our turquoise tea kettle to fill it with water.

"No coffee this morning?" I asked her.

"I have a test today in Design 1. It's the last one before the final, and coffee makes me too jittery on test days. Tea helps me focus."

Instead of using pre-packaged bags or k-cups, Marnie specially crafted her teas with herbs and spices. She was the only reason we had such an extensive collection of herbs and spices in the kitchen, primarily because I just used ingredients from Marjorie's shop.

"What are you making today?" I asked her, suddenly remembering I also had a test today. I hadn't studied, and the class, Survey of Western Art, was killing me. I thought about using my powers to cheat off of someone, but I knew that would come back to bite me in the butt.

"It's a chai tea blend for focus and energy. Kind of a 'Pass That Test' blend," she laughed softly. "I use black tea as the base and then add allspice berries, cinnamon, cloves, cardamom, fresh ginger, and vanilla bean, along with some pink peppercorns. For a little extra sweetness, I finish it with honey from the bee store a few blocks over. Tupelo honey is good, but I think the black sage blend adds something special. Want some?"

"Why not? Might help me out today."

She poured us both mugs of tea and took a seat across from me at the table. Her calico cat, Margo, jumped up on the table to greet her. She meowed a few times softly and then moved into Marnie's lap. Margo was a thin little thing—much less fluffy that Marjorie's cat. Her fur was mostly white with pale patches of grey and brown running down her neck to her tail. She typically only slept in Marnie's lap, because she preferred Marnie to anyone else in the house. Even then, she was more active than lazy. She would spend hours darting around the house like a wild animal, jumping from the couch to our kitchen barstools like she was playing some kind of game.

I appreciated the silence of the moment. It was nice. We sat there eating our Pop-Tarts and drinking our tea for a few minutes before Marnie spoke.

"You know, the first time I did my own tarot reading, I pulled Death," she told me. "I was 11, and I freaked out. I thought the card was a dark omen, and I didn't even look up the meaning. I just flipped. So I hid the box of cards in my drawer, hoping they wouldn't be able to find me."

"I could see it being scary for an 11-year-old."

"Over the next week, I was a paranoid wreck. I thought danger lurked around every corner. Finally, my dad realized something was wrong. I confessed it all to him."

"So, he explained the meaning?"

She nodded. "It felt like the end of the world at first. Then, when I looked closer at it, it was a new beginning. See, we moved from Texas to Alabama about a month before school was starting, which meant everyone else had already selected their electives. The choir was full, which was the elective I wanted. Instead, I got placed in an art class."

"Your new beginning," I smiled.

"It led me to this path, being here at SCAD. Maybe this is your transition from choir to art."

I grabbed her hand and gave it a small squeeze. Who said Marnie didn't have superpowers?

"Why is the morning always so early?" Emily groaned as she emerged from her bedroom wearing an oversized T-shirt that hung down to her knees. Her curly hair was matted into a messy bun on the top of her head, and she had a smear of black mascara down one cheek.

"There's tea on the stove," Marnie offered.

"Thanks, pal, but I need coffee," Emily yawned.

"Don't you mean creamer?" I corrected her.

"Shut up," Emily barked.

"More tea for me," Marnie told her. She allowed Margo to jump from her lap before getting up to grab a navy thermos from a nearby cabinet. She poured the remaining liquid from her teapot into the thermos and returned the teapot to the stove.

"You going in early today?" Emily wanted to know.

"Yeah, I have a test in Design 1," Marnie replied. She attempted to brush a clump of white cat fur from her burgundy sweater but gave up after a few moments. "Wish me luck," she said, fastening her brown shoulder bag over her shoulder.

"Good luck," Emily and I said in unison.

"Bye, Margo, be good," Marnie called to her before departing.

"Come sit on the couch with me," Emily demanded. She finished stirring about half a cup of French vanilla creamer into her coffee, and then she moved to the couch in the living room.

"I don't want to talk about it," I told her.

"Sit! I need a comfy seat in the morning. You know this."

"Fine, but only for a minute. I also have a test today, followed by a showdown with Maeve." I slumped into the black leather sofa, allowing it to swallow me. It was comfortable, and for a few seconds, I contemplated staying there all day.

Emily took a slurp of coffee/creamer from her pink Disney princess mug and then started her interview. "You didn't tell us the whole story last night, did you? Quinn wouldn't ask you to dinner just to break up with you. You were already broken up. Plus, I saw his face at the party. He got hit with the Emlyn feels," she winked at me.

"I told you, it's over."

"I know, but you didn't tell me what happened."

"Maeve happened."

"What? She showed up at Spenkie's? Why didn't you tell me?!"

"We can't get Marnie involved in this. I already hate that Maeve knows who you are. We don't need anyone else in the line of fire."

"I'm your best pal. You have to tell me everything." She looked down into her coffee and bit her bottom lip. "What did little miss psycho do?"

"She threatened to kill Quinn and almost drowned him."

"At Spenkie's?"

"Oh yeah. For bonus fun, Maeve can somehow control water. I'm not sure if she used the water in his body or if she summoned it, but she was going to kill him. It was really close, Emily, and I couldn't do anything to stop it."

"Poor Quinn. He really just can't catch a break."

"You think?" I glared at her. "The worst part is things were going so well with Quinn before Maeve showed up."

"Tell me!"

"It was just a good conversation. Quinn even asked me about magic like he was coming around to the idea. Our back and forth was effortless. We both could feel the electricity between us. The spark is still there."

"Then, Maeve tried to kill him."

"Yup. He got out of there as fast as he could."

"Did he say anything else?"

I nodded. "Quinn told me he still loves me, but as long as I'm a witch, we can't be together." I buried my face in my hands, allowing myself about five seconds of self-pity before I got up.

"That's harsh, girl. He'll come around, though. You'll see."

"I can't think about it right now. I've got to prepare for today. I might need to cleanse my aura or something."

"For the test?"

"The real test today won't be on medieval art," I told her. "Maeve is a bigger risk than before with this drowning ability. I need to check in with Marjorie and let her know what I found out."

"But you guys are ready for her, right? You spent all day preparing yesterday. So, you're good, right?"

"In theory," I told her. Emily furrowed her brow with concern. I decided the least I could do was fake it. "You're right. We have a plan—a good one. We'll come out on top."

"Probably not the right time to bring this up, but have you thought about taking the deal? What if you just gave her Blaine? I mean, you wouldn't have to worry about her or the Ainbertach Coven ever again. You could have a normal life. You could be with Quinn."

"I thought about it a lot last night. After everything that happened with Quinn, part of me wants to take the deal. During the ceremony, I asked the Goddesses to show me my fate. It seems unlikely this incident with Quinn isn't related. But no matter what I want, we can't give her Blaine."

"Why not?"

"Even if Maeve had the power to remove me from the list, there's no way she could convince Blaine not to retaliate. A novice witch and a human outsmarted him. Insult to injury, he's been trapped inside a trophy for a year. Blaine's big thing was fame and honor—I just don't see him forgiving this."

"So then we might have two evil witches trying to kill us," Emily realized.

"Exactly. Don't worry, though," I assured Emily. "Marjorie and I will take care of this. Everything will be fine."

I made it to my Survey of Western Art test minutes before our professor locked the doors to the auditorium. I was thankful for the extra scantron I kept in my backpack. An additional few minutes in the bookstore would've cost me a whole test grade. Of course, I knew I wasn't going to do well on this test. It was 150 multiple-choice questions over the medieval period in Europe. Fifty of those questions were images we were required to identify. I only knew ten of them. If I was lucky, I'd make a C.

Focusing on the test was nice. It somehow eased my anxiety. As soon as I turned in my answer sheet though, the knot in my stomach reformed with a vengeance. I sent Emily a text, yearning for a little pick-me-up of a positive comment. She'd usually send something like, "C's get degrees," but I remembered she had a class around this time. She was probably busy.

Marjorie instructed me to head straight to the shop after my test, but I felt drawn to Forsyth Park near my Dad's house. He was at work, so I wasn't sure what I was hoping to accomplish by visiting our home. Maybe I missed it.

Before the townhouse, East Gordon Street had been home for my entire life. My house was a yellow Victorian situated across the street from Whitfield Square. Before I met Marjorie, all I knew was the house was passed down on my mother's side. After meeting Marjorie, she told me the house had formerly belonged to Patrick Finnerty, my great grandfather. He purchased the land and built the house in 1890 for himself and his wife. Their son, Daniel Finnerty, was my grandfather and Marjorie's husband. When Daniel and Marjorie divorced, my mother, Rhiannon, was 15. Mom went to live with Marjorie. They bought the magic shop and the townhouse next door.

Years passed. My mother met my dad, and the two moved in together. Marjorie said they lived in an apartment for a while, but then my grandfather died. He left the house to Mom. She and Dad moved in, and I was born a couple years later.

Seeing the yellow house brought up so many memories, and I realized how much I missed living there. Emily and I had played countless games of hide-and-seek on that front porch.

I sat down on the steps and looked out to Whitfield Square, which had often served as my quiet place for homework and reading. I knew I should've been with Marjorie preparing for the coming fight, but something called out to me. Something wanted me at the house. I got up and traced the architecture of the house with my eyes, following the long white railing around the patio and up to the second story master balcony.

"Mom?" I asked, hoping some magic would allow her to respond. My eyes watered. "If you're watching, please send me your strength. Maeve is strong. She's stronger than me, and Marjorie is scared. Please, help us get through today."

"Emlyn? There you are. I expected you half an hour ago," Marjorie scolded as I stepped into the shop. Maeve would be there in about 30 minutes, and Marjorie was anxious. I could smell lavender in the air. She probably lit incense in the back, hoping the lavender would calm her. It didn't seem to be working.

"There was something I had to do," I responded, pulling my witches' robes over my head. It was the same cloak I'd worn during my ritual made of floor-length, wool fabric. The cloaks were traditional witch garb, making the meeting with Maeve feel more official. Plus, the numerous pockets were great for concealing dozens of potion bottles.

Marjorie motioned toward the front counter where she'd arranged a group of vials for me. I grabbed one of each color and placed them in different pockets.

"'Perplexity & Puzzlement' is the darkest, 'Fire Power' has a yellowish tint, and 'Flu-Like Symptoms' is the thicker mixture," she reminded me. "You have the dimension spell?"

I nodded and pulled my index card from my pocket. Marjorie nodded and showed me hers.

"I've arranged the crystals in a line here. We must be on one side, and Maeve must be on the other. Your quartz is here." She pointed to the table next to me. I grabbed the crystal and placed it in one of my pockets. "This is the last resort. Conjuring this spell will probably drain all our energy and power," Marjorie told me.

"Got it. Is Tephi at the townhouse?" I asked Marjorie.

"Yes."

"What now?"

"We wait."

Silence filled the room for about five minutes, but then I couldn't stand it. Emily was right about Blaine. I'd been questioning the deal Maeve proposed all day, and the idea was gnawing at me.

"Let's just give her Blaine. No questions and no fighting," I exclaimed. "We might not win here, Marjorie. I told you what happened last night. She's strong."

I watched anger grow in Marjorie's eyes. My statement practically made her wild grey hair stand on end. "You know why we can't do that. It's already been decided." Marjorie pursed her lips outward, and the rest of her face appeared to sink down in annoyance.

"There's another option. What if we stripped my powers? If I was human, they wouldn't need to kill me."

"Have you gone insane?" Marjorie threw her hands in the air, dashing over to me. She placed both hands on the sides of my face. "I understand your heart is broken, and you blame magic. But right now, when our very lives are on the line, is not the time for you to get cold feet."

"She's right, you know," Maeve's flat voice reverberated off the walls. "Your lives are on the line. So, no tricks witches."

Maeve took a few steps in from the front door. Her hair was pulled back into a single braid like Katniss from *The Hunger Games*. She looked like a cross between a warrior princess and a superhero in her skintight, black leather pants and knee-high boots. She wore a flowing, forest green tunic top layered under a golden corset embroidered with an intricate Celtic knot over the chest. Attached to her hip was a rounded athame. The knife was the only visible weapon she'd brought, but she could have hidden potions and powders in other places.

"You're early," Marjorie accused. She was good at faking confidence. Her entire demeanor shifted in a matter of seconds. Now, she was speaking from a place of power.

A sly smile appeared on Maeve's face. "You couldn't just take the deal? You 'good' witches are all alike. 'We have to make a plan. We have to stand our ground. Don't give in to evil.' For once, can't you just follow instructions?"

I reached into my pocket and placed my fingers around a vial of "Perplexity & Puzzlement." Marjorie had the essence of poppy hidden in her robes. The plan was to hit Maeve simultaneously with both potions. When, or if, it worked, we'd bind her hands and feet with zip ties. Assuming her drowning power was tied to her hands, she'd be contained for a while.

"We just want the opportunity to talk before we make the exchange," I told her.

"To be honest, I'm glad it's going this way." She started circling the store, noting her surroundings. Even being in a foreign place, Maeve didn't look at all worried. "I don't know why I bother making threats. Maybe I love building the drama too much," she said to herself. "It's the intensity of a situation, you know? I always go for the 'suffer first' strategy when a kill is much quicker."

"Maybe you're not as powerful as you think you are," I jeered at her. Before Maeve could respond, we threw our potions at her. They broke at her feet, releasing a weird mixture of scents into the air like pot-pourri mixed with chicken noodle soup.

"How quickly should these work?" I whispered under my breath. I wasn't sure if anything was happening. As far as I could tell, Maeve was unaffected.

"Big mistake," she growled. She locked her jaw, narrowed her eyes on Marjorie, and made a crushing motion with her fist. Immediately, the wall behind Marjorie started crumbling. Small chunks of plaster and drywall came tumbling down, knocking books and relics to the floor with them.

"Marjorie! Look out!" I screamed before tackling her as a heavy wood panel crashed into the space where she had been standing. We hit the floor hard and crawled behind the main counter near the back of the room. Maeve's anger was focused on the shop for the time being. She was toying with us, destroying everything she could.

"I said you'd be sorry if you tried to double-cross me!" Maeve screamed. "Didn't I warn you who you were messing with?" The walls of the shop quaked. I quickly realized the glass counter was a terrible place for us to find shelter. I pulled Marjorie up, and we wove through the destruction toward the doorway between the shop and Marjorie's back room.

"What power is this?" I shouted over the sounds of chaos filling the shop.

"I don't know. Telekinesis, probably," Marjorie shouted back. We both threw "Fire Power" potions at Maeve but only set fire to the books at her feet. It was a minor distraction, which led to Maeve returning her attention to us. She sent the shelving unit above our heads crashing down, shattering the glass counter next to us.

"The potions don't work on her," Marjorie yelled. "You have to go back."

"What do you mean?"

Marjorie took a step forward, threw a clear vial on the ground, and then held her hands out as if she was holding up something substantial. As the ceiling collapsed, chunks of wood, plaster, and insulation bounded off the space in front of Marjorie's hands. She must have created a force-field of some kind.

"Go back and warn us!" Marjorie screamed.

Maeve noticed the force-field and took it as a new challenge. Everything was crumbling around us.

"Our magic doesn't work on her!" I argued.

"Your magic is about you, not her! It's our best chance, Emlyn," Marjorie urged. "Do it!"

"I can't! You know I can't go back more than a few minutes!"

"Give me Blaine, Múireann!" Maeve commanded, positioning herself directly in front of the force-field. She placed her hands on the other side of the force-field, so her hands were mirroring Marjorie's.

"I'll die first," Marjorie declared.

Suddenly, everything stopped. All the debris flying around the shop dropped to the ground, and disintegrating walls held firm. We didn't let down our guards, though. Marjorie stood her ground, holding up the shield with everything she had. I took a step forward, putting myself shoulder-to-shoulder with Marjorie. My eyes locked on Maeve's hands. I knew Marjorie's spell was protecting us from falling objects, but I didn't know if it would keep Maeve from drowning us.

"If you die, I won't get Blaine back," Maeve snarled.

"Looks to me like it's all about power," I said, finding my confidence at last. Admittedly, it was more comfortable to appear confident behind a force-field. "Who has it, and who doesn't."

A smile returned to Maeve's face. "I couldn't have said it better, Emlyn. The illusion is that you have the power." She backed up toward the front door, careful not to take her eyes off mine. "See, you may think holding Blaine over my head gives you control, but you're wrong."

"Not from where I'm standing," I spat back, ignoring the feeling of dread growing in my stomach.

"I need you alive, or at least one of you." Maeve opened the door to reveal Emily's motionless body on the front porch. "But, I don't need her."

"Emily!" I screamed. She was completely still, and I couldn't tell if she was breathing. I didn't think before moving. I just rushed from the protected space toward Emily's body. "Is she alive? I'll kill you if you've hurt her," I shouted through tears. I stopped in the middle of the room, a few steps in front of Maeve.

"She's alive," Maeve snickered. "For now." She grabbed Emily by the arm and dragged her into the shop until she was lying between us. Maeve produced a small tube from a compartment in her boot, held it under Emily's nose, and Emily started coughing. Her eyes rolled open and instantly found me in the room.

"Emlyn!" she cried out in a weak voice. "She grabbed me on campus. I'm sorry."

"Everything is going to be okay," I blurted. "You're going to be fine!"

"Yes, she'll be fine," Maeve started, "As long as I get what I want." She pulled the athame from its sheath on her hip and pressed it against Emily's neck. The curved blade reflected the sunlight shining through the new gaps and holes in the roof.

Emily stiffened her body, but she didn't yield. "Why is it always so violent with you?" she choked out.

"I like her. She's plucky." Maeve kneed Emily in the stomach, and Emily crumpled into the fetal position on the floor. "I will kill her, Emlyn."

My knees felt weak, and I could feel my muscles tightening from anxiety. I didn't know what to do. The options weren't many. To me, there was only one left. So, I turned to Marjorie.

"Go get Blaine," I muttered.

"No."

"Marjorie!" I heard Emily cry out from the ground beneath Maeve's feet. She was as surprised as I was.

"What do you mean 'no'?" I demanded. "Go get him."

"We cannot create another enemy for ourselves. If you give her Blaine, we will all die today."

"Whoa," Maeve seemed to applaud Marjorie's stance. "I didn't see that coming. Good for you, Múireann."

"Marjorie, how can you say that? We follow the old ways— 'Harm None.' You're willing to sacrifice Emily to save ourselves?"

"The life of one cannot outweigh the lives of many," Marjorie said. She looked down at her feet, refusing to meet my eyes. "It's not only you and me. Think about everything, and everyone, Blaine knows about."

"Marjorie…" I didn't know what to say, but I knew I wasn't going to let Emily die.

"I'm bored with this," Maeve butted in. "What's it going to be, Emlyn? Tick-tock."

"I'm sorry, Marjorie," I breathed. "Maeve, I'll tell you where Blaine is."

"Emlyn, no!" Marjorie interjected.

"We have him in a safe in the back room." I glanced at Marjorie, who looked utterly defeated. I tried to apologize with my eyes, but I knew there was no going back.

"In a safe?" Maeve looked confused.

"He's trapped inside a track trophy."

Maeve's jaw locked. "You trapped Blaine inside a trophy?! He's been locked in a trophy in there for an entire year?" Her eyes went black, and fire blazed from her hands, revealing another terrifying power. She hurled four or five balls of fire at the wall beside us, causing flames to dance up the already-damaged bookcases.

"Bring him to me now," Maeve ordered as fire continued to blaze between her fingers.

"Marjorie?" I couldn't leave Emily's side.

"You did a stupid thing, Emlyn," Marjorie barked before disappearing into the back room. It would take her about two minutes to get the safe open. I just hoped Maeve kept her word and would let Emily live.

"No funny business, Múireann. I'll still kill the girl. Actually, both girls, if need be," Maeve yelled after Marjorie. In no time, Marjorie reappeared with the women's track trophy in tow. She glared as she handed Blaine over to me.

"I hope you know what you just did," Marjorie whispered to me.

I showed Maeve the trophy. "We trade at the same time," I told her, reaching out to Emily. Maeve nodded in agreement. She grabbed Emily by the arm and dragged her up from the floor.

"Easy, easy!" Emily yelped. "I'm a person, not a doll." Emily grasped my hand, and I held out the gold trophy for Maeve. She wrapped her fingers around the base and pulled at it. I pulled Emily away from Maeve. We darted back to Marjorie, who had created another protective shield.

"You were seriously going to let me die?" Emily griped at Marjorie. I ignored Emily's comment and took a few seconds to check her body for significant wounds. She wasn't physically hurt.

"Take your prize and leave," Marjorie demanded, also ignoring Emily's comment.

I pulled the last potion from my robes—the "Flu-Like Symptoms"—and aimed it at Maeve. I knew it wouldn't do anything to her, but it felt better than doing nothing.

"Leave? Why would we leave?" Maeve smiled a wicked grin. "I know my darling Blaine would love a chance to execute his foes." She stroked the trophy a few times and whispered something to it.

"You told Emlyn she'd be safe if she gave you Blaine," Emily reminded Maeve. "You told us your word was good."

Maeve laughed. "My word is good. Unless your magical ability is blurting out every thought in your head, you have no powers. Your opinion means nothing, human. I offered to leave Emlyn alone, if she would give Blaine up freely. Instead, she planned to strip me of my powers. That breaks the terms of our arrangement. Instead of letting you go, Blaine and I will exact our justice." Maeve started exploring the shop—what was left of it. She was searching for something.

"Justice?" I scoffed.

"It'll take her a while to get Blaine out, right?" Emily whispered to me.

"Umm."

Maeve found what she was looking for. Amidst the chaos covering the shop's floor, Maeve retrieved a half-broken jar, filled with a familiar yellow powder. I recognized it immediately: sulfur. In an instant, I knew her plan.

"It won't work, will it, Marjorie?" I asked in a panic. She didn't answer.

Last year, I had used sulfur more than once to deflect unwanted spells. I utilized flakes from a chunk of sulfur in a healing satchel to break the spell keeping Marjorie in a coma. The second time, I used sulfur powder to break a curse Blaine had cast on Emily. It made sense that sulfur would aid Maeve in banishing the magic I cast to trap Blaine inside the trophy, but I couldn't let myself believe it would be that easy.

"Oh, it'll work," Maeve winked and flipped her braid over her shoulder. She set Blaine's trophy on what had survived of our griffin table and conjured a ball of fire in one hand.

"We have to stop her." I took a step forward, ready to tackle Maeve to the ground, but Marjorie held me back.

"Keep her close, Múireann," Maeve sneered without pausing her spell. "Or this fireball has a new target."

Maeve sprinkled a tablespoon of sulfur powder into the flame, sending a terrible rotten egg stench through the magic shop. Each time a clump of sulfur met the dancing fire, it sparked. The fire continued to build with intensity after each tiny explosion.

Suddenly, I heard Marjorie's voice in my head. "When Blaine appears, it will distract Maeve. Sneak out the back door. Take these potions and slip out the door."

Marjorie silently passed Emily and I both a vial while Maeve focused on her spell. Marjorie continued, "She won't be able to track you for at least a few hours after you drink the potion. You must find a safe house. Once there, find the spell on the last page of the spell book. Use it to protect yourselves."

"What about you?" I whispered.

"Do as I say, Emlyn."

Maeve bathed the trophy in the sulfur smoke, and then she sprinkled more powder over the head of the stature. She kissed it and smiled.

"Be free, my love," she commanded.

We all looked at each other with wide eyes. "'My love?'" Emily blurted out. "Didn't she say she was Blaine's sister?"

Before we could say another word, sparks began flying from the trophy. A bright green light blasted through the room, and then Blaine was standing in front of Maeve. He looked exactly the same as the day when we fought a year ago—the same way I remembered him in my nightmares. The hem of Blaine's long, black robes brushed the floor. The hood was loose around his neck, accentuating his rigid jawline. He had green eyes just like Maeve, which was why I had believed they could be siblings. Seeing him now, though, he was almost the opposite of Maeve with his olive skin and dark black hair.

"Maeve?" Blaine exclaimed in his deep, rich voice. I'd forgotten how deep his voice was. He seemed shocked at the sight of Maeve. He probably hadn't been aware of his surroundings while he was trapped. There was a weird excitement to Blaine's voice. Was it longing?

Seeing him standing in front of us brought back the anger and fear I thought I had successfully worked through. I felt the betrayal all over again, and I wanted nothing more than to send him back to his trophy prison.

"Leave, while you have the chance," Marjorie's voice rang out inside my head, but I wouldn't leave her no matter how distracted Maeve was. She and Blaine were swept up in their reunion, which was definitely not the family kind.

"Blaine," Maeve whispered. She ran her hand down the side of his face, brushing his high cheekbone before tracing his lips. "I found you."

Blaine responded by wrapping his arms around Maeve's waist. He pulled her up to him, and she reciprocated the movement by standing up on her tippy-toes to kiss him passionately. It was like watching an evil Romeo and Juliet be reunited.

We were all thinking the same thing, but Emily was the first to speak. "Well... I did not see that coming."

Chapter Six

"If she isn't Blaine's sister, who is she?" I muttered under my breath.

"Someone worse," Marjorie answered without looking at me.

"His girlfriend," Emily echoed.

The romantic reunion unfolded, and we savored the few safe moments we had before Blaine and Maeve remembered we were also in the room. Fighting Maeve had been impossible. Now we also had to fight Blaine. Our odds of survival were growing weaker. Still, I wasn't going to sacrifice Emily or Marjorie to save myself. Either we all lived, or we all died.

"I have a gift for you, love," Maeve smiled at Blaine after they broke their embrace. The corners of his mouth tilted upward, and he moved his hand to caress Maeve's cheek.

"What is it?" he wanted to know.

"Remember your mark? The stupid girl who trapped you?"

Blaine's smiled flattened. Anger appeared in his face at the very reference to me. Then, when Maeve motioned to Marjorie, Emily, and I standing across the room from them, Blaine's eyes turned black with hatred.

"Emlyn." Blaine's voice was sharp and pointed like a knife. "You took away a year of my life."

"You tried to kill her!" Emily snapped.

An amused smile spread across his face at the sound of Emily's voice. "It's good to see you, Emily. Spirited as always, I see." His gaze shifted to Marjorie. "And you—you made it through the coma. Tough old crow."

"Ready for a rematch?" she spat back at him.

"A rematch?" Maeve laughed. "You barely survived the first time."

Blaine retrieved his athame and pointed its razor-sharp blade toward us. It was pitch black and attached to a bone handle. I'd felt the sting of its edge pressed against my throat once before, and the mere sight of the knife made me feel sick to my stomach.

"Oh, she'll get a rematch. They all will," Blaine stepped forward. "I have just the potion for the occasion."

I hoped I was wrong about the potion he was referencing. Blaine's gift was that of an empath. He could read and manipulate emotions, which meant he could force emotions on you. Blaine could plant the seed of any emotion in your mind to grow. He had built feelings of attraction and love in my mind, creating a wedge between Quinn and me. Then he'd convinced me that Quinn was the evil guy.

The night Blaine captured Quinn and me, he drank a brew that enhanced his powers, allowing him to cause physical pain. Empathic abilities alone weren't enough to cause pain, but this potion he used was powerful. It felt like being burned inside your body, like your organs were boiling. Once Blaine hit you with the pain, there was little else you could think about.

"My potion?" an evil grin formed across Maeve's lips. The pit in my stomach expanded as my fears were confirmed. I'd never been able to figure out how Blaine created that potion. I tried to recreate it many times, but I determined he must have bought it from a witch with a unique ability in brewing potions. Knowing Maeve created it was another blow. How many more special magical abilities did she possess?

"It worked like a charm last time. Let's give these witches a show," Blaine winked at Maeve and pulled a small vial from the pocket of his robes containing a red mixture. He popped the cork off and drank the bottle dry.

Maeve clapped with delight. "They won't survive."

"I told you to leave before this happened!" Marjorie's voice rang out in my head. One glance at Emily told me she was frozen in fear. She'd experienced evil spells before, but this was a life or death fight. I was terrified, but I pushed negative thoughts from my mind.

"Doesn't it feel wonderful?" Maeve murmured coquettishly.

"Do you feel your power growing?" She ran her fingers through Blaine's thick black hair and kissed his neck.

"Now to use it," Blaine jeered. His eyes taunted me as he shifted his focus to Emily. A second later, Emily toppled over in pain. Her screams filled the shop as Marjorie darted to her side, attempting to use a powder mixture to counter Blaine's magic. I knew it wouldn't work. The fire would only stop when Blaine wanted it to.

"Blaine! This is between you and me!" I shouted at him before freezing him in place. There was a brief moment when I didn't think my powers would work. The night he attacked Quinn and me, Blaine was wearing a medallion that blocked my freezing abilities. I couldn't remember what happened to it, but apparently, Blaine didn't have it with him now. To my surprise, Blaine's body immobilized, and he was still as a statue. Emily's screams ceased, and I felt a moment of relief, knowing one of our foes was susceptible to our spells.

"Blaine?" It was the first time I'd ever heard concern in Maeve's voice. She waved a hand over his eyes, trying to wake him. Being impervious to my abilities, Maeve had never seen my powers work. It also meant she didn't know how long the freeze would last.

"He can't hear you," I declared. Seconds later, I realized that it had been a stupid decision to mock Maeve.

"Unfreeze him NOW!" Maeve grabbed me by the throat and shoved a fireball in front of my face. The heat radiating off the fireball was painful; I couldn't imagine how terrible it would've been if the flames were actually touching my skin. I tried wriggling away, feeling like a fish on a hook, until Maeve's grip on my neck tightened to where I couldn't breathe. "I said now!"

Maeve's furious demand suddenly exploded into an agonizing yowl. The fireball in her hand disappeared as she collapsed onto her knees. I fell to the ground beside her, clutching my neck with both hands. It ached, but I could finally breathe. I looked up to find it was Emily who freed me by stabbing Maeve in the leg with a shard of glass. She was standing behind Maeve with a wide-eyed, shocked expression plastered over her face. Blood was dripping from her hands—she must have cut them in the process—and she was holding them together tightly to keep the blood from flowing out. Her wound was nothing compared to Maeve's oozing calf, though.

"You miserable human! How dare you touch me!" Maeve grunted as she clutched her leg. To our advantage, the wound seemed painful enough to keep Maeve from using her powers. I grabbed Emily by the wrist and pulled her toward Marjorie, hoping Marjorie could recreate the protective bubble for us.

We hadn't taken more than a couple steps toward Marjorie when I heard Blaine unfreeze behind us. "You'll pay for this!" he snarled. We turned to face them both in time to see Blaine tear the sleeve off his robes. He was tying it around the cut on Maeve's leg to keep the oozing to a minimum.

"Let's get out of here while they're distracted," Emily whimpered.

"You're not going anywhere!" Maeve yelled. She used what I hoped was the last bit of her strength to bring down the wall behind us, destroying the entrance to the back room completely and nearly crushing us in the process. We jumped out of the way and used what was left of the counter as protection. The only exit now was the front door.

"We need to stop the bleeding," Blaine told Maeve, ignoring us altogether. She was losing blood fast.

"No. Finish them," Maeve demanded. She picked up Blaine's knife from the ground and shoved it into his hand.

"What now?" Emily whined softly.

"Now you die," Blaine grimaced. He positioned himself in front of the counter where we were, ready to attack. At the same time, Maeve was ripping the piece of glass from her calf. I felt sick.

Time was running out, and I searched my pockets for anything useful. I had one "Flu-Like Symptoms" left, but there were no additional options. No magic sword appeared in my robes like in *Harry Potter*. Then my fingers found another solution. I scanned the wreckage of the shop and located the danburite, apophyllite, and quartz crystals. They were still relatively close together. I nudged Marjorie, showing her my quartz. She pulled hers from the cloak as well, reading my mind.

Now was the time to be brave. I popped up from my crouched position behind the counter to meet Blaine at eye level. "Let them go. It's me you want."

"Do you really think I'd let them go?" Blaine sneered. Seeing him up close was difficult. It brought back feelings of disgust and embarrassment, reminding me of a time I thought I was falling in love with Blaine. He played me well. Hopefully, I'd live to return the favor.

"I'm giving you one last chance to just leave us alone. Get out of here."

"Are you really that blind? You've already lost."

"Maybe. Maybe not." Wasting no time, I leaped over the top of the counter, launching myself into Blaine. Fiery pain met me. Instead of tackling him to the ground, I dropped to the ground at Blaine's feet, clutching at my abdomen. I wouldn't give Blaine the satisfaction of screaming.

"Kill her, Blaine. You'll return a hero!" Maeve was in my peripheral vision, trying to pull herself up from the ground. She'd wrapped Blaine's sleeve around her leg and seemed to ignore the pain as she played cheerleader for Blaine. "There's nowhere to run now, Emlyn," she cackled.

Blaine grabbed the shoulders of my robes and pulled me up to his face. The burning sensation seemed to lessen for the moment. However, Blaine was smart enough to pulse the agony through my body enough to keep me from freezing him.

"Just do it," I slurred at him.

"I don't know. Seems too easy for you," Blaine hummed. "Maeve, don't you think it'd be better for her to watch her friends go first?"

"Absolutely." Maeve produced a fireball in her hand and turned to take aim against Emily and Marjorie. "Wait? Where did they go?" Maeve screeched.

By the time she discovered them, they were in the opposite corner of the room. In throwing myself at Blaine, I'd given them enough time to reform the line of crystals needed for the dimension spell. The only stone missing was about four inches from Blaine's right foot.

"We won't be dying today," Marjorie barked before dodging a fireball.

While Blaine was distracted by Marjorie and Maeve, I smashed the vial of "Flu-Like Symptoms" into his face. The surprise factor and the tiny shards of glass in his face were enough to make Blaine drop me. I knew time was the most important thing now. It'd be about 30 seconds before the symptoms started. I hadn't taken a shot of flu to the face, but proximity still infected me.

"What did she do to you?" Maeve cried. She ran to Blaine's side, dropping her second fireball. She kicked me hard in the stomach, which just made the nausea worse. It was already building up, and I wasn't sure how much longer I could keep from throwing up. I forced myself to grab the yellow crystal next to Blaine's foot. I tossed it toward Marjorie and Emily before Maeve noticed what I was doing.

"Stop her," Blaine choked out as Maeve examined the glass in his cheeks. By the look on his face, Blaine was feeling more uneasy than I was. I crawled toward Marjorie and Emily, but Maeve kicked me once again and grabbed me by feet. I couldn't keep it in anymore. I threw up, spewing the contents of my stomach close enough to Maeve for her to jump back in disgust.

"What the hell?" Maeve exclaimed.

"Um, Maeve?" I could hear Blaine's weak voice.

"Emlyn, grab my hand!" Emily yelled. She grabbed me and tugged me toward them, and I heard Blaine hurling on the floor behind us. I wasn't far behind him. As soon as we made it behind the line of crystals, I let another round of sickness escape.

"Did you poison him?" Maeve snarled. There was a hint of fear in her voice I hadn't heard before. Blaine was on all fours, unable to control himself. His dose was much bigger than mine. I couldn't imagine how bad he felt. Maeve knelt down beside him with her hand on his back. "What did you do?" She sounded panicky. I knew we had seconds left before Maeve caused the entire shop to collapse.

"He's looking pretty rough, isn't he Marjorie?" Emily hooted. "Seems like he inhaled a lot of it."

"Right in the face," Marjorie answered.

"Maeve... I," Blaine's voice wailed out before toppling over again.

"Oh, my Goddess! Blaine?!" Maeve shrieked again.

"He's dying," I laughed, attempting my best Maeve impression. "He's got minutes left."

She turned to us with fury in her eyes. Maeve raised her hand, ready to drown us or throw a fireball at our heads, but she promptly dropped her hand when Blaine collapsed. He was lying on his side, still vomiting. Maeve's focus was split between Blaine's moans and the scattered ingredients around the shop as she looked for an antidote.

This was the only time we had to make the spell work. It had to be now, even though I couldn't keep from heaving for more than a few moments. I remembered what Marjorie said about the power we'd need to transport Maeve through dimensions and wondered if my body would keep up. I was cold and hot at the same time, my stomach ached, and I was on the verge of throwing up again.

We were huddled together to one side of the shop, among the debris. Emily pulled me into her lap and handed me a brown paper shopping bag. I grabbed the piece of quartz from my pocket and gave it to her.

"We have to hold this," I managed to get out.

"Keep it together, child," Marjorie told me. She pulled out her notecard with the spell written on it, and I did the same. "We all have to say the spell."

"But Maeve isn't affected by your spells," Emily interjected. "Won't this just piss her off?"

"The spell isn't for her," I stammered.

"We will need all the power we have, which includes you, Emily," Marjorie instructed. "Hold on to Emlyn and me tightly—as tight as you can."

"I don't have powers," Emily argued loudly. Maeve must have heard her, because suddenly her attention was back on us.

"What do you think you're doing?" Maeve screeched. She waved her arm, and chunks of the building came crashing down again. Marjorie was ready for it this time. As soon as Maeve's arm moved, Marjorie threw white dust in the air above us and thrust both her palms up.

"Stop!" she ordered, and an invisible force-field held above us, bouncing debris away from us as we worked. The challenge seemed to infuriate Maeve. She tore apart the shop with more force than ever, sending everything possible hurling towards our heads—bookcases, pieces of glass, the griffin table.

"My spell won't hold against this," Marjorie said. "Together!"

"Aperire ostium, pontem," we all chanted. I was barely holding on.

"I don't know what any of this means!" Emily said.

"You don't have to understand it," I started. "Oh god…" I threw up again on the floor in front of us.

"It must be now!" Marjorie urged. The entire structure of the shop was coming down. "Aperire ostium. Pontem. Iter ad celeritas lucis," we read.

"Don't let them get away!" Blaine's voice rang out alongside Maeve's insane-sounding screams. Sizeable chunks of the roof caved in, barely missing Blaine, who was in the fetal position, trying to keep himself from exploding again. "Watch it, Maeve!"

We ignored the sounds of destruction and pushed to finish, "Quod non-sit ei!"

Then everything was black as if existence faded, but I could still hear Maeve's enraged cries in the darkness. Her sounds were fragmented, though, and there were other words, too. I listened to my voice, in addition to Marjorie and Emily's cries. We were repeating the spell for a second time, but this time it was in English.

"Open a door. Build a bridge. Travel at the speed of light. As I will it, let it be."

As our words echoed across the emptiness, I realized we must have died. The collapse of the shop must have been too much for Marjorie's force-field. We were likely crushed under the weight of plaster, wood, and roofing materials. If I was honest, it came as a slight relief. Still, I expected less pain. The nausea and body aches from the potion hadn't subsided yet, and I felt residual pain from the fight—especially Blaine's scorching of my insides.

"Dammit," Marjorie's grouchy voice broke through the darkness, and I felt a wet nose push against my cheek. I opened my eyes to see Jeb's snout in my face. His warm body was lying next to me on a hard, cold surface. The world was in color again, and I recognized the bright cherry cabinets around me. We were in the townhouse. We survived.

"Emily? Emlyn? Are you here?" Marjorie called.

"I'm here," I choked out. Moving was tough, but I lifted myself into a sitting position. Jeb's face was full of concern. He was glued to my side. "I'm okay," I assured him, but I knew I'd be feeling the effects of the fight for days. Blaine and Maeve flashed into my mind, and I remembered we were still in danger. I search my cloak for the concealing potion Marjorie gave Emily and me. I downed its contents as quickly as I could. They wouldn't know where we escaped to. For all they knew, we could've transported ourselves to Canada. Then again, our townhouse was a simple place to start.

Marjorie appeared above me. Her demeanor was still on high alert. "Did you drink the potion?"

I nodded. "Where's Emily?"

"Here!" Emily's voice shouted from the laundry room.

"Take your potion quickly!" Marjorie instructed.

"Done."

"Good. We've bought ourselves a few minutes, but that's it. They'll be tracking us," Marjorie announced. "Get up—get up both of you. There's no time to lose."

"What's the hurry?" Emily questioned. The dimensional spell, which we used as a transportation spell, must have affected Emily differently because she stood up and made her way to the living room with no trouble. That or the flu was reacting poorly to the other magic.

I clutched the side of the counter and pried myself up. Jeb kept his eyes on me, likely convinced I was about to take another spill. Tephi and Margo wandered out from one bedroom, and Tephi darted toward Marjorie as soon as she saw her, letting out a few desperate meows.

"We're not safe," Marjorie told us, ignoring Tephi's greeting. She grabbed an empty laundry basket and headed to the kitchen. She thrust open the cabinets and started tossing all the nonperishables into the container. "Get packed. We need to be out of here in five minutes or fewer. Blaine and Maeve will not stop until they get Emlyn."

"I can't leave," Emily finally chimed in with a scowl. "The semester is almost over. Finals are less than a month away."

"Some things are more important than finals." Marjorie moved to the fridge now.

"We know," I gave Emily a resigned look. "We'll get packed."

"No, Emlyn. I'm not going. This isn't about me. This is a magic thing," Emily stood firmly. Her speech was echoing Quinn's. "I've been in danger before, but this is different. I'm trying to start my life here, and mine doesn't revolve around magic. I'm not going."

"No! Are you daft?" Marjorie slammed her fists down on the countertop. "Try to understand. No spell makes this go away. They know where we are. They know who we are. All of us. If we stay, we die. Unfortunately, this includes you too, Emily. Maybe you didn't ask to be part of this, but Maeve and Blaine will kill you to get to Emlyn. They'll take great pleasure in it, too. This isn't a game. It isn't what we faced last year. Maeve is a powerful witch. Maybe I was the only one who saw the damage she dealt?"

Emily looked away, unwilling to admit the truth in Marjorie's comment. We all saw how powerful Maeve was, and I knew Emily was just as afraid as I was.

"Best yet, she can't be touched by our magic," Marjorie continued. "We have one straightforward but tough choice at the moment. We run."

A low growl from Jeb interrupted Marjorie's speech. Something was moving outside. Jeb quickly and stealthily padded to the front door to investigate as we stood in silence, dread filling each of us.

"They found us," Marjorie said calmly.

"What do we do now?" I asked her.

"You two get down." She grabbed a butcher's knife from the drawer and slowly moved around the kitchen island to the front door. Emily crouched down, hiding in the shadows. I hoped they would leave her be if she was out of sight. I couldn't hide, though. I grabbed another knife and moved toward the front door in the opposite direction from Marjorie. If we played on both sides, we had a better chance.

"Together," I told her. She nodded in response, and we positioned ourselves strategically on either side of the door. Jeb stood alert in front of the door, and we waited. I told myself we had the element of surprise on our side, assuming Blaine couldn't feel our anxiety.

The lock clicked open, and I tightened my grip on the knife. Adrenaline built back up for a second time, pulsing through my chest. As the door creaked open, I couldn't help feeling guilty. "Harm none" was the cardinal rule of our religion, and I was prepared to stab someone with a kitchen knife. I wondered if the extenuating circumstances justified my actions or if it was all the same in the eyes of the Goddesses. I took a final calming breath and then darted from my hiding place toward the opening door.

"Holy crap!" a female voice yelped, causing me to jump back at the last second. Mexican food and soda spilled all over the entryway rug.

"Marnie?" I was so relieved to see her face, I dropped the knife and threw my arms around her. She pushed me off, revealing a less than cheerful demeanor. It was fair. Marjorie and I tried to attack her.

"What the hell is going on?" Marnie demanded.

I jumped back, composing myself as Emily jumped from her hiding spot.

"We're just so happy to see you!" Emily exclaimed. She ran up and hugged Marnie as well. "Sorry about your dinner. It looked like it would be tasty."

"Y'all just attacked me with knives!" Marnie accused.

"It's a long story," I explained.

"One we don't have time for. Emlyn, Emily, we need to pack. Three minutes," Marjorie interrupted.

"Sorry we attacked you. We had a good reason," Emily said before begrudgingly slinking toward her room.

"Where are you going?" Marnie pressed. "What's wrong?"

"Emlyn, now!" Marjorie commanded.

"I'm coming!" I yelled back at her as she hauled the hamper of food out to her SUV.

"I wish I could explain, but I can't."

"You came at me with a butcher knife. I think you can spare a few minutes to explain," she pushed. There was a fierceness in her I hadn't seen before.

"We can't get you involved. Just trust me; you don't want to know." I gave her an apologetic look and then trotted off to my room. I heard her slam the front door shut, which I assumed smeared guacamole and sour cream all over the entryway, and Marnie chased after me to my room.

"Emlyn, what are you guys running from?" Marnie asked.

"I already told you, I can't tell you. It would put you at risk." I smushed about a dozen shirts, four pairs of jeans, all my leggings and yoga pants, four pairs of pajamas, a drawerful of underwear, and a dozen pairs of socks into my bag. When I moved to shoes, I packed as many as I could fit while still leaving room for toiletries.

"Is the better question: who are you running from?"

"Why do you assume we're running?" Marjorie shoved her head into my room, being nosey and reminding me to hurry. It was the first time I noticed how rough Marjorie looked. Her wiry hair frizzed in every direction, and her face was drenched in sweat. Dust and debris left a brownish tint on her skin, and her clothes were stained from the blood. It didn't look like her own blood. I guessed it was from Emily's hands when she stabbed Maeve with the glass.

Marjorie didn't wait for a response from Marnie before barging into my room with another laundry basket. She headed straight to the trunk under my window and started raiding magical supplies.

"You were both ready to stab me when I walked through the door," Marnie told Marjorie. "Emily's hands are both cut pretty badly. You all look like you've been through a natural disaster or something. Now you're all packing. This pretty much looks like fleeing." She motioned to me as I shoved one last pair of boots into my bag.

I knew Marjorie didn't want Marnie involved, but I also knew Blaine and Maeve could use Marnie against us if they wanted. If they discovered the townhouse belonged to Marjorie, Marnie would be a sitting duck in the house alone.

"You shouldn't stay here after we leave," I told Marnie.

"Who is it? A new coven? A rogue witch? Maybe a revival of the New Forest group? They had a big following in the '30s."

The knowledge Marnie had shocked me. Until this point, we were told Marnie saw Wicca as a religion alone. It was a practice for her only in a spiritual sense and not in a physical one. I didn't think she believed in actual magic. Did Marnie have powers?

"Don't respond, Emlyn," Marjorie insisted.

"It's the Ainbertach Coven. Only one of the witches after us is a real member, though. The other was never officially initiated. He just has a vendetta," I spilled to Marnie.

"Do you not listen?" Marjorie exclaimed. "You just painted a target on Marnie's back."

"She's already in danger living here. She has to come with us," I argued.

"So, we can protect her? We barely escaped with our lives."

"It's better than leaving her here."

"Marnie is better off moving into another house downtown and finishing the semester. They don't know her, Emlyn. She's still safe."

"The Ainbertach Coven is after you?" Marnie frowned.

"Yes," I told her. "We just fought them off. They destroyed the magic shop, and we barely escaped. We have to leave."

"Where are you going?" she wanted to know.

"We have no idea where we are going," Marjorie told her.

"We need to find a safe house," I interjected.

"Splendid idea," Marjorie said sarcastically. "Let's just poof one up. Emlyn, we'd need a hundred charms and spells to even think about hiding from Blaine and Maeve."

"Guys," Marnie interrupted. "I know a place."

Chapter Seven

I was in a basement, I thought. Labored breathing was the only sound in the dark, empty room, but I knew it was a basement because of the smell. The aroma was cold and damp, reeking of wet earth, fresh-cut wood, and salt. It could have been a workshop, maybe, but it reminded me of the playroom Emily's parents had in their basement. Where ever I was, I wasn't alone. Another person was breathing hard beside me, sounding congested. I thought it might be Emily.

Everything seemed calm until I heard footsteps above us. My companion's hand reached out to me in fear. They grabbed the back of my shirt like we were in a haunted house, waiting for someone to jump out at us in the dark. The difference here being the danger was real.

"I don't want to hear your excuses, Stephen," an agitated female voice erupted. I knew the voice. It was dripping with antagonism and a hint of insanity. "Let me spell this out for you. You find her, or you can explain to headquarters why you couldn't. They aren't as understanding as I am, Steve."

"I'll find them, I will!" Steve responded in a hurried, high voice. Even from the basement, I could hear he was terrified of Maeve. "I'll notify all our contacts in the southeast, ma'am."

"Yes, you will. Now get out of here, and cut the ma'am crap."

A door slammed, and my gut instinct told me it was time to get upstairs. I crept forward in the darkness, taking baby steps and using the wall for support. Soon, I realized we were in a wine cellar, not a basement. Long bottle necks lined the surrounding walls, which made me question where I was. Who would have a wine cellar, and why would I be in one spying on Maeve? I took another step forward. I jumped when my comrade's hand grabbed me by the arm and pulled me back.

"Don't," Emily's voice quietly pleaded. It confirmed my suspicions, but at the same time, worried me. Why would Emily be anywhere close to Maeve again? Surely Marjorie

and I would never allow her this close to danger. I tried not to dwell on it. I knew I needed to get upstairs. Something urged me to confront Maeve head-on.

I squeezed Emily's hand and gently removed it from my arm. I rubbed her shoulder to let her know everything would be okay. Then, using touch as my guide, I slid past the wine bottles until my fingers reached a stone wall. Following the hard lines of stone, I reached a small, narrow staircase. I took my first step, cringing at the tiny creak that escaped from under my feet. Had someone heard? I took another step, careful to balance my weight against the rickety wood. After another step, the sound of a door opening above me sent me leaping back into the cellar, rolling my ankle on the way down. Fear masked the pain. Seconds later, I was relieved when the entrance remained shut—the sound must have come from somewhere else in the building.

I massaged my twisted ankle in the darkness, hoping it wouldn't affect my ability to take out Maeve. I was listening for my next opportunity when instead, I heard Blaine.

"I'm surprised you let Stephen live," Blaine joked. His deep voice was unmistakable. It caused all the hairs on the back of my neck to stand on end. Emily slid up close beside me, grabbing my hand as if sensing my unease. We quietly listened in the darkness.

"He's an idiot, but he's our best psychic," Maeve spat back. "If I killed him, headquarters wouldn't be happy." I imagined her pixie face turned downward. Her silver-grey hair would stand in stark contrast to the angry red color of her cheeks.

"If he's our best, we have a problem." The snarky undertones to Blaine's voice were interesting. "It was a fib, though, right? You haven't alerted headquarters that we failed a second time? They still think we're waiting for the right moment to attack?"

"Of course, Blaine. Can you imagine what they'd say? We'd be cut in an instant if they knew that girl outsmarted both of us."

"She's proving to be more and more intriguing, isn't she?" I didn't like the sound of his voice.

"If I didn't know any better, Blaine, I might think you were into this girl." Maeve didn't seem to like the way his voice sounded either. *"Maybe last year wasn't just an act? Maybe you really have a thing for red-haired, light witches?"*

"Someone's jealous," Blaine chuckled, unable to hide his amusement.

"Someone needs to remember who he's dealing with." Frustration bubbled to the surface as the tone of Maeve's voice dropped. *"Don't forget, I put my name on the line to spare your life with HQ. If we don't deliver, you won't be the only one they punish. We're both gone. Not trapped in a trophy. Dead gone."*

"Lighten up, babe. You're gold to this coven. They wouldn't risk an asset like you."

"I'm serious, Blaine. I saved you once. I won't be able to do it again."

"We're going to find her. I'm going to kill her. Then we'll both be in the coven's good graces. I'll officially be one of the team."

"Are you blind or just stupid?" Maeve snapped. It sounded like she slammed something down on a table or countertop. *"This isn't about your initiation. It's about her. It's what she could become."*

I jolted awake, feeling disoriented but not nauseated anymore. Marjorie, Emily, Marnie, Tephi, Jeb, Margo, and I were all packed into Marjorie's SUV. Once Marnie told us our destination, we took less than five minutes to gather our belongings and zip out onto U.S. Highway 80 toward Alabama. Our target area would typically be a six-hour drive. Still, Marjorie wanted to take a longer route to avoid big cities like Atlanta. We'd choose mostly back roads and spend as little time as possible on the major highways. The longer distance would tack on four or five more hours, but it felt like a necessary detour. We knew Maeve saw the SUV that night in Bonaventure Cemetery, and Marjorie was worried about her tag being traced. Maeve would likely utilize all her resources, including psychics, which meant Atlanta would be an accessible area for them to locate us in. The Ainbertach's southeast headquarters was likely in Atlanta.

We each took a cloaking potion except Marnie—she wasn't on Maeve's radar for the moment and we needed to conserve the potions we had. We couldn't be traced magically, but there were other ways for her to find us. If she was as closely aligned with the Ainbertach leaders as she claimed, there could've been many people at her disposal. If my dream was a vision and not a dream, it seemed Maeve had some authority. The unknowns, like Maeve's resources, were the reason Marjorie insisted we leave our phones behind. She promised we'd stop at a store to get "burner" phones, like something out of "Weeds" or "Breaking Bad." We all begrudgingly left our phones, along with the ability to tell our families we were okay. As soon as the news hit about Marjorie's shop, I knew Dad would flip out.

It was an odd feeling, leaving everything behind. I'd been in danger before, but this was different. I wasn't the only target anymore, and we were now dealing with an enemy we couldn't fight.

What was worse, I seemed to be pushing all my loved ones away. Emily was furious with me for "ruining her life." I tried to explain the goal was to protect her life, but she was giving me the cold shoulder. About an hour into the drive, she passed out into a deep sleep. Her snores were loud, but she was keeping Tephi comfortable. The two were napping on a pink, paisley duffel bag as a pillow. It surprised me she could sleep in the cramped space. Emily and I both had bags under our feet and two laptop bags between us in the back seat. Jeb and Margo were curled up in the only open corner of space in the back, surrounded by boxes, trash bags, suitcases, and laundry baskets containing all our possessions. We left behind more than imaginable, but Marjorie emphasized we'd be back. She told us this was a temporary solution, but I didn't know if I could trust it.

"What part of Alabama is it again?" Marjorie asked in a hushed voice. She and Marnie were up front, and Marnie was navigating the old-school way with an actual paper map. I was astounded at how quickly Marnie jumped into action after hearing we were in danger. I'd been under the assumption that Marnie didn't know about active magic. It seemed she knew a lot more than we initially thought. She actually thought we didn't know about active magic. Even more remarkable was how quick Marjorie was to trust Marnie. The mere mention of a safe house was all Marjorie needed. We didn't talk about where it was until we were an hour into our drive. Marjorie had insisted that we wait; someone could've been listening.

"Remlap," Marnie responded briefly. "It's my granny's house."

"I see." There was a moment of tension before Marnie spoke again.

"Right or wrong, the house is well protected."

Marjorie's lips seemed to curl downward at the mention of Marnie's grandmother. I waited for Marjorie's response, but she didn't speak again until she noticed I was awake.

"You were dreaming," Marjorie stated.

"Yes," I yawned, stretching my arms above my head. It was a futile attempt with the lack of room available. Jeb's ears perked up at the sound of my voice, and I reached backward to pet him. His brown eyes locked with mine as if he was checking on me. I smiled at him and nodded.

"Were you traveling?" Marjorie wanted to know.

"Traveling?" Marnie questioned, wide-eyed. I suddenly felt guilty about the secrets I'd kept from her.

"Emlyn's gift is time manipulation. In addition to freezing time and people in it, Emlyn can travel forward and backward, especially when she's unconscious," Marjorie blurted out before I could respond.

"Really?" Marnie turned back to me, almost in disbelief. "That's rare. Does it run in your family?"

"No," Marjorie took back control of the conversation. "Emlyn is the first recorded witch in our family with the ability. Telekinesis has always been the Finnerty power—a fairly common one. Her mother had it."

"Common but useful," Marnie commented.

"Oh, yes. You should have seen Rhiannon. She was so powerful. I'd like to see that silver-headed swine take on the three of us."

"Does foresight run in our family?" I asked, suddenly realizing I didn't know much about it.

"Prophecy is rarer for the Finnertys, but not unheard of... We had a few cousins who could levitate," Marjorie laughed as if she was stuck in a memory.

"Levitate? What good is that?" Emily butted in, suddenly awake.

"It's not," Marjorie snorted. "You know, it was fun though. Every Halloween, they'd ride around on broomsticks to keep the stereotype alive. It scared the bejesus out of their neighbors."

"My aunt Rosie told me she was an animal psychic," Marnie giggled, joining in on the fun. "She used to help me talk to cats."

This tickled Marjorie even more. It was most I'd seen Marjorie laugh. I was almost worried she was having a mental breakdown.

"Marnie, I knew your Aunt Rosie. She was no animal psychic. She was a psychometrist."

"A psychiatrist?" Emily questioned.

"No, a psychometrist," Marjorie snapped. "A token-reader. She drew foresight from objects. For example, she'd take that necklace you're wearing in her hands, and then it would conjure an image of your face. In a flash, she'd know half your life."

"Sounds like your powers but better," Emily blurted out.

With that, the happy-go-lucky storytelling portion of the trip concluded as Marjorie's nostrils flared and jawline tightened.

"To answer your question," I interjected before a fight broke out, "I'm not sure if I was traveling. Maeve and Blaine were there, but I was in a wine cellar. Something felt off."

"Write it all down," Marjorie instructed. "Scents, conversations, everything. It might become useful."

"How much longer do we have to be in this car?" Emily wanted to know.

"It looks like close to five hours," Marnie told her.

74

It was almost 9 p.m., and a little less than half the trip was over. It might have been the gigantic fight for our lives, or maybe it was the magically-induced flu, but I was wiped out. It felt like we'd been running forever, and it still didn't feel like we'd put enough distance between ourselves and Savannah.

"I'm hungry," Emily complained.

"Hush. We've only been driving for four hours," Marjorie barked.

"And I haven't eaten since class this morning when Maeve nabbed me," Emily informed her.

"Jeb should probably go out soon," I agreed with Emily, trying to smooth over our friction. "It's probably as good a time as any."

"Fine," Marjorie sighed. "We'll find a superstore to stop at, hopefully one with cell phones. Emlyn, you should also find a payphone while we're there."

"Me specifically?"

"I saw your father drive by the shop on his way home from work. He saw the destruction. I imagine he went by the townhouse and found we were gone."

"That would've been three hours ago! You mean he's been trying to call me for three hours, and you didn't stop earlier?"

"Have our parents been trying to call us too?" Emily wanted to know.

"The shop made the 9 o'clock news. Everyone's parents will find out, so I suggest you all make a call home," Marjorie gritted her teeth. "You might also want to know: the police will call it occult violence."

"Did your foresight tell you that?" Emily crossed her arms in the back seat.

"No, but police always call it occult violence with magic shops," she told us.

I looked at Emily, trying to study her face for a reaction. Her parents weren't overly religious, but they attended church when they were in town on Sundays. Emily's parents knew I was unconventional, but I guessed the occult reference to my grandmother's shop wouldn't go over well.

Especially because Emily would need to explain why she wasn't in Savannah anymore. Dad wouldn't be happy either. He never wanted witchcraft to be a part of my life. At least I wouldn't have to lie. I assumed Marnie's parents knew about magic too. To Emily's parents, this was their only daughter running away to become part of a crazy witch coven.

"Pull off at this next exit. There's a big supermarket up ahead," I instructed Marjorie, and then I turned to Emily. "Maybe you can tell your parents you don't know anything about the shop? Maybe you're just away at Teach for America or something?"

Emily rolled her eyes at me and then twisted her body away.

We found ourselves in a small town called Phenix City, situated right on the line between Alabama and Georgia. The store was on the Alabama side, and on our way there, I noticed it looked like any other small southern town. There were a few smaller grocery stores on the way to the big one, along with some mom-and-pop antique shops and a barbeque restaurant boasting the best ribs in town. At this time of night, everything was closed. When we finally reached the superstore, it surprised us to find there was still a payphone out front. It was that old.

"We'll make better time if we split up, and I do not want to be here for more than 30 minutes. So, pay attention," Marjorie ordered as she pulled into an inconspicuous spot in the back. I found it ironic that she was trying to keep to the shadows in the back when we all looked like we'd been through the ringer. We'd used wipes to clean ourselves off the best we could, but we looked like disaster victims. I didn't dare mention it, though.

Marjorie started barking orders. "This is the last stop we will make. No more bathroom breaks, snack stops, or other nonsense after this point. Emlyn, you'll take Jeb for a walk and then use the payphone to call your father. Marnie and Emily, you'll get food. Each of you should also make a phone call. Switch out spots until you each have a chance."

"What are you going to do?" Emily demanded of Marjorie.

"I'm going to get each of us a cellphone. Now, as far as food: aim for canned items or the boxed dinners that come with the meat included. I know it's not healthy, but it lasts longer. Don't forget cat food and dog food. There's a deli inside. Order what you'd like for dinner."

"Where are we going to fit all this food?" Emily groaned, referencing the lack of space in the car.

Marjorie rolled her eyes. "Emily, you might not have realized, but I'm a great deal older than you. I perhaps know what I'm doing. We'll get a cargo box for the top of the car and transfer our luggage onto the roof. Questions?"

Everyone, including Emily, was silent. Less than a minute later, we split up. Before I knew it, I was dialing my father's cell at the payphone with knots growing in my stomach at each unanswered ring.

"Sam Perry," Dad's monotone voice answered. In two words, he conveyed how utterly depressed he was. Guilt wasn't the word to describe what I felt. He was probably expecting a police officer or the hospital.

"Dad."

"Emlyn?"

"It's me."

"Thank God. I thought—what happened at the shop? Where are you?"

"I'm fine. There was an attack."

"What did your grandmother do? I'll kill that woman."

"It wasn't her fault. It's the coven. It's back."

"When are you going to stop this, Emlyn?"

"Dad, please. You know it's not that simple."

"It could be if you let it."

"I didn't call you to fight, Dad. I wanted you to know we're safe. Marjorie, Emily, Marnie, and I are all okay. We're heading to a safe house."

"A safe house? Where are you?"

"We can't stay in Savannah. It's not safe for us. The girl who attacked me might not know about you, but I think you should leave early for your business trip. Just get up and leave first thing tomorrow."

"This isn't going to ever stop, is it?"

"We're going to work out a plan, I promise. I just need you to be safe."

"Strip your powers like your mother did once. Make it like it was before. If Marjorie takes away your powers, you won't be a target anymore. You can end this now and come home."

"It's too late for that." My eyes watered, but I pulled myself together when Marnie walked out of the front door of the superstore. I knew my time was up.

"It's not. We could—."

"I have to go now, Dad. Please, just know I'm safe."

"Emlyn—."

"I love you."

Coins clanged in the machine when I slammed the phone down, and I took a minute to recompose myself. Luckily, Marnie didn't comment or get too close before I signaled her over.

"Phone is all yours," I told her.

"Joy," she smiled as she approached.

"Yeah, the conversation didn't go super well. At least Dad knows I'm safe."

Marnie nodded. "I know what it's like, having a parent who doesn't understand magic." It was the first time I could remember Marnie ever bringing up her parents. She had never talked about them before. Now that we were entirely out of the broom closet, I was getting to know a completely different side of her.

"Are your parents non-magic?" I asked.

"Not completely. My dad is half magic, like you. He has powers, but they're focused on herbs and mixtures. He was always giving me and my mom smoothies and teas, or making creams and salves for us."

"What about your mom?"

"No magic. My sisters and I were raised around magic with her consent, but in case you were wondering, one-quarter magic does not a witch make. None of us have active powers," Marnie sighed. "Still, Mom never really understood the practice, and she never supported it the way my dad needed. My folks split when I was 10."

"Oh, I'm sorry. I didn't mean to—."

"You didn't. And it's fine. They're both remarried now. Both to people who understand them better."

We both chuckled to ourselves, and I wondered what would've happened if Mom and Dad split when I was young. They were great together, but I wondered how different life would've been if Mom had continued practicing magic when I was growing up. I pushed the thought from my mind.

"I better call them," Marnie told me. "One of these calls is about to go a lot better than the other."

"Good luck."

"Oh, I almost forgot," Marnie slid a piece of paper into my hand. "Emily might be pissed at you, but she thought you might want this."

"What is it?" I asked as I unfolded the scrap to reveal a phone number.

"It's Quinn's. She noticed you didn't copy it from your phone."

"She loves to meddle, doesn't she?"

"I think she was right, though," Marnie told me. "He'll want to know you're okay."

We were in the car another five and a half hours, and I spent that time mulling over the decision to call Quinn. I couldn't keep my hands off the piece of paper with his number on it. My fingers constantly fiddled with it inside my hoodie pocket. I wanted to contact him. Marnie was right that Quinn would want to know I was okay, but it didn't seem safe contacting him. Part of me was convinced Quinn was better off not knowing anything and just assuming I was dead. I knew if I contacted him, Quinn might be hard to shake. He might want details I couldn't provide. A worse thought was him rejecting me if I called. Maybe seeing the destruction of Marjorie's shop would be the final bit of evidence he needed to eradicate me from his life. He wouldn't be wrong.

On the other hand, Blaine knew Quinn. Even if Quinn wasn't living in Savannah anymore, he was only an hour away. I wouldn't put it past Blaine to use my feelings against me again, and it was also likely that Blaine held a grudge against Quinn. I owed it to Quinn to warn him and to do what I could to protect him.

My internal argument continued until we turned onto a gravel road. I finally looked out the window and realized we were in the middle of nowhere.

"Get ready to lose cell service," Marnie announced.

"Wait, what?" Emily jerked forward. "I can't use my phone?"

"There's a better signal at the house, but it won't be great. There's no wi-fi either. Granny wasn't up with the times."

"What?!" Emily snarled. "This is like a nightmare!"

"Not to freak out, but how can we do any kind of research without the internet?" I echoed Emily's concern.

"I bought some hotspots at the store," Marjorie muttered. I could feel her eyes rolling. "God forbid you spend some time reading a book."

Emily slumped back in her seat, looking defeated. She was quiet most of the car ride. I guessed the conversation with her parents hadn't gone well. After the call, Emily's eyes looked puffy, and her cheeks were red. She still wouldn't say a word to me, though.

The gravel road was about 45 minutes away from the nearest highway. I hadn't been paying too much attention to my surroundings, but it seemed like the last fast-food restaurant or grocery store I saw was back near the exit. This was remote. The winding, rocky road suddenly became paved again as we passed along the ridge of a mountain. We couldn't see much in the night's dark, but the stars were brighter than I'd ever seen them over the ridge. There were some houses sporadically placed along the road, as well, but they looked nothing like the homes in Savannah. They didn't look similar to each other, either. They drastically varied in design from grand brick buildings to humble colonials to trailer homes.

A mile or so down the road, we must have driven past a pasture of cows or horses, if the smell was anything to judge by. It reminded me of visiting the petting zoo as a kid. The "farm" smell excited Jeb. His tail started up fast, thwacking anything around him, including people. He jumped over the back seat into my lap to get a better look out the window.

"Jeez, Jeb," I scolded him and tried pushing him back. Margo fled, finding refuge with Marnie in the front seat.

"It smells so bad," Emily complained as the stench of manure filled the car.

"We're in the country. The proper country," Marjorie told us. For those of us who had grown up in Savannah, the charm of farms and livestock wasn't a massive part of our South.

"The smell doesn't reach the house," Marnie assured us.

We took another gravel road into a thicket of woods with no lights or houses. The scenery was like the beginning of a horror film as we bumped along.

"Be honest—you're about to murder us, aren't you?" Emily asked in a sarcastic but pointed tone.

"It's just through this section of woods, and then it's about two miles down," Marnie assured us.

I couldn't wait to get out of the car. The animals were restless, and I needed to stretch my legs. Pretty soon we came to the foot of a long, packed-dirt driveway leading to a faded blue house. It was a welcoming one-story ranch-style home with white shutters and wood paneling all the way around. About eight windows were lit up with a dim light in the carport, acting as a lighthouse in the darkness. We could see a large doghouse, two wicker rocking chairs, a wicker swing attached to the ceiling, a dozen wind chimes, random tools thrown about, and a pile of decaying boxes. Bushes and flowers lined the front of the house and the exterior of the carport with several stone pathways leading out into unlit areas.

An old barn sat to the left of the house in the shadows. Even in the dark, I noticed the barn's brown paint was chipped, revealing rotting wood underneath it. I imagined how rustically beautiful it must have been in its glory days with fresh color and bright white trim. Maybe there would have been five or six horses housed inside, or even a small herd of goats. Now, there was a gaping hole in one wall and in the roof. The gate looked so rusted, I could probably push it down.

Out beside the barn, there was a long patch of dirt that created a rectangular garden, but the plot was empty. It was probably a vegetable and herb garden at one time. Even empty, it was inviting, practically asking for some fresh seeds. I didn't have a green thumb—I killed every plant I tried to keep—but Mom was great at it.

The grass and forest stretched into the night, and I was surprised by how relieved I was. This place felt safer than anywhere we'd been since the fight with Maeve.

"It's certainly isolated," Marjorie commented in a low voice.

"Creepy is more like it," Emily corrected her.

We started down the driveway, which was lined with crepe myrtles. They weren't in bloom, but I imagined the drive was beautiful in the spring. Almost immediately, the silence was broken by a pack of howling dogs who came running at the car. Five mangy pups were galloping toward us, barking their heads off, which motivated Jeb to join in. He trampled me once again. His hair was standing tall on the back of his neck, and the commotion quickly sent both cats into hiding. Margo buried herself under Marnie's seat, while Tephi attempted to use Emily as a shield.

"Jeb, calm down!" I ordered, using all my strength to pull him from the window. "Marnie, I thought you said this place was empty?"

"Those were Granny's dogs," Marnie laughed, seeming in good spirits. The dogs followed us all the way up the driveway until we reached the carport.

"Who takes care of them if your granny isn't here?" I asked.

"The groundskeeper. He's here every other day. The hounds have always been a little wild, so they pretty much do what they want. It's one of the perks of living on 80 acres in the middle of nowhere."

"Groundskeeper?" Marjorie and I asked in unison, suddenly worried about another person knowing where we were.

"Totally trustworthy. He knows about magic, and he was always a good lookout for Granny. He even took care of her when she got sick," Marnie explained.

I nodded. A tall, black German Shepherd jumped onto Marjorie's door, leaving muddy paw prints under his giant feet. His nub of a tail was wagging ferociously.

Marjorie's jaw locked, "This will be a long trip." She took a deep breath, composing herself. "Grab everything you can carry. We'll get everything unpacked, and then Marnie can show us to our rooms."

"Can't we unpack tomorrow?" Emily complained.

"No."

Jeb bounded out of the car into the pile of dogs, instantly bonding with a thin, blonde pup with a curled tail. The dark German Shepherd sniffed at Jeb fiercely but seemed to accept him in a matter of seconds. The dog's fur was coarse and long with a little greying around the snout. I guessed he was the old man of the group. He and one other dog seemed much older than the rest. His companion was a broad, brown Labrador Pitbull mix. He was just as tall as Jeb, but his shoulders were much more extensive. His bark was deep, echoing his dominant stature.

"The older guys are Oz and Hub," Marnie said as we scooted out. "The other three are Boots, Dakota, and Max."

Boots was a short, stumpy dog with black and white fur and long floppy ears. Her body was long and thick like a hotdog, and she stood a few inches from the ground. In drastic contrast, the blonde dog, Dakota, was slender and tall. She resembled a Husky mixed with a German Shepherd with her curled tail and pointed ears. Her snout was long, seeming to smile up at me before she nipped at Max like she was trying to keep him away from me. Max was also some sort of lab-pit mix, but smaller than Hub—maybe 50 pounds. He was brown with a white stripe down his forehead, which formed a white crown on his chest. Max was the happiest to see us. He practically drenched Marnie's hands in slobber when he greeted her.

I stroked Dakota a few times before she and Jeb took off chasing each other in the darkness. It seemed the whole pack was grateful for company. If they weren't playing, they were sharing playful licks or seeking attention by leaning their bodies against us. While the cats were less enthusiastic about our new companions, I was happy to see them.

"How much of this is your grandmother's?" Emily wanted to know, gesturing to the fields and forest surrounding us.

"Everything you can see. It goes on for about 80 acres… I think," Marnie answered. "Most of the land has charms protecting it, but there are three acres that are cloaked completely."

"Completely? How and why?" I asked.

Marjorie's eyes narrowed toward Marnie. I didn't understand this new tension between Marnie and Marjorie. I'd never seen Marjorie seem so irritated to be in a place before, especially one that was so safe-guarded. It reminded me of the first time I met Marjorie at her shop. Even though Marjorie knew who I was, I'd never met her before. I certainly didn't think she was my grandmother. She was cold toward me when we first met because she knew my father was against me using magic. After Mom died, Dad asked Marjorie not to reveal herself to me. She kept her promise. I was the one who found her.

"See the wind chimes strung up at the end of the driveway?" Marnie motioned to a bronze pole. It was barely visible, but in the moonlight, I could see the outline of feathers and several chimes dangling from it. "There's a totem like that every 25 yards, acting as a fence around three of the acres. It protects the house, the barns, and a pond that's a little way back behind the house. The wind chimes block all magic."

"Do we have to activate it?" Marjorie asked.

"No. It's a force field. It blocks people from seeing magic from the outside but allows us to continue using magic on the inside. The bubble is always active. There's also an emergency spell we can use to lock down the perimeter if we need to. The spell works two ways, though. No one in or out."

"Wow, that's some intense protection," I commented, feeling wholly safe for the first time in days.

"She needed it," Marjorie grumbled. "Let's get inside."

Marnie ignored Marjorie's comment and led the way into the main living space. It just screamed "grandmother's house," which was a little surprising. I expected to find spell books, jars of herbs, crystals, candles, statues of goddesses, or something magical in the house. Instead, there were copies of Southern Living and Reader's Digest on the coffee table. The furniture was pristine, as if they had enlarged it from a dollhouse. The sitting room's love seat and wingback armchairs, which were positioned cozily in front of a small brick fireplace, were decorated with pink floral accents.

There were dozens, if not hundreds, of picture frames all over the house. Photos of family members covered the walls, the shelves, and the mantle. Some people looked older; I thought they might be Marnie's grandparents when they were 25 or so. Many of the pictures were of young children, though. I suspected I'd find a few of Marnie around the house if I looked. There were also various knickknacks cluttering the remaining empty space. Many items featured the word "Nana" or "Granny," reminding me of gifts I used to make for Dad's mother.

We passed through the sitting room into a small kitchen, decorated with bright, white appliances. The white cabinets and counters contrasted with a cherry oak table in the middle of the room. There was still a surprising lack of witch stuff. Three ceramic containers were labeled, "Salt," "Sugar," and "Flour," instead of herbs we used frequently. They were placed next to a stainless-steel knife set in a white block of wood. A red rooster cookie jar provided a much-needed splash of color to the room, but it was still so typical. This kitchen looked too polished and pristine for eye of newt.

I was curious to explore the rest of the house, but we didn't waste any time. We were all exhausted from travel and anxiety. After dropping all our canned goods in the kitchen to be stored in the pantry later and prying the cats from the SUV, we were ready for bed.

"Alright. I'm done," Emily announced. "Where am I sleeping?"

"So, there are only three rooms," Marnie explained. "Two of us will share the master if that's okay."

"You and I can share," Emily blurted out, ensuring she wouldn't get stuck in the room with me.

"Emily and I will take the master. It's straight down this hallway. Marjorie, you can take the guest room, which is down to the left. Emlyn, you get the kids' room. It's the first door on the right."

We each nodded in agreement. I grabbed my pillow off the kitchen table and pulled my backpack over one shoulder. Emily didn't hesitate. She headed off to the master as soon as Marnie finished speaking.

"Let's get to sleep," Marjorie ordered. "We'll figure out shower arrangements in the morning."

Jeb and I retreated silently to the kid's room, an ironically cheerful room with pink and purple wallpaper and lamps lined in pink lace. The metal-framed bed was a full rather than a twin, which was a happy surprise. I pushed about 30 stuffed animals to the floor, messing up the perfect arrangement they'd been in, and I set my backpack down on a nearby dresser.

I wanted to fully appreciate the nostalgia of the room I was in. They kept it shipshape, which I guessed was a memento to a time when Marnie and her cousins were young enough to appreciate all the pink. I often wondered what it would have been like if I had known Marjorie as a kid. I couldn't imagine her creating a space like this for me at her house, but it was also hard to imagine what Marjorie was like 10 years ago.

"Bedtime," I whispered to Jeb, who in response jumped onto the bed and curled up at the foot of the mattress. I peeled my dirty clothes from my body, replacing them with a pair of pajamas. I needed to shower, but I was too fatigued. I crawled under the covers, turned off the light, and begged my brain to allow me a few moments of rest. My body was exhausted, my muscles felt weak, and my eyes were heavy. My mind wouldn't stop zooming. I couldn't get Quinn out of my head.

"Oh, for goodness' sake," I scolded myself. I sat up in bed, ran my fingers through my hair, and pulled my knees up to my chest. "This is dumb, Emlyn. You're so dumb," I told myself. Jeb lifted his head and gave me a long stare.

"You're right. It's just a text," I commented to Jeb as if his gaze was the approval I needed. Before I knew it, the piece of paper was unfolded, and Quinn's phone number was punched into my new phone. I kept the message brief.

Me: *I'm safe.*

About ten seconds later, my phone was ringing.

"Crap, crap, crap," I gasped. Jeb abandoned me, setting his head back down on the bed. He was tired. There wasn't time to think as the phone buzzed once and then twice. I answered on the third. "Hello," I whispered, hoping not to wake anyone else. I threw the pink quilt over my head to conceal my voice like I was in high school again.

"Emlyn?" Quinn's voice quivered on the other line.

"It's me."

"What happened? That magic store was on the news. After what happened at dinner—I thought that girl might have... I thought you were dead." Quinn's voice was shaky. He was talking fast, slurring his worries into phrases.

"I'm okay. We all made it out."

"We're really talking right now? I'm not making it up?" The line was suddenly voiceless, filled with muffled breathing. It sounded like he might be crying.

"Quinn, please don't be upset anymore. I'm okay—safe even." I winced a bit at my lie.

"All I could think about was the last thing I said to you. I was out of line, Em. If that had really been the last thing I said to you..."

"You don't need to apologize. Maeve attacked you and almost killed you. Your reaction was normal. You had every right—."

"I didn't have the right to criticize your life, especially when I wanted to know more about it. You aren't the one who attacked me. You tried to save me, and I repaid you by lashing out. I was afraid."

"But I put you in that situation. I knew Maeve was out there, and I put you at risk by being around you."

"It doesn't matter anymore. Emlyn, when I thought you were gone, all I felt was regret. I regret the way I treated you when I found out you were a witch. Even more so, I regret that we didn't spend the last year together."

"We both know there's more to that story."

Quinn wasn't listening. "I need to see you. I'll drive back to town tomorrow morning. I'll skip my classes. You're at the townhouse, right? What time can I come by?"

"Quinn, slow down," I interrupted.

"Sorry. I'm getting ahead of myself. What day works best for you? I'm free all week."

"You don't understand. No day works for me."

"What about this weekend?"

"Quinn, you were right before. My life is dangerous and crazy. You can't be a part of it."

"But you won. That counts for something."

"We ran."

"Ran?"

"We couldn't beat her. Maeve's too powerful, so we left town."

"What do you mean? You're gone?"

"I can't tell you where, but I just wanted you to know I'm alive."

"When are you coming back?"

"I don't know. We're working on it. I know this is a lot to take in, but I need you to do something for me."

"How can I help?"

"You need to find a magic shop or something spiritual. You need to purchase fluorite, black obsidian, and hematite."

"What for?"

"They're gemstones. Just buy them. You need to carry them with you all the time until I tell you otherwise."

"Fluorite, obsidian, and what?"

"Write them down, Quinn. Fluorite, black obsidian, and hematite."

"Okay, okay. Are you going to tell me why this is so important?"

"They'll protect you from being found or hurt."

"Protect me from that girl? You really think she'd come looking for me?"

"No. Blaine's back."

Chapter Eight

Sometime before sunrise, I gave up on sleep, retreating to the carport where the pack of dogs was snoozing in the fresh morning air. The side door creaked open as I exited the house. I was bound for the large swing chair, and I was dragging a giant blanket with me. Our presence alerted the blonde dog, Dakota, and her friend Max. They greeted us with thumping tails before stretching themselves awake.

I patted Dakota on the head as Max and Jeb greeted each other. I climbed into the swing and pulled the large comforter over myself. It was colder here on the mountain than it was in Savannah. We weren't that much further north, but it was still more than I was used to. A light breeze sent a chill through my body. I pulled the comforter up to my chin as I listened to the wind chimes sing. I tried to focus on the noise alone and push all the other thoughts from my head.

My mind wandered, focusing in on the dream I had in the car the previous night. There had been a repeat performance of the vision during my attempt at sleep after I contacted Quinn. The recurrence made me think I'd been time travelling. It felt real enough. The stale stench of dirt from the wine cellar was stuck in my nostrils. I sorted through the memories, trying to determine if anything differed from the previous dream. I couldn't remember anything new. The goal seemed the same in both: I desperately wanted to climb to the top of the stairs to reach Maeve, but both times I had woken up before anything further happened.

A cold nose on my arm surprised me. I looked down at Dakota, who was staring at me with her bright brown eyes. She lifted one paw and placed it on the comforter over my hand, trying to pull it toward her. I obeyed, scratching her ears and stroking her back.

"You're a good girl, aren't you, Dakota?" I asked her. She brought her face close to mine and gave me a sweet little lick on the cheek. "You don't really look like a Dakota to me, though."
She jumped into my lap on the swing, and we sat there for a while in silence. Jeb and Max were chasing each other around the yard, fighting over a deer antler. One by one, the other dogs joined in the fun, but Dakota stayed with me in the swing.

"Made a friend, huh?" Marnie appeared after a good 30 minutes of silence. She was standing in the doorway, dressed and ready for the day in a pair of forest green jeans and a T-shirt. Her dark blonde hair was loose at her shoulders, and Marnie hadn't bothered with contacts. Instead, she was sporting a pair of thick-rimmed glasses. I was thankful to see she was carrying two white coffee mugs.

"We're bonding," I told her.

She walked over, handed me a mug of tea, and then sat down on a wicker chair next to me. "To calm the mind and energize the body."

Seeing Marnie, Max galloped back toward the carport and practically climbed into her lap. Jeb followed him, seeming disappointed when he saw Dakota in my lap. He shot me a concerned look but then quickly took off to play with the other dogs again.

I sipped the tea, and it tasted like autumn. It was warm and filled with spices. "This is perfect, by the way."

"Why, thank you," she smiled. "You looked like something was on your mind when I walked out. Want to talk about anything?"

"How long do you have?" I asked her.

"Depends on how long Marjorie lets us stay outside. I'm not sure she slept at all. She's been in the sunroom since I got up an hour ago."

"Yeah, I tried to sleep, but no luck," I paused, taking another sip of tea. "How's Emily?"

"She's still sleeping. I'm sure she'll come around soon. It'll all work out."

"I hope so, but she's so angry."

"So we have to retake a semester. It's not the worst thing in the world."

"You're right about that."

"Everyone, join me in the sunroom!" Marjorie's voice crashed through the house, shattering the illusion of serenity I was enjoying outside.

"Here we go," I sighed, pushing Dakota's warm body off mine. She begrudgingly jumped down and ran to attack Max out in the yard. It was a fun game to her—torturing the smaller, brown dog—and Max seemed content with the arrangement. I lifted the blanket, letting out the warmth I'd been wrapped in, and I followed Marnie into the house. We passed through the kitchen into a new section of the house I hadn't seen last night. A set of French doors in a small dining room opened into a brightly lit area with antique wallpaper, resembling scrolls or aged paper.

This room was decorated much more like a witch's house. The windows stretched from the floor to the ceiling, inviting sunlight into every nook and cranky. It allowed no room for shadows, which must have been perfect for maintaining the lush greenery growing in every corner. Planters were all over the place with shrubs, small exotic trees, brambles, fresh herbs, winding vines, and vibrant flowers.

I finally noticed Marjorie to our left. Apparently, I didn't get the memo because she was also dressed and ready. The brown color of her long-sleeved, full-length dress matched the earthy tones of the room. She was settled in at a four-seat wooden table with her hands gripped around another white coffee cup. Behind her was an old-school chalkboard with Blaine and Maeve's names scribbled at the top. Just seeing the names caused anxiety. Under each of their names, Marjorie also listed their primary powers and any additional knowledge we had. There wasn't much.

"Well, sit down," Marjorie urged, standing up. She pointed to a bentwood couch near the middle of the room, which she'd positioned to face the chalkboard. Under other circumstances, I would've taken more time to appreciate the furniture in the room. The couch was ornate, made of elaborate twists of twigs and vines, with brown cushions that matched the color of Marjorie's dress. I liked the vibe in the room because all the furniture was constructed of natural materials, from the bookshelves to the two rocking chairs opposite the couch.

"Where's Emily?" Marjorie demanded.

"Still sleeping," I told her.

"Emily?" Marjorie called through the open doorway, her voice cracking in anger. "Now!"

"I'm coming!" Emily sounded defeated.

"Anytime now," Marjorie pressed.

Emily finally appeared in the doorway, fresh from sleep. Her hair was knotted into a messy bun on the top of her head, and her eyes were barely open. She yawned as she walked into the room and slumped over into one of the rocking chairs.

"I need coffee," Emily complained. She reached down to the bottom of her oversized T-shirt and used one corner to wipe her eyes. "Did we get creamer?"

"Not now, Emily," Marjorie scolded. "You can get it later."

"Marjorie, maybe we could all take a few minutes to wake up for the morning before we break into planning mode?" I added on Emily's behalf.

"Don't get complacent here, thinking we're all safe." Marjorie's jaw tightened.

"Marnie's grandmother has this place super protected. Why wouldn't we be safe?" I asked.

"As powerful and motivated as Marnie's grandmother was to stay hidden, there are always ways into a safe haven. If we allow ourselves to waste time, we're giving Maeve time to find us. She won't be wasting any time."

"I just wanted a cup of coffee," Emily interjected.

"Shush!" Marjorie bellowed. "I want you all to understand the gravity of this. Maeve is unaffected by our magic. She may also be able to see through the magic that protects us. We need to get to work."

"Well, Maeve is pretty much unstoppable. Her fireballs are pretty scary, too. They looked painful. I'm glad I didn't get hit by one of those," I admitted.

"She can also destroy a building by just looking at it," Emily grunted, looking down at the bruises painted across her arm.

"Her gifts are all active then?" Marnie asked.

I nodded. "I think so. The drowning thing Maeve did at dinner was instantaneous, and there's also that potion."

"What potion?" Marjorie asked.

"The one Blaine took that turned his powers violent. It was the reason he could cause physical pain instead of emotional pain. I've been researching that potion for a year, and I can't find anything on it. There's no herb for that."

"She's like mega-ultra-witch," Emily said under her breath.

"Blaine then," Marnie commented, "that's where we start."

"Exactly what I was thinking," Marjorie responded. "He's the weaker link."

"As long as he doesn't have that potion," I added.

"His gift is empathic abilities. What else do we know? Emlyn, you've spent more time with him than any of us. What can you tell us?" Marjorie wanted to know.

"Not much, really. Blaine's dad could manipulate the earth. He trapped Mom in quicksand to subdue her."

"We may be able to track the family name and the power if Corwin is his real name. When I researched his family last year, there wasn't much to find, unfortunately. They either have made little impact on the magical community or Corwin isn't Blaine's true family name."

"That would make things trickier." Marnie scrunched her nose in thought.

Marjorie wasn't willing to accept our lack of information. "Is there anything else? Anything specific to Blaine?"

I thought back to the weeks I spent with Blaine, and to my embarrassment, my eyes watered. I was ashamed of it all. They weren't fond memories, mostly because I started to fall in love with Blaine. I was in love with his lie. That, paired with magically induced affection, created a nasty mix. I'd suppressed as much of those memories as I could. Now, I needed to bring them back.

"Power," I told them. "He's all about the power. Before he tried to kill me, Blaine told me the way his father killed Mom wasn't honorable. Blaine called it the easy way out, which is why Blaine trained me like he did. To him, I was too easy a target as a fresh witch, and Blaine wanted glory."

I looked over at Marnie. She'd never heard the entire story before, and I wondered if she'd judge me later for the part I played.

"He wants a seat at the top," Marjorie pondered out loud. "He's motivated by dominance and command."

"He also enjoys hurting people. I think he feeds off the pain. He could have just helped me be a better witch, but he played a game. He wanted me to feel something for him before he killed me. Think about it: he poisoned me at the dance and brought me back. Then he attacked Emily and Quinn when he didn't have to."

Emily's face flushed red at the thought of her experiences last year. Emily was Blaine's homecoming date. His charisma charmed her as well. The attack she suffered was brutal, too. She spent the better part of an hour clawing herself bloody in an attempt to keep a swarm of hallucinated rats at bay. The memory of it must've been hard for Emily.

She jumped from her chair, crossed her arms, and stomped one foot down. "I'm done with this. I'm not a witch. Let me know when I can go home." She turned on her heel and headed out toward the kitchen. I heard the creak of the side door opening, and then it slammed shut. The commotion sent Margo fleeing from her hiding spot under the couch and into Marnie's lap.

"Temperamental little—," Marjorie huffed.

"Leave her," I interjected. "She's dealt with a lot, and she's right. This isn't her fight." I turned to Marnie. "It's not yours either, you know. You can go home. They don't even know who you are."

She looked down at her hands and stoked Margo's back. The cat's loud purring was the only sound for a few moments as Marnie contemplated her options.

"Our families were all part of the same coven once," she decided. "We protect our own."

Marjorie smiled and nodded at Marnie.

"Presumably, Emlyn is still Blaine's mark. He'll need to eliminate her as quickly as possible," Marjorie noted. "Even if Maeve has some pull with the Ainbertachs as she claims, the coven still won't tolerate a witch who can't fulfill orders. He's weak in their eyes right now. I'd expect he's on a strict deadline."

"You said he went after Emily and Quinn last time," Marnie added. "He'll probably do it again. Should your father be warned? Or Quinn?" I could tell she hesitated to mention Quinn, knowing my feelings at the moment.

"Dad left for a business trip. He'll be in California for a week. By then, I think Blaine and Maeve will have moved efforts out of Savannah. Quinn's in Statesboro at school and I sort of already warned him," I explained. I flushed red and bit down on my lower lip.

"How much did you tell him?" Marjorie's voice was shrill.

"Nothing specific. I only told Quinn that Blaine was back, and I gave him a list of crystals to buy."

"Alright. Good." Marjorie started pacing, which made me uncomfortable. I wanted a break from this challenging discussion. Being outside with the crazy dogs and just breathing in the frosty air sounded terrific.

Marjorie didn't need a break, though. "For argument's sake, let's say Blaine won't waste time with Quinn. He needs to locate you as soon as possible."

"If he doesn't kill me soon, I'm sure the coven will kill him," I said, feeling surprisingly numb to the topic of my own death.

"That's good for us, right? It's one less foe to fight," Marnie asked.

"No," Marjorie corrected Marnie quickly. Her tone was less patient than before. "When we lose Blaine, we lose our way to Maeve. He's the way in."

"So, we start with Blaine," I trailed off. "How?"

"A truth spell?" Marnie threw out. "When someone broke into our cabin, my dad used a truth spell to question a few suspects. I don't remember the ingredients, but I know it wasn't complicated."

"Yeah, truth spells aren't hard. I've seen one in the book before. We'd need Blaine in person to make the spell work, though, and getting him could be tricky," I thought out loud.

"Slow down both of you," Marjorie's voice snapped at us. "We don't need a truth spell. We have Emlyn."

Panic jerked through my system. I knew what she was referring too, and I didn't agree with her. "We've been through this, Marjorie. I can't do it." I stood up, hoping to calm the nausea building in my stomach while gaining a more dominant pose.

"You must, Emlyn. There are no other options," Marjorie pushed. There wasn't a hint of grandmotherly love in her voice. She was a war general, and I was the weapon she needed.

"Please don't ask me to do this."

"Can someone fill me in here?" Marnie asked, jumping up to strategically place herself between us as a buffer.

"Emlyn's powers allow her to travel back in time to relive moments," Marjorie explained. "And not just her own memories. Last year, Emlyn traveled back into one of her mother's past events." Marjorie was trying to use Marnie as a wedge, another person to convince me this was necessary.

"Marjorie, the last time we tried this, I was trapped for hours," I pled.

"You can do it without getting stuck," Marjorie insisted. "Besides, I got you out of it last time. I'll be here to get you out again if you need me."

The conversation was getting heated. "No, Marjorie. I won't!"

"I'm not asking, Emlyn!"

"Stop it!" Marnie interrupted. "Tell me what's going on. We can come up with a rational plan."

Marjorie and I glared at each other. We were both stubborn, each feeling victimized by the other. She begrudged me for not embracing my ability in this crisis. I resented her for pushing me into a power I wasn't ready for. It was the same fight we had when I announced I was done practicing that power. I wouldn't time jump again unless my subconscious was controlling the destination.

"Let's calm down. You said stuck. What do you mean stuck?" Marnie wanted to know.

"When Emlyn travels back, she can get embedded into a memory," Marjorie answered before I could speak. "If that happens, she can relive the moment in a loop, not realizing it's a memory rather than genuine life."

"Because it is real," I interrupted. "We're not just talking about watching a memory like a movie, and the memory I get trapped in isn't a pleasant one. I relive Blaine trying to kill me again and again, just like it's the first time. The pain and emotions are all real. I feel it all."

"Then what Emlyn? How do you propose we move forward?" Marjorie sneered, unwilling to empathize with me.

"We'll find another way to get the information. We just haven't thought of it yet."

"The other way means risking all our lives to capture Blaine without alerting Maeve to our position," Marjorie yelled. She breezed past Marnie and grabbed both sides of my face with her hands. "This isn't the time to be a coward child. Your mother would have done it."

"What if I get stuck in there forever? I could just be gone this time, doomed to be tortured for all eternity!"

"I'll be here to keep you grounded," Marjorie assured me.

"I can help," Marnie's voice added. Marjorie dropped the sides of my face as we turned to Marnie. "Granny grew kava kava root. It's the perfect herb for astral projection, relaxing the muscles and increasing brain activity."

"Kava kava root?" Marjorie smiled. "What an extensive library. Excellent."

"I'll brew it in tea with lavender and chamomile. In combination, I'd think those herbs would keep anyone calm. I'll get to work." She glided to a bookshelf behind her and pulled down a jar of brown dust. We watched her dart to the kitchen with Margo trailing at her heels.

"You really think this will work?" I wanted to know.

"Of course. We'll light some sage and create a circle of rosemary candles to promote concentration and brain activity," Marjorie muttered to herself, ignoring me for the most part. "Marnie, where did your grandmother keep her tapestries?"

Marjorie trotted off after Marnie, leaving me to sit with my thoughts. They were both trying to help, but neither of them understood what this would do to me. I was about to relive the worst night of my life—again.

I seized the moments alone to shower and mentally prepare for the time travel. Under the steaming hot water, I tried to focus my thoughts on the positive. There was a way to break through the Blaine memory; I knew I just needed to channel my strength into finding it. For the spell, I stayed comfortable, changing into a pair of yoga pants and a loose-woven sweater. By the time I was ready, the smell of sage and rosemary were already gathering in the sunroom. I wished the aroma was a feast being prepared. I knew the kava kava tea Marnie was making wouldn't be as appetizing as a turkey dinner.

Jeb and I settled ourselves in the middle of the room on a green tapestry, decorated with trees and animals. I wanted to focus on anything but the tea I was drinking. My first sip was enough to make me gag, but they ordered me to down the entire mug of liquid. After several nose-pinching gulps, I forced the mixture down. Marnie then instructed me to focus on my surroundings in order to cultivate a welcoming atmosphere for my powers.

So I stared at the golden feathers of a songbird depicted on the tapestry beneath me. Its tail stretched for inches until the feathers were hidden beneath one of four rosemary candles. We had positioned each to represent north, south, east, and west, surrounding Jeb and me in a circle of protection. Jeb was joining me for this spell, acting as my strongest source of grounding. Being my familiar, Jeb kept me protected from negative energies, which would hopefully keep me from getting stuck.

"Calm yourself, Emlyn," Marjorie fussed at me. "I can feel your anxiety from here."

"Because that's helpful," I fussed back at her. Jeb grunted at her before licking my face. I took that as him scolding Marjorie for stressing me out.

"Alright. Focus your mind on Blaine," Marjorie breathed in a more soothing voice. "Close your eyes and conjure an image of his face. What do his eyes look like? How about his nose? Once you've cultivated an illustration in your mind, imagine him speaking. What does his voice sound like?"

I followed Marjorie's instructions, allowing her words to replace the thoughts of doubt in my mind. Blaine's green eyes were easy to conjure up, and then I visualized the sharp lines of his face. He had a hard nose and rigid jawline. I painted his naturally tan skin and then added messy dark hair over his forehead and ears.

"Now, ask yourself, what did his first day with Maeve look like? Where did he meet her? What did they talk about?" Marjorie asked.

I repeated the questions, again and again, picturing both of their faces side-by-side. After a few minutes, the scents of rosemary candles and smoky sage faded into the background. The gentle ticking of the grandfather clock drifted out of my mind. Then even the warmth of Jeb's body disappeared.

When you're a child, darkness is terrifying. In the dark, monsters crawl out from under your bed and lurk behind the closet door. As you get older, you're supposed to learn that beasts and ghouls aren't real. Most people learn to enjoy the dark of night because it can bring quiet and peaceful dreams. Unfortunately, I wasn't like most people. The pitch-black emptiness surrounding me now wasn't the kind you drifted off into sleep with. There was no end to the shadow surrounding me, and I knew there was an actual monster at the end of this tunnel somewhere.

I took a step forward and stretched out my arms, reaching out into the nothingness. In this, I felt much like a child again. There was no running to Mom and Dad, though. It was time to look under the bed.

"Where did Blaine and Maeve meet?" I repeated the questions to myself again, trying to regain focus. "What did they talk about that day? Who was Maeve?"

With the questions burrowed securely in my mind, a door formed in the darkness, outlined by a thin veil of light. The fixture was made of stone, etched with symbols and words from top to bottom. The words weren't in English. They were Irish. Over the central doorway, the name Ó Fionnachta was engraved in large, ornate letters. Ó Fionnachta was our exact name—the Irish name of the Finnerty family. Roughly translated, our name meant "Fair snow." The four corners of the great stone door reflected our calling card with Celtic snowflakes woven together in curves and knots. It was apparent the door was mine.

The light from behind it was inviting, an oasis in the night, but I knew better. The rational part of my brain told me to wake up from this dream before it was too late. Instead, I reached for the door, wrapped my hands around its ornate silver knob, and twisted it open. This was the way time-traveling worked when I was conscious. A door would appear as the gateway to the past or future. I'd cross through the entrance as if I were strolling down a timeline.

I pried open the door and took a few extra moments to prepare myself for the other side. Even though it looked like light had been peeking out from behind the door, what waited for me was more darkness. My first step was cautious, but I quickly gained my feet. Now, there was no going back; the instant I crossed the barrier, my stone entryway disappeared. It was replaced with a kaleidoscope of colors zooming past me in all directions. I'd only seen pictures of the aurora borealis; still, it couldn't compare to the whir of energy swirling around my head. It wasn't just colors. Time was rewinding, waiting for me to pinpoint the right moment.

I thought about Blaine again, and the more I focused on the time we needed to see, the faster all my memories undid themselves. First, I was barraged with visions of the fight with Maeve and Blaine, but then time skipped back to the day Emily and I moved into the townhouse. This part was always hard for me to control. It was nothing like the time-traveling I did when I was asleep. Even though I should have had better control when I was awake, my subconscious seemed more attuned to my abilities. When I was sleeping, there were no doors to the past or future—I would just appear in another time. It was less disorienting.

The flashes moved faster and faster. As I poured my energy into thoughts of Blaine, I felt the worst possible memories entering my mind. I could feel those moments coming in the time stream, and my fears were only escalating the situation. A fiery burning sensation pulsed through my stomach. Fright took hold, and I was once again a child hoping the monster in my closet would stay hidden.

"Wake me up!" I screamed, longing for my message to reach Marjorie and Marnie in the physical world. I knew if they heard my pleas, they'd pull me from the vision before it took hold of me.

"Finally awake I see," Blaine's dark voice laughed behind me. "I thought I might have brewed that potion a bit too strong for you."

He was referencing a knock out potion he had used on me before dragging my unconscious body to the courtyard of my high school and chaining my hands to the ground. I looked up at Blaine, who was standing above me in his black robes. The lantern in his hand illuminated a few concrete picnic tables around us. Another light flickered on a table behind him, showcasing the altar Blaine had created for this sacrificial ceremony. There were gourds, gemstones, and coins displayed as offerings to the higher powers, meant to bring him success. Victory would mean killing me for the Ainbertach Coven.

"This isn't real. I'm not really here," I tried to say out loud to keep myself from falling into the memory too far. I couldn't get stuck again. I needed to take control of the situation. I repeated the phrase again, hoping the words would be audible. Still, I couldn't speak. Those weren't the thoughts on my mind that night.

Instead, I accused Blaine. "She was his target, wasn't she? So what, the coven decided, 'Hey, I know what would be neat. Let's get a father and son to kill a mother and daughter?'"

It was like a scene from a movie, and I knew it line by line.

"First of all, you don't make the orders right now. I do," Blaine's voice growled. I braced myself, knowing what was coming when Blaine clenched his fist tightly. I wasn't ready for it, though. Pain scorched through my body. It was like someone had drenched my body in gasoline and tossed a match in my lap. I tightened my fists and bit down hard on my lip, hard enough to bleed. I knew I didn't want to scream. I didn't want to give Blaine the satisfaction.

"It's a nice trick, right?" Blaine paused, gesturing with his hands. "It's a great little brew to intensify my powers."

Maeve made that potion for him, which frustrated me more. It also reminded me why I was reliving this memory. I needed to get past it. I tried to ignore the rest of the conversation, blocking out the back and forth of the night. I needed to see Maeve and Blaine together for the first time. I pled with myself to break the connection of this moment so I could move on from it.

When I felt his lips on my cheek, my skin tingled with anger. "Shh, wouldn't want to give too much away in front of lover boy," Blaine sneered.

In that instant, it was all over. Shame broke my concentration. The light from Blaine's lantern shined over Quinn, revealing fresh black and blue bruises. In addition to the physical pain he was likely in, Quinn had found out I cheated on him with Blaine at that moment. If that weren't bad enough, I also accused Quinn of trying to murder me.

Seeing Quinn like that, I lost myself. Maybe it was my shame. It could've been fear. With everything happening with Maeve, I agonized over whether warning Quinn had been enough to keep him safe.

"Quinn? Oh God, Quinn, I'm so sorry," I sobbed.

"Yes, boo-hoo, Quinn," Blaine echoed. "She cheated. She lied. She accused you of murder. Those are the thoughts to dwell on while you watch her die," he told Quinn before turning back to me. "It's time, Emlyn."

Then came the agony. Everything around me disappeared until it was all pain and darkness. Quinn and Blaine dissolved into the background as the smoldering sensation took over my body. My torso, head, and limbs felt barbecued. Screaming was the only solace I could find, and even that reminded me how alone I was as my voice reverberated back to me.

Then suddenly, it all stopped. I couldn't remember where I was. A voice woke me up. It was my voice. "She was his target, wasn't she," I spat out, referring to my mother. "So what, the coven decided, 'Hey, I know what would be neat. Let's get a father and son to kill a mother and daughter?'"

My flesh felt cold against the restraints holding me down to the earth. I didn't know why the cold was such a relief to my skin. I looked up to meet Blaine's eyes, which were intently focused on me as he stalked forward. The feeling of déjà vu as he approached only strengthened when he set his lantern down on the ground beside me. Looking down, I noticed my jeans were blood-soaked. I instantly remembered Blaine chasing me down River Street. Then the events leading up to my capture started floating back as the remnants of a dream. Still, this didn't feel entirely right. Something was off.

"First of all, you don't make the orders right now. I do," Blaine snarled before sending a burst of fire through my body. I'd been burned before, usually trying to cook, but this feeling of fire was different. It didn't come close to the sensation in my body now. It was inside me, filling me up. I bit down on my lip, drawing blood, trying to keep from screaming.

"It's a nice trick, right?" Blaine stood up to examine his hands. "It's a great little brew to intensify my powers. With it, I can make you feel physical pain instead of emotional stuff. As to your question," he said, leaning in toward me. "Yes, my father did kill your mother."

The words were hard to hear coming from his venomous mouth, especially when a day ago, I had romantic feelings for him. I felt sick—physically drained—and I tried to tune out his voice as he monologued.

"The initiation ritual is a chance to show the coven who you are; it's a real opportunity to shine," Blaine continued. "It sets your path as a member, and I don't want to be an ordinary witch. I was given an easy target with you, sure, but look at what I made you!"

It was all too gut-wrenching to listen to. I didn't want to be a part of the conversation, waiting for death. I needed to fight for my life, but my body felt weaker than I'd ever experienced before. The pain was hitting me hard, and it lingered even though the initial shock was gone.

Blaine's pompous ramblings were exhausting to comprehend, and I felt myself responding to Blaine's words without grasping what was being said. Then I heard the words "lover boy," and my brain zipped to Quinn immediately. I followed Blaine's line of sight to find a badly bruised Quinn bound to a concrete picnic table. The look in his eyes was something I never wanted to see again. It was complete and utter devastation.

"Quinn? Oh God, Quinn, I'm so sorry," I sobbed.

"Yes, boo-hoo, Quinn," Blaine echoed. "She cheated. She lied. She accused you of murder. Those are the thoughts to dwell on while you watch her die," he told Quinn before turning back to me. "It's time, Emlyn."

The blazing pain reestablished dominance in my body. I fought the urge to cry out for as long as I could, but my body gave out. I was tired of fighting against the pain, so I surrendered to it. I let the pain take me, and I allowed myself to scream against the torture.

As the invisible embers flurried through my system, I scolded myself, "You wanted to be a witch. Now, you'll burn like one."

Chapter Nine

People tell you the hottest burns make you numb before you can feel the flames, but this wasn't like that. It took a minute or two of intense pain before the sensation left my body. Maybe it was only a few seconds, but it felt like an eternity. My mind attempted to escape to other thoughts, but it kept coming back to the fire. I wondered if my skin was cracking and peeling.

"She was his target, wasn't she," my voice called out, acting as a catalyst for memory loss. The previous cycle faded from my mind, and suddenly, I didn't know where I was. The surrounding courtyard was vaguely familiar, but I didn't understand why I was there or why my body ached. I looked up to find Blaine standing across the way, holding a lantern that illuminated a sacrificial altar on a picnic bench behind him.

I continued to speak, accusing Blaine and his father of evil, but a strange voice trumped mine like a sound clip playing over this one. Staring into Blaine's eyes, I could tell he didn't hear the comforting voice echoing around us. The words were for me.

"By the power of Boannan and the Goddesses of the universe, I light a candle for my Emlyn. May it light her way through the darkness."

It was Marjorie. As soon as the vision of her face appeared in my mind, I realized what had happened. I'd been stuck in this twisted reoccurring nightmare again, and Marjorie was trying to save me.

"Bring Emlyn back to me. As this is my will, so mote it be," Marjorie demanded.

"As is her will, so mote it be," I repeated, closing my eyes to the scene in front of me. When I opened them, a small orb of light had appeared, and slowly, all the darkness of the memory evaporated into nothing. I looked over to where Quinn was formerly chained to a concrete picnic table, but he was gone. The chains holding me to the ground finally dissipated. I stood up, watching the elements around me—Blaine's altar, the concrete picnic table, the school itself—blow away in a mist.

The only thing left around me was my door. I bolted toward it, ecstatic at the sight of my Celtic snowflakes. "Marjorie?" I called out as I grabbed the metal doorknob, practically tearing the door down as I thrust it open.

"Marjorie!?" My body shot straight up from the floor in a rush. Immediately, the pain returned to my body, and I struggled to maintain a steady breathing pattern. My skin was sensitive—Jeb's head on my lap was even too much pressure.

"Thank Goddess," Marjorie sighed with relief. She plopped down into one of the wicker chairs, obviously exhausted.

I pulled up the sleeves of my sweater to examine my skin. Somehow there was no physical evidence I'd been assaulted. The fire wasn't real despite how it felt. "How long?" I asked. It was easy to tell it'd been a long time. When we started, it was a bright, early morning, and now it was pitch black outside. I looked from Marjorie to Emily to Marnie. No one wanted to speak.

"19 hours," Marnie finally said flatly. She backed up to give me some space.

"19 hours?" I'd never gone that long before, and my body was still reeling from the effects of Blaine's power. The scene I replayed was only about 10 minutes long, which meant I cycled through it more than 100 times. Not only was 50 percent of that being tortured, but I knew being in the travel realm for so long wreaked havoc on my body.

"Marjorie tried to get you out after an hour or so," Marnie admitted.

"We were worried you were stuck for good," Emily blurted out. She was no longer concerned with her pissed-off persona. I had scared her. They all looked scared.

"Well, girls, in the morning, we'll start preparations for capturing Blaine," Marjorie announced, ignoring me mostly. I couldn't tell if it was fear or disappointment in her voice. Either way, I felt guilty.

"Kidnap Blaine?" Emily questioned. "That doesn't seem like a smart decision."

"And what would you know about smart decisions?" Marjorie barked back.

"Marjorie, I agree," I spoke up in Emily's defense. "That can't be the only solution."

"We are out of options," Marjorie stood forcefully.

"We're at least safe here. If we leave—or worse, if you bring Blaine here—we might as well give Maeve our GPS location," Emily insisted, her face red with anger.

As they argued, Marnie jumped up, trying to get a word in. I wasn't sure what she was trying to say over Marjorie and Emily's yelling. They both thought they were right, and Emily didn't appreciate Marjorie treating her like an ignorant child.

"Hush, everyone!" Marjorie yelled, throwing a nearby jar of herbs against the wall. The shattering glass sent Margo and Tephi running from the room, and Jeb ducked down, angling his ears behind his head.

"Emily, if you ever want to get back to your life in Savannah, decisions must be made. We can't just wait around here." Marjorie was stern. "Emlyn, you rest for now. Marnie, help me research the proper truth spell."

"I can help too," I told her.

"It's best you give us some space."

It was painful for me that Marjorie didn't want me to help. I felt like a failure, and it was worse knowing Marjorie thought so too. Marnie shot me an apologetic look. Under normal circumstances, I knew she'd try to combat Marjorie's clearly dictator-like demands. Still, we all knew what was at stake.

So instead of helping, I went to my assigned bedroom and laid awake in bed for a couple hours. While it gave my body time to recuperate, my mind was far from rest. It searched for a better solution to defeat Maeve. Every option I concocted seemed too dangerous, though. We didn't have enough information to go up against Maeve yet, and kidnapping Blaine to get more details seemed just as treacherous.

"There has to be another way," I sighed out loud. "This would be so much easier if we had a dragon."

It was hard not to blame myself. If I could just get past the stupid night with Blaine—if I could understand what was blocking me—we wouldn't need to capture Blaine for the information. I knew I couldn't try again, though. My flesh still stung from being stuck in the nightmare last night.

I gave up around noon. There was only so much quiet time I could stand, so I got up. I pulled on a pair of jeans and a striped sweater and headed into the kitchen, hoping my allies were in better moods. The room was empty, aside from Tephi. She was sprawled out on the island out of reach from the dogs, who were scattered lazily around the house. My favorites, Dakota and Max, were curled up in a corner by the fireplace in the sitting room. If only life were that simple for all of us.

I grabbed an apple from the fridge and found Marnie studying in the sunroom. Her nose was buried in a book, and she barely noticed me as I entered the room. A notepad beside her was full of scribbles and sentences. It looked like she'd been reading for a while.

"How's it going?" I asked.

Marnie jumped at the sudden noise but calmed herself when she realized it was me. "It feels like I'm cramming for finals." She pulled the glasses from her face and massaged her temple.

"Anything helpful?"

"There's a translation issue, but I think I've figured it out. If I don't go crazy first."

"Is the spell difficult?"

"No. The hard part will be getting to Blaine without alerting anyone. A few spells can cloak a witch's essence or assign it to another person, but those are temporary fixes. They're also easy to break. It might be more reasonable to get Blaine alone and try to cast the spell quickly, but that creates a whole other mess of problems."

"But if we got him here, we could assign his essence to another person to make it look like he's somewhere else, right?"

"Is it possible? Yes. Is it likely? No."

"Why?"

"We'd need Blaine's permission to mess with his essence. Something about a witch's aura being personal—like you're the only one who can mess with you. It's a rough translation, but that's the gist of it."

"Not super promising," I paused. "Where's Marjorie?"

"Taking a nap," Marnie smiled to herself. "She dozed off a couple times before I finally convinced her to rest."

"I don't think she's slept since the fight at the shop."

"I haven't seen her sleep. Speaking of fights, how are you feeling?" she asked, closing the book in front of her.

"That's a hard question to answer." I flopped into a wicker chair diagonal from Marnie as if to illustrate my exhaustion. Jeb claimed the other wicker chair for himself, groaning as he settled in.

"It's a complicated situation."

I frowned.

"One that isn't your fault," Marnie added.

"On Samhain, I asked my mother for guidance," I told her. "I wanted to know which path to take. Whether I should focus on school—the plan I made before I was a witch—or if I should focus on witchcraft and protecting light magic."

"You think by asking for guidance, this is your fault?" Marnie's voice told me she didn't agree.

"All of this happened right after I finished my ceremony. Since then, nothing has been clear, and we've been faced with a lot of tough choices. I also can't seem to make the right decision when they present themselves."

"I think you're too hard on yourself." Marnie stood up and motioned for me to follow her. "Come with me."

"Don't we have to study?"

"The books will be there when we get back. There's something you should see."

Jeb and I followed Marnie out of the sunroom, through the kitchen, and onto the carport. The pack of dogs flocked behind us, ready to be outside again. Jeb paired off with Max and Dakota once again, and the three started a game of tag in the bright afternoon sun. Most of the dogs were barking and playing, enjoying the crisp fall day, but the big black shepherd was more interested in Marnie. He seemed wiser than the rest of them, and I wondered if he'd been a familiar to Marnie's grandmother. He watched her grab two walking sticks from the far corner of the carport, and immediately, he seemed to know where we were going.

"Here, take one." Marnie handed me a staff. Even though it was just a large stick someone found in the woods, it made me feel like Gandalf.

"Are we going on an adventure or something?" I laughed.

"Yas! Out into the country," she smiled. "I'm not sure how tall the weeds have gotten back there, so it could be like a jungle."

I trailed behind Marnie and the dogs as they zipped around the back of the house. We headed through a thicket of trees where the branches reached out in all directions, but there was a clear path for travelers. We wove between the twigs and trees as we headed to a small opening.

I wanted to ask where we were going again, but I decided not to disturb the quiet of the outdoors while we walked. Even the dogs were relatively quiet as they trotted around us with their noses to the ground.

Once we reached the clearing, I noticed a second barn. It was small and in worse condition than the one beside the house. As we passed, I could see a red, old-school tractor through the half-open barn door. I could barely make out an "I" and an "H" on the side of the machine and the word "Farmall" under the rust.

"That looks old," I commented. "Does it still work?"

"It's from the '60s, I think. It was my granddad's. They upgraded a while ago. The groundskeeper wanted something more modern."

"Makes sense."

After a couple more minutes, we came upon a surprisingly well-maintained meadow, which led to a perfectly round pond in its center. The grass was cut short, creating an inviting path to the pool of water. As we got closer, I realized a circle of river stones surrounded the semi-clear water, leading me to believe the pond itself was man-made. The water wasn't muddy like a natural pool of water. The sight of water excited the dogs. They bolted to it with their noses glued to the ground the whole time.

I followed Marnie up a slight incline to the edge of the pond. I wasn't sure of the significance of this space, but I could tell there was a strength here. Marnie looked out into the water for a few seconds as a breeze created ripples over the pond's surface.

"It's peaceful here, isn't it?" Marnie commented.

"Even with the pack of mutts running around."

Marnie laughed. "It's a meditation pond." She bent down and touched the water, wiggling her fingers around in it. "It's saltwater. Granny had it made."

I bent down to follow Marnie's example. The water was chilly, especially since it was in the shade. I guessed the temperature was in the 50s or 60s, but I didn't sense anything magical.

"What makes it a meditation pond?"

"The water balance is perfect. You easily float on the surface. As kids, we loved it, but it's really meant to activate your body's senses." She pointed to the river stones surrounding the pond. "These stones form a pentagram under the water."

"So, it's a magical, peaceful pool?" I asked her.

"She claimed it was where she did her best thinking. It gave her a sense of peace—a quiet place to call on her powers." She sat down at the edge of the water and pulled her knees into her chest, seemingly drawn into a memory. Seeing Marnie knelt down at his level, Max bounded over, planting himself right next to her. A smile spread across her face as she petted his head.

I followed her lead and plopped down beside her. Marnie was showing me this because she thought I needed a quiet place to collect my powers. I told her I was lost, and she was trying to help me find myself. More than anything, I felt like I needed a break. She gave me that too.

We sat there for a moment in the silence. Dakota wandered over and pawed at my hand, trying to pull it toward her belly. Jeb was off exploring with the other group of dogs. I could hear birds cawing at each other in the woods, and branches rustled as squirrels jumped from tree to tree. Marnie was right. Her grandmother had created the perfect sanctuary.

"Can I ask you something?" I said, biting my lower lip.

"Sure."

"I've noticed the way Marjorie talks about your grandmother like she doesn't like her."

"Oh." Marnie frowned a bit.

"Marjorie doesn't like her, does she?"

"Nope. I can't blame her, though. Many people from the old coven feel that way."

"Why? I mean, if you can talk about it."

Marnie didn't look away from the water. She stroked Max behind his ear as she spoke. "Granny handled things her own way sometimes. The coven didn't really agree."

"Her own way?"

Marnie paused for a moment. She took a deep breath and met my eyes. "My grandmother is Henrietta Thomson, the member of Marjorie's coven who started using her magic to kill dark witches."

"Yikes."

Marnie nodded. "She was with the coven a long time, and in the beginning, she followed the rules. She saved dozens of lives in the process, but she also saw many good witches die. To her, there was a flaw; dark witches have no problem murdering and manipulating. So one day, she ended the life of a dark witch for good instead of wiping his memory."

"She broke the law of the coven."

"Yup. There might be some fluidity in the words 'Harm None,' but murder isn't up for interpretation."

I thought back to training sessions with Marjorie and remembered she had talked about a rogue witch before. The witch was exiled from the coven. It must have been Henrietta. "I'm sorry, I shouldn't have pried," I told her.

"Don't be sorry. She's family, like it or not. And I have to respect her. She did what she thought was right, no matter what anyone else thought."

"That's true. Did your family exile her too?"

"My dad didn't agree with her, but he accepted her, I think. She pulverized a lot of dark covens. She was a badass."

"Jeez, covens? Like plural?"

"Not like the Ainbertach Coven, but she was powerful," Marnie smiled. I could tell she was proud of her grandmother. I would've been too.

"She wanted to protect the people she cared about," I could understand Henrietta's motivation. Sure, it was hard to think of turning your back on such a foundational law as "Harm None." It was the core of our religion, and it separated us from the dark witches. But who wouldn't kill if it meant saving the lives of those they loved?

"It may have been the wrong way, but it was her way," Marnie responded. She got up, brushed the dirt from her pants, and looked back in the house's direction. "That's why this property is rigged up so well. When my cousin Erica was born, Granny retired. She built this haven to protect her from other witches—both light and dark."

"The coven went after her?"

"Not really, but there were members who thought Granny's powers should've been stripped. They didn't think she deserved her magic."

"Like magic is a blessing?" My question was dripping with disdain. My current hate for magic was leaking out, and I immediately realized how insensitive my comment was. Marnie didn't have powers, and she probably wished she did.

"It's a gift—if you use it correctly. Granny used it to protect people. That's okay in my book."

There was bravery in Henrietta's story, even if she broke the rules. The more I thought about it, the more I realized Henrietta left everything she believed to make the world a safer place for witches and humans. I saw that same courage in Marnie. The moment we told her we were in danger, Marnie sprang into action. She hadn't been a part of the drama, but she sacrificed school and her goals to help us. She could've walked away. Blaine and Maeve didn't know her.

Everyone had shown nerve the past few days. Thinking back, Marjorie offered to sacrifice herself for Emily and me at the shop. Marjorie consistently illustrated her bravery and was always my rock in the hard times. Even Emily, who had no powers, stood up to Maeve with gumption.

I decided it was my turn to be brave.

—

"Courage," I told myself as I stripped down to my underwear. It was colder by the pond now than when I visited with Marnie during the day. Now in the dead of night, the absence of the sun gave my body instant chill bumps, and I knew the water would only make things worse. Jeb was by my side, ignoring the other dogs. They had followed me out to the water. Well, it was more that they led me back to the pond, because it was harder to find in the dark. The gang seemed excited about the night hike. It terrified me.

"I must be crazy," I said out loud as I took my first step into the ice-cold water. The shock to my system instantly made me think of *Titanic*. "Oh god, I'm gonna die."

Jeb whined in concern to my statement. He'd been watching me anxiously, ignoring the game of tag going on behind us.

"I'm exaggerating," I assured him, hoping I was right. I waded into the water deeper, my body trembling more and more with every step I took. It was painful being in the water, but I tried to ignore the stabbing cold. I made it to the center of the pond where the water was about six feet deep. It was easy to tread in, but I knew if things went wrong I'd drown.

I pushed the thought from my head. I was on a mission. Marnie had explained that this was Henrietta's place of deep thinking. She drew strength and power from the saltwater and the pentagram beneath it. So I figured, if Henrietta used this spot to meditate, I could use its strength to delve deeper into my mind. I was hoping it would be enough to get past the night with Blaine.

"See, I'm fine," I told Jeb. Then I thought about it again. "But, if it looks like something bad is happening, go get Marjorie."

Jeb whined at me. He didn't look happy.

I pushed through the negativity, though, closing my eyes and pushing my legs out in front of me to a floating position. I fully extended my arms and legs, pressing my fingers into the water. I allowed the liquid to take me over, allowing the surface of the water to create a dividing line across my body. As I floated on my back, the gentle rocking soothed my anxieties. Had I not been terrified and had the water not been freezing, this might have been relaxing.

I ignored fear, and instead, I focused on one question: how did Maeve and Blaine meet? My ears were halfway submerged, so I couldn't hear the rustling of the meadow beneath the dogs' feet as they wrestled. I couldn't hear the leaves in the breeze or the cicadas chirping. My not so steady breathing and the beating of my heart were the only sounds. So, I repeated my question to the drumming beat in my chest. Thump, thump, thump, until my body felt transported.

It was an odd sensation, but even with my eyes closed, I knew I was back in the unlit room. There was a distinct energy surrounding me. The vast emptiness was surprisingly comforting when I opened my eyes. This was the natural part. I was at least confident in my abilities to summon a path through time. It was all simple here with a door for the future and one for the past.

I stretched my arms forward and focused on the day Maeve met Blaine. In a few moments, the massive stone door materialized. I fought with myself briefly, wondering if there was a solution in the future instead. Marjorie would tell me that seeing the future sometimes changed the outcome. It didn't matter much. That door was harder to summon. I could only reach it through my subconscious. It had to be the past. So, I ignored my instincts—the screaming voice telling me to stay where I was. The voice said this was not worth the risk, but I reached for the door anyway, keeping Henrietta's courage in my mind. I hoped the bravery of my friends would guide me through the darkness I was about to fight, like my very own Virgil.

"I have to do this," I told myself. "For them."

I grabbed the silver knob and thrust the door open in one quick motion. I couldn't think about it for too long. I could only act. I leaped into the blinding light before me, and the memories kaleidoscoped by again, creating a wispy display of colors and lights around me.

"How did Maeve meet Blaine?" As the memories whirled past, I focused every bit of my being on that one question. Fragments of important moments whizzed by—the fight with Maeve and Blaine, my Dad's birthday, graduation from high school—but I refused to let anything distract me.

I painted a picture of Blaine in my mind, molding together the crisp green of his eyes, his obnoxious side smile, and his jet-black hair. I recreated the first day I met Blaine, hoping the energy of that moment would help me recall the day he met Maeve. I'd been immediately drawn to Blaine. Everything about him was mysterious and inviting. I later learned the attraction was a spell, but I had to admit part of it was likely real. I pictured the smirk on his face when he caught me staring at him during an English test and the confidence I felt when we practiced magic together. I cultivated the image of him as my teacher, the person I vanquished a demon with.

"Been traveling again?" Blaine's expression echoed in my mind, and I couldn't help but feel disappointed. I put everything I had into this travel, but it wasn't enough. I was back in the nightmare. I could've kicked myself for being so stupid—for choosing to go to the pond. Who cared if I was brave if I drowned?

I heard my voice respond. "She was his target, wasn't she? So what, the coven decided, 'Hey, I know what would be neat. Let's get a father and son to kill a mother and daughter?'"

My voice didn't sound right, though. Something was different about it. Then suddenly, I realized it was because the voice hadn't come from me. I opened my eyes to find I wasn't looking up at Blaine anymore. This time, I was hovering over myself. I was now the one holding the lantern in the other Emlyn's face. It was the first time I'd seen the look of fear on my own face. As the flame from the lantern danced in Other Emlyn's emerald eyes, I noticed how rough she looked. She was plastered with sweat and dirt and blood. I winced, seeing familiar cuts on Other Emlyn's knees and a nice gash on one of her legs. That one had left a scar.

It was hard seeing myself in that condition—sickening even. What was worse were the emotions I felt while watching Other Emlyn. There was an odd thrill of excitement in my stomach. There was *nervousness for sure, but more than anything, I felt enthusiasm and exhilaration at the pain I was causing. I was relishing it.*

It all became clear at once. I was Blaine.

"My father is weak. He has no lust for glory, and he knew he couldn't defeat your mother if she saw it coming. Still, it was a disgrace." I'd heard those words hundreds of times, but I'd never felt them before. This went beyond disappointment. Blaine was ashamed and embarrassed by his father.

I'd only experienced this kind of time travel one other time. Usually when I traveled back, I was myself reliving the moment, or I was a fly on the wall watching events play out in front of me. Something new was happening with my powers. I wasn't just in Blaine's body. I was inside his head, a place much darker than anywhere else I'd ever been.

"Sure, he made his mark, he was initiated into the coven, but he'll never be great," Blaine continued.

"I don't understand," Other Emlyn said defensively.

"The initiation ritual is a chance to show the coven who you are; it's a real opportunity to shine. It sets your path as a member, and I don't want to be some ordinary witch. I was given an easy target with you, sure, but look at what I made you!"

His final words resonated intensely with me. I wasn't able to see it before, but now, in Blaine's body of all places, I understood. The block in my powers wasn't about the trauma of that night, not entirely. It was Blaine's words: "Look at what I made you." Blaine was the first witch I met who wanted to help me with my craft. He represented the beginning of my training. Target practice with Blaine, as simple as it was, was the first time I controlled my abilities. Near the end of our relationship, I trusted Blaine completely. I believed in him and even loved him to some extent. Then I found out his magic was buried in darkness.

The moment he said, "Look at what I made you," something stuck in my brain, and I believed that Blaine's powers—his darkness—created my ability. But feeling the evil inside Blaine, I realized there was no way he influenced my magic.

I was a Finnerty. My power came from Ireland, rooted in nature and light. Our coven was of the old ways, and our magic was passed from generation to generation, dating back hundreds of years.

The Celtic magic I possessed was the same strength as my mother's, grandparents', and great grandparents'.

I closed my eyes. "The day Blaine met Maeve. Take me to the day Blaine met Maeve."

Then it was musty books, pipe tobacco, and furniture polish. The fresh smells filled my nostrils, reminding me of the restored historic houses in Savannah. The lighting in this new space was dim, filtered through stained glass light fixtures and windows. Looking down, I was sitting on a long, black wood bench with my hand, gripping the edge on one side. My fingers anxiously swirled over carvings in the wood.

Across from me in the wide hallway was a large black wood side table, etched with Celtic knots and antlers that erupted from each corner. Two Tiffany-style glass lamps were placed on opposite sides of the table, framing a detailed portrait that must have been four feet tall and three feet wide. The painting featured a man with silver hair and a stern look in his green eyes. His face looked familiar, even though it was apparent he wasn't from this time. The man was dressed in a cream tunic and an animal hide cloak that was wrapped around him several times. A brown leather belt was strapped around his waist to hold everything up. My eyes finally found the golden nameplate beneath the portrait, and I realized why he looked so familiar. He was Fáelán Ainbertach, the man who started the Ainbertach Coven. He was solely responsible for all the deaths the coven had caused since then, and probably for all dark magic in Ireland.

Fáelán's portrait meant I must've been at headquarters. I couldn't be sure which HQ I was in, though. They were everywhere, and the room's décor wasn't particularly telling. The foyer was expensively decorated, but I assumed they all would be. French doors leading outside were to my left, and a passage leading into a larger room was to my right. I couldn't see much aside from that.

The urge to speak suddenly overcame the unease I sensed. "Dad, are you sure you want to do this?" Blaine questioned. I was still in Blaine's head, and I suddenly noticed a familiar weasel of a man sitting next to me. The man looked like Blaine, but there was something greasier about him. It didn't help that Blaine's disdain for his father was reverberating around his entire body.

"Wasn't this your idea?" his father responded sharply. The accusation was clear. "Didn't you say this is how we secure our future?" Blaine's father lacked confidence. His tone was reluctant, as if Blaine had forced him into this situation. He didn't look dressed for a coven meeting either, looking more like a salesman than a witch. He wore black dress pants, a sports coat, and a red tie. I imagined any meeting with the Ainbertach Coven should call for robes, but I noticed Blaine was wearing a suit as well—all black.

"I believe it is, yes. We need this to move forward," Blaine stopped. He was careful to phrase his next words carefully. "I only want to ensure you're prepared to pay the price. I can feel how reluctant you are."

"I'll do what needs to be done, Blaine. Didn't I tell you to stop reading me?"

"There's no going back after this," Blaine warned. There was a slight amount of guilt in Blaine, backed up by a lot of anxiety. He didn't believe his father was strong enough to fulfill his oath, and he felt terrible for demanding so much. The overwhelming emotion was desperation. It was imperative for Blaine that his father succeeded, and Blaine wasn't convinced his father could. It would ruin Blaine's own chances for success.

I realized this moment must have been Blaine and his father's first meeting with the Ainbertach Coven. This was the day they asked to join the coven, and it was also the day Blaine's father would likely get assigned an initiation target. They'd assign him my mother, which meant Blaine only met Maeve half a year or so before I met him.

"We talked about this, Blaine. You made your case," Blaine's father looked down at his feet. "With your mother gone, this is the right family for us."

Family, I thought. Blaine must have manipulated his father into thinking the coven would be a replacement family for the wife and mother they lost. It was a low blow, using his father's grief as a bridge to evil. Then again, Marjorie's coven was her family. Maybe there was some truth to it, even if I couldn't imagine the kind of family the Ainbertachs would be.

"You and I need a place where we belong. We need structure and stability," Blaine said in an exasperated voice.

"Blaine. I know—."

His father's words were interrupted by two men in green and yellow robes embroidered with the same Celtic knots and deer antlers as the table.

"Alexander Corwin?" one of them questioned. He had a short, bleached blonde fro that stood out sharply against his brown skin. The other man was a classic Celt—curly red hair, a face full of freckles, and a porcelain-pale complexion. There was a look of determination on each of their faces. I guessed they were bodyguards for the leader, not that the leader would need them. I assumed he'd be more potent than the two of them combined.

Alexander licked his lips once and flattened his sweaty palms against his pants. He glanced at Blaine, looking for solace. Blaine nodded at him in assurance before Alexander stood up and faced the bodyguards.

"Yes, sir," his voice trembled.

"We are to take you to the drawing-room now. You'll receive your orders there."

"Yes, sir," Alexander stammered. He quickly scurried toward them, following them back into another room. Blaine watched with feelings of both excitement and regret as his father cast him one more glance.

Eagerness washed over Blaine. This was one step closer to fulfilling his plan. He needed his father to join the coven to add credibility to the Corwin bloodline. Every witch that practiced black magic wanted to join the Ainbertach Coven. It was a legend, and members were guaranteed certain comforts if they performed well. The demand for membership meant the Ainbertachs could be picky. They wanted impressive powers, which made being an empath a disadvantage. It wasn't the most powerful of abilities. Empathy would provide the coven with less information than a typical psychic. Blaine's father, Alexander, had the impressive power, though he had always squandered it. His ability to manipulate the earth was rare, and Blaine knew the Ainbertachs would want control of it. It would mean taking on a coward, but Blaine knew they'd make that sacrifice.

Guilt soon replaced his giddiness. Blaine had pushed this on his father, and he wasn't sure Alexander would survive if pitted against another witch. Alexander came from a line of dark magic, but his family never went so far as assassination. Sure, Blaine's father had manipulated people and hurt others when he needed to. But Alexander was a history geek at heart. He found no thrills in power or control.

Blaine knew his plan meant sacrificing his father along the way, and he was alright with the trade-off. Blaine hoped Alexander could make it in the long-term, but they both belonged to the coven now.

"It won't be as bad as you think." The girl's bold declaration broke Blaine's concentration. Suddenly, I felt a fluttering sensation in his chest when he saw the owner of the voice. It was Maeve. She was leaning against the hall table across from Blaine, radiating with confidence and strength despite her petite frame. It was an immediate attraction—I could feel the thrill inside him. A grin formed on his face as he took in her ashen, silver hair and green eyes. She was wearing a forest green corset over a tight black dress that ran halfway down her thighs, stopping about six inches from her knees. Black tights led down to a pair of black, old-fashioned Oxford heels. Blaine was so lost in the sight of her, he almost forgot to respond.

"What isn't as bad as I think?" Blaine finally managed.

"Assignment." Maeve's eyes were studying Blaine. As far as I could tell, it looked like Maeve was happy with what she saw. Her dark purple lips were pressed into a small smile. She pushed herself from the table, positioning herself directly in front of Blaine. "They won't give him someone he can't handle," she added.

Blaine was intrigued. "You've experienced this before I take it?"

"Been there, done that," she casually mused, looking toward the doorway Alexander and the guards had disappeared through. "He may not move up in the ranks, but it's not always about individual strength. After all, there's strength in numbers, and the coven's resources are vast."

"Some individual strength would be good," Blaine countered.

"True," she smiled. "I'm sure the leader will put him where he belongs. The higher-ups have a way of sensing power and putting it to good use."

Her words mesmerized Blaine as he imagined the day he would face the leader one-on-one. The way Maeve spoke piqued his interest. He tried to probe her mind for more information, but she had some sort of shield in place, blocking his abilities. For Blaine, the mystery made her even more attractive.

"Who are you?" Blaine wanted to know.

"Just another member of the coven." She gracefully moved toward him, taking a seat on the bench. The closeness of her excited him. He wanted to touch her, to feel if her vibrations were as powerful as he thought they'd be.

"For how long?" I cringed at his eagerness. "When did you get your assignment?"

"I was 15."

"The end of your training."

"Yes. I grew up in the coven, so initiation marked my completion. We only celebrate witches who make their marks."

"Fifteen," Blaine mused, "that seems young."

"You're 17, right?" Maeve smirked.

"Well, yeah. Still, I—who did you get? Did they assign you another young witch?"

Her smile widened, "Oh no. My mark was challenging—the leader of a small coven in the mountains north of here."

"The leader of a coven? But you were 15." Blaine was taken with every syllable Maeve uttered. He stared at her lips with intense concentration, wishing more than ever that he could feel her emotions. He wanted to share in the moment of triumph she had when she was initiated into the coven. The whole thing made me feel sick, and it didn't surprise me that Maeve could take out an entire coven when she was 15. It was disheartening, though.

"When you're raised here, they expect more," Maeve explained to Blaine. "Fiona Blackwater and her coven were undoing our efforts in the Northern Georgia mountains. My first project was to subdue her."

"That's incredible. You must have some power." Jealousy crept into his words as he realized his gift as an empath would likely never return the same rewards. Blaine wanted to be Maeve. He wanted her glory.

"She was one of many targets they gave me. This is a coven where power and success are rewarded," Maeve locked eyes with Blaine. She held up her hand in front of her chest and conjured a fireball.

"Pyrokinesis?" Blaine exclaimed.

"Partly." She doused the flame in her hand and skipped back over to the table, putting more distance between them. I decided Maeve was playing a game with Blaine—one Blaine wanted to win.

"Partly?"

"Tsk, tsk, Blaine. What fun would it be if I told you all my secrets right away?"

He was about to respond with a lame attempt at a joke, "I'll tell you mine if you tell me yours," but he stopped mid-thought. He had picked up on the same thing I noticed. Maeve knew his name. That wasn't entirely weird in itself, but she also knew how old he was.

"How do you know my name?" Blaine demanded. "Are you a psychic, too?"

"Not a psychic, but you'd be surprised at what I know," she smirked again and raised her eyebrows in a way Blaine thought was cute.

"Oh, really?"

"Sure," she said, inching closer. "You're an empath like your mother, but your father has the gift of geokinesis."

Maeve's quick dismissal of his powers made Blaine feel rejected. "Yeah, he's got the real power in the family," Blaine admitted.

"Some might say that, but something tells me you're the Corwin to watch."

The intensity in her gaze was evident. I was surprised by how in-sync their attraction seemed to be and alarmed by the knowledge Maeve had. Blaine didn't seem to be. He was curious, and he loved the playful banter and mutual chemistry.

"How do you know all that?" Blaine grinned at her.

"I have my connections in the coven. What they know, I know."

"That's not cryptic at all," Blaine laughed.

"It's no fun if I make it too easy for you."

"Give me something," Blaine begged. "What other powers do you have?"

"No way."

"How about a hint?" Blaine was using all his powers of charm—the cute half-smile and puppy dog eyes. I couldn't see him, but I saw the look on Maeve's face. She was loving it.

"Okay, how about this? Pyrokinesis for me is like the wands in the tarot."

"Was that supposed to help?" His laugh was loud and full of energy.

"That's all you'll get from me." She leaned in closer. So close, I thought she would plant a big kiss on Blaine's mouth. Luckily for me, they were interrupted.

"Miss?" The dark-skinned guard had returned. They were both so enthralled with each other, Blaine missed his entrance in the hallway.

The interruption was upsetting for Blaine, but it also reminded him why he was there in the first place. Blaine knew he should be there with his father as his father received his target. The dark-skinned guard must have been there to collect Blaine, which meant Blaine would have to put his interest in Maeve to the side.

Maeve didn't seem surprised by the disruption. It was weird, too. The guard focused on Maeve and didn't give Blaine a passing glance. I didn't think he was there to collect Blaine after all.

"Miss?" the guard asked. I could hear a twinge of fear in his voice.

"Harold," Maeve's tone hardened, transforming into something more authoritative than before.

"We're ready for you in the drawing-room."

Blaine was confused, and I was right there with him. Why was Maeve being called into the room with Alexander? It took longer than it should've, but the pieces finally formed in both our minds. Maeve nodded at Harold and then turned her back to Blaine. She held out her hand for him to shake, suddenly more professional than flirty.

"Be seeing you, Blaine," she said.

"I never got your name," he told her, waiting for her to fill in the blanks.

"I'm Maeve Ainbertach," she told him.

Water rushed into my nostrils and throat as my body flailed back into consciousness. Air. I needed air, but I couldn't reach it through the water. I was choking on it, and I could hear Jeb's anxious barking behind the sound of splashing water in my ears. I knew how to swim. I'd been to Tybee Island beach more times than I could count, but my body wouldn't or couldn't cooperate. Blaine's memories were too vivid; it was like I was still inside him, unable to control my actions.

Fear—the real kind when you think you're going to die—rushed into my chest. I tried calling out to Jeb or to anyone who might hear me. The truth was out. I finally knew who Maeve was, and I was probably about to die before I could tell anyone about it.

"Emlyn!" Two bodies splashed toward me. Hands grabbed hold of my shoulder, and teeth chomped down on my underwear on the other side of my body. I flailed around as the water crashed over my nose and mouth. Nails caught my skin a few times as we made our way to land, but, finally, I made it to the edge of the pond. Instincts took hold, and I snatched fistfuls of grass and dirt in an attempt to claw myself out of the water. I coughed up liquid onto the ground as I gasped for air.

"Ainbertach," I choked out before spewing another mouthful of salt water.

"What?" Emily questioned. Her curly head was directly above mine. She rolled me over onto my back. "Do you need CPR? Does she look like she needs CPR?"

She was talking to Jeb, who was shaking water off himself after helping Emily drag me out of the water. I'd need to make him a steak or something.

"She's—. We have to—," I coughed in between thoughts. We couldn't afford to lose any information right now, and I needed to get it all out while it was fresh on my mind.

"Stop trying to talk. Just breathe, Emlyn."

Beneath her matted, pond-water hair, I could see the concern in Emily's eyes. Her hand was under my neck for support. Jeb also took on a protective role, squishing his body close to mine to share his body heat. I hadn't realized how cold I was before. Without the sun, being soaked in water was painful. Still, it seemed a lesser priority than the information I had to share. Everything was coming together.

"What were you thinking? Are you psycho?" Emily yelled at me once we were both in a standing position. Now that she was sure I was okay, she was ready to yell at me. "You could've died."

"We needed answers," I coughed out. "I didn't want to risk anyone else."

"So you risk yourself? You're lucky I followed you out."

"I am," I said. "How did you know I was out here?"

"I'm a light sleeper," her tone softened. "The hoard of dogs walking by my window woke me up. I saw you walking into the woods in the middle of the night. I was concerned."

The moment was perfect for reconciliation. Everything was perfectly positioned for me to make a big apology. Then Emily would apologize, like in a Lifetime movie. There would be a big hug and maybe some tears shed. I couldn't get into that now, though. I couldn't think about anything except Maeve.

"Earth to Emlyn," Emily started. "You look freaked out. What happened in there?"

"We're in more trouble than we thought."

Chapter Ten

"She's an Ainbertach?" Emily's voice quivered. "Like, we're talking 'Ainbertach Coven,' Ainbertach? Like the family."

Once again, Emily, Marjorie, Marnie, and I found ourselves piled into the sunroom. After my discovery, Emily and I didn't wait to wake up the rest of the group. The information seemed too big to keep to ourselves, so Emily and I wrapped ourselves in fleece blankets to combat the cold and convened another meeting.

"Yes. That's what I'm saying. I think I saw Blaine's father receiving his initiation assignment at one of the Ainbertach headquarters," I explained. Somehow, I was able to keep my teeth from chattering as I spoke. I'd spent about an hour in the water, and my skin was bright pink as the circulation returned to me. Jeb and I were curled up on the couch side-by-side, sharing body heat again. More than anything, I wanted to sleep, but we couldn't wait.

"Was there any indication to which headquarters they were at?" Marjorie asked.

"Honestly, no. I remember Blaine telling me the Atlanta location assigned him my name, though. If he and his father went to the same headquarters, we could assume Maeve runs the show in Atlanta."

"With how powerful she is, she may run the whole U.S," Emily chimed in.

"Atlanta makes sense," Marnie agreed. "This could be big news."

"Let's not get too ahead of ourselves," Marjorie interrupted. "For the time being, let's assume we're only talking about Atlanta and not the entirety of our country. She's powerful, yes, but the Ainbertachs are likely seated in tradition. They give men more authority than women."

"The patriarchy," Marnie grumbled. "Female witches are usually more powerful than male ones."

"As much as I'd love to talk about female power and overcoming stereotypical traditions, we need to stay on topic," Marjorie hissed. "Go over it all again, Emlyn."

I groaned. This was the third time repeating my story. "Marnie gave me the idea to use the centering energy of Henrietta's pond to travel back in time. I was able to get past the night Blaine tried to kill me, and I saw the day Blaine met Maeve."

"Which was extremely reckless and could have cost you your life," Marjorie chided.

"For the record, that wasn't the reason I brought you out there," Marnie added.

I ignored them both. "Blaine's dad, Alexander, was there to meet with the coven leader to receive his assignment. I think it was the meeting where Alexander was given Mom's name. At the end of the memory, Maeve ended up being the leader."

"Focus on your surroundings. Where were you? What did the place look like?" Marjorie pushed for more information.

"I was literally inside Blaine's head," I told them.

Emily made a loud choking noise. "That must have been pleasant."

"Blaine and his dad were waiting in a foyer inside the front door of the building," I continued. "Everything was well decorated. The windows were stained glass, the furniture was antique, and there was an oil painting of Fáelán Ainbertach."

"So, it looked more like a house than an office building?" Marnie wanted to know.

"My gut says yes, but I can't be sure. From my vantage point, I couldn't see much," I admitted.

"Why does that matter?" Emily asked.

"We're going to have to find it. Knowing what kind of building it is could help us narrow down a location," Marnie told her. There was a new boldness to her voice.

"Back to Maeve," Marjorie refocused the conversation. "What did they talk about? Repeat the discussion."

"She was cryptic," I frowned, thinking of the flirty way she talked to Blaine. The chemistry between the two was magnifying, even from the beginning. "The interaction was a power play, but there was a lot of heavy flirting. They were into each other big time."

Emily made another choking sound.

"She talked about her first assignment, correct?" Marjorie pushed.

"Yes. Maeve said it was the head of a coven in North Georgia. Fiona something. It was a weird last name."

"Blackwater," Marjorie told us. "It wasn't her true last name, but it's the one she used publicly. Fiona was from a Cherokee tribe of Native Americans in Georgia. They used tribal magic. It was all very earth-based. She was a good witch, though," Marjorie trailed off. It made me angry to hear the sadness in Marjorie's voice.

"And Maeve killed her," I grunted.

"I can't believe she's been the one in charge this entire time!" Emily blurted out. "How did we not know this?"

"We couldn't have known, but in a way, it's comforting," Marnie told us.

"How?" Emily wanted to know.

"It means she's the most powerful witch at that location. We don't have to worry about someone worse than her."

"At least in Atlanta," I added, not wanting to think about the other headquarters. The one in Ireland would likely have the most powerful son. I pushed it from my mind.

"She's still untouchable," Emily pointed out. "Did Maeve tell Blaine she was indestructible?"

"No. Like I said, Maeve was mysterious," I told them. "She showed him her pyrokinesis, but nothing else."

"So, now what?"

No one answered. We let the fresh information marinate, realizing there was a lot to take in. Nothing seemed helpful. If anything, it created a more significant challenge for us. With Maeve leading the Atlanta chapter, there was no way of knowing what resources they had.

My eyes drifted up to the chalkboard with Maeve and Blaine's names written on it. We had minor notes under both. Maeve's consisted of the words "fire power," "crushing power," "invincibility," and a big question mark. We needed to add "army of witches" and "power boost potion" to the list.

"Wait," I almost jumped out of my skin. "I'm having a thought."

Everyone looked up at me. I paused, thinking through everything once more before divulging my epiphany.

"Spit it out," Emily demanded.

"Maeve said something to Blaine about her powers," I announced. "She compared them to suits in the tarot."

"She did? What were her words exactly?" Marjorie wanted to know.

"She said pyrokinesis was one piece of her power, just like the wands are one suit in a tarot deck." I motioned toward the chalkboard where Maeve's powers were listed, seeing if anyone else came to the same conclusion I had.

"Of course," Marjorie groaned. "How did we not see it?"

"It's obvious now, isn't it?" I agreed.

Emily looked around the room, feeling left out. "You wanna fill me in?"

"Maeve is an elementist," Marnie smiled.

"A what-ist?" Emily questioned.

"An elementist," I echoed. "It means Maeve can control the four elements."

"Like earth, wind, and fire? How did you get that from what she said?" Emily didn't read tarot cards, so she wasn't putting it together like the rest of us.

"The suits of the tarot are based on the elements," Marjorie explained.

"They're like the clubs, spades, hearts, and diamonds in playing cards," I clarified.

Marjorie walked over to the chalkboard, erased our scribbles under Maeve's name, and wrote the four elements. "If Maeve has control over the four elements, fire would stand for the pyrokinesis."

"Water's easy. Maeve can drown people with the snap of her fingers," I added, thinking back to the night Maeve threatened Quinn. "That's the cups."

Marjorie recorded it on the board.

"So, air and earth are left," Marnie said.

"Maeve destroyed the magic shop pretty easily. Could that be air like the wind?" Emily suggested. "It was like a tornado."

"Or she crushed it," I offered.

"It could be either, I suppose," Marjorie commented. "It felt a little more like an earthquake, but that would leave air. I'm not sure what we've seen from Maeve that leans toward air."

"What tarot does that represent?" Emily wanted to know.

"Swords," Marnie answered.

"Maybe we just take a sword to Maeve," Emily growled.

"It probably wouldn't hurt her. If she's invincible to magic, a sword might not do much."

"Unless…," Marjorie started a thought. "What if she's not invulnerable to our magic? What if it's a power?"

"What do you mean?" I didn't follow.

"What if Maeve uses the power of wind to surround herself with a protective shield at all times, guarding herself against unwanted spells?"

"Would that be a good thing?" Emily asked. "It still means she can't be touched."

"If it's an ability, there's a way around it," Marnie pointed out. "But I'm not sure what that would look like. I guess we could try to disable it."

"I doubt we could create a spell strong enough to incapacitate her ability to protect herself," Marjorie frowned.

"What if we turned the power around on her?" I asked, suddenly putting together a plan.

"Become invulnerable ourselves?" Marjorie tried to follow.

"There was a medallion Blaine used to keep me from freezing him. His father, Alexander, used the same medallion on Mom to block her telekinesis. We could use it to block Maeve's wind ability."

"How do we get something like that?" Emily asked.

"I believe we could make one ourselves," Marjorie told us. "It must be a blessing cast over the pendant, to protect the wearer from the effects of a specific ability."

"So we just make one of these medallion things, and then one of you can cast spells on her? Nice!" Emily rejoiced.

"Yes. Emlyn could freeze her long enough for Marnie and me to perform a binding spell," Marjorie clapped. "This can work."

"Wait. Bind Maeve's powers?" Marnie interrupted. It was maybe the first time I'd heard anger in her voice. "I know we all want to follow 'Harm None,' but this isn't a typical case. Maeve is an Ainbertach. Didn't we just talk about her single-handedly destroying a coven at age 15? She's responsible for more deaths than we could count. Eliminating her permanently would be a step toward taking down the coven. It's for the greater good of all witches."

We were all silent for a minute. There was truth in what Marnie was saying, even if no one wanted to admit it. Wouldn't things be better without Maeve around?

"I don't think I could kill someone," Emily finally said. She wouldn't be the one responsible, but she was speaking for the group. I didn't want to kill anyone either. Still...

"She has a point, though," I said, refusing to make eye contact with Marjorie. "We trapped Blaine in a trophy, but he came back. We can undo magic."

"We will not take on the principles of Henrietta!" Marjorie snapped. When she got angry, more of Marjorie's Irish accent came out. Now, she was fuming mad. She took a taller stance, trying to appear more substantial than the rest of us. At 5-foot-4, she wasn't very menacing, but I knew better than to cross her. "We will not turn our backs on the laws of the coven."

"I wasn't suggesting we kill her," Marnie backed off. "We just need a more permanent solution."

"You seem full of ideas," Marjorie spun her words angrily. Marnie wasn't her favorite pupil at the moment. "What do you propose?"

"I don't know," Marnie shot back. "But we can't just remove her powers and hope that does the trick."

"I just want my life back," Emily moaned. "How do we do that?"

"What if we sent her to another dimension?" I interrupted the yelling match. "It's the spell we used to transport ourselves to the townhouse during the fight. It was supposed to be for Maeve, but we realized magic didn't work on her."

"That sounds like a difficult spell," Marnie commented.

"It's tricky. I'm not going to lie. It would be tough. But if we got a little more magic on our side, we could do it."

"Couldn't she find a way back?" Emily asked.

"Not if we bound her powers first," I smiled, feeling like we finally had a real plan.

"That... sounds promising." Marjorie smiled as well. "It won't be easy. We must develop an iron-clad plan. It will require getting through Blaine and all the other witches at the headquarters."

"Research mode," Marnie suggested.

"We need to know how many witches Maeve has at her disposal, and where the physical location of the headquarters is. Atlanta is a vast place. It could be in any number of locations."

"Emlyn could go back again. She could use some of Maeve's memories to find all that information," Emily proposed.

"It's too risky. This recent success was Emlyn's first, and we don't know enough about her abilities. It's possible Maeve could sense Emlyn's presence in her mind. We must do this ordeal in phases." Marjorie ran a hand through her crazy grey hair. She furrowed her brow as she silently worked things out.

We sat in stillness and silence, watching Marjorie's eyes trace the words on the chalkboard. After what seemed like ten minutes, Marjorie moved to the bookshelves on the other side of the room. She scanned the rows of volumes and started pulling random spines from shelves. After collecting the ones she wanted, Marjorie carried her stack back to us, struggling not to drop one of the giant books before reaching the coffee table. She plopped them down and turned to me.

"Did you get a good look at the medallion Blaine used?" she asked me.

I nodded. I'd seen the pendant about a hundred times in my nightmares and time traveling. I'd held it in my own hands after snatching it back from Blaine. Unfortunately, I couldn't remember what had happened to it. Still, I could picture it perfectly.

"Good," Marjorie handed me two books from the top of her stack. "Take *Magik Artifacts* and *Enchanted Objects*. I need you to identify the exact pendant he used. We must find another one."

"You think it'll be in these?" I wanted to know.

"It's a starting place." She shoved the two books into my arms, which had finally returned to their standard, pasty-white color. Marjorie turned her attention to Marnie, passing her three books. She listed off their names as she placed each one in Marnie's hands. "*A History of Magical Abilities*, *Elemental Magik*, and *Ancient Celtic Bloodlines*. Start with Maeve's power of wind. It would be nice if we could all use magic against her. See if you can find a weakness. Once you've finished, you can move onto her other abilities. Last, you can move to the family line. Perhaps the key is with the family itself rather than in Maeve."

"Lucky me," Marnie sighed.

"What about me?" Emily blurted out. "I'm just as good at studying as these guys."

"I assumed book work wasn't your thing," Marjorie teased. "Wasn't your stance that you aren't a part of this?"

132

"Rude," Emily rolled her eyes. "Give me something to do."

"Try to locate the headquarters in Atlanta. Conduct a search for large estates surrounding the city. Perhaps a rich suburb? It's likely been paid off for a long time. It wouldn't be under the Ainbertach name either."

"Like search online? I so got this," Emily mused. "I used to be so good at digging up dirt on people in high school. This should be easy."

"The property would be worth millions, I'd assume, maybe more. Compile a list for Emlyn to look at. She may recognize something from her travel," Marjorie instructed.

"Just saying, but there are a lot of multi-million-dollar homes in Atlanta," Emily cautioned. "There's a lot of rich people there."

"This one would be grand. The Ainbertachs have untold wealth. The headquarters in Ireland is lavish. Look for the most expensive houses first. It probably houses dozens of witches," Marjorie told her.

"I'm so pumped!" Emily grinned. "We're gonna take this girl out!"

"I admire the enthusiasm, but it's premature," Marjorie scanned each one of us. "Get to work in the kitchen. I'd like some time alone here to follow up on some ideas by myself."

"Ideas?" I wanted to know.

"I'll call you once I've finished."

Marjorie wasn't about to let us know what she was up to. So, we took our orders and marched to the kitchen like a small Wiccan army. Marjorie pulled the double doors to the sunroom shut behind us. She had also kicked Jeb and Margo out of the room. I was worried whatever she was working on wouldn't be pleasant.

"How quick do you think we can get all this knocked out?" Emily eagerly asked as we settled in around the kitchen table. Marnie took the metal teakettle from a cabinet, filled it with water, and set it on the stove.

"All what?" I watched as Emily set up a hotspot on her burner phone and connected her laptop to it.

"Like the research part, and then the planning part. How fast do you think we can get rid of Maeve?"

I hoped Marnie would pipe in to save me from this answer, but she stayed quiet, chopping herbs for the tea. Margo was next to her on the counter, inspecting the slew of ingredients Marnie had gathered.

"I'm not sure, Em," I admitted. "Hopefully, it'll be soon." I tried to remain optimistic, but I knew it wouldn't be as fast as Emily wanted. I felt guilty for taking her away from classes, home, and the guy who wanted to be her boyfriend.

"I've only missed a couple days of classes so far. Maybe, if we get done in time, I won't have to retake anything."

"That would be nice. I was so ready to be done with A Survey of Western Art." Her voice sounded more optimistic than I'd heard it in a while, so I didn't burst her bubble. It might be weeks before we could go back to Savannah—that was if we survived.

"The more we find out, the faster we can form a plan," Marnie chimed in as she set three mugs on the table in front of us.

"Then, let's get to it!" Emily opened an internet browser and got straight to work. Seeing Emily's determination, Marnie grabbed her tea and dove into the fattest of the books Marjorie had handed her.

The research felt remarkably like schoolwork, but this was more life and death than failing an Art History test. My job was to locate the medallion Blaine used to deflect my powers or any other magical object that acted similarly. I couldn't remember reading about any other objects that guarded against abilities, but I'd also never been looking for them. I opened *Magik Artifacts* first, which was probably the more difficult of the volumes Marjorie gave me. There was no index, so it would take more work. Luckily, the chapters were labeled by type of object, so I could start with amulets.

Blaine's was gold if I remembered correctly. Or was it copper or bronze? Whatever the material was, I definitely remembered the details etched into the medallion. There was a crescent moon inside a triangle, and each point of the triangle had a shining star. It was distinct in my mind, and I knew I'd recognize it if I saw it in the book.

Two hours later, I'd scoured the entire book with no luck finding the pendant. I'd sorted through hundreds of drawings and photographs to no avail. None of the images matched the one in my mind, and each minute of failure added to my anxieties.

I looked over to Marnie, who had filled several pages of a notebook with scribblings and questions. It was obvious why she received a full ride to SCAD. Emily gave up her search after finding hundreds of multi-million-dollar homes in, around, and outside of Atlanta. Pictures were limited, so there wasn't much for Emily to go on without another lead. She'd compiled an extensive list of possible locations, and had now moved on to YouTube videos.

"I'm not getting anywhere with this," I complained, closing the book in front of me. I let my head fall onto the table to dramatically illustrate my frustration.

"I've got some good notes on the Ainbertachs that might come in handy," Marnie offered.

"Weaknesses?" I asked, hopeful.

"No…"

"Information on Maeve?" I tried.

"Maybe? Fionn Ainbertach is the current leader of the coven. He was born in 1976, which would likely make him Maeve's father or uncle. He took control in 2009 when his father, Faolan, passed away. I can't find any current information on Fionn, though. A witch who died in 2013 wrote a lot of this stuff. That was before Maeve would've taken control of Atlanta."

"So, this is all pointless," Emily exhaled.

"Not pointless," I reassured her. "We just haven't found our lucky break yet. Marjorie might find something."

"I'm never going home, am I?" Emily shouted, slamming her laptop shut with a loud thwack that sent Margo scrambling from Marnie's lap.

"Margo!" Marnie jumped in surprise, as all the dogs in the house jolted awake at the sudden noise. It was chaos from there. Thinking Margo was playing a game, Max and Dakota bolted toward her. In response, Margo scurried across the room and hurled herself onto a bookshelf. She frantically clambered from shelf to shelf, putting more distance between her and the dogs at her heels. All the way up, she knocked down books, picture frames, and decorations.

Marnie sprang into action immediately, running to Margo's aid. "No! Bad dogs," Marnie scolded them. "You all know better than to chase her." She grabbed Margo in her arms as I shooed the dogs out to the carport to give the cat some space.

"She okay?" I asked.

"Yeah. Margo was just scared."

"I'm sorry," Emily frowned. "Did they break anything?"

Marnie leaned down and grabbed a few items off the floor. "Everything looks okay except this picture frame." She showed us a picture of her with Henrietta. It must have been old because Marnie looked about 10. Her hair was cut short, and she was wearing a blue dress with red strawberries patterned across it. Her grandmother was wearing a matching kerchief around her hair.

"I can pay for a new one," Emily offered.

"No, it's fine," Marnie told her. She placed the photo back on the shelf, cracked frame and all. "It's not your fault. Margo's been jumpy since we left the townhouse."

"She's not alone," I added, grabbing a book from the floor. "I think we've all been on edge." I dusted off the spine, flipped it to the cover to put back in its place. The moment I saw the image on the front, I could've jumped for joy.

"This is it!" I shouted, unable to hide my enthusiasm. "This is the symbol I've been looking for!" The moon, triangle, and stars were in the center of the cover. The only difference was they weren't on a medallion. I was sure I was right, though.

Marnie grabbed the book from me to examine what I'd found. *"West African Folk Magic,"* she read the title of the book. "The medallion is African?"

"It doesn't make sense to me either, but we finally have a lead!"

Marnie smiled to herself and glanced at the picture frame. "I see what you did there, Granny."

"If it's West African magic, does that mean we have to fly to Africa?" Emily wondered out loud. "That'll be such a long plane ride. Plus, I don't have a passport."

"Lots of magic here comes from other places, so we might not have to go that far," I told her. "Like our Celtic magic is from Ireland, but Celtic magic is prevalent all over the United States."

We circled around the book at the kitchen table, and I started flipping through the pages, hoping for an illustration.

"There it is!" Marnie caught a glimpse at it in the middle of the book. It was an exact illustration of the one Blaine used. Underneath the drawing, there was a small inscription.

"It says the symbol is used for protection in the folk tradition of Hoodoo," I announced.

"You mean Voodoo? Like New Orleans?" Emily asked. "I'd be so down to go to New Orleans. I have a cousin who looks just like me, and we went to NOLA last year during Jazz Fest. My parents go every year. The best part was everyone thought my cousin and I were twins, so they thought I was 21 just like Kaitlyn."

"No, it's not Voodoo. It says Hoodoo, with an 'H,'" I corrected.

"That's disappointing," Emily said. "I could've used a vacay."

"Here, I've got it," Marnie said, reading from her phone. "Hoodoo is a traditional style of Black American magic based on the spiritual beliefs of West Africa. It says the practice was created during the time of slavery here in the United States. Its roots are in African traditions, but they mixed with many forms of religion, such as Christianity, Catholicism, Native American beliefs, and Voodoo."

"So, it's a giant mixture of beliefs?" Emily asked.

"Sort of, but that's the most basic way of looking at it," Marnie explained. "It says Hoodoo utilizes spiritual and natural magics from herbs, roots, animal parts, and crystals to manifest desires and intentions."

"So, we just need to find a coven of these witches and ask them for help. Does it say where to find witches who practice Hoodoo?" I asked, hopeful this lead would pan out.

"Um… it says Hoodoo originated in the South, but once the Great Migration happened, Hoodoo spread across the country. They could be anywhere."

"Maybe Marjorie will know of a coven," Emily was excited.

"So, this is really good, right?" I felt cautious about getting my hopes up. "We just need to find a coven, get a medallion, enchant it, and then go after Maeve."

"Heck, yes!" Emily shouted. We high-fived in a moment of victory, but Marnie didn't seem as excited by the news. She was still reading the article on her phone. I realized there might have been more to the Hoodoo covens.

"Marnie, does it say if Hoodoo is light or dark magic?" I asked, hesitant to hear the answer. The excellent feeling deflated.

"It doesn't say," Marnie admitted. "I'd assume it's like any practice. It probably varies from coven to coven."

"Wait. So, if Blaine got a necklace from them, they're probably bad, right?" Emily determined.

I sighed. "That's a definite possibility."

"Many practice light magic," Marjorie's voice surprised us from the other side of the room. We all jumped at the sound of her stern statement. "I have connections to one coven, not too far from here." Marjorie told us. "My coven helped them disperse an evil being a long time ago. He was a nasty character, and they needed magic different from their own to release his spirit."

"So, they owe us?" I asked.

"I wouldn't lead with that," Marjorie told me.

"Where are they?" Emily wanted to know.

"I'll get to that," Marjorie clarified. "I know it seems we should celebrate, but we have much to discuss, and time is running thin."

No one argued. We followed Marjorie in silence to the sunroom. The remnants of her spell-casting were still visible on the coffee table; it was covered in herbs, candles, and oils, leaving a sharp scent in the air.

"Take a seat," Marjorie motioned to the wicker furniture.

"Didn't you hear? We got a lead! Why are you so down in the dumps?" Emily finally asked. We were all thinking the same thing.

"It is a splendid thing, and it gives us another job to do. However, retrieving the medallion is not the only task we must accomplish. I've weighed all our options, explored various outcomes, and delved into the choices we have before us," Marjorie said.

"Why is that bad? We know what to do next," I enthused.

"I have a plan. You won't like it."

Chapter Eleven

Marjorie was right. I hated the plan she'd concocted, and I told her I wouldn't follow it. There was no way I'd do something so stupid and dangerous. But it didn't matter in the end, because nothing went according to plan. Everything escalated in a way we couldn't predict, and the result sent us running again. Only this time was worse. When we left Savannah, we were all together. Now we were fragmented into pieces.

"It's not your fault, Emlyn," Emily ended the hour of silence.

My knuckles were white from my grip on the steering wheel of Marjorie's SUV. I hadn't loosened my hands since we left Henrietta's house. I had spent the entire hour dwelling on what would've gone differently if Marjorie listened to me. I tried to tell Marjorie it was a terrible plan, but she wouldn't hear it. And now...

"We shouldn't have left her," I said, wiping pools of water from my eyes to see the road. "We could've found another way. It shouldn't just be you and me."

"There was no other way, Emlyn," Emily consoled me. Half of me knew she was right; the other half was still in shock. "Maeve's guys almost got all of us. Marnie handed them Marjorie, and I thought we were next."

Emily was right next to me in the passenger seat, but I refused to look at her. I kept my eyes on the black pavement in front of me as we blazed southbound down a three-lane highway.

"We could've fought harder. We could've found another option."

"No, Emlyn. If we had stayed any longer, you'd be on your way to see Maeve, too. We're not ready for her yet."

"Stick to the plan," I said stiffly, echoing Marjorie's last words as the day replayed in my mind.

—

After mapping out Marjorie's plan, which took hours to perfect, we found a little time to rest before a full day of spells, potions, maps, and charts. I'd argued a lot, spending hours trying to convince Marjorie there was a different path. Marjorie was unmoving. She told me she was the one with foresight, so I needed to trust her judgment as she assigned our tasks. In theory, the plan could've worked, but we didn't expect Maeve's agents to show up at Henrietta's house like they did.

Marjorie had assigned my role in private, so only I would know the specific details about the Hoodoo coven. Marjorie told me about the last known location of the coven and its leader, Azariah Imamu. They were in New Orleans, just as Emily had suspected. When Marjorie worked with them, the Hoodoo coven owned a small magic shop nestled right outside the French Quarter. Marjorie thought they might still have the storefront.

Emily's job was to handle the logistics of getting us to New Orleans—lodging and transportation—while I prepared potions and spells for our visit. We weren't supposed to tell Marnie about New Orleans, though. Marjorie explained that the fewer people who knew about our mission, the safer Emily and I would be. Marjorie even took a memory potion to make herself forget about the Hoodoo coven after we spoke.

We were going over the plan in the sunroom again—Marjorie was thorough—and I should've sensed something was wrong. As the four of us chatted in the sunroom, Marnie seemed stiffer than usual. Her jaw was locked and tense—the opposite of the Marnie I knew. She was usually a calming presence, but this version of Marnie was edgy and hyper-focused. In hindsight, I should've known something was coming. Initially, I thought Marjorie's plan bothered her, but I never asked her about it. One minute Marjorie was discussing potion options, and the next Marnie was behind me with a kitchen knife against my neck.

It took everyone, including me, a few seconds to realize what was happening. It didn't seem real, but it was. Marnie's had a plan of her own, and it was playing out. Jeb was the first to jump up, immediately snarling at Marnie.

"Marnie, what are you doing?" Marjorie's movements were steady, despite her shocked tone, as she and Emily positioned themselves in front of me. She didn't need to ask though. We all knew what was happening.

The cold blade against my throat was almost electrifying as its sharp edge nuzzled against my skin. I'd been in this situation before, but it was still terrifying. Of course, it was different this time. This time it was Marnie who held my life in her hands—my friend and confidant.

"Everyone, back up," Marnie's once soft voice barked out with newfound authority. There was no point in speaking, even if I hadn't been afraid of the blade.

"Marnie, what the heck?" Emily screamed.

"She's betraying us." Marjorie spat the words out like venom.

"You know being a loner witch doesn't work anymore, Marjorie," Marnie told us. "So, when the opportunity to join the Ainbertachs came around, I took it. It's not personal."

"Just like your grandmother," Marjorie jeered at Marnie.

I couldn't see Marnie's face, but her grip on my body intensified with the mention of Henrietta. Jeb's growls intensified, but he knew he couldn't attack Marnie.

Marnie ignored Marjorie's jab at her grandmother. Instead, she called out to someone in the other room. "I've got Emlyn."

Two men appeared, and Jeb turned his snarls to them. His teeth were bared, and the fur on the back of his neck was standing two inches high. I recognized one man as Harold, the blonde-haired black man who worked for Maeve. The other man was tall—probably 6-foot-5. He was bald, with a long black beard and pale ivory skin. His eyes were pools of aqua blue.

They were both in jeans rather than robes, but what they lacked in pockets they made up for in pouches attached to their belts. They were likely armed with potions and powders galore, along with athames.

"Figures," Marjorie insulted Marnie. I wasn't sure why she was laying it on so thick. "You aren't witch enough to take us on yourself."

"Shut up, Marjorie. Learn when you've been beat. And don't try anything funny. No freezing or weird potions. Maeve wants Emlyn for herself, but it's not a requirement we bring her in unharmed."

"Harry, this Marnie girl was serious. She really cornered the witch Maeve is after," the bald man motioned toward me with the knife against my throat. He seemed happily surprised. "Do we know who these other people are? I thought our orders were just to find the time manipulator."

"The old lady is the grandmother," Harold explained.

"Old lady?" Marjorie huffed.

The bald man took out his athame and ambled toward Emily and Marjorie. Jeb immediately blocked his way and snarled at him. I'd never seen Jeb look so vicious, and it seemed to scare the bald man.

"Come on, Daryl. You afraid of a dog?" Harold jumped to the lead and snarled back at Jeb before kicking him hard in the chest. Jeb flew backwards into the wicker coffee table behind Marjorie and Emily. I wanted to run to his side, but I was still locked in Marnie's grip. Jeb whimpered but didn't move.

"Jeb!" Emily shouted, immediately dropping to his side. I could only watch helplessly. "What is wrong with you?" Emily got up to punch Harold in the stomach, but he grabbed her arm and spun her into a headlock.

"That one has a mouth," Daryl laughed.

"Get the old woman," Marnie ordered.

"You both really need to work on your people skills," Emily grunted under Harold's bicep, always one to fight back. "You can't just go around kicking dogs and insulting grandmas like this."

I looked to Marjorie, hoping she had something up her sleeve to take care of all these guys, but Marnie read my mind. "Marjorie, you'll also want to drop whatever potions you have hidden in your pockets, or your granddaughter gets it," she ordered.

Daryl moved forward to restrain Marjorie, who resisted for a moment, but then gave herself up. She scowled at Marnie. "We trusted you, you wretched girl. What would your aunt think?"

"She probably saw it coming. I was close to Granny," Marnie moved us both a few steps forward.

"How could you put your family through this again?" Marjorie asked her as Daryl removed several vials from her robe pockets. Harold and Daryl secured Emily and Marjorie with zip ties and sat them down on one of the wicker chairs. I was next.

"Again? When did it ever stop? Our family was always scorned for what Granny did, even though she was right! Think about it. When you found out where we were going, you were angry. Even you, who helped me move in with your granddaughter, couldn't let me forget for a second who my family was. We were supposed to be friends."

"We thought so too," Emily scoffed.

142

"It doesn't matter. My granny was right, and I need to be with witches who respect my abilities." Marnie nodded toward Harold and Daryl.

"You don't have any powers," Marjorie protested.

"Do you really think a descendant of witches has no powers? It may be humble, but it's respectable enough: potion-making," Marnie said shortly. "I'm not just good at making tea."

"You'll be rewarded for this." Harold stepped forward, offering Marnie two sets of zip ties for me. "It's Marnie, right?"

Marnie nodded.

"We look forward to you joining us, Marnie," Daryl echoed. They were enthralled with her. I wasn't so much impressed as I was shocked. Being on the other end of the knife, I couldn't really feel much, though. I focused on escape. I knew an opportunity would present itself soon.

"I'm eager to see if Maeve feels the same way."

They all grinned at each other before Harold turned his attention to me. "How should we restrain this one?"

"We can't risk her freezing time on us," Marnie assessed. "There's some essence of poppy on the top shelf behind you. We should give her some before we tie her up."

"Good thinking," he said. Harold turned to the bookshelf while Daryl kept his eyes locked on Marjorie and Emily.

"One wrong move from either of you and our trip back to HQ will not be—," Daryl's threat was cut off by Marnie's sudden shriek. It was my moment!

It was Tephi who came to my rescue. She pounced onto Marnie's shoulder, digging her nails deep into the soft skin of Marnie's neck. Marnie yelped and dropped the knife as she instinctively reached up to pry Tephi off. Harold and Daryl spun around, ready to react, but they weren't fast enough. I froze the room as soon as the blade left my throat. The rest was a scramble.

I pulled Tephi's frozen body from Marnie's shoulder, unhooking her claws as quickly as I could, and ran to Emily, Marjorie, and Jeb. I removed my magic from them, leaving the rest of the room still. "We have to go now!" I ordered as Emily and Marjorie reanimated. I grabbed the knife Marnie had dropped and used it to cut the zip ties that bound their wrists and ankles.

Marjorie took Tephi from my arms and darted to the back room to grab her things. Emily did the same, scurrying to the room she'd been staying in. A brief feeling of relief rushed through my system. Jeb, who was still lying on the floor, was still alive. His brown eyes met mine, and I helped him up to his feet.

"Thank Goddess," I exhaled, pulling all 100 pounds of Jeb into my arms. I stumbled out of the sunroom, through the kitchen, and into Marjorie's SUV, barely making it with all of Jeb's weight. As I loaded Jeb into the back, I realized the other dogs were gone. Marnie must have known this fight would happen and shut the pack in the barn. I kicked myself for not noticing it as a sign. Part of me also wanted to take Dakota and Max with us, but I knew we didn't have time or room.

Emily busted through the door seconds later, moving faster than I'd ever seen her before. "I got your bag, too," she yelled out of breath. She tossed the two bags into the backseat and slammed the door shut.

"Can you drive? You need to hit the gas the moment we're in," I instructed. I didn't listen for a response before tossing the keys at her. I heard the roar of the engine come alive as I re-entered the house. I knew it shouldn't have taken Marjorie this long to get her things. A nagging voice was telling me something was wrong, and about three steps into the kitchen, my fears were confirmed.

"Wouldn't leave without grandma, would you?" Daryl laughed. His thick arm was wrapped around Marjorie's body so tight I worried he'd break her in half.

"Get your hands off her!" I screeched.

"Emlyn, get out of here," Marjorie barked at me.

"She won't be getting far," Daryl hissed before tossing Marjorie onto the sofa. Harold and Marnie came barreling out of the sunroom. Harold darted to Marjorie on the couch, quickly overpowering her to hold her down. Marnie took a defensive stance next to Daryl.

I had tenths of a second to react—to decide which plan to follow. Marjorie had insisted I was the part of the plan that mattered most. She told me I needed to locate the pendant. I was the witch to take down Blaine. I didn't want to leave Marjorie. No part of me was okay with leaving her to the torture Maeve would almost certainly subject her to. Fighting Daryl could lead to me also being captured, which would mean the end for all of us.

"Go, Emlyn!" Marjorie urged right before Daryl darted forward to grab me. I froze him and Marnie at the same time, hoping to buy more time. Instead, my magic only decelerated Daryl's steps forward like he was moving in slow motion. He was adapting to my powers somehow.

"You can't worry about me, Emlyn," Marjorie exploded, sensing my hesitation. "Stick to the plan! I believe in you, Celtic girl!" Tephi ran to my side and jumped up on my leg, angrily meowing and hissing. She wanted me to save Marjorie, but I couldn't. All I could do was grab Tephi and flee. She clawed at me as we escaped through the door to the carport. Tephi wasn't going to leave Marjorie of her own volition, but I knew they'd likely kill her if she stayed.

"Go!" I shouted the moment my butt hit the passenger seat.

"Marjorie?" Emily probed.

"We have to leave," I told her. Daryl burst out of the house. I hit the lock button on the doors about a second before he grabbed the handle. "Go, go, go!" I yelled.

Emily screamed, instinctively punching the gas. The engine roared, and the tires squealed as we took off, but Daryl held on, his feet dragging against the ground as we accelerated forward. I was afraid he'd get in somehow, but after a minute of Emily's crazy, zig-zag driving, he let go, falling into the dust.

———

"Stick to the plan," I repeated to myself.

"Take this next exit," Emily's voice returned me to the present—about an hour out from Henrietta's house. Emily and I had changed positions once we reached the main road so Emily could navigate.

"We should keep going," I argued.

"No. We need to grab some food and ditch this car," Emily contended. "They know we're driving a black SUV with Georgia a plate. We're sitting ducks in this thing."

"It doesn't feel safe," I told her. "They're going to find out we're headed to New Orleans, I'm sure. We have to beat them there, get the medallion, and get out fast."

"Stop. Marjorie is smart. You and I are the only ones who know the Hoodoo coven is in New Orleans, plus Marjorie made us the cloaking potions again."

"So? You guessed New Orleans before Marjorie ever confirmed it."

"They might send someone to New Orleans, but probably not Maeve herself. We can handle this." Emily seemed determined. "Now, take this exit. Remember, Marjorie made logistics my job."

"Fine." I got in the right-hand lane and took the exit for Bessemer, turning under the highway to pull into a small shopping center. The area consisted of two fast-food restaurants, a grocery store, a dollar store, a nail and hair salon, and a gas station. All the buildings were made of old, red brick. I parked in the back of the grocery store lot, putting distance between us and the other cars.

"Did you get us a rental car?" I wanted to know as got out of the SUV.

"No credit cards, remember?" Emily fussed at my negligence.

"That'll make things more difficult. How did you get us a hotel without a credit card? Did you make a fake one?" I asked.

"Wow, yeah, that would've been a good idea. But no, we're staying at Janice's family condo in the French Quarter, which requires no deposit because I didn't tell her we were staying there."

"Are you kidding?" My face flushed red with anger.

"It's fine. At the Halloween party, Janice asked if I wanted to go to New Orleans one weekend with her in November. Her parents left it off Airbnb for the month because Janice told them she wanted to have a girls' weekend."

"And how do we know she didn't pick this weekend?" I grumbled.

"She was so worn out after her party, she'll be giving herself a weekend of recovery before she hits up NOLA. Trust me." She shot me a sly smile. "Kind of crazy to think that party was less than a week ago. So much has happened since then."

I didn't like the plan. It left too much up to chance. Emily's smile told me there was more to the story, though. "What are you not telling me?" I questioned her. "And what car are we taking?"

"I've got it handled." She pointed to the grocery store. "Why don't you go grab food? I'll wait out here with Tephi and walk Jeb."

146

"I don't like this." I grabbed my duffle bag and found my wallet. I didn't have much in the way of money, mainly because I couldn't use the card Dad gave me. "How much money did Marjorie pack in the car? Do we have any cash?"

"There's $1,000 in cash, along with a bunch of gift cards she bought to places like gas stations, fast-food chains, and grocery stores. There are also three $200 Visa cards." She handed me a plastic bag filled with multi-colored plastic. "Cash would've been better, though. Why didn't she just take it all out in cash?"

"Most banks have withdrawal limits. She probably got what she could from an ATM and used her daily spending limit to buy the cards," I pulled out one of the Visa cards. "Want anything special?"

"Something crunchy, and something sweet. Also, the beasts are probably hungry too." She motioned to Jeb and Tephi. I nodded in agreement and then trotted toward the large "Family Market" sign flooding the dark parking lot with light. There were a few other cars—some were nice, and others didn't look drivable. Several pick-up trucks, in particular, had seen better days. They were probably work-trucks since we were out in the middle of nowhere. I hurried through the parking lot into the store, trying to shield my face from the two white cameras prominently displayed on the front of the building. I knew I was being paranoid, but I wasn't taking any chances.

The place was empty for 8 p.m. on a Friday. A few people were wandering through the aisles, but only two employees were working the check-out lines. The store, to my dismay, didn't have self-check-out. I'd have to talk to someone.

I grabbed a cart and quickly darted through the aisles. I filled the cart with boxes of cheese crackers, sour candies, a family-sized bag of pretzels, and a couple oatmeal cookies. The more substantial items were protein bars, beef jerky, oranges, bananas, lunch packs, gallons and bottles of water, cheese sticks, pre-made sandwiches and fried chicken from the deli section, dog food, cat food, and a two-liter of diet soda.

"Road trip?" a blonde, high school-aged girl asked as she scanned my items. She was wearing an Alabama baseball cap, which shielded her face from me as she stared at her cell phone in between scanning. I'd selected her for that reason, hoping she'd be so annoyed with my presence that she'd ignore me completely.

"You guessed it." I repositioning myself so the credit card reader was blocking my face.

"This is a lot of food."

"My brother and sister eat a lot, and my parents don't want to stop again," I told her, painting the picture of a crazy family road trip in her brain.

"I have a little brother," the girl said as she scanned my cheese crackers, "I totally get it."

It felt like it took her forever to finish everything. The need to flee never left my mind. I knew we should've kept going. We should've taken back roads instead of the main highway to Louisiana, but it was what it was. My only reassurance was that Daryl and Harold didn't seem to have a car close to Henrietta's house. They likely weren't able to follow us immediately.

"$168.52," the girl finally announced.

I slid the Visa card, hoping she wouldn't notice it was a gift card.

"Are you guys from here?" She made direct eye contact now. So much for not being remembered.

"No, we're from Mississippi, heading up to New York City," I lied.

"Oh, my god. I love New York!" the girl smiled at me, handing me the receipt. "Y'all have fun."

I grabbed my cart and bolted, doing my best to make it look like I wasn't running away. The slight panic I felt from being out in the middle of the parking lot escalated when I saw Emily hugging someone by the SUV. Dread rushed through me, and I hurried back a little faster. If she ran into someone out here, it could compromise our position. My brain raced through the possibilities of who it could be, and whether we would be able to trust them.

Then I saw the Chevy Silverado.

"Emily," I grunted to her when I was within speaking distance. My jaw locked.

"Oh, Emlyn. There you are." She smiled an innocent grin.

"What is he doing here?" I yelled, parking my cart behind Marjorie's SUV. I meant it to illustrate my unwillingness to get inside Quinn's truck.

"We need a ride, Emlyn," Emily insisted.

"Not from Quinn! Why would you even think this was okay?" My fury only seemed to grow the more I talked. Heat was radiating from my face. Emily knew what being pulled into this witch drama was like, and I couldn't believe she wanted to drag Quinn into it too.

"Look, I volunteered," Quinn jumped in.

"You didn't know what you were volunteering for," I snarled.

"Calm down, Em!" Emily tried.

"How do you expect me to calm down right now?"

Instead of responding, Quinn wrapped me in his arms, giving me a tight hug. "I know you're pissed, but I'm just glad you're alive," he admitted.

Had ferocity not been operating my brain, the embrace might've felt nice. It had been a long time since Quinn held me, and I needed a good hug and a shoulder to cry on. The warm feeling was brief, though. There was a ball of anger in my chest that I couldn't ignore. I pulled away from him.

"You're both insane!" I hollered.

"Emlyn, I know this was a surprise, but try to think this through," Emily reasoned. "This was the best idea we came up with."

"You dragged my ex into a life-threatening situation. That was your best idea?"

"I know all the risks," Quinn inserted himself into the conversation I was intentionally leaving him out of. "It was my choice. I couldn't sit around and do nothing while you and Emily go through this."

"I can't let you get involved in this," I told him, my voice calming a bit. "Emily, what made you think this was a good idea?"

She shot me a crooked, "I'm sorry," smile. "Well, technically, Marjorie decided we should call Quinn. I only made the arrangements," Emily sheepishly responded. "He was supposed to pick us up from Henrietta's house. Luckily, he was already on his way when those goons got there."

"Lucky?" I was spinning. "Look, just find another option."

"We don't have one," she insisted.

"Blaine doesn't know my car," Quinn interjected. "And because my parents have different last names, you wouldn't be able to track the plate to me. It's under my Mom's last name."

"It's not a chance I want to take. Blaine knows you and I were connected. It's easy to dig up both your parents' information."

"But Maeve also saw Quinn dump you at dinner," Emily reminded me. "As far as they're concerned, Quinn wants nothing to do with you."

"There's nothing flashy about the truck that would give us away," Quinn added.

"The license plate will show it's from Savannah. Dead giveaway," I pointed out.

"Nope. The truck was my granddad's. It's registered in a city north of Atlanta."

"It doesn't feel right," I expressed weakly.

"We can't rent a car, we can't steal a car, and we can't take Marjorie's SUV anymore. Time is a factor. We still have to get to New Orleans, and we need to get there fast," Emily told me apologetically.

"This is the best plan," Quinn confirmed.

We said nothing for a minute as I let it sink in. Quinn and Emily knew I'd fold. Emily stroked my shoulder for a second and then grabbed the grocery cart from me.

"Yes! You got pretzels," she praised me, changing the subject. Emily grabbed the bag and put it under her arm before loading the rest of the items into the cab of Quinn's truck.

Quinn followed her lead and started transferring our travel bags.

"Jeb and Marjorie's cat can sit in the back with—," Quinn continued, hoping someone would volunteer for the riding position. The truck had an extended cab, but it was going to be kind of cramped back there.

Emily beat me to it. "I'll take the back," she said. "That way, I can cuddle with the floofs and take a nap."

"I can't believe this is happening," I huffed as I collected Tephi from the SUV and transferred her into the truck. She wasn't happy, letting out a dull growl when I lifted her from her hiding place under the seat. She didn't like car rides.

I claimed a package of sour candies from the grocery bags and took the front passenger seat, swiveling my body away from Quinn. Minutes later, we were on the road again. I had a break from driving, at least, even if I wasn't happy about it. With my focus shifted from driving to our predicament, I got lost in obsessive thoughts.

When I couldn't concentrate on the future—the drive, the mission, my companions, Marjorie's capture—any longer, I allowed memories of the past to drift into my thoughts. A week ago, I wouldn't have believed I'd be heading to New Orleans with Quinn. It'd been a long time since we'd gone on any kind of trip together. In high school, there weren't many opportunities to get away, but it was only a 20-minute drive to the beach.

"Are you still mad?" Quinn finally asked, keeping his voice soft as to not wake a snoring Emily.

"Obviously," I told him.

"Maybe you're at least a little happy I'm here?"

"I'm not."

"Come on, Em."

"Maybe a little...but not enough to make it worth you being here."

"Fair enough." He let silence creep back into the car for a few moments. "You thinking about Marjorie?"

"Yeah. Also, our trips to Tybee Island," I admitted. "I guess all of us in your truck brings back memories." My eyes didn't leave the trees whizzing by as we passed them on the highway.

"Makes sense," he smiled. "Maybe this time you'll manage not to turn lobster red from the sun."

"Probably not. Irish, remember?" We both knew the sun was my real enemy. SPF 100 wasn't even enough to protect my pale skin.

"What was that restaurant we always ate at? The place with the seafood nachos."

"Dockside Café. Good food."

"I take it this trip won't be like those."

"There's still time to drop us off at a rest stop and go home," I offered.

"Nope."

"Quinn, I'm ruining your life."

"No, you aren't."

"Be honest, Quinn. Think about everything that's happened over the last year."

"I'm a grown-up, Emlyn. I get to make my own choices."

"You didn't choose to have a girlfriend who was a witch. You were just dragged into the aftermath."

"I choose to be here now."

"Think about school. What about football?"

"They'll still be there when I get back."

"Football won't. You'll be kicked off the team for leaving mid-season."

"Maybe not, but it's my choice."

"Quinn, you have a life to live. Just drop us off somewhere. We'll be fine."

"I won't do that."

"Quinn, please! For me, just stop this." I was in tears now, despite my attempts to sound calm and reasonable. I hated it when my emotions betrayed me. I wiped my eyes while checking the back seat to make sure Emily was still asleep.

"Don't you get it? I'm doing this for you," Quinn almost shouted, then caught himself and lowered his voice. "Football and school will always be there. You might not be. Do you think I could live with myself if anything happened to you when I could've helped stop it?"

"Exactly, this is dangerous! I have magical powers, and you don't. What makes you think you could help in this position? I've already endangered your life twice. Let's not do it again."

"You're frustrating. You know that?"

I didn't respond.

"Whether or not you and I have a future, I care about you. That means when your best friend calls, saying you both need a ride to New Orleans in a life or death scenario, I'm your guy."

"You guys are so dramatic," Emily yawned, interrupting suddenly. "It's so mushy-gushy, too. Could you just not? You both want the best for each other. You love each other. Deal with it."

I quickly wiped my eyes. "Did you have a good nap?" I asked her.

"No. I feel more tired. Can we get a motel for the night?"

I checked the map we were using to navigate. "Yeah, we probably should. I don't think we'll get to New Orleans until 2 a.m."

"Bourbon Street would still be wild." Emily smiled.

"Exactly," I groaned. "We need a good night's sleep."

"We're staying on Bourbon Street?" Quinn wanted to know.

"According to Emily." I didn't hide my disapproving tone.

"Our friend Janice's family has an Airbnb that'll be empty," Emily told him. "It's the perfect plan. Bourbon is loud, crazy, and full of distractions. We'll be able to stay under the radar, easy."

"She has a point." Quinn grinned. "Might even be fun."

"Let's stop off the main highway tonight then." I ignored the "fun" comment. Quinn still didn't understand the danger we were in. "We'll need to be way off the grid, though." I grabbed the map and tried to find our current location. I'd never used a paper map before, so it was a bit of a struggle.

"Where are we anyway?" Emily asked.

"Somewhere in Mississippi," I yawned.

"That's specific."

"Oh, here we are. It looks like we could take this next exit. There's a lake nearby, which means there are probably cabins for rent, or a cheap motel at the least."

"A cabin?" Emily didn't seem pleased.

"What? It's secluded, and it's not like you need cell reception."

"I mean…" She trailed off without finishing.

"Emlyn is right," Quinn interjected. "It'll be isolated, which is good for us."

"Fine. I've obviously been overruled," Emily sighed. She slouched back in her seat. "How did people survive like this for so long? It's so boring without a real phone."

We took the exit, and the bright lights, billboards, restaurants, gas stations, and buildings faded away into the darkness of the night. After about 20 minutes, the paved road transitioned to gravel as we drove farther from the highway. The simplicity of our surroundings made me feel safer. Even the jostling of the car on the uneven road was comfortable.

"Take that bridge over there," I instructed Quinn, pointing to a small wooden structure wide enough for only a single car. We crossed over the lake, rocking back and forth on the rickety bridge as we headed into a thicket of woods. A rusted metal sign with a small cabin painted on the front directed us deeper into the forest. I told myself a cabin would be beautiful, imagining the classic log motif and furniture designed with antlers. At the very least, there'd probably be a bed and a couch, which was all we needed.

"This is how all scary movies start," Emily groaned. "Let's just go to New Orleans tonight instead."

"It is creepy," Quinn nodded. "You think anyone's been murdered out here?"

"Oh god, Quinn. Why did you put that in my head?" Emily scolded.

I ignored them. "Follow this road. The cabins must be down that way."

Quinn frowned. "You can use your magic to keep the ghosts and murderers away, right?"

He tried to hide the fear in his voice, but I knew he was serious. The guy loved to watch scary movies, but he rarely slept after seeing them.

"I'll cast a protective spell over the cabin for the night," I told him.

"Like a force field?" Quinn wanted to know.

"Kind of. It won't be impenetrable, but it'll keep negative energies and spells from entering our space, in theory."

"Ghosts are like negative energy," Emily assured him.

We rolled up to the cabin area, and Jeb immediately started whining with excitement. He was fed up with being in the truck—we all were. Although, I wasn't thrilled with the location. The structures weren't the Lincoln Log cabins I'd imagined. Instead, they were just eight little wooden boxes dropped in the middle of the woods, each numbered sloppily in white paint.

"They look tiny," Emily complained.

"It's not that bad," I argued.

"I can always sleep on the floor," Quinn offered.

Emily just sighed in reply, slouching back into her seat. Even Tephi seemed grouchy as she emerged from underneath the seat, producing a low moaning/growling noise. My guess was she had to pee.

Quinn pulled his truck alongside a metal machine at the front of the campground. A single lamp-post stood to its left, creating an orange circle of light around it. A quick assessment of the lot was enough to tell us we were practically alone there. There was one other car—a white Saturn—parked at the far end. I decided it couldn't have been an agent of the Ainbertachs, though, because there was a significant dent in the rear bumper. It didn't seem like Maeve's style to keep damaged cars in her fleet. Besides, black was probably more her color. I imagined her people driving BMWs, or maybe the new Buick.

"I'll go pay," Quinn offered.

I shook my head. "No, I should go. I can freeze someone if they try to sneak up on us."

"Unless it's Maeve," Emily kindly pointed out. "Then, your powers don't work."

"Very true, yes. Thanks, Emily."

I opened the door and slid out of the truck. It was a few degrees colder by the lake, causing goosebumps to appear immediately. It looked like Cabin No. 1 was the farthest away from the main road, which was the ideal location, but the owners of the Saturn had already picked that one. My next choice was three doors down: Cabin No. 4, which was right in the middle and away from the other guests. According to the signage, the cabin was only $125 for the night, which was great. It was all done through a machine, which was also pleasant. The unfortunate news was we needed a credit card to pay for it.

"It's a no go," I grumbled as I climbed back into the truck.

"They're full?" Quinn asked. "It doesn't look full."

"We need a credit card. The machine won't take cash."

"Crap. What about a gift card?" Emily offered.

"It holds an extra $100 on the card until the park ranger can inspect the cabin. Our cards won't cover the difference."

"Then we use a credit card," Quinn said, seeming confused.

"We can't use any of ours," Emily said. "Maeve can probably track our info."

"She's a witch, not the FBI," Quinn argued in a tone that made it clear he thought we were being paranoid.

"We don't know what connections she might have. Maeve could have law enforcement in her pocket," I explained.

"You really think so?" Quinn asked. "That seems extreme."

"Well, they really want to kill Emlyn," Emily added.

"Okay, then use my card." Quinn pulled a black leather wallet from his pants pocket and produced a silver credit card. He passed it over to me.

"Blaine and Maeve both know you," I shook my head. "It'd be too easy to tie you to us."

"Come on, they're tracking my last name, and once again, this card is in my mother's name. Even if they can track credit cards, it would take them a while to put the pieces together. We'd be gone before they could find us."

"What if we just broke in?" Emily offered.

There was a moment of silence as we all pondered the idea.

"I don't like it," I told them. "It's not worth the risk of getting caught."

"Looks like this is the best option," Quinn placed the card in my hand. "We'll just shower, sleep, and skedaddle."

I reluctantly took the card and felt guilty the entire three minutes it took me to get the key for the cabin. My gut was telling me this wasn't a good idea, but I didn't see any other options. That seemed to be a recurring theme in my life right now.

We unloaded the truck, balancing armfuls of groceries in each hand as we stumbled into the dark cabin. Luckily for us, the interior of the cabin was much homier than the exterior. There were even two bedrooms, which earned a happy cheer from Emily.

"Thank goodness!" Emily smiled. She plopped grocery bags onto a small, maple wood coffee table and took off toward one room. Jeb chased after her, leaving Quinn, Tephi, and me alone in the living room.

"Guess we know which room she claimed," I laughed.

"I'm just happy to be off the road. I was getting sleepy," Quinn told me.

"There's only one bathroom, but I'm not gonna complain," Emily called out. "Who's taking the other room?"

Quinn and I exchanged an awkward look. A little more than a year ago, the answer would've been easy, but now it was uncomfortable.

"You take the other bedroom, Emlyn," Quinn told me, reading my mind. "I'll sleep out here on the couch."

There was a sofa in the center of the room, accompanied by two chairs, the coffee table, and two end tables. They pushed the outdoor aesthetic hard in this place. There were paintings of fishermen and hunters on the walls, and the lamps on each end table featured antlers and fish.

"You came to our rescue. The least I can do is give you the better bed," I told him.

156

Quinn shook his head at me and tossed a duffel bag onto one armchair. He let himself collapse onto the couch.

"So, I'm like a hero then? You must owe me big time." He shot me a charming half-smile, and I, of course, flushed red. I immediately broke eye contact and headed toward the kitchen in the other direction.

"I've got a few things I need to do around the cabin—the force-field. Why don't you fight Emily for the shower?"

He didn't respond, and I ignored the awkwardness, focusing on magic instead. It was a lot less complicated. I set my bag down on the bistro-style kitchen table and sorted through the herbs, jars, vials, and books Marjorie and I had packed. This was our emergency bag, and we'd luckily put it together before Marnie called the Ainbertachs. We'd stocked the entire SUV earlier in the day with handy objects and ingredients, including defensive potions, charms, and pendants.

Most importantly, we packed lava stones, meant to ground and protect. If the mystical properties of these rocks were tapped into correctly, the lava stones would cultivate mental and physical fortitude. When mixed with formidable gemstones—black tourmaline, labradorite, fluorite, and black obsidian—and sage, the combination should guard the cabin. I designed the mixture to protect us from both physical and mental attacks. I knew they wouldn't do much against Maeve, but I pushed the thought from my mind.

"Can I help with anything?" I almost jumped at the sound of Quinn behind me. "Emily beat me to the shower, so it'll be a few minutes."

"Um, yeah. Sure." I handed him several small sachets. "Fill these with the lava stones. They're the rough ones with holes in them."

Quinn looked confused by the myriad of items on the table. "What is all this?"

"Gemstones and rocks mostly."

"So, a bunch of rocks will keep all the bad people out?"

"In theory."

"Ghosts, too?" he asked.

"Sure," I smiled at him, taking a handful of gemstones to add to the bags Quinn filled. "Can you help me disperse these around the cabin?"

"You bet. Where do you want them?"

"One in each corner, and two along the main walls. The goal is to create a barrier with the stones."

"Interesting." He grabbed three sachets and headed toward the two bedrooms in the back. I took the remaining three bags and dropped one onto the hardwood floor in the kitchen before moving on to the living room.

"I still don't get how a bunch of rocks are going to build a force-field," Quinn commented when we met in the middle of the house. "How does that work?"

"It's nature-based magic. We use the essences of plants, minerals, and animals."

"Animals?" he choked over the word.

"Not whole animals," I gave him a disapproving look. "We used hairs or nails—the things that grow back. Like these sachets also have turkey feathers in them."

"Oh," he laughed a cartoonish giggle. "Feathers."

"Shower's open," Emily called out with gusto from the back room.

"You're up," I told him. "I'm going to cleanse the cabin if you need me."

"Cleanse?" He asked.

"I purify the space with smoke from sage, lavender, rosemary, and valerian root," I told him as I walked to the kitchen and pulled a neatly tied bundle of dry herbs from my bag.

"I think I've seen this before. You wave it around, right?" Quinn chuckled at his own simplistic explanation. It seemed like he was trying to connect with me, at least.

"Movies and TV shows use this a lot," I told him before lighting one end of the bundle on fire. He watched as I allowed the flame to fully engulf the end, and then I blew it out.

"That's a powerful smell," Quinn complained. "No wonder the negative energy stays away."

"Yeah, it can take some getting used to." I liked the scent, personally. The lavender was my favorite. It always reminded me of the first time I walked into Marjorie's shop. She burned lavender candles and incense for the soothing energy. It often produced more robust visions for Marjorie.

"This could take a while," I told Quinn. "Your shower is waiting." Quinn took the hint and retreated to the bathroom with his bag, leaving me to my task.

By the time he finished, I'd moved into Emily's room, which offered me some sanctuary from the unease of being around him. Emily was another matter, and she wasn't timid about sharing her opinions.

"You're totally still in love with each other." Emily was delighted. She sprawled out in the middle of the bed's green comforter with Jeb by her side. They were watching me as I covered the matching green curtains with my smoky mixture.

"Can you please drop this?" I begged, ignoring eye contact and focusing on the smoke.

"Well, he didn't come here for me." She paused to eat a handful of pretzels. "He's here for you, and you're pushing him away to protect him. It's classic romance stuff, Emlyn."

"He feels obligated to be here. That's all. He shouldn't die over a false sense of duty."

"Who says he's going to die?"

"You know what I'm saying. Quinn's only here because he feels guilty."

"Nuh, uh. The word you're looking for is 'love,' sweet-cheeks."

"Well, I don't have time for love," I told her. "I have to find these Hoodoo witches, save Marjorie, and get rid of Maeve. All of this I have to do while keeping you and Quinn safe. I need to focus on what matters right now, which doesn't leave a lot of room for romance."

"Your life is like the plot of a movie."

"Maybe a tragedy," I offered.

"Whatever the genre, it means you and Quinn will get back together."

"Or he dies."

"Okay, but let's just say we all survive. It'll be you and Quinn in the end."

"What end?"

"When we defeat Maeve, and this is all over."

She was optimistic. I understood it. There was an ending for her and for Quinn, but this wouldn't ever be over for me. Defeating

Maeve would only make me a more significant threat and a bigger target for the coven. Maeve's family would have personal reasons to kill me now, not just professional ones. Thinking about how powerful Maeve was, it scared me to imagine the abilities her brother and father might have.

Marjorie and I had discussed it, and we'd accepted the truth. If we escaped from Maeve's powers with our lives, Marjorie and I would still be in the game, battling and hiding for the rest of our days.

"You know, I think you should know—" I began, only to be interrupted by a high-pitched scream. It was Quinn.

"NOPE!" his terrified voice rang out from the other room. I felt my eyes get big as they locked with Emily's. We immediately darted through the open door toward the source of the scream. Jeb took off in front of us, barking all the way out.

"Quinn!?" we shouted in panic before he toppled into us in the hallway. He hit me square in the chest, and we both fell to the ground.

"Holy crap, Quinn," I coughed from underneath him, trying to catch my breath after getting the wind knocked out of me. "Where are your clothes?"

Quinn scrambled to reposition the towel around himself as Emily grabbed my hand to pull me upright.

"Emlyn. Front door," Quinn choked out. His usually cheerful face was tight and frowning, his jaw clenched. He pointed towards the living room, his hand shaking. I couldn't see into the room from the hallway, but I could hear Jeb running back and forth in there. He wasn't growling, which was reassuring.

"You two stay behind me." I motioned for Emily to pull Quinn over to her before I peeked around the corner. While the front door was wide open, I didn't see anyone. "Quinn, did you open the door, or did someone else open it?" I asked.

"There's a doll," he trembled.

"A doll opened the door?" I asked.

"This is about a doll? You really are such a 'fraidy cat," Emily told him.

"I opened the door," Quinn corrected. "There was a doll."

The hairs on the back of my neck pricked up. "What kind of doll?" I wanted to know.

"A weird one, like something out of *American Horror Story*."

My adrenaline was spiking like crazy; I could feel my heartbeat in my ears. "Tell me what happened."

"When I was getting out of the shower… I heard someone knock on the front door," Quinn tried to explain. Talking seemed difficult for him. "I thought… it was the other campers."

"You went to answer the door in your bath towel?" Emily gave him an incredulous look. "You couldn't call for one of us to open the door? Like maybe the one with the powers?"

"It's not like I was naked," Quinn justified.

My thoughts weren't on Quinn's modesty. I was more worried about why Jeb didn't hear the knocking. He should've gone ballistic at the sound of someone knocking. It made me think there wasn't anyone at the door. It might've been magic—magic meant for Quinn's ears.

"What happened when you opened the door?" I asked, turning to face him and Emily.

"No one was there—," he began.

"You said there was a doll," Emily interrupted.

"Can I finish? When I opened the door, I didn't see anyone, so I figured it was a tree limb. It was a little creepy, but I didn't freak out because Emlyn did her spell. I headed back to the bathroom, and then the knocking happened again."

"Why didn't you come get us?" I pushed.

"Yeah, this is the part of the movie where you die," Emily scolded him.

"Well, half of me thought it was dumb kids messing with us," Quinn told us.

"What kids?" Emily asked.

"That's when I found the doll lying on the porch."

"And you came screaming," Emily poked at Quinn. They nagged back and forth for a few moments back and forth until I interrupted.

"Be quiet a minute," I ordered. "I'm going to check out the front door."

"Emlyn, shouldn't I be the one—," Quinn attempted, but I waved him off.

"She's the one with the powers bro," Emily said under her breath. "This is something she has to handle."

Emily was right, and even though I didn't want to be the one inching toward danger, I was the only one who could remotely handle a witch bursting through the door. Jeb stayed a few steps ahead of me as I crept forward. He made it about two seconds before me and quickly let out a low growl from deep in his belly. Fear trickled down my spine. A sudden heaviness grew in my chest. Sadly, it was a feeling I was getting accustomed to.

Finally, the doll came into view, and I understood why Quinn didn't like it. I'd pictured an old-fashioned porcelain baby doll like the ones they used in movies to scare people. It was almost worse that this doll was different. The form was less lifelike—rougher and more primitive. Its body was a hand carved wooden cylinder. One end was rounded into a ball to represent the head. The lower half of the doll's body came to a point. The details were delicate—someone had spent a considerable amount of time etching slender grooves into the sides. Maybe to represent clothing, it was wrapped in thinly braided rope.

"It's a Voodoo doll," I blurted out, immediately regretting it. I should've kept it to myself, saying it out loud felt like I was adding to its power. Quinn and Emily would soon come to the same conclusion I had.

Someone knew we were headed to New Orleans.

Someone knew we were in the cabin.

Chapter Twelve

"Get me a broom," I barked, keeping my eyes locked on the doll. This was a message from someone, and I wasn't about to touch the figure. There was no telling what kind of magic was attached to the item. I also couldn't leave it on the stoop.

"Is it the Ainbertachs? It is Maeve?" Emily squeaked out.

"What kind of broom?" Quinn wanted to know.

"We can't be sure of anything yet, Emily. Just get me a broom—any broom," I ordered. I'd transformed into an army general. Tension was thick in the cabin, but it didn't matter right now. I had to make us safe, which meant I needed to stay sharp and hard like stone. "I also need the jar in my bag labeled sulfur dust."

Jeb remained by my side as Quinn fetched the broomstick, and Emily dug through my bag to find the jar of sulfur.

"It's Maeve, isn't it?" She panicked again. "I can't believe Marnie would give us up like this. She didn't even know we going to New Orleans. How did they find us here?"

"I don't know," I admitted as I grabbed the yellow dust from her. The jar smelled of rotten eggs, which usually made me gag, but I was too focused on the doll to notice the stench. I pulled out a handful of dust and sprinkled it over the figure. If this was a Voodoo doll, there was a chance it was made to represent one of us. Quinn was the one who heard the knocking, so odds were the figure would be assigned to him. I hoped the sulfur would break the connection.

"What's the yellow stuff you're using?" Quinn wanted to know. He approached the door and handed me a plastic broom with green bristles. It definitely wasn't what I'd call a besom—a traditional witch's broomstick—but it was the best we'd get in the cabin.

"It's brimstone dust—sulfur," I explained. "It'll banish any spells on the doll. Then I'll sweep it off the porch with the broom and that should defuse any lingering magics."

"That's interesting." Quinn seemed to be coping with his fear better. I hoped my knowledge of magic made him feel safer. As far as he was concerned, I could handle anything. Emily was there for the fight with Maeve, though. She knew the truth.

"Are we safe here?" Emily asked as I shut the front door and fastened the chain lock into place.

"I think so," I lied. There was no use scaring my friends. Someone knew we were hiding out in the cabin and that someone was likely a witch. We moved to the couches in the living room, suddenly too tense to sleep. I plopped down on the couch, positioning myself toward the front door. Jeb wasn't ready to lie down yet. He was restless, pacing the floor along the exterior walls of the cabin.

"I think we should leave," Emily blurted out. "If someone knows we're here, I don't want to be here." She was on high alert. I noticed her eyes scanning the cabin, watching for movement.

"What do you think, Emlyn?" Quinn asked. He took a seat next to me and looked up, waiting for a reaction. I wondered if he wanted proof that I could handle this.

"We shouldn't have used Quinn's card." Emily flung herself into the armchair closest to me.

"I don't think it's Maeve. It's probably not related to the Ainbertachs—not directly, at least," I told them. They looked at me blankly. "We're just assuming Maeve can track our cards because she's so powerful, but it's not likely. I think the more realistic theory is that Maeve can trace our essences. Marjorie's cloaking potion should protect us as long as we take one every six hours. Everyone took one, right?"

Emily and Quinn nodded.

"Then the card is the only explanation," Emily argued. "How else would they know?"

Quinn shook his head. "But even if they had tracked the card, it would take time to get here."

"Not if they teleported."

"That's a thing?" Quinn gasped, weirdly excited. "Why didn't we do that?"

"Yes, teleporting is a thing, but it's hard to do, especially with more than one person," I told them both. "I don't think they traced the card. Maeve's people don't know where we are."

"How do you know?" Emily asked.

"Whoever left the doll wasn't strong enough to break my protection spell. The power of the coven wasn't behind this person. Also, Maeve really wants me dead. Why would she leave a Voodoo doll outside the house instead of just breaking in?"

"To mess with you?" Quinn offered.

"Because she's crazy," Emily suggested.

"I think it's a message," I announced.

"From who?" Emily asked.

"I'm thinking the Hoodoo witches."

"You did say it was a Voodoo doll," Quinn agreed.

"I think Marjorie might have got in contact with them somehow. Maybe they know we're on our way?" My theory seemed to soothe Emily and Quinn's fears. It didn't help me any, though. This idea didn't explain how the witches would've known we were in the woods. Unless they were following us, they wouldn't know where we had stopped on the way to New Orleans.

"Could it also be someone trying to kill us?" Quinn's fear got the best of him. "Let's not rule out ghosts or zombies."

"Sure, that's another theory."

"Oy vey," Emily sighed.

"I think someone would've attacked us by now if they meant to," I reassured them. "Luckily, the protection spell should also work against malicious spirits. That includes ghost, zombies, and even ghost zombies."

"Oh, good," Quinn smiled.

"I do think we should all sleep together in the living room. Just to be safe."

"So, we're staying?" Quinn wanted to know. It was hard to tell if he was relieved or not.

"So much for getting my own room," Emily groaned.

"It would probably be good for us to get some rest. I'm not sure when the next opportunity will be," I told them. "Besides, we've got a big day ahead of us in New Orleans."

Emily passed out asleep next to me about an hour later. We were sharing a mattress on the floor that we had dragged out of one bedroom. Quinn took the couch. Everyone was quietly snoozing around me. Even Jeb and Tephi were curled up by my feet. I envied them. No part of me could sleep. Emily's snoring and Jeb's panting didn't help, but they weren't what was keeping me awake. I felt ready for an attack. There was this need to be prepared for the worst, because I was now responsible for the well-being of everyone else in the cabin.

I also had Marjorie on my mind. I still couldn't believe we'd left her behind. It wasn't right, and there was a lot of guilt paired with my exhaustion. I wanted to know she was alright.

So, I slipped out of bed quietly and moved to the kitchen where I'd left my supplies. I grabbed my black obsidian scrying mirror, along with a few candles. Our mirrors had been carved out of the same piece of stone, which connected them—I should've be able to channel Marjorie's energy. It was kind of like the Beast's magic mirror from the Disney movie.

I'd gathered the bare minimum of items needed to create an altar. Typically, I'd use gemstones and herbs in addition to candles to harness the power of the scrying mirror, but I was low on supplies. Two white candles would have to do. I used the island in the middle of the kitchen as a barrier between myself and my sleeping friends, pressing my back up against the cabinets and sitting crisscross-applesauce on the floor. Facing the small stove, I created a make-shift altar.

Under other circumstances, the cabin probably would've been a fun place to stay. I imagined Marjorie, Emily, Quinn, and even Marnie all sitting around the living room waiting on a batch of oven-made s'mores to bake. Marjorie would insist on including more traditional bites into the evening. She'd make some fire-roasted sausages with a batch of Irish soda bread to munch on. It was Marjorie's favorite meal. She made it every year on St. Patrick's Day, along with shepherd's pie and corned beef and cabbage.

The memories of Marjorie helped me focus on her. I imagined her wild, loose hair. She wore it long and without restraint. Her smile reminded me of my mother's—mostly gums but incredibly genuine. Marjorie wasn't one who smiled often, but I'd seen it a few times.

With this illustration in my mind, I pulled a lighter from my pocket and ignited one of the white candles.

"This light is mine, shining bright as a beacon in the night," I lit the other candle. "This light is yours, burning hot but out of sight." I placed the obsidian mirror between the two candles. "Let the mirror be my guide from earth to earth and sea to sea. By this light, I conjure your image to me," I whispered. "Let my eyes become yours to see. My body feels what may be. Together as one, witches we; I conjure your image to me."

I paused for a few moments, holding Marjorie in my mind, but the mirror remained black.

The magic wasn't working, so I tried again.

"Let the mirror be my guide from earth to earth and sea to sea. By this light, I conjure your image to me." I was louder this time, maybe because I thought I could force my way into Marjorie's mind that way. "Let my eyes become yours to see. My body feels what may be. Together as one, witches we; I conjure your image to me."

"Emlyn?" Quinn's voice made me jump, yelping in surprise.

"Don't do that," I snapped at him.

"Sorry, I didn't mean to scare you like that." He looked from me to the candles and understood he'd interrupted. "Were you doing a spell?"

Tears formed in my eyes. I quickly wiped them away.

"I was trying to reach Marjorie," I told him. "But wherever she is, she's blocked from my vision."

Quinn sat down next to me on the floor.

"You were calling her?"

"Kind of. I was trying to see through her eyes and channel her senses."

"Did it work?"

"No, which means I won't be able to find her. We have no idea where she is." The weight of it all suddenly felt like stones strapped to my back. "How am I supposed to do this?"

He didn't answer. Instead, he pulled me into his side and wrapped his arms around me. "You can do this." He stroked my hair.

"I'm not good at being strong," I admitted to him.

"You are one of the strongest people I know. Remember, I was with you when you defeated Blaine the first time. You were brave, and you beat him."

"I was lucky."

"It's more than that. You can do this, especially with some help from your sidekicks. Remember, you've also got Emily and me."

"Exactly, and I have to keep the two of you safe. Everyone is counting on me, and I don't think I can do it. Maeve has been a witch her entire life. She's stronger than me."

"So what? We believe in you for who you are, not what you are. It has nothing to do with your magical abilities. I believed in you before you were a witch."

The words sounded beautiful coming from his lips, but they didn't reassure me any. I knew the truth of it. "This isn't school or a career, though. I don't think you understand—this isn't just something challenging, like a really hard class. A class, I could handle. This is life or death. If I'm not prepared, I don't fail a test—people die. You, Emily, Marjorie… Maybe it would have been better if I never found out I was a witch."

"Maybe, but just saying, people would kill to freeze time like you can. And the whole time-travel thing is really cool."

"The powers are great, but the price is too steep. What if I lose her, Quinn? What if I lose all of you?"

"You won't. Maybe Maeve's stronger, but you're smarter. She doesn't stand a chance."

Then, for the first time in more than a year, Quinn and I kissed.

Chapter Thirteen

The feeling of dread I'd grown accustomed to receded by the next morning. Newfound energy replaced it. My body practically gyrated in my seat the entire drive into New Orleans. My skin felt electric. Part of it was nerves for sure. We were tracking down a new coven of witches; we didn't know if they were the ones who sent us a message in the cabin, and we didn't know if they'd be friends or foes. This would be a defining moment in the mission to defeat Maeve. A more significant part of me was elated by being close to Quinn again, which I knew was a an enormous distraction. I couldn't help it, though. He made me feel hopeful for the future.

We arrived in New Orleans around noon after eating a late breakfast on the way in. The giant stack of pancakes smothered in a half-gallon of syrup did little to drown my nerves. The closer we got to the French Quarter, the more anxious I felt.

"I'm back! NOLA!" Emily excitedly announced as we pulled into a parking deck.

"You understand this isn't a vacation, right?" I reminded her.

"Yeah, this is a serious mission. I can still enjoy my surroundings, though," Emily explained. "And we have to eat, don't we? It would be dumb not to eat good food while we're here. When in Rome, right?"

We ignored Emily and searched for a well-camouflaged area of the parking deck. We surrounded ourselves with other cars and parked out of view of the more noticeable cameras. There was no way to know what other cameras were hidden, but Quinn backed the truck into the parking spot and removed the license plate as extra precautions. On our way into town, Quinn had found a costume shop. He suggested Emily and I purchase a few items to disguise ourselves. It was a good idea, but as I got out of the truck, I regretted it.

I pulled my wavy red hair into a low bun and then mashed it into a platinum blonde wig. The hair was straight as a board and layered into a sharp V at my back. Emily's wig was also straight, but her hair was shoulder length and black.

"These aren't super comfortable," she complained.

"We can't risk people remembering you guys," Quinn told us, handing me Jeb's leash.

Emily rolled her eyes. "Because walking down the street with a dog and cat is so discreet. They've seen Jeb."

"It's the best we can do, Emily."

"Stop bickering," I barked at them. "We get to the house as fast as we can. The less time we're out in the open, the better I'll feel."

"Jeez, you don't have to bite our heads off," Emily said. "You sound like Marjorie."

Quinn locked eyes with me. "We'll behave."

"Emily, can you carry Tephi?" I asked.

"As long as she keeps her claws to herself," she told me before scooping Tephi into her arms. "We have to go for a walk, now, girl. Believe me, you'd rather not touch the ground."

Tephi yowled once but didn't fight Emily's grip.

We each grabbed all we could carry from the back of Quinn's truck and made our way out of the parking deck. We were several blocks away from Janice's Airbnb on Burgundy Street, and the busy atmosphere was jarring after the isolation of Henrietta's house. There were so many people crowding the stores and sidewalks that they spilled into the road in some places. We'd selected Bourbon Street as our primary walking route—it was the most crowded—and it was one big party. Everyone was carrying plastic cups and wearing beads, even though we were months away from Mardi Gras.

I worried that we looked crazy as we hauled our many bags and pets with us, but no one noticed. We weren't nearly as wild as our surroundings. I was sure we passed a snake charmer on our way in, and there were kids sitting on the sidewalk drumming on plastic buckets for tips. A horse-drawn carriage passed us on one side, reminding me of home.

I thought I'd see more similarities between Savannah and New Orleans. Both were historic, tourist-filled cities. They both had "haunted" pasts and were described as beautiful Southern sites. The architecture was similar and yet different. There were some quaint cottages, but most of the buildings were two stories with beautiful balconies on the top level. Most had ornate iron railings, some woven into leaves or knots, and there were colorful baskets of flowers in each opening. Beneath them were restaurants and bars. I imagined there were boutiques and shops along the other streets, but Bourbon seemed to be a place for food and drink.

"Do you smell how good the food is? I need some shrimp," Emily announced.

I nodded in agreement and then considered her statement. There was the aroma of decadent seafood, but underneath there was also a smell like the remnants of a party. Forgotten beads and empty cups were sunk in pools of unknown liquid along the sides of the street. Jeb seemed very intrigued by the smells, though—both pleasant and sour.

"After we get settled in," Quinn suggested.

"He's right," I agreed, knowing in reality there wasn't time to sit down and eat. Our priority was clear, and I needed to contact the Hoodoo coven as soon as possible. Marjorie had told me where to find the tourist shop they managed. It was like Marjorie's shop, with hokey charms and things displayed in the front for humans while they hid the real stuff in the back. I'd just have to convince the witches I was magical, too. I was lucky to have an active power—I could freeze the room to show them my abilities.

I hadn't mentioned the Voodoo doll again since the night before. Still, I was also hoping the Hoodoo coven already knew we were on our way. If they were expecting us, it might solve the mystery of the doll outside our cabin.

"How much farther?" I asked Emily, who was leading our parade. We had veered off from Bourbon Street onto a back road, so I figured we were close.

"We're here. It's this duplex here, the unit on the right," Emily pointed.

I'd expected a hole in the wall—something subtle. This looked like something straight out of a magazine. The building was a two-story double townhouse painted a dark aqua color, and it featured finely crafted cherry wood finishes. Each unit's entrance was a mirror of the other, with small windows dividing the two front doors. Flowers, ferns, and moss made the house look more like a beachfront property than a duplex tucked away in a New Orleans alley.

"This is beautiful," I said.

"Yeah. Janice's family does it right," Emily nodded.

"It's bigger than I expected," Quinn added. We shot each other a look.

"Only the best for my boos," Emily winked. "Come on."

She led the way into the house, and there was a moment of relief as we crossed the threshold. We'd made it. Tephi leaped from Emily's arms onto the back of a leather sofa, and Jeb dashed toward the middle of the room as soon as I unclipped his leash. They both scanned their surroundings and seemed to approve. I did too. It was just as elaborate as the exterior, featuring faded, antique-like wallpaper on every wall to compliment the polished hardwood floors. There was modern furniture in the living room and dining area, and a butcher-block island divided the kitchen from the rest of the open floor plan. At least a dozen small appliances nestled among dark wood cabinets.

"Didn't I tell you? This place is boujee, and I love it," Emily sighed happily. "Follow me upstairs to your rooms."

"Isn't this a little much? I thought the point was to be low key." Quinn looked pointedly at the crystal vase on the center of the coffee table.

"Please," Emily groaned. "We're here on a secret mission. There's nothing wrong with embracing the finer things. It's not like the Ainbertach Coven will know we're here based on how the place is decorated. Besides, we might die soon. Live a little."

"Where are our rooms," I interrupted, moving the conversation away from her "we might die soon," comment.

"There are three rooms, so we each have our own! I'm going to take the master," she blurted out. "If that's okay?"

"Fine by me," I told her. I wasn't worried about our sleeping arrangements. By the looks of this place, all the rooms would be beautiful anyway.

"A room is a room," Quinn also agreed.

"Great!" Emily was in her element, and she was super pumped to be in New Orleans no matter the circumstances. "Emlyn, the room on the right is yours. It's decorated with wine bottles, paintings of wine, and mostly purple hues. I think it'll be a good fit. Plus, it's a queen bed, so you and Jeb will enjoy the space. Quinn, you get the oceanic scenes across the hall."

"Nice," Quinn told her.

"Do you ever wonder why every house always has an ocean theme somewhere?" Emily thought out loud.

"I hadn't spent a lot of time on the subject," I laughed. "What is the theme of your room?"

"French Bistro. I'm all about those beignets," Emily told us. I envied her enthusiasm. Had this been a leisure trip, she would've been the perfect travel companion.

"So, how about we dump our stuff and reconvene downstairs in ten minutes?" I offered.

Quinn and Emily nodded in agreement, grabbed their bags, and disappeared into their respective rooms. Jeb and I quickly found out our wine-themed setup was more than accommodating. The furniture was a distressed white color; the lamps were blown glass, and everything else was made of wine bottles or corks.

I threw my duffel bag onto the plum bedspread and dug through its contents. "Alright, I'm going out to meet other witches," I told Jeb. "Meaning, I should probably be prepared for anything, right?"

He let out a small whine as he jumped onto the bed, plopping down on a pile of too many decorative pillows. He yawned once and then set his head down on one side of my bag.

"Get some sleep bud," I told him before returning to my task. My black messenger bag was already packed with some necessities: my athame, leftover vials of "Flu-like Symptoms," sulfur, three bottles of essence of poppy, and a supply of versatile powerful crystals: pointed clear quartz, yellowy-orange citrines, a few chunks of obsidian, several tiger's eyes, bloodstones, and amethysts. I checked the battery level for my e-reader to make sure I'd have access to the digital copy of my Book of Shadows for the next few hours. Then I tucked my pepper spray in the front pocket of my bag where I could grab it quickly. Predators came in both the human and magical varieties.

I looked at myself in the mirror and realized something was off.

"I don't look ready for a party, do I?" I pointed out, remembering how Quinn and Emily described Bourbon Street. I replaced my yoga pants and T-shirt with a pair of dark skinny jeans and a green crop top. I traded my ballet flats for combat boots, added some bright red lipstick to my lips, and secured the blonde wig over my ginger waves once again. This time I was able to use bobby pins and make the wig sit more realistically.

"Better," I nodded at my new reflection in the mirror. The outfit would keep me more hidden, but I worried the Hoodoo witches wouldn't take me seriously while wearing it. It was a risk.

I left Jeb upstairs asleep and found I was the last to arrive downstairs. Emily and Quinn were already planted on the couch, but they were still in travel clothes.

"Woah," Emily muttered when she saw me. They both looked surprised, which made me flush red.

"Too much?"

"No way," Quinn blurted out.

"I just need to change now," Emily mused. "I didn't know we were going full Bourbon first thing. It makes sense, though. We'll blend."

Quinn jumped over the outfit conversation and moved straight into business. "What's our plan from here?"

"I've got to find Azariah Imamu," I explained. "Marjorie said the coven's main house is in a residential part of town, away from the tourists, so I probably won't be able to find it. But, they do have a small tourist shop on the outskirts of the French Quarter."

"How will they know you're telling the truth when you ask for help?" Quinn questioned.

"I figure I'll just ask for Azariah. Maybe then they'll know I'm not a tourist," I told him.

"Do we know where the shop is?" Emily asked.

"Well, it's a Voodoo shop," I offered.

"Babe, there are a lot of Voodoo shops here," Emily informed me.

"It looks like there's a vampire shop somewhere, too," Quinn added as he scrolled through search results on his phone. "And lots of ghost tours."

"Marjorie said they called the original shop Sòsyè. I looked it up on Google, but it doesn't look like it's around anymore," I told them.

"So, they're gone?" Emily groaned.

"There's a replacement shop called The Root of Magic. I'll start there," I explained.

"Maybe it's the same owners, or maybe they know the previous owners at least. Where is it?" Quinn wanted to know.

"Royal Street—a bit of a walk from here," I admitted. "I've got my supplies ready. I might be gone a while."

"She's using the word 'I' a lot," Emily said.

"I noticed that too," Quinn agreed. "Emlyn, you know you aren't going alone, right?"

"It's safer if I go alone," I assured them.

"No way!" Emily shouted, looking ready to race me to the door.

"We're stronger together, which means we're safer all together," Quinn added.

"It's too risky," I told them, unwilling to budge. "Witches rarely respect non-magical people. Bringing you could hurt our chances."

"I don't like it, Emlyn. It's not a good idea," Quinn argued.

"You coming isn't a good idea. What if agents of the Ainbertachs left that doll? If they know we're here, you should stay hidden. It's safer."

"This sucks," Emily flopped down onto the leather sofa, disturbing a sleeping Tephi. "We deserve a little fun after all this mess."

"It's not about fun, Emily. This is about protection. I have to keep you safe."

"Which is why we should go with you," Quinn reasoned. "We're no match for witches on our own. Together, we can at least help you if things go wrong."

"That's an excellent point, Quinn," Emily mused. "Emlyn, if you leave us here alone, we're defenseless."

Ten minutes later, the three of us turned onto Bourbon Street, headed to Royal. Emily had changed into a short romper. It seemed chilly for the crisp autumn weather, but she insisted she'd be fine. Quinn stayed in his travel clothes. He packed a supply bag of his own, though, filling it with kitchen knives, a can of hairspray, and a lighter.

"I love this city!" Emily cheered as we passed by a group of bachelorettes in matching tank tops. They were each carrying bright green, grenade-shaped cups in their hands. Emily's spirit was contagious, and they cheered back at her. It all made me feel too visible.

"Glad someone is having fun," Quinn laughed as we walked down the street, weaving in and out of the crowd.

"Too much fun," I grunted. One bachelorette handed Emily her grenade cup, and I watched her gulp it down. "She knows this is serious, right? It's life and death stuff."

"She knows, but she's also been through a lot. You both have," Quinn offered. "Is having a little fun such a bad thing?"

"Maybe. It depends on how many of those green things Emily drinks."

"You could stand to lighten up a bit, too, you know."

"I'll add it to my list of things to do."

"We should take this next right turn over there," Quinn changed the subject.

"You mean by the man holding the snake?" I cringed at the giant python wrapped around a street performer's neck. It was the second snake I'd encountered on this street. Had the area not been crawling with people, I would've frozen the slithery reptile as we walked by so it couldn't jump out at me.

"That's the one," he laughed at me. Ghosts scared him, but not snakes. He was crazy.

"Emily! It's this way," I called back to Emily, who had fallen behind as she met a new group of friends. She was carrying a different cup now.

"Coming!" she yelled, hustling across the brick street to meet back up with us. "Are you guys having fun? I just met the sweetest gals."

"It's a blast," I quipped.

"Anyone else hungry?" Emily wanted to know. "I'm feeling some fried shrimp, maybe a po'boy. Maybe Quinn and I could stop off at this restaurant while you go talk to the witches?" She pointed to a gigantic sign with shrimp, fish, and lobsters painted on it.

"I'm definitely hungry too, but we should stay together," Quinn told her.

"But it's lunchtime. The shop will still be there in an hour."

"So will the shrimp," I interjected. "You're the ones who convinced me it's safer to stay together. Now that you're out, we're not separating."

"Fine."

"I'll buy lunch on our way back," Quinn offered.

"It'll probably be like 2 o'clock by then," she groaned. "Fine. How far is this shop?"

"We're almost there," I told them. "See, it's right down there on the end."

A pink stucco cottage with teal trim finally came into view at the end of the street. Hanging above the front door was a small wooden sign revealing the name of the shop, The Root of Magic. It was the one building without a balcony, seeming bare in comparison to the two structures framing it. Next door, the balcony featured ornate green railings under large planters filled with orange flowers. The simplicity of the magic shop was understandable, though. I knew Marjorie's shop didn't bring in a lot of extra revenue. I assumed the coven, like Marjorie, made money in other ways.

"It's not what I expected," Emily said.

"Looks can deceive," I told her. I was more concerned about the feeling the shop gave off. It wasn't warm or inviting. It seemed closed off and private, making me suddenly self-conscious. This might have been a locals-only establishment. Some covens didn't take kindly to strangers, especially if two of those strangers were non-magical.

"Are we going in?" Quinn asked.

"Yes, but use this if anything goes wrong," I handed out vials of "Flu-like Symptoms."

"What is it?" Quinn held his vial up to the light and examined the potion inside.

"It's your way out of there if something goes wrong," I explained.

"Really? How?"

"Just throw it on the ground in front of someone," I told him.

"Does it blow up?" He looked concerned.

"No. It makes people sick. They'll be distracted."

Emily laughed. "Believe me, it does the trick. Blaine was vomiting in 10 seconds flat."

"So was I." My face flushed red, and my stomach churned at the memory.

"Oh," Quinn trailed off. "I'll be sure not to drop it."

"Good plan. Alright—game faces, team," I ordered. "Let's do this."

When we reached the teal blue door, I took a deep breath in before pushing it open. It wasn't heavy. We stepped across the threshold to meet display after display of Voodoo items. Multicolored pre-made Voodoo dolls covered in bright feathers and plastic beads sat in a basket on the table directly in front of us. They weren't as authentic-looking as the one at the cabin.

"Come on, let's fan out," I told them. Emily and Quinn nodded, and we split off into different parts of the shop.

I was right about the inventory. Several spell jars were placed on the table next to one with the Voodoo dolls. Tourists liked the idea that a mixture with instructions could produce magic. Usually, the spells never worked, but they were fun for non-magic people. The labeled jars covered a range of vague wish-fulfillment, including "To Find Success," "To Obtain Power," and "To Find Love." Love was a popular topic at magic shops, I knew. In my year working for Marjorie, dozens of tourists came in every month looking for love spells. Lust was actually more accessible to conjure than love, but neither spell lasted long when the feelings weren't real.

Emily moved toward the front counter where the cash register was positioned. The case under it contained assorted jewelry and popular gemstones. From behind Emily, I could see mostly amethyst items. The purple gemstone was well-liked and often used because it encouraged peace and tranquility. Quinn found a wall filled with seven-day and ceremonial candles. Some were associated with spells— courage, love, confidence, energy — and others were simple. Witches often used single-colored candles for general spell work.

We reformed our united group and headed toward the back of the shop. I figured they hid the real stuff behind the showy items. When we found a wall dedicated to plant roots, I thought we were getting close.

"I haven't heard of some of these," I told them both. "And look at these. Snake skins and venoms, tarantula exoskeletons, butterfly wings, animal skulls… I wonder what they use these for."

"This is creepy," Emily blurted out. "Why would you possibly need tarantula skins?"

Before I could shush her, another voice beat me to it. "They represent cycles of life — the ever-changing and ever-evolving."

I spun around, on high alert. Behind us was a tall, thin Black woman with dark yellow-brown, umber skin. She looked to be in her late 20s, with thick, black feed-in braids she wore in a high ponytail over her right shoulder. Gold hoop earrings framed her face, and a matching gold statement necklace draped elegantly against the front of her violet cotton jumpsuit. Strappy gold wedges completed the look.

"My bad," Emily said in an apologetic voice.

The woman didn't respond. She eyed us accusatorily, likely assuming we were just another group of obnoxious teens interested in the occult.

"Can I help you find something?" she asked more politely.

"I'm looking for an amulet," I told her.

"Amulets are in the back, next to Jaz," she told us.

"Jaz?" Emily asked.

The woman pointed to the right back corner of the shop with a crooked smile. I followed her finger to find a large terrarium with a colossal ball python. He was draped over a log in his habitat with his head pointed straight at us. When he stuck his tongue out, I immediately shuddered.

"Careful, he's creepy," the woman said with a smirk before heading back to the cash register. She pulled out her phone and started scrolling through one of her apps.

"I think we made her mad," I told Emily and Quinn in a low voice. "Not the best first impression."

"I got this," Emily assured us. "You look for the amulet. I'll smooth this over."

"Maybe you shouldn't," Quinn said.

"Hush." She spun around and waltzed over to the counter. She smiled big, and I heard her ask the woman where to find the best po'boy in the French Quarter. Emily wanted that sandwich.

I didn't follow the rest of the conversation. Part of me wanted to get out of the shop immediately for fear that Jaz would somehow attack me through the glass of his tank. The other half of me knew we needed to find the amulet. I'd have to face the snake to win my prize.

"This is like snake number three today," Quinn laughed at me. "You're really not having a lot of luck here."

"Let's just get this over with." I grabbed the burner phone from my pocket and showed Quinn a photo of the amulet. "This is what we're looking for. Pay attention to the crescent moons and stars."

We searched for a few minutes, checking the front and back of every pendant hanging up. If we got lucky, I wouldn't have to get the Hoodoo witches involved at all. There were dozens of varieties, but nothing matched.

"It's not here," I sighed after double-checking three times.

"Maybe ask Emily's new friend?" Quinn suggested.

"Guess so."

I scurried away from Jaz, happy to put some distance between the two of us as I returned to the register. Emily and the woman seemed to have hit it off, discussing recipes.

"Emlyn, Nia recommended some great foodie spots for us to check out later," Emily smiled. "Nia, this is Emlyn and Quinn."

"Your girl here is into her food," Nia grinned, suddenly much more approachable than before. Emily had her own kind of magic.

"We all appreciate a good meal in this group," I smiled, trying to connect.

"Well, the brewery scene here is pretty great too if you're looking to get away from Bourbon. I'd highly recommend the Hawk Warrior Double IPA. The brewery's within walking distance."

"We'll look into that," I told her. "Thanks."

"Sure. Did you find an amulet you like?" Nia asked.

"Unfortunately, no. I'm looking for a specific one," I pulled the photo up on my phone. "Do you carry one like this?"

She picked up the phone and analyzed the photo. After a minute or so, she shook her head. "I haven't seen one like it. Maybe another shop will have it. You should check the stuff in this case, though. There are some gorgeous pieces." She pointed down to the counter in front of us and then showed us the rings decorating her fingers. One was in the shape of a feather that glided across two of her slender fingers. On the other hand, she wore three different bands set with various gemstones. "I get all my rings here."

"Too cute, girl," Emily told her. "I might need to get a couple myself."

"It has to be this one," I told Nia, ignoring Emily's comment.

"I'm sorry I can't help," Nia apologized.

"Are there any other shops in town that might carry it?" Quinn asked.

"It's possible," Nia said. "There are a lot of niche places in the French Quarter and Garden District. I couldn't tell you for sure, though."

"Does anyone else work here? Someone else we could ask?" I pushed, not ready to take no for an answer. This had to be the right place. We were close to something. I could feel it.

"The owner might know, but she's tied up right now. Maybe you could come back tomorrow?"

"Azariah?" I showed my hand. "The owner is Azariah Imamu, right?"

Nia's face tensed, her jaw tightening with concern. "Azariah? What do you know about Azariah?"

"I was told she was the person to ask for scarce items," I hinted. "You know, back room type stuff."

180

"Kaiya!" Nia called out without responding to me. "I need you out here." Urgency was present in her tone, but she didn't sound panicked. I took that as a good sign, but I kept my guard up just in case.

"What is it, babe?" a soft female voice called back. Seconds later, another woman entered the room. Kaiya's sepia skin glowed against her maroon pixie cut and dark brown crop top. She had a curvy, athletic figure, which she stressed by placing both hands on her hips upon seeing Emily, Quinn, and me. The short-sleeved top was cute, but it also showed off muscular biceps and toned abs. From the looks of her, I didn't want to face her in a fight.

"These three asked me about Azariah," Nia told her. Apparently, I'd crossed a line by mentioning the name. I wondered if they were feuding covens, and I'd entered a battleground.

"Look, this is a total misunderstanding. My grandmother—," I tried to rectify the situation, but Kaiya cut me off.

"Who are you?" Kaiya asked, her voice suddenly harsher, which seemed to strengthen her Cajun drawl. "Who told you about Azariah?"

"I should've started this differently," I scrambled for the right words.

"She was talking about an amulet. She seemed mad we don't have it," Nia announced.

"No," I told them.

"You aren't looking for an amulet?" Nia asked.

"I am," I admitted. "But I'm not mad you don't have it. Disappointed is more—."

"What amulet?" Kaiya demanded.

"She's a witch too," Emily blurted out before I could continue.

"Emily!" I snapped.

"What? You are," Emily stated.

Kaiya's eyes narrowed, and her brow furrowed. "Who the hell are you?"

Nia took a more defensive stance, putting additional space between our two groups. They were ready for a fight, which was the opposite of what I wanted.

"Whoa," I cried out, throwing both hands over my head. Quinn and Emily did the same. "Look, we came here looking for help."

"We come in peace," Quinn emphasized.

"My grandmother is Marjorie Finnerty. She told me to ask for Azariah because they worked together once. She thought Azariah could help us now," I explained.

"Finnerty?" Kaiya asked.

"Yes," I nodded. "At the time, my grandmother was part of a Celtic coven in Georgia."

"Celtic Witches," Kaiya muttered to herself.

I couldn't read her. Her muscles were still tense, and her jaw locked. She whispered something to Nia, and, luckily, I saw Nia relax. She shot our group a smile—an olive branch.

"You're all witches then?" Nia wanted to know.

"Nope, she's the only one," Emily admitted. "We're her sidekicks."

"Yeah, we're part of the team," Quinn echoed.

Kaiya wasn't buying it, though. She smirked, "Like you'd be able to help her."

"Kaiya!" Nia scolded after elbowing Kaiya in the side.

Kaiya brushed it off. "What was it you thought Azariah could help you with?"

"We need an amulet."

"And Marjorie assumed our coven would have it?"

"She suggested we come to you for help, yes. She said Azariah is your coven leader and that she'd remember our family."

"She was the coven elder," Kaiya told us, "but she died three years ago. I'm her daughter. I run things now."

Emily was the first to speak.

"Aw, I'm sorry girl. Losing your mom. That's rough."

"We didn't know. I'm sorry," I echoed. I was always awkward in these situations. I never knew the right thing to say.

"I was six when the Celtic witches came to help us," Kaiya continued, ignoring our condolences. "Dark Hoodoo witches cursed our coven."

"Were they super strong or something?" Emily asked.

"No, but they developed a spell immune to Hoodoo magic," Nia explained quickly. "Celtic magic differs from Hoodoo. They could dispel the curse."

"Oh, that makes sense," Quinn nodded.

"So, now you come seeking repayment?" Kaiya changed the subject.

"We seek help," I corrected. "You don't owe us anything, and we know that."

Kaiya paused and scanned us carefully before replying. "What's with the wigs? Who are you hiding from?"

"We just thought we'd be discreet," I answered vaguely.

"Really?" Kaiya wasn't buying it. She signaled to Nia, who spun around toward the register. We watched her open a drawer in the counter and grab a small vial of blue liquid. Meanwhile, Kaiya walked to the front door and flipped the deadbolt.

I suddenly felt vulnerable. My heart started beating faster. Emily reached for the back of my shirt with her fingers, pleading with me to make this alright. "We're not looking for trouble. We just need the amulet, and then we'll be out of your hair. You'll never see us again."

"You have the wrong idea," Nia said, holding the vial up for everyone to see. Kaiya grunted in response to Nia's generosity, which I assumed meant Kaiya didn't agree. Nia continued anyway, "however, we don't make a habit of sticking our noses into unsafe situations. We need to know what's really going on, and you wearing disguises suggests there's something to worry about."

"I could argue that not knowing is better sometimes," Quinn offered.

"No," Kaiya insisted.

"You could be lying about who you say you are," Nia said. "It's happened before."

"Look at my hair," I pulled the blonde wig off to reveal my red curls. "I'm a Finnerty."

"It's a simple test," Nia smiled. She handed the potion to me. "Drink up."

"How can we trust you aren't about to poison her?" Emily screeched.

"What is this?" I asked.

"Nothing dangerous," Nia smiled. "I'm an aura reader. This potion puts the pieces together more clearly."

I looked from Quinn to Emily. They both shook their heads, "no." I drank it anyway. It tasted like strawberries, which was nice. I wasn't as fond of Nia's gaze focused on me, knowing the terrible things she'd likely find out.

"What do you see?" Kaiya pressed.

"It's muddled, but I'm not here for these vibes," Nia announced after a minute or two of silence. Her eyes widened. "There's danger. They should leave."

"You heard her." Kaiya unbolted the door and pointed out.

I understood the response. This was dangerous, and it wasn't fair to ask Kaiya's coven to get involved. Still, this was the last stop before defeat, and I couldn't let Marjorie down. "Please help us," I begged. I pulled the photo up on my phone and shoved it into Kaiya's face. "I'll pay whatever you want. This is all I need."

"I don't want your money," Kaiya insisted. "I want you out."

"Marjorie saved you once. Now she needs saving," I told her. The anger bubbled up in me. "I'm not asking you to fight. I'm asking for a trinket. You don't have to do anything!"

Kaiya shut the door again. "Saving from who?"

"You don't want to know," Emily blurted out.

"Whoever it is, there's a lot of power there," Nia told her.

"The Ainbertach Coven captured her," I blurted out. I wasn't sure if telling them the truth was the best play, but it was all I could think of.

"Out!" Kaiya yelled. "You couldn't pay us enough to turn against that coven."

"She's right," Nia added. "I'm all for helping a fellow female, but that's a line we can't cross. I'm sorry."

"No one needs to know you helped us," I interjected.

"I'm a great secret keeper," Emily agreed.

"Just leave," Kaiya argued.

"Even if we wanted to help, we couldn't," Nia told us.

"Why not?" Emily wanted to know.

"Because—"

"Stop it, Nia. Leave it alone," Kaiya ordered.

"Are you saying you can't or won't help us?" I pushed.

"Look, my mother was the only one who could make those pendants," Kaiya finally told us. "She only created a few of them, and they were for exceptional customers."

A knot formed in my stomach. Blaine's family owned an amulet, which meant they knew Azariah. There was a chance we were in danger with Kaiya and Nia. I pushed the thought from my mind.

"Still, you have to know where one of them is," Emily questioned. "Maybe you could just point us in the right direction?"

There was silence suddenly as the couple studied us. Nia and Kaiya turned to each other. My anxiety was through the roof, wondering what was going unsaid between them.

"Nia and I need a moment to chat privately," Kaiya finally spoke.

"Give us a few minutes," Nia smiled, and she followed Kaiya into the back room.

"Can't anything be easy?" I moaned when the two were out of sight.

"Well, *that* went well… What happens if they decide not to help us?" Emily asked.

"We'll find another way," I told them, sounding much more confident than I felt. There was no other option, but I couldn't tell Emily and Quinn that. "There's always another way."

"But, best-case scenario: they get us an amulet." Quinn offered. "Then what?"

"Then we find Marjorie and face Maeve," I told them.

"Then, we go home!" Emily added.

Quinn ignored Emily's enthusiasm. "I thought you couldn't reach Marjorie through your mirror thing?"

"I'll figure it out," I told him. It was another problem I had to solve—another weight on my back. I'd focus on one thing at a time, though.

Quinn didn't push the subject. He remained quiet as Emily occupied herself browsing jewelry at the counter. I kept my eyes locked on the doorway to the back room where Kaiya and Nia were. When they reemerged, the looks on their faces worried me. They were stern and kind of determined. They didn't look mad, which was good, but I had a feeling they'd formed a bargain. I didn't have time to make deals. I could've doubled over with anxiety had Quinn not squeezed my hand as they approached.

"We've decided," Nia announced.

"And?" Emily looked up anxiously.

"If you do something for us, we'll get you the amulet you want," Kaiya announced as she wrapped her arm around Nia's waist protectively.

"Name it," I told her, soaking up confidence from Quinn's closeness.

"There's an item we need from an old doctor's office, and we haven't been able to retrieve it," Kaiya told us.

"Why can't you get inside?" Emily asked.

"It's not about getting in," Nia corrected her.

"Let me guess: it's haunted by some spirit or demon," I chimed in.

Nia and Kaiya both smiled. "Spirit—we think," Nia said.

"Suddenly, I feel right at home," I muttered.

"A ghost?" Quinn almost audibly gulped.

"No problem. I can banish a spirit."

"This is different than your average haunting," Kaiya explained. "We can handle ghosts. Dr. Rufino is an unusual case."

"He's a doctor?" Emily asked.

Kaiya shook her head. "Dr. Claude Rufino was a pharmacist. In the 1800s, when the pharmacy opened, Rufino became known as the man to see for unique cures. When the other doctors and pharmacists in the city failed, Dr. Rufino would proscribe alternative remedies cultivated from Voodoo and Hoodoo practitioners."

"Oh, god. I hate stories that start this way," Quinn said. "He experimented on people too, didn't he?"

"Shush, Quinn," Emily snapped at him.

Nia took over. "It worked well for a time. It was a standard exchange of goods between the witches and himself. He paid local practitioners fair wages to keep his shelves supplied with potions. Then he started realizing how much money he could make, because no one else could replicate the medicines he was offering customers. So, like any like any capitalist, he started raising prices."

"Typical," Emily agreed.

"His wife and children lived in a beautiful, grand home," Kaiya interjected. "And the witches were still living in shacks. My great, great grandmother was one of them."

"She made potions for the pharmacist?" I confirmed.

Kaiya nodded. "Precious mixtures. Rufino's most expensive remedy, in fact."

"What did it do?" Quinn asked.

"Clelia had the gift of rejuvenation," Kaiya explained.

"She made zombies?" Emily asked.

"No, she didn't reanimate the dead. Typical that you associate Hoodoo with zombie-making, though," Kaiya grumbled in a thicker Cajun accent. "Her spells brought new life to the sick and newfound youth to the old."

"That's amazing. I've never heard of anyone having that ability before," I admitted. "Why wouldn't her magic be documented?"

"You really need to ask that question?" Kaiya seemed offended. "Think about who does the documenting. They weren't seeking out my great, great granny back then."

Nia placed her hand on Kaiya's shoulder to calm her. "People from all over Louisiana started visiting Dr. Rufino. His fame grew, and all the while, Clelia remained underpaid and unknown. She wasn't in it for fame, but she wanted a better life for her family, so she asked for more money."

"I'm sure he did the right thing," Emily said sarcastically.

"He refused," Kaiya told us. "Clelia threatened to sell the potions herself and cut Rufino out of it, which wasn't the smartest move."

"This doesn't sound like a happy ending," I frowned.

"He killed her, took all the potions she had left, and left my great grandmother an orphan," Kaiya told us. "My great grandmother tells the story that Rufino took eight vials. The price tag was ridiculously high, so only a few customers could afford them. We think there are at least two of her potions left."

"That's what we want," Nia told us.

I took a minute to think through the entire quest. It seemed simple enough: defeat the evil and gain the prize. I had a feeling we were missing information, though.

"That's easy! Right, Emlyn?" Emily sounded relieved.

I shook my head. "If it were that easy, they would've found the vials ages ago."

"He's been around our magic too long," Kaiya told us. "Our magic has no effect on him—he can absorb anything we throw at him."

"Yes. It seems we might need a little Celtic magic," Nia smiled slightly.

"There's one more hiccup, though," Kaiya admitted. "As your non-magical boy here guessed, Dr. Rufino experimented on some of his less affluent patients."

"Called it!" Quinn exclaimed.

"There are probably a dozen additional ghosts besides the good doctor," Nia told us. "They don't like to be disturbed."

"Holy crap!" Emily practically yelled.

"A dozen ghosts?" Quinn wasn't happy. "There's no way!"

Quinn tried to meet my gaze to make sure I agreed with him, but I wouldn't meet his eyes. I didn't want to upset him, but there was no other option. I needed to get the amulet or die trying.

"Our coven can back you up with the smaller ghosts, but you'll have to handle Rufino before you can get to the potions. He won't let you take them without a fight."

"I need one of your people at our Airbnb to keep my people safe," I told them.

"Emlyn, wait," Quinn argued. "Shouldn't we take a minute to talk about this?"

"I'll watch over them," Nia offered, ignoring Quinn's pleas. "Kaiya and I can meet you at your place, so Kaiya can walk you to the doctor's office."

"What time?" I asked.

Kaiya smiled. "Let's make it the witching hour."

Chapter Fourteen

"So, you're just going to walk into this blind," Quinn criticized. "Emlyn, you didn't even take time to think about it. You just agreed on the spot. Now you're on the hook to banish a violent ghost. Do you even know how to fight a ghost?"

"Not particularly, but I trapped a demon inside a crystal once. After that, getting rid of a poltergeist should be cake. You don't need to worry about this," I assured him as I minced a sprig of rosemary into tiny pieces. I didn't want to be fighting with Quinn. I needed to be focusing on the intentions of my banishment bags—taking in the earthy sensation of the black rock salt and the piney freshness of the rosemary.

"Aren't enough people trying to kill you? I don't think it's a good idea to press our luck."

"He's got a point, Emlyn," Emily agreed. "The Ainbertachs are out there. What if using this much magic alerts them to your position or something? That's a thing, right?"

"And we still don't know who left the Voodoo doll at the cabin," Quinn added. "More unknown danger. We need to be going into this with open eyes. We need a plan. There are too many enemies out there."

"I'd forgotten about the Voodoo doll," Emily frowned.

"Which is why we need the amulet, guys," I explained as I divided the finely cut rosemary into four sachet bags on the kitchen counter in front of me. "It's a ghost. It's not a werewolf or a demon. This, I can handle. Need I remind you, this is the only way we have to defeat Maeve."

"Wait, are werewolves real?" Emily interjected.

"I don't think so," I told her.

Quinn got us back on track. "There's got to be another way."

"There isn't Quinn, and I know this sounds scary, but it's not that bad. All I have to do is follow this spell. Once I deliver the rejuvenating potion to our Hoodoo gals, we can find and save Marjorie."

"Okay, so say fighting this doctor guy is the best plan," Quinn reasoned. "Then Emily and I should go with you."

"No way," I said bluntly. "Emily, hand me the devil's claw."

She sighed and collected a jar from the kitchen table. I pulled four spider-like twigs from the container and dropped them into a mortar. In the summer, devil's claw had long green and silver stems with fresh-looking leaves. When the plant was harvested in the winter, though, they looked like thorny insects with branches extending in all directions. I crushed them with my pestle inside the mortar.

"We just don't like the idea of you going alone," said Emily, trying a softer approach.

"I don't like the idea of you going ghost hunting with me. Do you know how dangerous that could be for you?"

"It's dangerous for you, Emlyn! We don't know these witches," Quinn argued. "How do we know they're not working for the Ainbertachs?"

"I'm sure Jeb will sense if they're a threat or not when he meets them," I tried to assure Emily and Quinn again, before pouring my crushed devil's claw into the four pouches. "There's a lot we don't know right now. We have to take some of it on faith."

"Well, while you're gone, you're also leaving us with a stranger. Not really safe," Emily groaned.

"I'll leave you some defensive potions in case something goes wrong."

"Or we could just go with you," Quinn pushed.

"You don't have powers. You're too easy to hurt or possess," I explained, starting to lose the calm demeanor I'd been maintaining.

"Emlyn, please." Quinn wouldn't stop.

"Listen to him, Emlyn," Emily pushed too.

"I said no!" I yelled, slamming my fist onto the marble countertop. Suddenly, I couldn't keep it together anymore. "I am the one carrying the weight of all this. I am the one who has to make everything right. Not you. So, stop arguing with me. I'm in charge here because I'm the one with the powers."

"That doesn't mean you get to make all the choices alone," Quinn shot back.

"Yes. It does. They are my choices to make because I am the only one who can stop all this. One wrong move means we're all dead, so please, get out of the kitchen so I can finish these spell bags."

"Jeez, Emlyn. You need to chill," Emily told me.

"I need quiet," I shot back at her.

They didn't say anything else. I could tell my friends were hurt, but I didn't have time to feel guilty. Emily was treating this like spring break, and Quinn was in over his head. They couldn't understand the burden. The only thing that could help Marjorie was the amulet, and I knew Dr. Rufino was the only thing standing in our way. There was no time for second-guessing.

My friends reluctantly left the kitchen as I walked over to the fridge to collect a plastic baggie of stinging nettle. To most people, stinging nettle was a common weed with coarse, fiberglass-like hairs. Touching those hairs was a no-no. Without gloves, the little hairs stuck to skin, causing a burning sensation. The fresher, the better, and I was lucky that Nia's garden had been well stocked. I slipped on a pair of latex gloves and carefully pulled the leaves off the stem. Once I finished with the stinging nettle, I moved onto the less painful ingredients.

The quiet was a nice change. As I added comfry root, blood meal, and garlic to each sachet, I focused on the need to banish Dr. Rufino from the pharmacy. I infused each ingredient with purpose. I topped each bag off with a bloodstone, pulled the drawstrings tight, and kissed each one to seal the spell.

With the bags finished, I moved to my room, silently passing Quinn and Emily in the main living area. They didn't speak, which was awkward, but I didn't have time for another argument with them. So, silence was better.

Just as I finished transferring my spell pouches into my messenger bag, a small knock on the door broke the silence of my room. I quickly pulled the satchel over my shoulder and took one last look in the mirror. I needed to remind myself of what a strong woman I was. For ghost hunting, I had selected a more flexible outfit than the one I'd worn earlier on Bourbon Street—a pair of black jeans, a tank top, and a hoodie. I'd pulled my wild hair into a ponytail, refusing to wear the wig for a fight.

"Showtime," I muttered to myself.

"Emlyn, our babysitter is here," Emily jeered from downstairs. I could hear Jeb barking in the living room. Everyone was awkwardly waiting for me at the foot of the stairs. Emily and Quinn were pouting, but it relieved me to see Jeb sniffing at Nia and Kaiya rather than growling at them. He seemed a bit distracted by whatever Nia was toting in her paisley-patterned casserole carrier, but I still took his friendliness as a good sign.

"Hey guys," was my generic greeting. My mind wasn't focused on pleasantries.

"You ready?" Kaiya asked me, seeming as uninterested in hellos as I was.

I nodded, even though I wasn't sure. I hated this side of witchcraft—the fighting-evil side of things. I far preferred the spell-crafting, spiritual side of magic.

Kaiya and I were dressed in similar comfort-based, ghost-fighting clothes, but Nia looked ready for a house party. She was wearing a long-sleeved, purple and gold turtleneck tunic dress with a pair of old-fashioned oxford heels. She had bejeweled temporary tattoos on her cheeks. One was a tiger, and the other had the letters "LSU" in bright purple. Opposite her casserole dish, Nia was carting a purple and gold picnic-style cooler.

I met Nia's eyes. "You sure you're good staying here?"

"Of course," she responded, waving her hand at me. "I brought a few local brews Emily might want to try. Since she's such a foodie, I also brought some leftover gumbo for her to try."

"You're an angel," Emily said, jumping over to Nia to help with her casserole dish. "This looks and smells amazing!"

"The secret is frozen okra. I also mix in a few tablespoons of bacon fat to really pump up the flavor," Nia smiled, handing the dish to Emily.

"How did LSU play today?" Quinn asked Nia.

"We beat Alabama 17 to 14," she cheered. "Geaux Tigers!"

"You guys are looking good for the National Championship this year," Quinn told her. He'd moved on from stubborn ex-boyfriend mode to college football mode. I'd spent quite a few Saturdays watching the Georgia Bulldogs play. Quinn was a die-hard fan.

"I get more anxious every time we play," Nia laughed. "Alabama was a big concern. You guys root for UGA?"

"Definitely," Quinn told her.

"Oh, yeah!" Emily echoed from the kitchen. She'd already broken into the gumbo, serving herself a healthy portion. "Does anyone else want some of this?"

"I'll grab some in a minute," Quinn told her, turning back to talk sports with Nia. I hoped Nia could keep Quinn's mind off the ghosts. She seemed optimistic and relaxed, so there was a chance her good mood would rub off on Quinn for the night.

Nia sat down on the couch, propped her feet up on the coffee table, and cracked open a silver can from her picnic cooler. "I think we're good here, Kaiya," she announced.

"Divine actually." Emily came out of the kitchen, pulling a spoon out of her mouth. "This is delicious."

"Oh good," Nia took a sip of her drink. "It was a tweak on an old recipe."

"We'll leave you to it then," Kaiya said, ignoring the food chatter. She walked over to Nia on the couch and pecked her on the cheek.

"You two be careful," Nia told us.

I locked eyes with Quinn and knew he was angry that he wasn't coming with me. I wished I wasn't leaving on such bad terms with him, but I couldn't gamble with Quinn and Emily's safety. My biggest concern was the other witches who would be joining us. I couldn't control what they would do, and I didn't know the full story. The potion was powerful, sure, but I didn't understand why they needed it so badly. Quinn coming would've made me feel safer, sure, but it was easy for a ghost to possess a human. The chances of a spirit possessing a witch were slim. I couldn't focus on expelling Dr. Rufino if I were worried about protecting Quinn.

"Be safe," he nodded at me.

The night was colder than I expected, and I instantly wanted to return inside for a thicker jacket. I didn't, though—I didn't want to face Quinn again. It surprised me to see the chill air wasn't enough to kill the vibes of the French Quarter. It was bustling. There was an energy around us I'd never seen before. Even Savannah, which was a tourist town with a lot of nightlife, didn't know this kind of party.

"The hair is much better this way," Kaiya broke the silence between us as we followed the neon lights on Bourbon Street.

"Oh," I instinctively reached up to feel my hair. "I like it this way too."

"This is your first time in New Orleans?" she asked in a tone that was only slightly snarky.

"Yeah," I told her. "I wish it was under better circumstances. It seems like a fun place."

"It's definitely an experience. All of New Orleans isn't like this, but everyone should do the French Quarter at least once."

"Reminds me a little of Savannah. There are the touristy things you need to experience, but the locals know the best spots off the beaten path." I paused. "Do you enjoy living here?"

"I'm over it."

"You thinking of moving?"

"Not possible."

"What do you mean?"

"The coven and shop are here. I have to stay too."

"Duty," I commented flatly, suddenly understanding Kaiya's stern demeanor. She wasn't that much older than me—probably six years or so. I couldn't imagine having an entire coven dropped on me in my 20s. I was barely making it through this mission.

Kaiya didn't respond, so the conversation ended there. It felt like Kaiya had opened up more than she wanted to, but I couldn't be sure. I didn't mind the lack of conversation, though. It gave me more time to think. I was mentally sorting through everything I knew about ghosts. Savannah had plenty of its own stories—sightings at local restaurants and hauntings at the cemetery. The historic district was filled with local myths.

The stories from Celtic magic and folklore were a bit different from the Southern ghosts. Part of our legends featured banshees—the beautiful, ghostly women who wailed over imminent deaths. We could track even the headless horseman to Irish stories. Folktales aside, I knew ghosts were typically spirits who didn't or wouldn't leave our human dimension. The longer their souls stayed in this plane with no purpose, the more susceptible they were to being taken over by dark energies. One of our jobs as witches was to help those lost souls move on, banishing the evil that would eventually turn good souls into malevolent ones. My mission for the night was to help Dr. Rufino move on—even though he sounded like he'd been a terrible human before he became a ghost.

"So, what's your deal?" Kaiya asked, breaking my concentration as we turned into a back alley. The sounds of the street faded as the party disappeared behind us.

"What do you mean?"

194

"Don't be coy. You've got the Ainbertach Coven on your trail, your granny is in trouble, and you're using humans as your backup. There's a story there."

"Oh…" I trailed off, not sure how to respond. Quinn's worries echoed in my head, but I pushed them aside. "Have you ever dealt with the Ainbertach Coven?"

"No. I've heard about them, obviously, but our magic isn't high on their radar. Hoodoo is a neutral ground for them. We aren't strictly light or dark."

"Are *you* neutral?" The question was much more pointed than I meant for it to be.

She noticed my tone and paused for a minute before responding. "We keep to ourselves."

"Meaning as long as the coven is picking off Irish witches, it doesn't concern you?" I could feel the heat in my voice.

"We're here," Kaiya ignored my comment. She pointed toward a group of people sitting on the curb a few yards down. From the single lamppost, I could make out the shape of a dark storefront. Compared to the two red stucco buildings framing it, the navy building looked squatty and unfriendly. Two large bay windows jutted out on either side of the front door, like a shop from a Victorian village. I imagined the windows would've been display cases if the structure wasn't a doctor's office. A wooden sign hung over the front door, depicting the two snakes and the winged staff from the medical symbol. I just hoped there weren't any snakes inside the pharmacy.

Three people were waiting by the porch—two guys and a girl. One man was probably eight inches taller than the other two. From what I could see in the darkness, the tall man was lanky with beige skin, while the other man was short with deep brown skin, massive biceps, and a long beard. The girl was petite, her skin a russet, reddish-brown.

"Is this her? The Celtic witch?" the shorter guy asked.

"Jeez, man. Way to make an impression," the taller one interjected. I noticed a tie-dyed Grateful Dead shirt when he turned and extended his hand to me. "I'm Jordan. This is Chad and Kim," he said in a cheerful voice. His accent sounded more like a Mississippi-southern accent than a Creole one.

"Emlyn," I told him, offering a smile. Jordan shook my hand while Chad and Kim nodded at me. They didn't seem enthused by my presence.

"Where's Nia?" Kim wanted to know. I noticed right away that her voice didn't match her small stature. Her tiny features, hidden under pitch-black hair, were the opposite of her forceful voice.

"Emlyn has non-magical people traveling with her," Kaiya told them, not hiding the annoyance from her tone. "Nia will keep them safe while Emlyn helps us."

"Good deal! So what's the plan, boss?" Jordan asked. I immediately knew I liked Jordan. He seemed calmer than the others, which might've been because he was a few years older. I guessed he was in his late 20s or early 30s.

"Emlyn's going to take care of the doc. Then she'll deliver the rejuvenating potions back to us," Kaiya said matter-of-factly. I waited for Kaiya to elaborate on the rest of the plan before I realized she was finished.

"Wait," I rattled out as the adrenaline began pumping. "I thought we were all going in together? You and your people are supposed to take care of the other ghosts."

"Exactly right. We do that from out here," Kaiya explained. "Since Rufino knows our magic, we can't cross the threshold or else he'll be able to interfere with our spells. It'll be better if we stay here while you go inside."

"Better for you, maybe. I didn't know I'd be going in alone."

"You agreed to do this," Kaiya snarled.

"But I was under the impression—"

"Stop," Kaiya ordered. Chad snickered, making it clear that people rarely disagreed with Kaiya. The whole group seemed to find humor in my challenging her authority. "Look, our bargain was for those potions. If you want to back out now, fine, but you won't be getting the amulet."

I suddenly realized I was cannon fodder. This coven didn't care what happened to me. Kaiya had the upper hand, though, and she knew it. "I guess I don't have a choice then."

"I'll go in as backup," Jordan offered.

"You will not," Kaiya scolded, cutting her eyes at him.

"What's the security like in this place?" I changed the subject.

"Cops drive by occasionally, but not often. It's not a high-traffic area, so people won't be an issue either," Jordan explained. "Chad and I used bolt cutters on the door lock, so you're ready to go." He motioned to Chad, who said nothing.

"How much time do you need for your spell?"

"Five minutes," Kim answered.

"I'll be ready."

Kaiya's group started arranging a circle of plant roots on the sidewalk in front of the door, and I took a few steps back to give them some space. I cracked opened an energy drink and took a few gulps as I watched Kim outline the roots with black salt. Chad met Kim in the middle of the circle with a small vintage birdcage, which they filled with four of the tarantula exoskeletons Emily had been creeped out by earlier. Chad whispered something under his breath, and then he nodded to Kim.

From what I could tell, Hoodoo magic dealt with a lot of symbolism, utilizing objects from nature to craft a spell with the outcome in mind. The cage seemed obvious—a trap to keep the ghosts from escaping. I wasn't sure about the exoskeletons.

"Want a lollipop?" Jordan was suddenly next to me, catching me mid-thought. He pulled a lollipop from his pocket, stripped it of its wrapper, and plopped it into his mouth as he waited for my response.

"Lollipop?" I questioned.

"Ex-smoker," Jordan laughed. "Keeps me from wanting a cigarette."

"Smart." I took a sip of my energy drink. "No, thank you, though. I'll stick to my drink."

"Kaiya's not so bad, you know."

"I'm sure she's not."

"What's your power?" Jordan stretched his arms behind his back as if he was preparing for a race.

"Time manipulation."

"No kidding," he exclaimed with a bright smile. "That's wicked magic. Badass."

"It's cool when you get the spells right," I tried to laugh.

"For your sake, I hope you get it right. This ghost is no joke, girl."

The hairs on the back of my neck pricked up. "Have you faced the doctor before? Was it bad?"

"All of us have tried to get those potions. Unfortunately for Kaiya, we've all failed. Two of us almost died trying. I damn near broke my neck when it was my turn."

"Are these potions really so important? That's so irresponsible! She risks the lives of her coven members over something she's never even seen before?"

"Don't be too quick to judge, girl." Jordan's smile turned to a frown. He ran a hand through his long, dark hair and bit his bottom lip. "Kaiya's kid sister needs the potion."

I flashed back to our conversation about being stuck in New Orleans. Kaiya's responsibility was to her sister. They had to stay because of the safety a coven offered them. I suddenly felt ashamed thinking badly of Kaiya. This fight wasn't for her. It was for someone she loved.

"I had no idea. Is Kaiya's sister…?"

"Dying?" He nodded yes and sighed. "We're all counting on you, Red."

They weren't the only ones, which only made my nerves worse. The pit in my stomach felt like it could swallow me whole.

"Jordan, Emlyn, we're ready," Kaiya called. Jordan bit down hard on his lollipop and started crunching the candy off the stick. He raised an eyebrow at me and then jumped to his spot in the circle between Chad and Kim.

"You got this girl!" Jordan cheered. I appreciated his enthusiasm, but Kim glared at him. She clearly didn't trust me. I was a stranger, which made me dangerous, but they needed me just as much as I needed them.

Kaiya met my gaze. "Once we begin our chant, you're good to go in."

I nodded.

"Our casting should keep the lesser spirits from manifesting," Kim explained. "As you probably know, it might not last long."

"So, if the ghosts show up, it's time to go," I commented.

"Not without the potion," Kaiya scoffed.

I took a deep breath to balance myself. "What does the vial look like?"

"We aren't 100% sure what it'll look like, but the bottles should feature a star inside a triangle somewhere. It won't be easy to find. Dr. Rufino would've kept it with the other rare and expensive items," Kaiya explained. "Take care of Rufino first is my suggestion."

"Needle in a haystack it is." I turned around to face the front door, took a deep breath, closed my eyes, and tried to calm the crazy drumming of my heart in my chest. I could taste adrenaline in the back of my throat—a sadly familiar coppery tang. I knew I could handle the ghost, but there was still a chance this was a trap. It occurred to me that the Voodoo doll could've been sent as a warning to stay away from the Hoodoo coven.

"Good luck," Jordan's voice echoed as I cautiously climbed three concrete steps up to the stoop. I waited there until the chanting started. The language sounded a little like French, but some words were strange. As they spoke, I could feel their collective energy beaming out. Kim, Kaiya, Chad, and Jordan were all in sync, and I only hoped it would keep the ghouls away.

The door was heavier than I expected, but I pulled it open. My eyes adjusted to the dark fairly quickly, but it was still difficult to see. Dark velvet curtains were draped over the windows, allowing only slivers of light into the pharmacy. A few stray beams of light from the open door illuminated a cluttered interior, revealing a much more difficult task than I had bargained for. Finding the potion wasn't going to be easy.

I switched on my flashlight and quickly reviewed my surroundings. Kaiya's coven made it sound like Rufino would appear quickly. I wanted to prevent him from catching me off guard. I scanned the entire room, again more slowly, this time paying more attention to details. There were thousands of glass jars and potion vials lining the shelves and walls. Some were built-in floor-to-ceiling units, and other shelves were about 6-feet high, positioned to create aisles in the museum. I'd never seen so many containers in one room. Finding a single bottle with the star and triangle was daunting.

I didn't like how quiet it was. It was almost more upsetting than being attacked, because I knew when Rufino jumped out he'd catch me off-guard. I took one last look at the street outside the shop before letting the wooden door thud closed behind me.

"I know you're in here," I called out, keeping my voice steady despite the trembling of my jaw. My free hand was tightly wrapped around a banishment bag. "Come on out. Let's get this over with."

It seemed the coast was clear for the time being. I wondered if Dr. Rufino only revealed himself to Hoodoo witches. I turned my attention to the first shelf on my left and headed toward it. The floor creaked under my feet as I walked, sending jolts of panic up my spine. The jars and vials were on the outermost shelves, lining the exterior walls of the room, and they were kept on the highest and lowest levels. It seemed whoever designed this museum wanted to keep the more interesting medical antiques at eye level. When I made it to the first shelving unit, I dropped to my knees and groaned at the number of potions.

"How do you eat an elephant? One bite at a time."

By the fourth case, all the shelves were running together. I'd found countless vials of lavender oil and sandalwood powder. The more unique ingredients—goat teeth, caterpillar hairs, sting of scorpion, duck claws, and assorted reptile eyeballs—kept things interesting. The clock on my burner phone said it'd been 30 minutes, but it seemed like hours.

"New strategy," I announced to myself as I stood to stretch my legs. "If I were a valuable potion, where would I be? I probably wouldn't be out in the open, right?"

I crossed to the back of the room, honing in on several cabinets with doors and drawers. As I dug through them, I cringed when I realized I'd found the "blood" drawer.

"Jeez, this is gross," I made a gagging sound as I held up a jar of pig's blood. The blood had turned black from age, and it looked like some had even evaporated out of the half-full jar.

Suddenly, a massive crash escaped from the back of the building. I cried out and jumped, dropping the jar and splattering the contents all over my combat boots and jeans. The mess—and the realization of what was on my clothing—wasn't on my mind, though. I locked my eyes on the white door leading to the patients' exam room in the back. Something was in there, and I knew it was likely Dr. Rufino. I had avoided that back room intentionally, hoping if the doctor was in there he would leave me alone. I noticed now that the door was cracked open, but I couldn't remember if it was open or closed when I first entered the building.

I grabbed the banishment bag I had set down on top of one of the cabinets, and took cover behind a glass display case to my left. There wasn't movement in the room that I could see, but the hairs on the back of my neck told me Dr. Rufino was back there. Another bang confirmed my suspicions.

I took a cautious step forward as I loosened the drawstrings on my spell bag. Even over my heavy breathing and thumping heart, I could hear small scratching sounds coming from behind the door. The sounds grew louder as I crept forward. Thinking quickly, I formed a simple plan. I'd burst through the door, freeze the ghost, and cast the banishment spell in one swoop. The only bad part was, I needed both hands for this spell, so I'd need to put down the flashlight.

I set it quietly down on the hardwood floor, keeping it pointed at the white door. Giving up control of my one source of light felt like being swallowed by darkness, even with the beam angled towards the white door. I stood in place for a minute, waiting for my eyes to adjust. The scratching noises continued, sounding more like scraping at this point. The time was now. I needed to move.

"One, two," I counted, psyching myself up for the fight. My fingers loosened the opening of the banishment bag, making it easy to toss the contents onto Dr. Rufino. "Three—."

I lurched forward, ready to attack, only to realize the assault was coming from behind. The front door slammed shut, and I jerked my body around to face the noise. The shock threw me off my game. Instead of freezing first, I threw the banishment bag at the shadowy figure in front of me.

"Blood stone, blood meal, stinging nettle," I chanted, hoping I'd have enough time to cast the entire spell.

"Whoa!" Jordan yelped.

"Jeez! What the hell, Jordan?" I stomped over to him, secretly relieved.

"Girl, what did you throw at me?" He brushed a few ingredients from his shoulder.

"I just wasted one of my banishment bags on you," I scolded him. "What are you doing here? Didn't Kaiya tell you to stay outside?"

"Aw man, I'm sorry. I didn't mean to scare you. We got anxious—you've been gone 45 minutes."

"Have you seen all the bottles in here?" I motioned to the magnitude of potion bottles surrounding us.

"I would have looked by the cash register, personally. It seems like a good spot to hide valuables."

"Thanks for the heads up," I grumbled. I was mad at myself for not assuming the same thing. I hadn't checked those shelves yet.

"Kudos, by the way." Jordan offered me a thumbs up.

"For what?"

"We didn't even hear the fight out there."

"That's because it hasn't happened," I grunted. "This is honestly feeling like a wild goose chase. Are you guys just setting me up?"

"Wait, you haven't seen him yet?" Suddenly, Jordan was less mellow. "Not good."

"Nope, which is why wasting one of these banishment spells isn't good," I bent down to see if I could salvage any of my ingredients on the floor. "Although he might not show up at all. Can you give me a hand with this mess?"

"Oh crap!" Jordan cried out. "Emlyn!"

Immediately, I felt Jordan's hands push hard against my body, toppling me over onto my right side about a second before a translucent being slipped between us. I ignored the pain in my side and rolled onto my feet, locking my eyes on Rufino. I'd imagined ghosts to be wispy phantoms, but he wasn't. Apart from the feverish look on his face and being able to see through him, Rufino looked normal from his well-groomed mustache to his lab coat.

"Dr. Rufino?" I blurted out, hoping to gain a few extra moments to form a new plan. The game was about to change, because now I had Jordan to consider.

"You're just gonna talk to him?" Jordan whispered from behind me. I ignored him.

"Dr. Rufino, I came here for a potion you have in your pharmacy," I announced, taking a few steps to my left. I wanted to put space between myself and Jordan. If I could get Rufino focused on me alone, maybe Jordan could get out of the building. "I think you know the mixtures I mean. I want the potions Clelia made for you."

It appeared name dropping Clelia wasn't the right move. My statement sent Rufino into a rage. He craned his neck backward and released a high-pitched shriek as his eyes seemed to bulge out of his head. He zoomed toward me, but I dodged his attack, positioning myself to freeze him in place. As he swirled around to face me again, I tried to freeze him. Unfortunately, nothing happened.

Panic hit me. I tried again, and nothing happened for a second time. I didn't know why, but my ability had no effect on him. Would my banishment spell work?

"Get out of here, Jordan!" I yelled. My voice seemed to wake him up from his shock, and Jordan scrambled to find a hiding place.

I jolted backward, trying to lead Rufino away from the front door to give Jordan an opening. When my fingers found a second banishment bag, I spun around suddenly to face Rufino head-on. I was ready to throw the contents of the bag at Rufino, but he was faster. Suddenly, his cold fingers were around my throat. His touch felt like frozen electricity against my neck. This was a twist—one I wasn't counting on. Rufino shouldn't have been able to grip my throat like this. Ghosts weren't corporeal. Some could take physical form for a few seconds. Others would animate objects, like ropes, to strangle people, but Rufino's fingers were holding firm against my skin.

"Witches are not welcome," his rough voice thundered, reverberating around the office.

As I gasped for air, I dropped the banishment bag to the ground and attempted to pry his fingers off me. I scraped and scratched at them, panicking for an escape. There were supplies in my messenger bag to repel evil—a small vial of holy water from the Cathedral of St. John the Baptist in Savannah. I couldn't access any of them, though, without first removing Rufino's hands from my neck.

"What's up, doc?" Jordan had crept up behind Rufino. He was holding a jar over his head and thrust it down in an attempt to knock Rufino over the head. The blow failed, passing straight through Rufino's translucent body. The distraction itself was a success, though. As Rufino laughed at Jordan's attempt at bravery, he loosened his grip on my neck long enough for me to wiggle free and search my bag. I quickly felt around for the glass vial, seizing it in the nick of time. Before he knew what was happening, I smashed the holy water at Rufino's ghostly feet.

With a shriek, Dr. Rufino disappeared, and at the same moment, I grabbed Jordan by the shoulder. We ducked behind a counter for cover. It was hard to focus on anything specific. My throat throbbed. Swallowing was painful, and I knew casting my spell would be difficult.

"Why are we not fleeing?" Jordan yelped.

"We have to get that potion," I screeched at him.

"How?"

I had no idea, and before I could come up with a response, a low rumbling sound took over the room. I peered around the glass counter to see dozens of ghosts swarming around the room in a swirl of translucent blues and yellows. I only had two banishment bags left.

"Oh man, Rufino must have blocked our spell," Jordan was freaking out. "We're gonna die. We'll get possessed."

"No, we aren't. I'll take care of the ghosts, but I need you to watch the room. Find Dr. Rufino," I commanded in a raspy, likely hard to understand voice.

Jordan nodded reluctantly. I squeezed his shoulder briefly to wish him good luck and then jumped out into the middle of the room with the ghosts. They charged me, but many passed right through me. They weren't as powerful as Rufino, so they did little more than disorient me.

"Witch," Rufino wailed from somewhere behind me. "Get out of my office!"

I grabbed one of my last banishment bags and poured its contents into my hand. Figures racing around my head, making me dizzier by the second, and the stinging nettle tingled in my hand. I knew what had to be done. I tossed the contents from the banishment bag above me into the air.

"End all movement. I banish you!" I yelled as loudly as I could with my damaged vocal cords. Then I froze the room, and luckily, everything came to a sudden stop around me.

"What magic is this?" Rufino bellowed. Because Rufino hadn't frozen before, I'd gambled that he wouldn't understand what was happening.

"They're crossing over, Dr. Rufino," I smiled at him. "You've lost."

Rufino snarled at me, "How dare you? They were my patients. They owed me everything!"

He bolted toward me in a gush of blue light, but I dodged his attack and threw myself toward the counter where Jordan was hiding. Jordan grabbed my arms and pulled me toward him.

"What did you do to the ghosts?" he wanted to know.

I ignored his question. "Where did Rufino reappear?"

"What?" Jordan didn't understand.

"After the holy water—," I was cut off mid-sentence as a wire coil dropped from the ceiling. It wrapped around my torso and pulled me up toward the ceiling.

"Bring my patients back!" Rufino ordered.

"Where, Jordan?" I squeaked out as the coil constricted my movement. My bindings grew tighter by the second, but Jordan didn't seem to understand what I needed from him. Jordan was retreating, scooting his body across the floor as fast as he could away from Rufino. I needed help, and I wondered where the others were. Did the coven know the spell stopped working? Was this the plan all along?

Then the ghosts reanimated. Rufino looked around the room and let out a billowing laugh. "Looks like I haven't lost at all!"

"Jordan. Where," I used the last bit of air in my lungs.

"By the soda machine," Jordan shrieked just before the ghosts swarmed him. They were wild, angry spirits, and I assumed Rufino was controlling them.

"Emlyn, do something!" Jordan yelled. "Kaiya! Chad! Kim!"

Jordan was on the ground, and Rufino hovered over him, likely preparing to possess Jordan's body. With it, Rufino could stay corporeal as long as he wanted, and he wouldn't be stuck inside the doctor's office anymore. Still, I knew there was only one thing I could do to help him. I ignored his calls. Instead, I focused intently on the moment I threw the holy water on Rufino. I took the deepest breath I could with the coil crushing my sternum.

"What's up, doc?" Jordan's voice repeated. It was the courageous Jordan once again, getting ready to slam Dr. Rufino in the head with the jar. I was elated to see this scene play out again. As Jordan's blow slid through Rufino's transparent form, I grabbed my holy water once again, and I smashed it at Rufino's feet.

This time I grabbed Jordan by the shoulder, and we ran toward the vintage soda machine on the other side of the room. Ignoring the agonizing sensation in my throat, I barked out orders.

"In about three seconds, all the ghosts will be here. Rufino will reappear right here by the soda machine. All I need you to do is hide behind it. Then toss the contents of this banishment bag on Rufino when I tell you."

The rumbling sound started, and I could see fear explode in Jordan's eyes.

"My magic doesn't work on these guys," Jordan argued.

"But mine will—only with your help. You can do this." I darted out toward the swarm of ghosts once again and checked to make sure Jordan was in position. He looked terrified, but he was all I had. For this plan to work, I'd need him. I lowered myself to my knees and waited for my moment, closing my eyes and blocking out the sensation of ghosts flowing back and forth through my body.

"Blood stone, blood meal, stinging nettle, away is where your soul must settle," I muttered quickly and quietly under my breath. "By rosemary, garlic, and comfry root, I cast you out of this institute."

"Witch," Dr. Rufino called. "Get away from my patients!"

I poured the contents from the final banishment bag into my hand and thrust them above my head. In the same second, I jumped to my feet, froze the room, and spun around to see an angry Rufino hovering about a foot away from the soda machine where Jordan was hiding.

Jordan peered out, and I nodded at him, hoping he would take my cue.

"What magic is this?" Rufino asked, shocked once again at the room of frozen ghosts.

"Our magic," Jordan exclaimed. He dumped the contents of the bag over Rufino as I chanted.

"Blood stone, blood meal, stinging nettle, away is where your soul must settle. By rosemary, garlic, and comfry root, I cast you out of this institute," I spoke as powerfully as I could muster with my damaged throat. Rufino was glued in place under the weight of the ingredients. "And if you try to fight my spell, devil's claw will drag you straight to hell."

Dr. Rufino's mouth widened into a black void. Soon his entire shape disappeared. A white light flashed, lighting up the entire front room and knocking Jordan and me to the floor. The last thing we heard from Dr. Claude Rufino was a mournful wallow.

"Jordan?" I sat up and brushed debris off myself. I assessed the damage, and there wasn't much to report. Besides my sore throat, I had a cut on my arm, but it was nothing compared to the claw marks I'd got from the demon on Abercorn Street.

"I'm here," Jordan coughed.

"Jordan, what happened here?" Kaiya's stern voice broke into the room.

"Emlyn did it," Jordan beamed, emerging from the back of the room.

"Ghost is no more," I told her, wincing. I was feeling the full intensity of my throbbing neck now that the adrenaline was wearing off. "We did it together," I added, shooting Jordan a smile.

"Jordan, what a stupid thing to do. You shouldn't have left the circle," Kaiya scolded.

"If it weren't for him, I would've died," I told her.

"The spell didn't work, Kaiya," Jordan explained. "All the ghosts were here."

"Yeah, Kaiya, what happened with that?" I pulled myself up from the ground and brushed dirt from my jeans.

"You were gone a full hour," Kim pointed out. "That's a long time to keep a spell going."

"The spell failed about five minutes after Jordan left. We don't know why," Kaiya clarified. "Did you find the potion?"

"We didn't find it, but Jordan thinks it'll be close to the register," I told her, hoping it had survived.

She jetted past me to the register. The rest of the group followed, and the search began. Everyone shuffled through drawers, tossing out unwanted vials and jars. About five minutes passed before Kaiya found what they were looking for.

"It's here! It's really here!" Kaiya declared. She produced two small glass vials and turned to her friends with a broad smile on her face. "There are two left."

The entire group rejoiced. As I watched them hugging and trading fist bumps, I smiled to see them so happy. It felt good to know that Kaiya's sister would be okay.

"Thanks, Red," Jordan turned to me.

"Yes, thank you," Kim echoed in a soft voice. Tears were rolling down her cheeks.

"I'm happy I could help," I told them. I paused, hoping not to ruin this special moment for Kaiya's team. "About the amulet I need?"

Kaiya turned to me. Her smile faded and was replaced with a look of guilt. "A deal is a deal, and you got me the potions I needed."

"I told you she was the witch for the job," an all-too-familiar, dark-roast-coffee voice smirked behind me.

"You were right," Kaiya agreed. "And as I told Emlyn, a deal is a deal."

"Blaine," I let the name roll off my tongue dully. Kaiya had betrayed me. I was part of a deal she'd made with Blaine.

"Hello, Emlyn," Blaine locked eyes with me and flashed me a charming smile.

"I should've known," I scolded myself.

"Don't feel bad, Emlyn. Kaiya's a good double agent— compelling. Unlike your girl," Blaine stated matter-of-factly.

My heart could've stopped in my chest. It was a worse feeling than facing Dr. Rufino. "What are you talking about?" I questioned him.

"Marnie."

Chapter Fifteen

Three Days Earlier.

"Take a seat," Marjorie motioned to the wicker furniture.

"Didn't you hear? We got a lead! Why are you so down in the dumps?" Emily finally asked. We were all thinking the same thing.

"It is a splendid thing, and it gives us another job to do. However, retrieving the medallion is not the only task we must accomplish. I've weighed all our options, explored various outcomes, and delved into the choices we have before us," Marjorie said.

"Why is that bad? We know what to do next," I enthused.

"I have a plan. You won't like it."

"Great," Emily sighed, plopping down onto a chair. Marnie and I took a seat on the center couch. I felt deflated. This wouldn't be good. I could tell from Marjorie's demeanor she was nervous. She was fidgeting, twisting her waist-length hair in her fingertips.

"We all have roles to play here, and they must be played exactly as I describe," Marjorie began. She walked over to the chalkboard she'd been brainstorming on. Words like "amulet" and "power-stripping" were listed together, along with Maeve's powers.

"Tell us what you're thinking," I pressed.

Marjorie shook her head. "I need you to understand that I've looked into dozens of options, Emlyn. This is the right plan."

"Go ahead, Marjorie," Marnie urged. "We'll listen."

"I will explain the first part of the plan to all three of you." Marjorie paused. "Then, Marnie will need to leave the room for the second half."

Marnie looked just as surprised as I did.

I spoke up. "What are you talking about, Marjorie? Marnie's part of the team. We'll need her help."

Marnie nodded. "I know the risks, and I want to help. We're better off working together."

"You will help," Marjorie explained. "You'll be joining the Ainbertach Coven."

"Are you on drugs?" Emily blurted out, which I thought was a fair question.

"You can't be serious, Marjorie," I exclaimed. I turned to Marnie, looking for her reaction.

"I am serious, Emlyn," Marjorie said. "She's the only one who could fill this role. Maeve knows the rest of us."

"Come on! That's ridiculous!" I shouted.

"It makes sense to have someone on the inside," Marnie responded, sounding much more confident in the plan than I was.

"Marnie!"

"It does," Marnie pushed. "It's a smart idea, but there's a problem. I'm not a witch."

"You are," Marjorie scoffed. "You come from a lengthy line of witches."

"I do, but they're light witches," Marnie pointed out. "Powers or not, my family has always fought the darkness. Why would they believe I want to join their coven?"

"Easy: your grandmother."

Marnie's lips pursed. "She killed dark witches. She broke the laws of our coven, but she was still a light witch. She still wanted to fight dark magic."

"Don't get angry," Marjorie walked in closer. "Just think about it. She helped rid the world of evil, and then her entire coven turned against her."

"Yourself included."

Marjorie pushed past Marnie's comment. "Wouldn't it be easy to weave the story of a young witch who turned to dark magic to avenge her grandmother? You grew up with Henrietta. She was a powerful woman who only wanted to rid the world of dark magic. In exchange for her passion and dedication, our coven of light magic persecuted your family."

"I'd buy it," Emily admitted.

"Stop," I demanded.

"What? It's a good story," Emily said.

"I don't like it. Do you know what would happen to Marnie if they find out she's double-crossing them? They would kill her. Might I also point out that Marnie doesn't have powers? How can she join the coven with no magic?"

"Of course Marnie has powers," Marjorie rolled her eyes.

"She does?" Emily asked.

"Potions," Marjorie announced.

"Potions are my power?" Marnie was confused.

"Have you ever met another witch who knows more about the properties of herbs, oils, or plants?" Marjorie asked. "Marnie, the mixtures you create are perfectly balanced. They must be magic. That's your ability."

"I make tea."

"No. You make potions. Brew Maeve a muscle-relaxing tea, and she'll believe it's a potion."

"Not to dampen anyone's hopes, but the Ainbertach Coven is selective about who can join. There's an entire initiation process, as we know," I reminded everyone. "Why would they just welcome Marnie into the group?"

"Because Marnie will tell them where we're hiding," Marjorie revealed.

"My head hurts," Emily groaned. "I don't follow."

"Maybe Marjorie should explain the whole plan without us interrupting," Marnie suggested. "Then we can poke holes in it."

Marjorie nodded. "Once we've all settled into our roles, Marnie will contact the coven. They'll likely have seers scanning for energy. Tell them where we are and tell them your story. Offer the three of us up in exchange for membership to the coven. You decide when the time is right, because we can't see it coming. It must be a surprise to us. Emlyn and Emily, you will have go-bags ready in your rooms. You'll be ready to leave, but not so ready that the coven's agents think we knew they were coming. All the other essentials, we'll pack in the SUV."

"Where are we going?" I asked.

"I'll explain that part of the plan later. Marnie can't have any knowledge about that part. The fewer memories I need to block from any psychics, the better. We can't have big chunks missing from your mind. It'll look suspicious."

"Okay, that makes sense," Marnie nodded.

"Now, this is also incredibly important. Marnie, you're going to attack Emlyn."

"What?" Marnie and I said in unison.

"Your objective has to be kidnapping Emlyn. If the coven's agents notice one hesitation, it could throw off the entire plan. You must attack her in a way we won't see coming. Can you do that?"

"I guess," Marnie looked down at her feet. "I don't want to hurt anyone, though."

"It'll all be for show. We'll all know it, but it has to be convincing. Emlyn's tough. She can take it."

"Gee, thanks," I huffed.

"We will react in the moment, and one way or another, we will get Emily and Emlyn out of here. They'll take Jeb and Tephi with them to keep them safe."

"What about Margo?" Marnie asked.

"She's your familiar, so she may remain with you. You may also leave her here for the groundkeeper to take care of until we're able to return. They would kill Jeb and Tephi for belonging to me and Emlyn."

Marnie nodded.

I sat in silence, absorbing everything Marjorie was saying. There were a lot of pieces I didn't agree with—most of them, actually. I suddenly realized a person missing from the plan. "Wait, you only said Emily and me."

"That's correct," Marjorie turned away from us. "Maeve will trust Marnie much more if Marnie impresses her. She can't join the coven empty-handed. I'm staying behind, so Marnie can offer me to Maeve."

"Absolutely not!" I threw my arms up. "How is this a plan? This is crazy!"

"Emlyn, sit down and don't worry. Maeve won't kill me."

"You don't know that," I was so mad I was crying.

"She won't give up her leverage. With me as a hostage, Maeve can draw you out of hiding. I'm too valuable to kill."

"What if she tortures you?" I asked, still feeling hysterical.

"Wounds heal."

I couldn't believe what I was hearing. This was the worst plan, and I couldn't get behind it.

"Emlyn, there aren't a lot of other choices," Marnie mumbled. "I don't like the plan. Really, I don't, because I'm the one who has to pull it off. But what else can we do?"

"She's right," Emily chimed in.

"Emlyn, this is about saving everyone. If you want to go home again and feel safe again, this is the only plan," Marjorie told me. "Once Marnie and I are at the headquarters, we'll have a better idea of what we're dealing with. We can prepare you. The scrying mirror will allow us to communicate securely."

"They likely wouldn't allow you to use any magic, Marjorie," Marnie speculated. "You'll be in a magic proofed room, I'm sure. I'll have to take the scrying mirror."

"So, that leaves the saving part to Emlyn and me?" Emily asked. "Remember, I don't have powers. I'll help, but I'm not a superhero."

"Emlyn and I will get to work creating defensive potions for you to use on Maeve's minions," Marjorie told her. "Once you make it inside the headquarters, you'll have Marnie and me as backup."

"The best-case scenario would be getting Blaine out of the way," Emily added. "That pain thing he does is terrible." She cringed, remembering.

"That's not his real power," I explained. "He has to drink a potion to manifest that ability. If we catch him by surprise, he's just an empath. We could defeat him pretty easily."

"I could even switch that potion with essence of poppy," Marnie suggested. "We can knock him out before you even get inside. It leaves us clear to take out Maeve together."

"Perfect," Marjorie said. "We still have some details to iron out, but this is all good."

"We're really going to do this?" I asked, hoping Marnie and Marjorie would come to their senses. They all nodded in agreement.

"I guess that settles it then," I sighed.

"Marnie, I need to go over Emily and Emlyn's task," Marjorie told her.

Marnie nodded. "Understood."

"I must press the importance of everyone sticking to the plan, one last time," Marjorie added, looking at each of us in turn. "Our lives depend on this going right."

Chapter Sixteen

"Marnie," Blaine said.

"The girl who betrayed us, held a knife to my throat, and kidnapped my grandmother?" I asked incredulously.

Blaine smiled and waved his finger at me. "Tsk, tsk. Let's not play games, Emlyn. You might've been able to fool everyone else with whatever spell or potion you used, but not me."

"What exactly are you saying, Blaine?" I held my ground.

"What's going on here, Kaiya?" Jordan interjected, making me remember Blaine and I weren't alone. Jordan, Kim, and Chad were sporting confused faces.

"You all know Blaine," Kaiya said. "He and his family have been our allies for a long time. He suspected Emlyn would seek our coven's help. Blaine suggested we have Emlyn help us get the potions, and I agreed to give him Emlyn after she banished Rufino."

"We had a deal!" I snarled at Kaiya. "You told me if I got the rejuvenating potions, you'd get me a medallion. You lied to me, and worse, you handed me over to the people trying to kill me!"

"Hold on a second. I held up my end. Blaine is the only person I'm still in contact with who still has one of Mom's amulets," Kaiya reasoned. "You and Blaine have unfinished business. I did and said what I needed to, but don't call me a liar. I followed through."

"Man, that's low," Jordan frowned.

"She did what she had to do," Kim whispered, nudging Jordan with her elbow.

"You should all go," Blaine told them. "Emlyn and I have things to discuss. I'll check in shortly."

"I don't know, man," Jordan hesitated. It seemed our near-death experience had bonded us, but I knew witches. The coven would win out. Nothing was more important than loyalty in a coven.

"Come on, Jordan." Kaiya's voice was rigid, and he obeyed. They filed out the door with Kaiya at the rear. As she left, she turned to Blaine. "I'll meet you back at the address I sent you. Nia is watching Emlyn's friends and familiar. Take all the time you need."

Blaine nodded without breaking eye contact with me. Nauseated wasn't the right word for what I was feeling. I was too stubborn to cry, but facing utter defeat was painful. Not only did Blaine have me, but he also had everyone I loved. Kaiya would serve

Quinn and Emily up to Blaine on a silver platter. I wondered if I could text Emily without Blaine noticing. There was a chance I could get them out before Kaiya returned.

"How does pizza sound?" Blaine asked nonchalantly.

"Um?" I responded, confused.

"We need to talk, and I'm hungry. I'm sure a pizza joint is open."

"Look, I'm sure it's fun for you to drag all this out, but I'd prefer we get it over with. When is Maeve getting here? How much time do I have?" I hoped if I got him talking, I could distract him and get a text out.

"Oh, that's why you look so gloomy. Maeve isn't coming. She doesn't know I'm here."

The heavy beating of my heart slowed a bit. I could take Blaine in a fight. "You're bringing me in yourself then? Looking to gain back her respect?"

"No need to be rude, Em. Now, calm down," Blaine lifted his hand in my direction, and a relaxed sensation washed over me. Blaine was manipulating my emotions. "I'm not here to kill you. I want pizza, and I want to talk."

"You expect me to believe that? Don't use your empath abilities to make me calmer. I have a right to be tense."

"Have it your way then." All at once, my anxieties and fears hit me. I could barely think straight. Blaine sighed and gestured to the door. "Can we get out of here now? Someone is bound to find this office in disrepair, and it's best we aren't here when that happens."

"Why would I willingly go anywhere with you?"

"If you prefer I call Maeve, she and about a dozen cronies can be here in no time," Blaine nudged me with a grin. "Pizza or Maeve? What's it gonna be, lover?"

I cringed. It was such a terrible reminder of the past. "I guess I'll take the pizza."

"Good. Follow me."

I contemplated escape routes the entire walk over to VC Pizzeria. Kaiya and Nia were with Emily and Quinn, which would make fleeing more difficult. I knew turning back time wouldn't help. Reason one: I wasn't sure how long Blaine had been waiting for us. Reason two: I didn't know if I could rewind an entire day. Once time got to a certain point, all I could do was watch it unfold. It left few options. I just hoped Quinn and Emily would be okay.

Once we reached the small café, Blaine selected a table on the patio, a round, iron structure with wobbly chairs. A group of rowdy guys were seated next to us. I wondered for a moment if I could get help from them, but they seemed far too gone to be useful.

"Meat lovers?" Blaine suggested.

"Whatever is fine," I responded.

"You're probably one of those pineapple people, aren't you?"

I didn't answer.

"Meat lovers, it is."

He put in our order when the server came by. Blaine was pleasant and charming, just like he always was. The poor waitress believed his act, but I didn't.

Blaine cleared his throat. "That brings us to the main topic of conversation."

"Which is what? What are we doing here, Blaine?"

"We're about to have a conversation over pizza."

"So, you try to kill me, and now you're feeding me? What game are you playing this time?"

"No games. I need your help getting rid of Maeve."

There was no hesitation in his voice or hint of humor, but the words were ridiculous. I paused a second, waiting for the punch line.

"You're insane. How stupid do you think I am?" I stood up, opting for a more confident position.

My raised voice attracted attention from the group of guys behind us. They chimed in with a couple laughs and "Yeah, she's not stupid!"

"Sit down and let me elaborate," Blaine said calmly. "You have no reason to trust me, but you can at least listen to what I have to say."

I didn't respond.

"Either I'm telling the truth, making me a powerful ally in defeating Maeve, or I'm lying. If I'm lying, Maeve will be on her way here anyway, so you might as well enjoy a slice of pizza." Blaine pulled a chain out from underneath his shirt and revealed the medallion I needed. "You can't stop her without this. Kaiya told me you were desperate to find it, which I'm guessing means you figured out Maeve's abilities."

"Yes. Maeve's an elementist," I blurted out. I slammed myself back into the metal chair, realizing I had no choice but to listen to Blaine. I hated to admit it, but I was very interested in what he had to say. "More importantly, Blaine, we figured out who Maeve is."

Blaine smiled. "Smartypants."

I ignored the little rush of butterflies his smile caused, kicking myself for feeling it at all.

"She's an Ainbertach, Blaine. Why would I believe you want to get rid of her? Maeve is your ticket to the top of the Ainbertach Coven. She's the head honcho, and I know how much you crave power. She's the key."

"Believe me, she's not. I've become a joke because I couldn't kill you. Not only did I miss my mark, but I'm also still alive. My girlfriend begged her father, the leader of the entire coven, not to kill me. They granted me a second chance, which makes me look beyond pathetic. My father—the coward—is more respected in the coven than I am. Do you know what that's like?"

I rolled my eyes at him. "Really? That's why you want to get rid of your girlfriend?"

"It's the only way I can rise above this situation. Until she's out of the picture, I'll only be seen as her pet."

"The amount of misogynistic bull crap you're spouting right now is crazy. You can't handle living in Maeve's shadow, so you want to kill her? That's so cold, Blaine."

He narrowed his eyes at me. "Like you're one to talk. Didn't you accuse your own boyfriend of being a killer and then cheat on him? Anyway, I didn't say 'kill.' We can just… misplace her."

"Still, eliminating Maeve won't save your standing with the coven. You'd be in a worse position than me. It's no fun having your life threatened. Take it from someone who's been on the run for a week. I think I'm developing acid reflux from the stress."

"You know me better than that. I have a plan that will promote me to the top of the Atlanta branch and simultaneously erase your name from their hit list."

My first reaction was excitement. A brief image of life without fear flashed into my head, but it quickly deflated. My rational mind knew there was no way Blaine could pull that off.

"How could you possibly accomplish that?"

"Easy." He shot me a charming smile as our waitress dropped the pizza off at our table. Blaine pulled a cheesy triangle from the pie and took a big bite. "We'll kill you too," he said casually, after swallowing.

"Keep talking."

"Part of my deal with Kaiya was obtaining one of those rejuvenation potions."

"I'm sure she didn't want to hand that over."

"I told her if she didn't, I'd give Maeve your location. Without you, Kaiya wasn't getting any potion. She was smart to accept my offer."

"That was for her sister. You manipulated her."

"It worked, didn't it?"

I glared at him but moved on. "Why do you want the potion?"

"While Kaiya uses her vial to heal the living, we'll use our vial on a dead body."

"I don't follow."

"Using rejuvenation on a corpse reverses decomposition, making a cadaver look like a newly dead body. Since I figured you'd be opposed to killing someone—"

"Obviously."

"—I knew we'd need a backup. All we have to do is glamour the corpse, similar to the little illusion spell you used to disguise yourself. Then we fashion the body to look like you—magical essence and all—and poof. Problem solved."

"Great for me, but that doesn't really work for you," I pointed out. "Maeve would be gone—locked away in a mystical dimension without magic for the rest of her life. I don't see Fionn being cool with that. You know because he's her father? Also, he's the leader of the entire Ainbertach Coven. He'd come after you. You really don't think he'd blame you for losing his daughter?"

"Wait, is that your plan for Maeve? Smart, Em," Blaine laughed. "If you pull it off, she'll be gone for good."

I could've kicked myself for letting our plan slip to Blaine. "Back to your idea," I deflected.

"Right," Blaine took another bite of pizza. "Well, you have a good point about Fionn, but I think I can sway his thinking. Say you clean out the entire Atlanta headquarters and trap Maeve in an alternate dimension. Fionn would have no choice but to admit how powerful you are."

"Still not seeing how this helps you." I gave in and grabbed a slice.

"Don't you get it? When I tell Fionn that I've killed you and avenged Maeve's banishment, my first failure will be irrelevant. We'll have the body as proof, and then we get you out of there. You go back to your cushy life, and I take over the Atlanta chapter, restoring it to its former glory."

Blaine was obviously impressed with himself. I wasn't so sure, though.

"I still don't see Fionn so easily glossing over the loss of his daughter."

"Eh," Blaine shook it off. "I'm not sure how much he really likes Maeve. He's all about the boys, even though she's more powerful than all her brothers. Fionn assigned her the Atlanta headquarters, which isn't nearly as important as the European headquarters—London, Rome, Scotland."

"Brothers? How many?" I wondered how much information I could get out of him.

"Four. Maeve was the only girl. Fintan, the oldest, is powerful, but the others don't have impressive active powers. Fintan will be the next leader to take over in Ireland. He'll be 'The Ainbertach.'" Blaine grabbed another slice of pizza, then met my gaze. "I know you think you're tricking me out of information, but I'm speaking freely because we're partners now." Blaine winked.

"It's an interesting plan," I told him, breezing over the partner comment.

Blaine smiled. "Ah ha! You're starting to believe me. You're considering that I might not be trying to kill you." It felt like he was flirting with me. He was acting like he hadn't lied to me, betrayed me, and plotted to kill me.

"So, how would all this happen? And don't get excited or anything. I'll hear you out, is all."

Blaine grinned. "We stay here in New Orleans one more day. I tell Maeve I'm following up on leads. Kaiya and her coven help us prepare for the fight. They'll locate materials for the dimension spell, power stripping, sleepy potions, and whatever else you might need.

You and I head out to the cemetery to bless the amulet. I'm assuming you would use it to block Maeve's force-field?"

I nodded.

"It'll have to be powerful to work. Even the amulet has its limits. It'll take both our magic to enchant it."

"Great."

"Then we split up. You take the medallion, and we'll all reconvenc at the mansion."

"Which you'll provide directions to?"

"Of course. You and your people will need to take out the outer defenses. The less powerful witches, who do our grunt work, have locations they'll be posted at. While I keep Maeve in the kitchen, your girl Marnie can eliminate the witches on the inside. It'll be relatively easy because everyone loves her for bringing in your grandmother." Blaine stopped mid-thought. "Which, by the way, I put Marjorie in a coma, and no one seems to remember that."

"You're not really helping yourself here, Blaine," I grumbled at the memory of Marjorie in the hospital.

"Right. Okay, so there's a secret entrance to the kitchen through the wine cellar. That's where you come in and freeze time. We take out Maeve together."

"Wine cellar?" I suddenly remembered my dream. Emily would end up in that wine cellar with me. "I don't like putting my people in danger. Emily and Quinn don't have powers. I think you should be more involved in this process. Maybe get Kaiya's people to join?"

"Lover, that's as involved as I'm going to be."

"I thought we were partners? If you aren't going to play an active role—"

"I hate to point this out, but without me, you've got no plan. You don't know where the estate is, how many people we've got, where the secret entrance is, or the layout of the property. If you don't want your friends in danger, find other people to help you," Blaine answered in a tense tone. "I'm just telling you, I'll have Maeve in position."

"Fine, but I'll need everyone's help to be able to rip the folds of time to send Maeve into another dimension. Marjorie will need to be there too. The three of us will have to combine our powers to banish Maeve."

"God, that's confusing—so many M's: Maeve, Marnie, Marjorie. Why so many M's?"

"I'm serious, Blaine," I pushed him. "We're talking about serious magic."

"Yes, Em! I'll get your grandmother. Jeez," he assured me. "I thought you were a time-witch. Shouldn't dimensional stuff be easy? You didn't seem to have trouble with it at the shop."

"That didn't work out as intended," I admitted. "We only transported ourselves a few blocks away."

"You were only a few blocks away?" Blaine laughed. "Maeve was convinced you were halfway across the country. She was so mad. I think your magic worries her."

"Bull," I argued. It could've been true, though. In the dream I had, Maeve told Blaine this situation wasn't about initiation anymore. She said it was about me and what I could become.

"That's the basic plan. What do you think?" Blaine asked.

"We'd be free to go? All of us?" I asked, biting my lower lip.

"You, Grandma, Marnie, Emily, Quinn, and the herd of animals you travel with."

There was no way to trust Blaine. He'd tricked me before, and the odds were against him wanting to help us. It wasn't smart to team up with the person who had tried to kill me a little more than a year ago. The most significant part of my mind screamed that I shouldn't do it. With Blaine, there was bound to be a twist or a trap—there had to be. Selling Emily and Quinn on the idea would also be rough, considering the physical and mental damage had Blaine caused us.

Weirdly, I didn't think Blaine was lying to me. In Blaine's mind, power outweighed all other objectives. I remembered because I'd been inside it. If Maeve was the thing keeping Blaine from rising to the top, why wouldn't Blaine want her gone? He was evil. Love wasn't high on the list of priorities for him.

"Wait, you've been following us from the beginning, haven't you?" I suddenly realized. "You knew we would come here…You left the Voodoo doll!"

A sly smile spread over his face. "It was funny, wasn't it?"

I shook my head. "No. We didn't find it amusing. How did you find us?"

"It's a long story."

"Tell me."

"When you teleported out of Marjorie's shop, Maeve and I split up. She went back to headquarters in Atlanta. I did some preliminary searches—I checked your dad's place and Emily's house, but then it dawned on me: you might want an amulet of your own."

I shook my head. "There's no way you figured it out that fast. Why would you even think of that?"

"I knew you'd be searching for a way to defeat Maeve. If you figured out what powers Maeve has, you'd probably remember the medallion I have that blocks powers. My dad used it on your mom. I used it on you. So why shouldn't you use it on Maeve? It was a logical thought process, although I wasn't 100% sure."

"But wait, you didn't have the medallion when we fought at Marjorie's shop. I thought it disappeared when you were trapped in the trophy."

"You'll never believe this, but Maeve located it when she went looking for me. When I didn't check in, she searched the high school, knowing that's where I'd planned to do the ritual. She found the medallion in the lost and found."

"The lost and found…" I couldn't believe it.

"Anyway, I figured that would be your plan, so I called Kaiya. We made a deal," Blaine smirked. "At that time, I planned on killing you. It wasn't until I met back up with Maeve in Atlanta that I realized I was being scorned by all the other witches. The whispers and laughs were humiliating."

"You poor thing." I rolled my eyes.

Blaine ignored my sarcasm. "Marnie reached out to us shortly after. We didn't take it seriously until she showed up with your grandmother. She was everyone's hero. Even Maeve was impressed, but I realized Marnie was a fraud right away. I thought about turning her in, but then my plan took shape."

"Less than a day or two to turn on the love of your life?"

"I'm an empath, if you remember. When people mock, hate, or pity me, I can feel it as if it were my own thoughts. I can only withstand it for so long. It's practically a psychic attack. Besides, this was just the catalyst. Maeve has been holding me back from the beginning. Why do you think it took so long for me to get an assignment? Why do you think she gave you to me? She had plenty of excuses, but in reality, Maeve wanted to pick someone she knew I'd beat."

"Guess it sucked for her when you never came back."

Blaine smirked at me. "Once I guessed your plan, it was easy, especially once Quinn picked you up. The doll was a simple conjuring spell. Simple, but hilarious."

The story made me feel nauseated. We hadn't covered our tracks at all. If Blaine had wanted to kill us, we wouldn't have stood a chance. It also begged the question: if Blaine could've handed us over to Maeve at the cabin, why didn't he?

"You turned on Maeve almost instantly. Why should I trust you now? How do I know you won't turn on me when the occasion presents itself? You'll do whatever it takes to get to the top. That's obvious."

"There are no guarantees, but I think the bigger question right now is, can you defeat Maeve without my help? I'm smart enough to know I can't do it without you. The enemy of my enemy is my ally, right?"

I sighed. "We've got a deal."

Chapter Seventeen

"Maybe I should go in first by myself. You know, ease my friends into the idea," I reasoned as Blaine and I stood outside the house, carting a big box of supreme pizza and a bag of soft, puffy beignets. It was blatant bribery—my lame attempt to distract my friends from our new partner. Delicious food had a chance of working on Emily, but I knew it wouldn't work on Quinn.

"Whatever you'd like to do, lover," Blaine laughed. "Either way, I'd imagine they'll be angry, but I'm sure you can make them understand. It's in everyone's best interest that I join the team."

"Blaine, don't call me lover, especially around Quinn. He hates you enough," I grunted. "Secondly… I thought maybe you could lighten the mood in there after I tell them. Maybe you could make everyone more agreeable?"

"Emlyn, I'm shocked," Blaine mocked. "You want me to use my powers on your friends? Wouldn't that be manipulating them? Now, who does that sound like?"

I shot him a dirty look. "Shut up and wait out here."

I took a deep breath and casually walked through the door. Emily, Quinn, Kaiya, and Nia were on the couch, playing some kind of card game. Emily and Quinn greeted me with relieved smiles, Jeb jumped down from the sofa and jetted toward me, but Kaiya and Nia didn't look up. I hoped they felt guilty.

"Hey, guys! Hi buddy," I scratched Jeb behind the ear with my free hand. I looked from Emily to Quinn, noticing they didn't seem mad or upset. I guessed Kaiya didn't mention Blaine. Part of me hoped she'd already told them. It would've made my job easier. "You guys want some pizza?" I asked them.

"Emlyn, finally!" Emily ran over and wrapped me in a hug.

"Is that for me or the pizza?" I laughed.

"You obviously." She laughed too before grabbing the box from my hand. "We were worried."

Quinn smiled at me. "Kaiya told us you were getting the medallion, but it was something you had to do yourself."

"He seems calm now, but you should've seen him when Kaiya came back without you," Emily teased. "This pizza smells so great. I'm gonna have a slice. Anyone else?"

"I didn't like the idea of you out there alone," Quinn protested.

"Kaiya told us you banished Dr. Rufino." Nia smiled. "You must be one bad witch."

"Thanks," I told her awkwardly.

Kaiya didn't waste time with pleasantries. "Is he with you?"

I nodded and intentionally avoided eye contact with Quinn.

"Who is 'he?'" Emily asked as she plopped onto the couch with her slice.

Kaiya eyed me. "Do you want to tell them, Emlyn? Or should I?"

I scowled at her before turning to Quinn and Emily. "Well, we have a new ally."

"That's great!" Emily exclaimed. "We need all the help we can get."

"Right. But you see, the circumstances are a little complicated. It's totally explainable, but it's a unique situation," I was stalling.

"It is another witch?" Quinn asked.

"Obviously he's a witch," Kaiya spat at him. "Another powerless human wouldn't be an ally."

"Kaiya, be nice," Nia scolded.

I ignored the side commentary. "Exactly. He's a witch with a lot of knowledge about the Ainbertachs—the Atlanta headquarters especially. So, he's going to be super valuable when we take down Maeve," I stammered over my words. "What I'm trying to tell you is… and you should keep an open mind…"

"Is he a serial killer?" Emily joked, not really paying attention to me anymore. She took a big bite of pizza instead.

"It's Blaine," Quinn blurted out. His face was suddenly tense and red, his jaw clenched. Emily spit out her pizza in surprise.

"What?" Emily yelled.

I spun around to see Blaine standing behind me in the doorway.

"You remember me then," Blaine smiled. "Good."

Jeb growled in a low, menacing tone at the sound of Blaine's voice. I looked back at Quinn and realized how devastated he must have been. I'd betrayed him once again. Emily looked shocked more than anything. I couldn't tell if she was mad or hurt.

"Before you say or think anything, please let me explain," I urged. "There's a—."

Quinn stood up. "There's nothing you could say. Blaine? Are you kidding?"

"I told you, there's a reason."

"He's got a point, Em. Teaming up with me? What were you thinking?"

I glared at Blaine, who apparently found it amusing to antagonize Quinn. I took a few steps forward, putting more distance between Blaine and me, and I tried to explain. Before I could say anything, Quinn shook his head at me and stormed out of the room.

"Quinn, wait!" I chased after him, but Emily grabbed my shoulder to keep me from following Quinn up the stairs.

"Don't. Emlyn, I think Quinn deserves some time alone to process this," Emily said. "This is a lot to spring on us."

"He didn't give me time to explain," I whimpered.

"I'm not sure we want an explanation."

"But Emily, listen. Blaine's going to help us get rid of Maeve. He's switched sides. He wants her gone as much as we do."

"Why would you ever believe that?" Emily scolded. "Did you forget the passionate make-out session we witnessed when Blaine was freed? How about the excruciating pain he subjected us both to?"

"Sorry about that, by the way," Blaine jetted into the conversation.

"Maybe not the right time, Blaine," Nia commented. "Their auras are all out of whack."

"Of course, my aura is out of whack!" Emily yelled. "Emlyn has teamed up with the evilest person I know. Forget about the times he's tried to kill ALL of us. He's going to be our ally now? How stupid are you, Emlyn?"

"That's our cue to leave these two alone." Nia dragged Kaiya and Blaine away from the confrontation into the kitchen.

Emily scowled at me. "You know what he did to Quinn and to me. He made you fall in love with him and then tried to kill you. What are you doing, Emlyn? How could you do this to us?"

The flood gates opened, and I broke down sobbing. "It's too much, Emily. I'm supposed to be strong and powerful and make these all these important decisions. Everything I do seems to be wrong.

Every choice I make is the wrong one, and I can't hold the world anymore. Emily… I can't carry it."

"Then why do you keep making these dumb decisions? You could've at least talked to us about this first, but you didn't. You came in ready to tell us what to do—again."

"You don't understand. We can't be democracy here. Sometimes I have to make choices because this whole plan depends on me and my magic. If I mess up, everyone dies. We'll never go home. If I can't save Marnie and Marjorie, no one will."

"Okay, so you're the captain, but you should still listen to your teammates. We might be able to help you make those tough decisions. I mean, what are you thinking with this? Do you remember what happened the last time you trusted Blaine?"

"I remember, but Emily—Blaine knows about Marnie," I told her.

"He does?"

I nodded. "Blaine saw through Marjorie's spell."

"Ohmigod. Did Blaine tell Maeve? Is Marnie okay? Did they kill her? What about Marjorie?"

"Blaine said he didn't tell Maeve. I think he's telling the truth."

"We can't know that for sure. What if Blaine killed her?" Emily was freaking out.

"It's not like that. Apparently, Blaine's been following us from the beginning. He's the one who left the Voodoo doll, and he got to Kaiya before we did. I don't think we have a choice but to work with him."

"Of course, he's behind the Voodoo doll. It's just like him to do something so sneaky."

"We should've guessed," I admitted.

"It still doesn't make sense, though. Blaine and Maeve seemed super into each other. Why would he want to hurt her?"

"It's about power. Maeve is standing between Blaine and a shot at the top. If he doesn't get rid of her, Blaine will never ascend the ranks."

"When she's gone, you really think he won't come after you again? You'll be standing in the way too."

"If we stick to Blaine's plan, I might not be. We could get our lives back and drop off the coven's radar. I really think this could work, but we can't do it without him."

Emily paused, bit her lip, and closed her eyes tightly in thought. After a few moments, she met my eyes. "You think this is the right call? Honestly?"

I paused and thought through everything again. "I do."

"Okay, then."

A flush of relief hit me. "Okay? Meaning, you're okay with it?"

"Okay is a strong word," Emily told me. "But if it's the only way, then we carry on."

I hugged her. It was a one-sided hug, but I was so happy to have her on my side. Emily seemed to trust my judgment, which I needed. I just wished I was as confident.

"What are you going to do about Quinn?" Emily wanted to know. "He's not going to come around so easily. He had it the worst last year."

"He's logical, right? He'll have to understand we don't have any other options."

"I think Quinn would rather die than work with Blaine, but I could be wrong."

"No, you're probably right. We might have to do this without Quinn."

"You'd pick Blaine over Quinn?" Emily seemed hurt.

"Again, it's not like that."

"I'm just telling you what he's going to think. Quinn loves you. Put yourself in his shoes. How would you feel?"

"It can't be about that right now. It has to be about the mission—defeating Maeve and rescuing Marnie and Marjorie." Emily nodded. "So, what's the plan, then?"

"Why don't you have Blaine fill you, Nia, and Kaiya in? I need to speak to Quinn." I motioned toward the kitchen.

Emily frowned. "A room full of traitors. You know, I thought Nia was a sweet gal. Now we know they've all been against us. How rude."

"They had their reasons, too. We're all just trying to survive."

"I'll go monitor the possibly evil people. You owe me so big after this is all over. I expect lovely gifts for every holiday, and maybe a few nice dinners."

"It'll happen, I promise." I'd buy her anything she wanted if I could just get us to the "after" part of this plan.

The next step was convincing Quinn to go along with everything. I took the stairs slowly as I scrambled for the right words to use. Everything I tried sounded like an excuse or a cop-out. In my heart, I knew this wasn't forgivable, but Quinn was more of a brain-person than a heart-person. The support Blaine offered was vital to completing our mission. We needed his medallion to take Maeve out. Not to mention, Blaine knew the property and the other witches we'd need to get through. Sure, things were hairy because Blaine had tried to kill all of us in the past, but he was our best chance of success.

With my stomach in my chest and my hands trembling with nerves, I paused at the door to Quinn's room. It reminded me of that night on River Street when I'd met him for dinner. This time there was no sympathetic waitress and no restaurant full of people. It was just Quinn and me.

I knocked gently on the door. "Can I come in?" I waited for a second, but there was no answer. I knocked again. "Quinn, I understand you don't want to talk to me, and I'm deserving of the silent treatment. It's not fair for me to put you in this position, but we need to settle this now. We've only got today to prepare. We leave for Atlanta tomorrow. Believe me, I want you to have all the time you need to process this, but we don't have that luxury right now."

Silence.

As I turned to leave, the door creaked open a bit. Quinn left a crack of space before he swiveled back into the room without making eye contact. I walked in as he took a seat facing away from me on the navy-blue bedspread.

"Quinn—?" I started.

"What do you want?"

"I know you're upset with me." He snorted at the statement but didn't respond.

I took a couple steps closer. "I know you feel betrayed, and you think I'm making a huge mistake."

"I do."

"There's so much more to the story, Quinn. If you would just listen, you might realize I've thought this through."

Quinn laughed angrily and stood up to face me. "You've got to be kidding me, Emlyn. You've thought this through? How—," he shook his head, stopping himself from completing the sentence. His face was flushed red with frustration, and his jaw locked.

"I told you, Blaine has insider information. We can't get in touch with Marnie or Marjorie, so we need his help."

"You're blind, you know that?"

"Please just sit down, and I'll explain everything."

"You know what? It doesn't matter. You've made it clear that you're in charge here. No one else's opinion is worth a thing."

"That's not what I'm saying."

"Save it, Emlyn. You can have Emily relay my orders once you assign me duties. I'll do whatever I need to do to get out of here."

"I'm sorry," I told him, trying to hold back my emotions. "I didn't mean to get you involved in this again."

"I got myself into this mess. I chose to be here. If I recall, you told me to stay away. At the time, I didn't realize it was because you're reuniting with your old boyfriend."

"Quinn, no. It's not—."

"You're wasting time now. You'd better go." Quinn pointed toward the door.

I nodded in agreement. Quinn was right. I needed to get back to work, and like I told Emily, my feelings for Quinn couldn't affect the plan. I wasn't choosing Blaine over Quinn. I was choosing the lives of everyone I loved over Quinn's hatred of Blaine. I hoped Quinn could come to see that.

I took a moment to quietly sob in my room and then wiped the mascara streaks from below my eyes and headed back down to the kitchen.

"Once we're all together, we'll combine our powers to banish Maeve to another dimension," Blaine announced. I had walked in at the end of the conversation. Now that we were moving forward, I was eager to see how everyone else was feeling about the plan.

"Ballsy scheme, Celtic witch," Kaiya exclaimed when she saw me walk in. "You really think you can pull that off? Even with Blaine, you're still banking on an old lady and three non-magic humans to back you up."

"It'll be tough, yes, but it's the best plan we have," I admitted. I realized I was using a soft, weak voice. I needed to sound more confident.

"Your coven will need to help," Blaine told her. "We'll need a stock of both offensive and defensive potions to thin out the Ainbertach witches. There are about 15 who live on the property, and another 20 witches live in condos and apartments close by. It's best we do this quietly," Blaine explained.

"Where is this place?" I asked.

"It's the north side of Atlanta, and the place is a fortress. It's four and a half acres of luxury and modern technology. There's a car vault, an art museum, a pool and spa, a gun range, a heavy-duty vault, three kitchens, two elevators, a bowling alley and game room, a wine cellar, and a command center,"

"Wait, what? Can I live there?" Emily blurted out.

"Hush!" Kaiya screeched.

"Rude," Emily told her.

"We can slowly clear the perimeter," I said. "Blaine will provide a map of all the security posts."

"You, Emily, and Quinn are going to get through all those witches?" Nia asked, seeming worried.

"Unless you have some witches who'd like to join us?" I hoped.

"I wouldn't put my people in danger like that," Kaiya scoffed. "Right, Nia?"

"I'm sure if you plan well enough, Emily and Quinn will be alright," Nia assured me. "The element of surprise is often stronger than magic."

"Compared to what we've been through in the past, this plan seems like cake," Emily laughed. "A few potions to knock out the minions, and then Emlyn and Blaine handle the rest. What's difficult about that?"

Emily was overcompensating.

I took a breath and found my confidence. "It won't be easy, but I think it's the very best plan we could have."

"So, we're taking on the Ainbertach Coven in a day and a half," Emily mused before biting her lower lip.

"The Atlanta branch at least," Blaine added.

Kaiya shook her head at the three of us. "You guys are crazy!"

"But, we'll help with all the spells you might need," Nia announced, putting her arm around Kaiya. "Right, babe?"

"Yeah, we got you."

"Emily and Quinn will work with you tomorrow," Blaine told them, before looking to me. "Is your guy going to be good with that?"

He'll do what needs to be done," I nodded.

"Kaiya, your family's gravesite is in a cemetery near Iberville, right?" Blaine confirmed.

Kaiya nodded.

"Emlyn and I will head there later this afternoon to bless this amulet properly to protect against Maeve. I suggest everyone takes a few hours of rest before we reconvene."

"Does everyone understand their role?" I asked. "Everything needs to be ready by tomorrow morning. Maeve is going down."

Chapter Eighteen

Once again, I found myself headed toward a cemetery.

It was a breezy afternoon in New Orleans, and the city was bustling with activity. Sunday brunch was being enjoyed in the balcony cafes above Blaine and me as we walked. I envied them as they drank orange juice from champagne flutes and munched on bananas foster French toast. I'd scarfed down a protein bar after a short few hours of sleep, and then we were off, heading to find Azaria's gravesite outside the French Quarter. Her burial site was the only place we could revise the blessing on Blaine's medallion, according to Kaiya.

The streets leading out of the French Quarter were quieter than Bourbon, allowing me time to think. My mind buzzed with questions and anxiety. I thought about the upcoming fight with Maeve, wondering how we'd defeat her. The plan seemed rock solid, but I knew things never went according to plan. I also agonized over Blaine's real intentions, especially after my uneasy, dream-filled nap. I was taken back to my high school once again, but this time Maeve and Blaine were trying to kill me. Blaine had used his pain ability to torture me as Maeve drowned Quinn.

"What's in that potion you take?" I broke the silence.

Blaine chuckled. "That's specific."

"You know, the one that turns your empath abilities into torture."

"Oh, that potion."

I waited for a moment, but Blaine didn't say anything else.

"Well?" I asked him as we crossed out of the French Quarter and across an eight-lane street. A large white church was situated on the corner of the road, featuring an ornate clock tower.

"Basic things: the bark of an oak tree, acorn, dried thistle, bay leaf, cedarwood, mullein flower, Tonka bean, and cinnamon."

"That's not it. All last year, I tried to recreate a version of it. I've tried all combinations of those ingredients. I added mint leaf for potency, and when that didn't work, I went with goldenseal root for extra strength. Nothing I've done can replicate the potion Maeve made."

Blaine smiled to himself. "Frustrating, isn't it?"

"So, there is more? What is it?"

Blaine grinned, "There's a secret ingredient that people would have a hard time obtaining. It's nearly impossible."

"Come on, Blaine. I thought we were partners? Don't you think that potion would help us in our fight? We could both take it. I'm not sure what it would do to my powers, but we know it makes you more powerful. It's worth a shot, isn't it?"

He was silent for a moment. "It requires a pure lifeline to Fáelán Ainbertach—a link to our original leader."

"A lifeline? You mean...?" I frowned.

"Blood. For the potion to work, we need a drop of Maeve's blood."

"That's so gross! You drank her blood? What are you, a vampire?"

"Please. Vampires don't exist, Emlyn. It's not that bad, either. You barely taste it mixed with all the other ingredients. I'll tell you, the mullein flowers taste the worst."

"That's sick."

"The powers it gives me are sick. The coppery taste of blood is the price. Admit it. If I hadn't slipped up and brought Quinn to the school, I would've beaten you. It was my pride that did me in. Very Odysseus of me."

"First of all, don't compare yourself to a Greek hero. He's much cooler than you. Second, that's cheating! You had the medallion and some super potion. Witch to witch, I win every time." I was slightly joking with him, but the more substantial part of me wanted Blaine to understand that I was stronger than he was. It was a power play.

"Wit often wins a battle, Emlyn. Strength alone isn't enough. Remember that."

Another eight-lane road stood between us and the cemetery across the street. We let the conversation drop as we waited for the light at the crosswalk to change. From here, I could see the distressed white wall that surrounded the cemetery and the impressive tombs reaching toward the sky. The gray marble and stone eerily guarded the bodies and decay beneath.

"You know, you never asked about it," Blaine said as we continued forward.

"Asked about what?"

"About me being trapped in the trophy."

"I guess I figured you wouldn't want to talk about it. Plus, I'm not sure I want to know. If I'm honest, I really hoped you were aware of everything. I wanted it to be a torturous existence after everything you put me through. The betrayals, the manipulation, the—"

"I get it. Jeez, there might be a little dark magic in there, Em. It wasn't that bad, actually."

"That's disappointing."

He ignored me. "At first, I was aware of everything. Quinn tricked me, and I saw the flash of green from your spell. When I woke up, everything around me looked giant. I knew the spell you used. It wasn't hard to figure out what had happened."

"Thanks for teaching me that spell, by the way."

Blaine tensed his jaw and nodded. "After a while, everything faded. It was like being in a deep, dreamless sleep. Time didn't matter. When Maeve broke me out, it was like our fight had just happened."

"So it wasn't torture. It makes sense. Our magic is based on the principle of 'Harm None.' Why wouldn't my magic create comfort in isolation?"

"That's what I'm worried about," Blaine admitted. "It won't be that way for Maeve."

"Are you feeling guilty?" I was shocked. "Do you not want to move forward with the plan?"

Blaine shook his head. "No. I'm just concerned about you."

"Me?" I was confused.

Blaine hesitated, "You're just such a goody-two-shoes. I hope you have what it takes to get the job done. I know Maeve, and she won't go down without a fight. Things could get complicated."

I felt offended. "I can handle it."

"Good." Blaine left it at that. We'd arrived.

It surprised me how different this cemetery was from the ones I was used to in Savannah. Historic homes and beautiful oak trees surrounded the one closest to my childhood home in the historic district. The police station and a church were on one side. There was a playground on the other, which was both creepy and inviting. The entrance was an ornate arch of stone with a large metal eagle on top, funded by the Daughters of the American Revolution.

The exterior of this cemetery wasn't grand like that. It was situated on a wide, busy street with run-down buildings on either side.

To our left, I noticed a semi-dilapidated structure with boarded-up and smashed windows. A chain-link fence protected the property from kids looking for mischief and squatters. Some modern-looking apartments were down the street a bit, but the builders clearly wanted to keep their distance from the graves.

Looks were deceptive here, though, as the grounds were immaculate. There weren't grave markers or statues like I was used to seeing. Many of the tombstones in Savannah's historic district had been damaged when Federal troops in the Civil War took up camp in the Colonial Park Cemetery. Some larger headstones and tombs remained, but the exterior walls of the cemetery were filled with misplaced gravestones. The soldiers had also changed dates and names on some graves.

I couldn't see headstones and burial plots from our position, but I could see large, house-shaped structures. Some reached toward the sky, displaying impressive white and black marble. They were tall and elegant—unique. I was a little excited to see them from the inside as we approached the metal gate.

"This one is locked," I told Blaine. "I think the main entrance is on the other side."

"It is," he said flatly, moving past me to get a closer look.

"So, let's head that way."

"If we go to the main entrance, they'll know we're inside."

"So? It's a tourist location. We'll pay the fee and head back to the right spot."

"We need some privacy. I think slipping in unseen is a better option," Blaine smiled and pulled a pointed tool from his pocket. "Cover me."

I frowned. "Woah. I'm not breaking into the cemetery!"

"Come on, goody-good. I thought you were willing to do whatever it takes."

"I am. This just isn't necessary. There's an entrance right over there."

"Just give me a minute."

I wasn't good at rule-breaking. As a child, I went through this phase where I confessed every little wrong-doing to my mother and father. If I ate a cookie when they told me not to, I'd have to admit what happened or I wouldn't be able to sleep. It was that bad. So, breaking into a cemetery made me feel like I was about to pass out. I scanned our run-down surroundings, searching for police officers or do-gooders who might report us.

"Relax, we're in," Blaine chuckled. "After you, lover."

I checked once again to be sure we were clear. Then I reluctantly slipped past the iron bars into the cemetery. Immediately, I was face-to-face with a giant square structure that was probably 15 feet tall. There were several rows of large rectangular boxes—house-shaped tombs—in lines around us with a small narrow path weaving through them.

"Come on, Azaria is this way," Blaine directed, seemingly unimpressed by the structures.

"Do you know why all the headstones are like this?"

"They aren't headstones. They're mausoleums."

"So no burials? Even the smaller ones are tombs?"

"Yup. New Orleans is below sea level, so instead of burying the dead where they can be washed to the surface during a flood, the dead are above ground, encased in these vaults."

"That's kind of creepy."

"Says the girl from Savannah. Haven't friends of yours found human remains in their basements?"

"Fair enough. I guess it's just weird to think about. It's beautiful, though."

Blaine was leading the way, so I didn't pay much attention to where we were going apart from the scenery. The marble tombs were hauntingly beautiful, and the mighty were mixed among the humble, which I thought was very cool. There were tall pillars decorated with carved angels and crosses, and there were also simple boxes constructed of brick. Each resting place seemed to have its own personality, as if to represent the person within.

"Here we are," Blaine announced. We came to a row of six structures. Two were comprised of brick and surrounded by iron gates and crosses. The other four were grey and white. I couldn't tell what material they were made from, but I guessed concrete and stone.

"This is where Azaria is?" I asked him.

"Well, they're family tombs, so it's not just Azariah. The Imamu structure is the third one down, with the two white vases on either side," Blaine said.

I took a deep breath. "Are you ready?"

Blaine nodded. He took the pack off his back and pulled a cream-colored altar cloth from it, which he laid down on the space directly in front of the Imamu tomb. Then he placed a golden bowl in the center to create an altar for our spell-casting.

"Here are the elemental candles and gemstones." Blaine handed me two plastic bags. "I think you should handle the air element during the spell because you'll be the person wearing the medallion."

"I'll take water, too. You light the candles for fire and earth."

Blaine nodded in agreement. The spell was rather simple. A colored candle, a directional position on our altar, and a gemstone represented each element. Together, Blaine and I would cleanse the previous energy from the amulet and then assign it new power.

We each took a seat, cross-legged, on opposite sides of the cloth. I took a deep breath as I grabbed Blaine's hands. "You ready?"

"You first, love."

"What in the world? What kind of heebie jeebie nonsense are you doing in my cemetery!?" A large, dark-skinned woman with her hair slicked back into a severe bun broke Blaine and me from our concentration. She was wearing a navy uniform, and must have been an authority figure. She worked here in the cemetery, and I was breaking the rules.

She looked as dumbfounded as I felt. Panic hit me, and I immediately scolded myself for listening to Blaine. He was the villain. Deciding whether or not to sneak into a cemetery was a choice I should have made myself.

"Get a grip," Blaine muttered. Instantly, relief rolled over my body as Blaine used his powers on me. He pulled himself up from the ground, brushed himself off, and took a few paces closer to the woman.

"Hello ma'am, how are you doing today?" Blaine reached his hand out to shake hers.

"Oh no, don't you play that with me. You're doing some kind of Voodoo magic stuff here. I'm not buying it! Get your stuff and get out. This is a historic site. It's not made for your satanic rituals!"

"You know, you're absolutely right. I'm sorry, we shouldn't be here. By the way, I'm Blaine," he smiled at her. Her stiff position shifted. Her arms uncrossed, and she shook Blaine's hand.

"Loraine," she grinned back. Her tone was suddenly soft. I'd forgotten how manipulative Blaine could be. It made me feel a little better about being duped by him last year. It also made me feel sick. I couldn't let my guard down around Blaine, no matter how kind he acted.

"Loraine? That's a beautiful name, and what a beautiful historic site this is. Are you with the historical society? I've thought about joining myself. There's so much history in this city."

Loraine giggled. "You should. It's a wonderful way to spend your time."

"I will definitely look into it," Blaine continued. He looked back at me, winked, and met Loraine's eyes again. "I'll tell my friend to pack our things. I really am so sorry we intruded. We didn't mean any harm."

"Well, I supposed I could let you stay. Just this once," Loraine gushed. "One history lover to another."

I could've face-palmed right there. It was sickening to watch.

"Would you really do that for me? It would mean so much!"

"Sure I will," she cooed back.

"I hate to ask because you've already been so kind, but do you think you could do us a tiny favor? I'd really owe you."

"I'd be happy to help any way I can."

"Could you make sure no one disturbs my friend and me for the next 30 minutes or so?"

"Well, I'm really not supposed to—," Loraine started.

"Please, Loraine. Just between us?"

Loraine smiled at Blaine, seemingly melting in her own skin at his charm. "Alright," she said. "But I can only get you 20 minutes. A tour group is scheduled to come through, and they get anxious if we keep them waiting."

"You're a doll, Loraine. I owe you."

"Stop by on your way out now, hun," Loraine told him.

He winked at her and watched her walk away. As soon as she disappeared behind some tombs, Blaine rushed back to me.

"We've only got a few minutes to get this done, so let's hurry," Blaine urged.

"That was gross," I told him. "It was a complete invasion of that woman's feelings. Did you make her love you? Because that's what it looked like."

"No. I diminished her hostility and gave her a more light-hearted demeanor."

"You practically charmed the pants off her. That's not right."

"Jealous much?" Blaine shot me a charming side smile.

"Hardly! I just think what you did was wrong."

"It worked, didn't it? And I only made her feel a slight attraction toward me. It was barely anything."

"I could've frozen her or something!"

"Look, you didn't step up. You were the one who froze. Now, we can argue about this for 20 minutes or we can cast this spell. What do you want to do?"

I took another deep breath to ground myself and cracked my neck on both sides. "Okay, you're right. Let's get this over with. Do you want to start?"

Blaine nodded.

"We call on the power of Azariah Imamu," Blaine began. "At the site of your human remains, we ask you to aid us as we cleanse a gift of your making from powers old to powers new."

"Encased in salt, we hope to break your spell," I chanted as Blaine held up a mason jar between us. Inside was the medallion, surrounded entirely with pink Himalayan salt. Blaine pulled the amulet out of the salt by its chain, slowly poured about a cup of salt into the golden bowl, and then placed the medallion on top.

I reached into one of the white vases flanking the Imamu tomb and grabbed a fist full of dirt and debris. I sprinkled the greyish brown detritus over the medallion.

"At the site of your grave, we break your spell," Blaine chanted before nodding for me to continue. It was time to invoke the elements, the base of Maeve's power.

"We call upon the power of the elements to cast this new spell," I chanted.

"A green candle is lit in the north," Blaine used a match to ignite his candle, "and fluorite represents the magic of the earth."

"A blue candle is lit in the west, and aquamarine represents the power of water," I followed his pace.

"A red candle is lit the south, and red jasper represents the power of fire."

"And finally, our chosen power, we light a yellow candle in the east and present you with celestite to represent air. It is the power of air we seek protection from," I cast. I used a match to burn the end of a common sage bundle. Once there was enough smoke, I pulled the medallion from the golden bowl and bathed every inch in smoke before placing it back in the mason jar.

"With our wish granted, we shall pierce the wind of protection created through the power of air," Blaine took the blue celestite crystal and tossed it into the golden bowl. I finished the spell by pouring the melted yellow wax over the top.

With Blaine's hands in my own, we both cast in unison, "May the wearer of this pendant break the barrier of air."

Chapter Nineteen

"Three dozen vials each of 'Perplexity & Puzzlement,' 'Fire Power,' and 'Flu-Like Symptoms' were all created following Emlyn's recipe. Another four dozen vials were filled with essence of poppy. We've crafted six protection pouches, ten concealment jars, and five of what we've named 'You Won't Feel a Thing,'" Kaiya explained. "Blaine told us there are 35 possible witches you'll be facing. This should be enough fire-power."

"Well, as long as you knock out some of the guards without alerting the others to your location," Nia pointed out.

"We're locked and loaded!" Emily exclaimed. "And of course, yours truly helped make all of them."

Kaiya glared at her. "You helped?" We were all standing in the condo's kitchen, gathered around the island. Emily was next to me, and Kaiya was on the opposite side.

"Well, I got the ingredients ready for you and opened the vials, didn't I?"

I ignored the squabble. "What about the power-stripping potions?"

"Nia worked on those." Kaiya pointed toward the kitchen table where Nia was seated across from Quinn. She had a large wooden crate sitting in front of her. Nia motioned to it and flashed a smile and thumbs up. Quinn, on the other hand, wouldn't meet my gaze.

"These basic ones are done. I recommend the four of us pooling our magic on a few of the vials for meant for Maeve. You'll need some extra strength for her."

I shook my head. "I have the potions for Maeve. Marjorie, Marnie, and I made them. They'll pack a punch."

Blaine shot Kaiya a doubtful look. "Are you sure, Emlyn?" he confirmed. "It might be good to have everyone do this together."

I shook my head. "This is Celtic magic. I trust it to save Marjorie and Marnie."

"Go with your gut. I like it. If that's the case, you've got all you need," Nia smiled.

"Excellent work, you guys," I scanned the room, trying to give everyone individual attention. "I really appreciate all the help. I couldn't have done this without you."

"We're happy to do it," Nia told me. "Taking on the big dogs is good for all of us in the long run."

"If she wins. I still think you're crazy," Kaiya blurted out.

"I know, Kaiya," I sighed.

"So, we're ready?" Blaine confirmed.

We all nodded in agreement.

"In that case, it's time for me to get back to Maeve. I've got preparations of my own to do in Atlanta." Blaine turned his attention to me almost apologetically. "Walk me out, Emlyn?"

I nodded again.

"Take care of yourself, Blaine," Kaiya said. "I don't want to hear you died."

"You could always help," Blaine winked at her.

"You know she won't do that," Nia laughed, moving to Kaiya's side and wrapping her arm around her girlfriend's waist before waving Blaine away with her other arm.

"See ya, Blaine. I'd say it's been nice, but you know..." Emily commented. She'd been speaking to him like that at every opportunity. I'm sure Blaine found it more amusing than offensive. I loved Emily all the more for it.

"See you soon," Blaine responded. He exited the kitchen with me trailing behind him. Quinn's eyes were on me as I left, practically burning into my back. Ever since we returned from the cemetery, he'd refused to make eye contact with me. He was good at shooting dirty looks, though. Honestly, I couldn't blame him. Being in the same room with Blaine was uncomfortable for me. I imagined it was especially bad for Quinn.

Blaine opened the front door and took a step outside, breathing in the crisp fall air. I couldn't believe it was November. We should've been studying for finals or dreaming of turkey dinner. Instead, I was standing on the front porch of an Airbnb with Blaine, my sworn enemy.

"You ready for this, lover?" Blaine asked.

I'd never get used to him calling me that. There were too many awful memories. Still, it didn't seem like Blaine would stop.

"Ready as I'll ever be. I'm nervous," I admitted.

"You'll be okay. You're strong."

"It's not me I'm worried about. None of my friends should be in this position. Maeve is ridiculously powerful—stronger than I am. I'm setting everyone I love up for failure. Everything could go wrong. What if—."

"We don't have a choice here, Emlyn. I don't mean to remind you of the obvious, but you're a target to the coven. That means everyone here is a target. You're doing what you must to survive. This is war. There might be casualties. Heck, I might not even make it," he joked.

I could tell he was trying to lighten the mood, but, for some reason, even the thought of Blaine dying was challenging to think about. There were so many unknowns wrapped into this as well. I didn't tell Blaine about the dream I had with Emily and me in the wine cellar.

"The estate is on the north side of Atlanta. You can't miss it. Remember, the place is a fortress—four and a half acres," Blaine illustrated with his hands. "Stay on your game."

I nodded. "I'll study the floor plan of the estate. You'll find out which witches are on duty. Then we'll come in fast and quiet. Just be in position."

"Don't you trust me?" Blaine shot me a charming sidelong smile, and I felt a twinge of attraction. I brushed it off, hoping it was Blaine messing with my emotions.

"I'll let you know after this fight."

"I probably deserve that," Blaine smirked. "Hey, I've got one more thing for you. You might need it." Blaine handed me a familiar red vial.

"Gross," I muttered.

"Just take it," Blaine rolled his eyes. "You might need it."

The thought of drinking Maeve's blood was sickening. Still, I was curious. "What would it do to my powers?"

"It affects everyone differently, lover. All I know is it will magnify your abilities."

"I don't want it."

"Emlyn, don't be stubborn." He grabbed my hand and closed it around the vial. "Consider it, at least. That vial could mean the difference between life and death."

I examined it in my hand. Amplifying my powers was alluring, but I didn't think it was a good idea. "I think you should keep it. Your powers benefit from it more than mine."

"You mean because I deal in emotions, not action? Thanks, lover. I have a few more stashed away, so don't worry about it."

"Fine." I shoved the potion in my pocket.

"Let's both make it out of this alive," Blaine nodded at me, and with that, he disappeared down the alley. It was weird how his absence was both comforting and nerve-wracking. I knew having him around made Quinn and Emily feel stressed. They didn't trust him, and I knew I shouldn't either. Still, he knew a substantial amount more about magic than I did. If I couldn't have Marjorie with me, Blaine was an oddly good ally to have—as long as he wasn't plotting against us secretly.

The thought of what tomorrow would bring was uncomfortable. I held up Blaine's potion and hoped the red color wasn't an ominous sign about what awaited us. If everything went according to plan, there wouldn't be bloodshed.

"Hey, girl!" a familiar, cheery voice rang out.

"Jordan?" I was surprised but thrilled to see the lanky hippie strutting up to our townhouse. A lollipop hung from his mouth, and he was sporting a different tie-dyed shirt, representing another jam band. "Kaiya and Nia are inside. Are you looking for them?"

"Nah, girl. I'm here to join the fight."

Chapter Twenty

The addition of Jordan to our team increased our odds slightly. We were seven people—four of us witches—against Maeve's army of 35. All of Maeve's soldiers were magical. Despite the overwhelming odds and Kaiya's objections, Jordan was determined to help. Jordan claimed that he owed me a debt from our experience with Dr. Rufino. Jordan also didn't agree with the way things went down with Blaine and Kaiya. I didn't know Jordan particularly well, but he seemed like a good-natured person—fair and honest. I liked him, which also made me feel guilty for roping him into this fight. To Jordan's point, though, I couldn't deny the help of another magical ally.

Jordan's ability was the power of deflection. It'd be handy against Maeve's fireballs, for sure. Hers wasn't the only power we were up against, though. Blaine described a mansion full of incredible abilities. A few of our opponents' skills were not-so-impressive, but we'd know more once we arrived.

"I feel too poor to even drive through this place. It's swanky," Emily mused as we passed through a hilly area called Westminster. "I bet you wish you could've gone to this high school, Quinn. Look at the size of that football stadium."

Quinn nodded. "This is a ritzy town, for sure."

It was ironic coming from Quinn. He grew up on the most beautiful street in the historic district of Savannah. The roads weren't made of asphalt; instead they were paved with brick. The houses were massive, with ornate facades and well-maintained landscaping. It surprised me Quinn hadn't attended a private school like the one to our left. It was impressive, with a vast baseball field next to the football stadium and tennis courts on our right. The message I was getting from this area was that the Ainbertachs had money as well as power and connections.

"I've got a theory about private schools, ya know," Jordan kicked in. "It's all a conspiracy. I won't get into it now because we've gotta stay focused, but remind me next time we're hanging out."

"You got it," I told him. I was still unsure there would be a next time. I enjoyed Jordan's enthusiasm, though.

"So, are we close to the spot?" Jordan wanted to know. "Nia's car isn't super roomy. Not that I'm complaining. I could just use a leg stretch."

We had—temporarily—traded Quinn's Silverado for something less noticeable. Nia had kindly offered her four-door Honda Civic. Quinn was driving with Emily riding shotgun, which left Jordan and me in the back. It wasn't uncomfortable for me, but Jordan was also a full foot taller than I was. Luckily, we weren't traveling with Jeb and Tephi. They were staying with Nia until we could retrieve them. I'd left my dad's phone number with her, in case we didn't come back.

"You're taking the next turn at Ridgewood," Emily told Quinn. "We'll follow that up to—up to a road that starts with a 'G' that I can't pronounce. Follow that to the Chattahoochee River."

"All the way to the river?" I asked. "That doesn't seem right."

"Okay, so the road ends before the river," Emily admitted. "I'm sure there's a house with access to the river for swimming or fishing or other outdoorsy stuff."

"Once we park, the hiking starts, right?" Jordan cheered. His excitement was pleasant distraction from my anxiety.

"Do you do much hiking?" Quinn asked.

"Not really, but you see a lot of tents where I live. I just enjoy being outside," Jordan smiled.

"We're not camping out, remember. We're just waiting for dark," I announced.

"Still, we'll get a little time under the stars."

"I like this guy," Emily exclaimed. "You put a positive twist on everything."

"Life's too short, girl," Jordan told her.

Quinn wasn't into the positivity. His tone was flat, "We're getting close. Keep your eyes open for a place to ditch the car."

"Where would one ditch a car?" Emily asked.

I wasn't sure either. We zoomed by several streets that shot off from the main road. The problem was, we had no way of knowing if they were utility lanes or if they were the driveways for eccentric billionaires. I didn't want to risk it in case of police patrolling the neighborhood.

Some shorter driveways revealed luxurious homes with swimming pools, tennis courts, hedge mazes, or massive fountains out front. I wondered how people could afford to live like this.

"Can you believe this place? I thought Savannah had some expensive houses, but this takes the cake. Who do I have to marry to live here?" Emily buzzed.

"A movie star," I muttered.

"I'm not much into politics," Emily didn't miss a beat.

"Hey, stop!" Jordan blurted out. "There it is."

I scanned the surrounding area, looking for the spot Jordan identified. I didn't see one. "Where?" I asked him.

"Right next to us on the right."

"There's no road there," Quinn objected.

"Nah, but look at how the trees are parted ever so nicely to one side. You pull in that way, and the trees on the other side will hide the car."

"Ummm," Emily said doubtfully. I agreed with her. I wasn't sure we could angle the car down such a steep incline without flipping it.

"I'm serious! It'll work. You guys haven't spent much time hiding cars in the woods, have you?"

"It's not one of my hobbies," Emily scoffed.

"Quinn, do you think you can get over there? Jordan is right. It'll work if we can get down there safely," I told him.

"One way to find out," he told me.

About a minute later, Quinn was maneuvering the car down the hill. His head was craned out of the window, ensuring we didn't damage Nia's car. Once he got down there, it seemed surprisingly easy to maneuver through the opening in the trees.

"Make sure you get as close to that clump of trees as possible. They'll shield," Jordan instructed.

Quinn nodded and did as he was told. Taking orders seemed to be Quinn's new normal. Even with Blaine gone, Quinn sulked. He didn't make eye contact with me or acknowledge me much. Emily was the one to fill Quinn in on the plans. I knew if all of us made it through this fight, Quinn and I would return to our non-speaking relationship.

"Leave the keys somewhere easy to find. Don't risk taking and losing them somewhere on the property," I told Quinn. "If things take a turn for the worse, you guys get out of here."

They all nodded.

"Don't worry, girl. We got this," Jordan assured me.

"Yeah! We'll be fine," Emily smiled back at me.

"Come on. Let's load up and head out," I ordered, feeling like a general. I hated having to play war rather than a best friend. It felt cold and cut off, but it was a coping mechanism. Now wasn't the time to be emotional. There was a chance we'd lose someone. I hoped if it came to that, I'd have the opportunity to trade my life for those of my friends.

The Ainbertach estate was about a mile away, nestled deep in the woods perfectly diagonal from our current position. The trek there wouldn't take us long, but we wouldn't attack right away. It was about 5 p.m. now, which meant we'd make it to the checkpoint by 5:30 p.m. Then we'd wait until nightfall. According to Blaine, most of the witches who didn't live on campus would be gone for the day by then. Our odds of success increased substantially without those extra bodies. So, our time of attack was 8 p.m., when we had the cover of darkness on our side.

"Everybody got their hiking boots ready? Time to get our steps in," Emily chirped. I wondered how much of her enthusiasm was due to nerves. I envied her, though, even if it was fake. My body was practically vibrating with anxiety.

"Everyone grab a protein bar and water bottle before we head out. We need to keep our energy up. Let's also take this hike easy; it isn't a race. There's no rush to get to the checkpoint," I reminded my comrades. I didn't want them to tire themselves out. It was easy to burn energy in a situation like this.

"Ma'am, yes, ma'am," Emily joked again. "Lead the way, Em."

I hoisted my messenger bag over my shoulder and headed into the woods. The sun was low in the sky, making the already-cold temperatures feel freezing. I didn't have much reference for what witches wore in battle aside from *Charmed* and *Buffy*. Those characters always wore cute outfits and shoes. With my clumsiness, I knew heeled boots weren't an option. Instead, I elected to wear long black yoga pants, a burnt-orange knit sweater under a larger leather jacket, and black combat boots. Emily was dressed similarly but with tennis shoes instead of boots.

I envied the boys. They wore jeans, which were likely warmer than our thin work-out pants. I'd eliminated jeans as an option, thinking they weren't flexible enough for kicking and punching.

However, if this fight came down to physical violence, I was a goner anyway.

The leaves crunched under our shoes as we descended further into the forest. Quinn and I were leading the pack, with Emily and Jordan trailing behind us. They were chatting it up as if we weren't heading toward a fight, swapping New Orleans stories.

"Favorite restaurant in NOLA?" Emily quizzed Jordan behind us.

"Donut sliders at District," Jordan's voice boomed. "It's the best thing I've ever tasted. Crave it all the time."

"You're speaking my language." I could practically hear Emily drooling.

"Next time you come to visit, I'll take you out to all my favorite foodie spots, girl. We'll eat our way through the city."

Emily cheered, and I did my best to tune them out. I quickened my speed to put a little more distance between the chatting and me.

"Jealous?" Quinn suddenly appeared right next to me. His smile and eye contact were surprising. I almost did a double-take to make sure he was talking to me.

"So, you're speaking to me again?" I avoided his accusation.

"Maybe," he smirked.

"Better than nothing, I guess. And yes. Emily and Jordan are just so easy-going right now. My mind is racing. I wonder if they're even taking this seriously."

"I know what you mean. I don't know how they're so calm. I've played in big games—championships and what not—but it's never felt like this."

"Well, this is life-or-death, and that was just interscholastic football."

"Life-or-death is so final, isn't it?"

I nodded. "We've been here before, though. We made it through."

"I threw a science experiment at Blaine's head. It wasn't exactly strategic. I'm honestly feeling worthless here. Did you hear the powers Blaine was describing? Telepathy, conjuring, necromancy, shape-shifting… they all sound intense. What's adaptation? Is someone going to evolve in front of us?"

I couldn't imagine how much scarier this was for Quinn and Emily. Other than the potions we made for them, they didn't have much in the way of defense.

"I think adaptation means that spells wear off more quickly than they normally would." I thought of Daryl back at Henrietta's house. "If it's the witch I think it is, he'll be difficult to deal with."

"I'm so out of my league."

"It's going to be okay," I lied. "You guys aren't going into the thick of it. You'll help us thin out the herd, and then you'll go back to the checkpoint."

"You really think this is going down the way we planned? No tricks from Blaine?"

"Yes." It was another lie.

"I don't see how you're trusting him again, Emlyn. After everything he did. Are you thinking this through properly?" Quinn's voice was still calm, but I knew there was anger behind his words.

"I'm trusting him because we must. We don't have another choice."

"Are you sure that's all?"

"What are you implying?" I wasn't controlling the tension in my voice anymore. Quinn's accusations were peeving me off, and I didn't like where this conversation was heading.

"Was it real a year ago between you and Blaine? Are you in love with him?"

I stopped dead in my tracks. "Are you kidding me?" My voice was louder than I intended, interrupting Jordan and Emily's conversation. They stared at us. I didn't care if I was causing an awkward scene, but Quinn did. He motioned with wide eyes that we should continue walking. Emily and Jordan must have realized it was smart to stay out of it, because they returned to their own conversation.

"Did you really just ask that?" The heat radiated from my face as we trekked on.

"Well, Emlyn, we never talked about it," Quinn admitted. "Maybe because I didn't want to know. You dumped me for him, didn't you? So, some of that must've been real."

"I didn't dump you for him," I corrected. "I thought you were an evil, murderous witch."

"Okay, but even before that, you were pulling away."

"I was not."

"Just be straight with me, Emlyn."

"Yes, I had feelings for him," I sighed, "but it all flew out the window when I realized what he was. Then all those feelings were replaced by guilt and shame. That's no secret, and I'm sure I've told you all of this before. You also know that Blaine can control emotions."

"So, there's no way to know if those feelings were real or not?" Quinn asked.

"Correct."

"It just feels like you were quick to trust him. Maybe there are some residual feelings left."

I rolled my eyes. "You're incredible. I'm trying to make decisions that will keep us alive. They have nothing to do with my emotions."

"I wouldn't be so sure."

"Let's see you make all these choices."

"I think I'd make different ones."

"How about we go back to not speaking?"

"Fine by me."

Quinn slowed his pace, falling back to the rear of the pack. I was fuming mad, which was not the preferred state of mind to be in before a fight. For someone who didn't want to work with evil witches, Quinn sure was doing a bang-up job of helping them. I was left questioning my own decisions. Maybe it was stupid to partner with Blaine. There was a chance we were all stepping into a trap. The thoughts rolled around in my head.

The final quarter-mile of our hike was a blur. We were heading toward a pin-drop Blaine had sent me—a random spot in the middle of the woods. It was close enough to see the property but still far enough away that we'd be safe from unwanted eyes. From the higher elevation, I could see a distinct line that'd been dug out, surrounding the coven's land like a winding snake. Blaine told me it was really a wall of magic—a secret alarm system. Blaine also said he'd deactivate it by the time we arrived.

"We're almost there, everyone. It's just at the bottom of this hill ahead. See where the tree line stops and then starts back up again? Be alert," I warned everyone.

"Isn't this supposed to be our safe spot?" Emily asked.

"According to *Blaine*," Quinn spouted off.

"That's comforting," Emily agreed with Quinn.

"It's safe. We're just in enemy territory. I want us to be careful," I told them.

"Honestly, Blaine's always been cool with our coven. He and Kaiya go way back," Jordan chimed in, acting as the peacemaker. I was thankful to have him.

The trees thinned as we descended until we were standing in a bare spot in the woods. It was mostly sand and loose dirt, similar to a riverbank. A few feet ahead of us, the tree line began again, leading toward the Ainbertach mansion.

"Stay away from the outline of the property until I test it," I instructed them, "We'll rest here until go time."

"You okay if I hand out dinner?" Emily asked. "That hike has me starved."

I nodded.

"Subs!" Jordan cheered.

"You ordered meatball, right?" Emily settled onto a large rock to one side of the clearing. She opened her bag and started pulling food from it. Jordan joined her, happily tossing his backpack to the ground. We had figured we'd need something easy to eat before the big fight. No sense throwing up from nervousness with nothing in your stomach. Subs sounded like the best option.

"Chicken tender sub is mine." Emily passed out the sandwiches. "Club is Quinn's, and turkey is Emlyn's."

While everyone else's focus was on dinner, I assessed the perimeter. I held my hand close to where the magical boundary would've been, and I didn't feel any sign that a spell was active. There was no change in temperature. I conducted a visual check from all angles, and there was no distortion of vision either. It seemed fine, but I still sprinkled some sulfur dust over a small area to play it safe. We'd cross the line in this section only.

The grand house was difficult to miss from this position. I could see it poking through the empty patches in the trees. Late fall wasn't the best time to hide in a forest. Still, it seemed we were hidden for the most part. The structure was about one and a half football fields away. I could make out a very fancy garden trail to one side and the outskirts of a stone encased pool on the other. From Blaine's notes, I knew the exterior also contained a gazebo, a hedge maze, and a fountain. I cringed at the amount of money and resources the coven must've used to pay for and maintain this place.

"Emlyn, aren't you going to eat?" Emily called out.

"Quiet!" I urged her.

"Sorry," she half-whispered back.

"Yeah, I just need to find something first."

Emily returned to her sandwich as I scanned the surrounding area. Finally, I found the package nestled behind the trunk of a large tree.

"He's kept his word," I confirmed to myself. I hated that I still needed to convince myself I made the right call. The package was wrapped in craft paper, held together with string. Tucked into the front was an envelope with the word "Lover" written on the front. I'd need to remind Blaine how annoying that nickname was, especially with the negative memories it evoked. Those flashbacks were probably why he continued to use it, though. Blaine was a villain. His temporarily being on our side changed nothing.

I ripped open the envelope to find a simple message: *Try to blend in. Maeve will be in position at 8:30 p.m. Don't be late and don't die.*

Enclosed with the note was a detailed map that showed all the witches that would be on duty at 8 p.m. and the powers they possessed. I crumpled up the letter and shoved it into my pocket. I'd put it in Emily's backpack where no one would find it. Inside the craft paper were four of the coven's robes.

"Here's your sub. It's turkey, your favorite." Emily tried to hand me the paper-wrapped sandwich. I shook my head no.

"Everyone needs to put these on." I handed Emily, Quinn, and Jordan each a green and yellow robe. They were the same ones I'd seen Harold wearing in my vision of Blaine and Maeve.

"I like the little gold antlers," Emily smiled.

"I'm like officially a Celtic witch with these knots," Jordan agreed.

"The robes will help us blend in. Stealth is key here," I told my friends before sliding the garment over my arms.

"I don't think I can wear my backpack with this. How will that work?" Emily asked.

"No backpack. Pick a pocket for each type of potion you're carrying. There are plenty. Just remember which kind is in which pocket."

"Oh, god. I'm gonna mess this up," Emily agonized.

"Don't worry, girl, you'll have all of us with you," Jordan chimed in.

I looked at the map Blaine had left for us once again and made a judgment call.

"About that—we're splitting up once we get in there," I announced.

"What!" Quinn was the first to object. "How many times are you going to do this?"

"Yeah, I don't think that's a good idea," Emily echoed.

"It is the better option, especially given this map Blaine drafted for us." I did my best to sound definitive and confident. "We'll split up to take care of the exterior posted witches, and then we'll meet back at the fountain."

"And we're sure we trust this map?" Quinn questioned.

Emily met my eyes, silently agreeing with Quinn.

"It looks legit, man," Jordan told him after looking it over. "He's drawn in all the coverage areas and the key facts about the witches."

"I agree." I smiled at Jordan, feeling thankful again for his presence.

"Now, the left side of the mansion seems like more firepower, though," Jordan commented. "Might want to take that side, Red. I can take the other side."

Jordan was right. If we took them on in order from our position, we'd encounter a psychic partnered with a telekinetic witch first, which seemed like a challenging pair. A little further down was a conjurer. Blaine's notes didn't say what she could conjure, but my imagination had plenty of ideas. The last witch on the more difficult side was Blaine's father, Alexander, who had the gift of geokinesis. He could manipulate the earth beneath your feet, turning it to quicksand where you stood. It was how he'd trapped and killed my mother.

The witches on the other side of the building weren't pushovers by any means, but it wasn't as bad. First, there was a telepath—a witch who could communicate through her mind. It was a passive power like Blaine's. Then, there was a necromancer at the very end of the yard, which didn't seem like a massive threat unless there were dead people nearby. I didn't see a graveyard on the map, and we didn't plan on killing anyone. The only real problem was the shapeshifter between the necromancer and the telepath.

"I don't like you taking on the shifter," I admitted. "He'll have surprise on his side. You don't know what he'll be disguised as. I'd have a better chance of avoiding his attack by freezing him."

"Still, girl. Geokinesis and telekinesis are no joke. I'm not afraid to admit, I'm not as strong as you are. I'd rather take my chances on the shifter."

I nodded in agreement. "I'll take this side alone then. You three work together. You'll have better odds that way."

"Are you sure, Emlyn?" Emily asked. "I don't like that."

"We're stronger together," Quinn reminded me. "But you're in charge. Whatever you decide is right."

There was a little sting in Quinn's words. I shifted my gaze from Emily and Quinn to Jordan. "Jordan, are you comfortable leading the group?"

Jordan nodded. "Three of us, working together? We've got this."

"So, we'll meet at this fountain when our witches are knocked out," I reminded everyone, pointing at the spot on the map.

My comrades nodded in agreement. Quinn and Emily headed back to the rock to gather their belongings and put on their robes.

"Jordan, hang on a minute?" I asked him.

"What's up, girl?"

I looked down at the ground. I needed to be strong, and I was worried that making eye contact with anyone would make me emotional. "Please protect them," I urged.

"With my life, girl."

Chapter Twenty-One

From my crouched position in the foliage, I set my sights on the first two witches on my list. They were set up near a carriage house in the very back of the property, on a path which would eventually lead to the pool. According to Blaine, the psychic's name was Harold. We'd encountered a Harold at Henrietta's house, and from what I could see in the darkness, this was the same witch. His short, bleached blonde fro was difficult to miss. He'd been a bully at Henrietta's house, but he wasn't as bad as Daryl, the other witch who came to the house that day.

It seemed Harold was one of two psychics working for Maeve, and it looked like he'd been demoted since the last time I saw him. I guessed Maeve didn't like failure, and she probably wasn't pleased that he and Daryl had lost us in Alabama.

Knowing there were two psychics, I took the precaution of downing a potion to block my mind from Harold's abilities. The mixture wasn't fool-proof. Harold would likely feel something coming, but it would be blurred. I only hoped it was enough to keep me and everyone else safe. Harold's partner was more worrisome, though. Natalie Vigero was a solid-looking brunette with long braided hair and a permanent scowl. She looked like she could probably beat everyone I knew at an arm-wrestling match, apart from maybe Quinn. On top of her muscles, Natalie had the power of telekinesis, an ability I was already familiar with. My mother was telekinetic, and Marjorie always bragged about her strength.

"This is bull," I could hear Harold complaining as I crept closer to them. "I can't believe I'm stuck out here with you. You know how long it's been since I've pulled the night shift outside? I should be sitting by the fire and resting up. I can't believe Steve is the favorite psychic now. It's insulting."

I remembered the name, Steve. Maeve mostly referred to him as Stephen, but he was the witch Maeve had spoken to in my dream. He was the other psychic. From the sound of it, Stephen was moving up in the ranks over Harold.

"Don't complain," Natalie barked in a gruff alto voice. "What makes you think you're special? You'll earn a spot inside just like the rest of us."

"Earn a spot inside? I've earned it again and again. Don't forget, you used to work for me, Natalie," Harold spat at her. He was angry and distracted by his frustration, which was good for me. It meant he wasn't paying attention to his ability.

"You screwed up, Harold. You're lucky Maeve didn't kill you for losing that witch, especially after Blaine lost her the first time. I don't know why you thought bringing that old lady would make up for such a stupid blunder. Pathetic."

"Oh? But it's perfectly fine for that twerp, Blaine. I guess if you're dating Maeve, you don't have to complete your missions. I'll tell you how he earned his spot."

Natalie elbowed him hard in the stomach. "Shut up! Do you know what she'd do if she heard you talking like that? Maeve would drown you in an instant."

"It's true."

"You're on thin ice, Harold."

"I—"

I plunged toward them. It seemed like the opportune moment; they weren't paying attention, and, luckily; they were facing away from me. Still, it wasn't the surprise I'd been hoping for. With one fling of her wrist, Natalie sent me flailing into the stone wall of the carriage house. I splatted onto the concrete, landing on my stomach with the wind knocked out of me.

"Nice reflexes!" Harold complimented Natalie.

"Which is how I'll earn my spot. Take notes, Harold. I'll be your boss soon."

"Humph," Harold scoffed. "Who is that anyway? Is that one of ours?"

Luckily, the hood of my yellow and green cloak had fallen over my head when I dropped to the ground. The attack was so fast, I don't think either of the witches noticed who I was. Harold was the only one who'd seen me in person, anyway. The blow had been painful, and it left me gasping for breath. Usually, I'd try to ignore the impact and walk it off without a sound. In this instance, however, I made a bigger show of my injuries than I was feeling. I let out a wail of pain, only loud enough for Harold and Natalie to hear.

"Aren't you psychic? You tell me who it is," Natalie muttered under her breath.

"They're blocked from me," Harold admitted.

"Of course I'm blocked!" I huffed, mimicking my art history professor's Appalachian drawl. "Blaine sent me to test your reflexes. I guess that backfired, huh? Mind giving me a hand?" I reached up, keeping my face shielded.

"This is just like that dude to 'test' us. Like he's one to judge. Poor recruit; she's cannon fodder against us," Harold ranted.

"Forgive him," Natalie murmured. She walked over to me and reached out to help me up. "He's having a crappy week. Sorry about the wall there."

"No problem," I told her. As I stretched my right hand out to take her arm, I used my left to splash a bottle of essence of poppy in her face, making sure not to inhale any of the fumes myself.

"Hey! What was that?" Harold cried out as Natalie dropped to the ground. A dose to the face like that was pretty much instantaneous.

I jumped to my feet, putting distance between myself and the sleeping potion before taking a breath of air. It seemed to take Harold a full 10 seconds to realize who I was.

"Wait. You're Em—"

I froze him mid-sentence. "I am."

I conducted a quick assessment of my surroundings to confirm no one heard the commotion we'd made. The air was still and quiet around us. My next witch was stationed on the far side of the pool, and, luckily, I couldn't see her position from here. It likely meant she couldn't see this post either.

It was time to do the problematic task—stripping Natalie and Harold's powers. I slipped the cork off the first potion, pried Harold's frozen mouth open, and poured the liquid down his throat. I did the same with the essence of poppy to keep him quiet the rest of the night.

When I unfroze his body, he was conscious for only a moment.

"What did you…" Harold passed out before he could finish his thought. He'd wake up human without powers. I hated doing it. It felt wrong to take away such an integral part of someone's life so easily. These people grew up as witches, and now they'd have to find new destinies. It seemed extreme in some ways to me. It was the way of our coven, though. The potion I used was the same recipe our coven had used for decades against dark witches. These witches chose life with the Ainbertach Coven. They had probably done far worse.

I walked over to Natalie and gave her the same potion. "It was an impressive shot. Breathing is still hard, and I'm sure I'll have a bad bruise."

I didn't waste any more time. Two were done, and I had two more to go before the meet up. I darted back into the bushes and trees to avoid the giant windows of the mansion as I made my way around the house. Past the pool was a covered flagstone patio with a grill and wicker furniture. The only lights were from strands of bulbs hung up around the perimeter of the covered area.

The cover of darkness and the shrubbery surrounding the pool area created the perfect hiding place for me. The path to approach the conjurer, Lillian O'Riley, was clear ahead. I'd never encountered a conjurer before, but she appeared less severe than Natalie. She was sitting on a stone bench beside the pool, staring into the light of her phone. From this distance and the limited lighting, I pegged Lillian at age 35. I guessed she was a new member, earning her dues just like Harold described. Judging by her last name and her thick, wavy red hair, I also assumed Lillian was a true Irish witch. She wore her hair like Marjorie—wild and long past her shoulders.

I grabbed another vial containing essence of poppy and slowly crawled toward her, keeping to the shadows. She seemed oblivious to her surroundings, which made me think this would be the easiest take-down I'd have all night.

"Lillian! Look out!" a familiar voice screeched out. My heart sunk, and my anxiety level sky-rocketed.

"Alexander?" Lillian turned towards me before I could react.

The voice belonged to Alexander Corwin, Blaine's father. He was supposed to be posted at the next checkpoint, but I hadn't checked to make sure. Why didn't I check? It made sense that Alexander would visit Lillian. It probably got boring out there standing by themselves. Why wouldn't you find someone to chat with?

As quickly as I realized what had happened, I was sucked into a newly formed pit of quicksand. I struggled for a minute, but my arms and legs were hopelessly stuck in the mud. I couldn't freeze my enemies or throw a potion. I was trapped. Crap.

"Oh my Goddess," Lillian exclaimed. "Who is that?"

"Blaine sent me over to test your reflexes," I tried my trick again. "I guess you're a better team than he expected."

"I don't think so," Alexander argued. His voice was like Blaine's, but greasier somehow. It might've been because Alexander looked like a weasel compared to his son. Alexander continued, "The focus has been on the Finnerty witch. He wouldn't waste resources on this right now."

Alexander approached me slowly and carefully. He'd always been the more cautious witch. He lifted the hood off my face, and I saw the light in his eyes when he understood who I was. I spat in his face.

"Call Maeve," Alexander muttered, wiping off his cheek.

"Are you sure you want her out here? Can't we get rid of the girl without involving Maeve?" Lillian wanted to know.

"She needs to be here," Alexander confirmed.

"Why?" Lillian groaned.

"Because I'm the Finnerty witch," I told her.

"Oh, my Goddess! Alexander, we caught the Finnerty witch! We're going to be promoted!"

"I wouldn't be so sure of that. Alexander got himself a Finnerty witch once before. It didn't seem to get you far, did it?"

"You killed a Finnerty witch?" Lillian asked. "Whoa!"

"No, I wouldn't say he 'killed' a Finnerty witch. More that he… facilitated her death."

"Shut up, you," Alexander attempted to speak over me.

"Lillian, call Maeve down here at once."

"See, Alex here is a coward. He made my mother kill herself, so he wouldn't have to. He gave her a potion," I told Lillian.

"The potion they give us in case we're caught? The one so we don't give up information?" Lillian sneered. "Really, Alexander?" She giggled to herself.

"I will kill you," Alexander exclaimed. He glared at me, probably debating how much trouble he'd be in if he really killed me. With little effort, he could've smothered me in quicksand or crushed me by turning the mud back into dry earth, but he was flustered.

"Too late, Mr. Corwin," I smiled.

Five minutes earlier, this time I knew to look for Alexander before I attacked Lillian. I waited in the shadows and the bushes until Alexander's skinny frame came into view. He was walking casually.

There was no sense of urgency or alertness to his stride, which meant I was still a secret. When he was about a yard away from me, I jumped out in front of him and froze him before he could take another step.

Now, he was the one stuck in a trap.

"Doesn't this scene look familiar?" I asked him after unfreezing his head.

"What the... who are you?" Alexander asked in a panic.

"It was too easy to lure you here." I echoed a phrase I'd heard Alexander say to my mother. I lifted the hood of my cloak to reveal my face. "Remember what you said? 'You can always count on a good witch to investigate the cries of a child in distress.' Now I'm the one catching you by surprise."

"Rhi—Rhiannon? But... but you..." A flash of recognition crossed his face. "You look like your mother. It looks like you weren't smart enough to stay out of it. Were you, kid?"

"I guess that makes two of us."

"I've always practiced magic. There was never an out for me."

"Not true. The day you met Maeve, I know you felt reluctant. You knew what this coven would ask of you. But you still let Blaine manipulate you into this life." I could feel rage bubbling up in my blood. It was a new energy I hadn't felt before, pushing through my skin. It was an ache—a pain. The man in front of me took my mother. He stole so much from me.

"So, you caught me off guard, and now you'll do—what? Strip my powers? Trap me in a lawn ornament?"

"You killed her." Tears of anger and sadness built up in my eyes. "She would still be here if it weren't for you. She wasn't hunting your people anymore. She'd stopped. She wanted children, and she needed magic to get them. She never used magic again after I was born! Not until she wanted another child—How dare you target her for that?"

"Oh, so it's revenge then? Are you going to kill me, good witch?"

"I'm not like you." I stepped back, threw a bottle of "Flu-like Symptoms" at his feet, and unfroze the rest of his body. "But, I will make my mark tonight."

262

Alexander doubled over in sickness, and in that instant, I thought of Henrietta. She killed for those she loved. Would it be so bad to rid the world of Alexander? Henrietta had broken the law of the coven again and again, but it made the world a better place. Was she wrong? Didn't Alexander deserve to die for what he did? I thought back on the memory I'd relived last year. My mother had begged for the chance to say goodbye to my father and me, and Alexander wouldn't even allow her that courtesy. I thought about the months my father and I had spent weeping over Mom's death. Who would weep over Alexander? Maybe Blaine, briefly.

A stinging sensation in my back immediately interrupted my vengeful thoughts. The throbbing sent me to my knees, and I cried out in pain. It was a feeling I'd never experienced before—an arrow protruding from my right shoulder blade. Lillian was behind me, holding a crossbow in her hands. It disappeared into thin air as Lillian darted to Alexander's side. He was already vomiting.

"Alexander, are you alright?" Lillian cried as she placed her hand over his back. He vomited again, and then he sunk to the ground and rolled over into the fetal position. "What did you do to him? Who are you?"

I knew better than to remove the arrow. Right now, it was blocking blood flow, but the minute I removed it, I'd lose a lot of blood. I needed to focus. Turning back time wasn't a possibility anymore. It took too much power. My strength was waning. Instead, I froze them both.

"Hubris," I scolded myself. "You stupid girl. You let revenge distract you."

This wasn't how this should've worked. I stripped Lillian and Alexander's powers and dosed them both with essence of poppy, but I had been reckless. I let myself get injured, and facing Maeve at half-strength sounded like a suicide mission. The wound stung, especially now that the adrenaline of the fight was gone. Moving my right arm was painful. I knew the injury needed attention and probably stitches, but I tried to focus on the task before me.

I froze the wound, pulled the arrow out with a yelp of pain, and spread an ointment of goldenrod and calendula—two plants with healing properties—into the cut. Like an idiot, I'd given Emily, Quinn, and Jordan all of the "You Won't Feel a Thing" potions. I ripped the golden cuff from the sleeve of my cloak and tried to patch the puncture while my blood was frozen. It was a temporary fix. I needed another set of hands to help.

My next step was to get to the fountain a little ways past where we'd entered the property. The others would meet me there. Then we could regroup. I just hoped to Goddess the others would make it back too. I pulled myself up, moved back to the bushes, and started my trek back the way I'd come.

Then the sirens rang out.

"Oh no," I whispered to myself, fighting the tears welling up in my eyes. "Please, no." The sirens could only mean one thing. They had caught my friends. With one hand securely holding the cuff of my cloak to my wound, I attempted to sprint to our meeting place. Between my injured shoulder and the heavy cloak, it wasn't very graceful, but I did my best. Stealth wasn't part of the equation anymore. I needed to get there fast.

I whizzed past Harold and Natalie, who were still asleep. Out of breath and panting like crazy, I finally came to the grey fountain in the back. Large stone cherubs were spaced evenly around the fountain's low basin, small streams of water pouring in from urns on their shoulders. I looked around, because I was the first one there.

"Come on. Come on," I bit my lower lip. Hoping, praying to the Goddesses that my friends were alright. I tried to ignore the ache in my arm and shoulder. My body throbbed, and I felt like I might pass out at any moment. Still, the only worry in my mind was for my friends.

"Please," I begged the darkness again.

One long minute of anxiety later, I saw shapes moving toward me. My heart leaped in my chest as Jordan, Quinn, and Emily appeared.

"Guys!" I yelled too loudly, running to meet them.

"Shh!" Emily hissed back.

They darted to the fountain, each out of breath, and we ducked behind the massive stonework, hoping the cherubs would act as camouflage.

"What happened?" I urged.

"The telepath must have warned someone about us before we could strip her powers," Jordan explained, panting tiredly. "We took her out, no problem, but she got a good look at us for several seconds before the essence of poppy hit. We were looking for the shifter when

264

the sirens started. One witch came at us—I'm not sure which one. We took care of him and ran back here."

"Are you okay? What did you use on the witch who was following you?" I demanded.

"Essence of poppy and 'Flu-like Symptoms,'" Quinn replied. "You're hurt?" He had seen the blood-soaked shoulder on my sweater.

I ignored the question. "Was it the shifter or the necromancer?"

"We don't know. The shape-shifting witch was next on our route. It was probably him," Emily explained. "Emlyn, we need to bandage that. What happened?"

"I took an arrow to the shoulder," I told her. "I'm fine."

"An arrow?" Quinn exclaimed. The concern in his voice was hard to miss.

"Y'all, we've gotta get out of here," Jordan interrupted. "There's gonna be more coming."

Quinn paused a moment and then spoke up. "We'll lead them away. Emlyn, stay here and hide until they pass. You're the one who needs to get to Maeve."

"What?" I shook my head. "What if they catch you?"

At that moment, I saw a group of three witches emerge from the backdoor of the estate and start looking around. We had maybe a minute left before they saw us. There was no time to plan.

"We'll get to the car. We'll make it out," Quinn assured me.

"I'm not fast enough," Emily objected.

"Yeah, you're probably right. You stay with Emlyn," Quinn said.

"We'll come back for your girls," Jordan assured us.

"But, I…" I started. There wasn't time to argue, though. I threw my arms around Quinn's neck and kissed him with tears in my eyes. "Be safe," I told him. He nodded, and they took off into the woods. It sounded like they were making more noise than necessary as they headed up the hill. Only moments later, Emily and I watched from our hiding spot as the coven members took off after Quinn and Jordan.

Then it was quiet. I could feel Emily trembling beside me. This wasn't what she expected.

"Are you okay?" I whispered.

"I didn't get shot by an arrow, at least," she replied. "We need to look at that."

"Not yet. It's 8:15 p.m., we need to get to the wine cellar first so I can be in position at 8:30. We'll try to bandage it up then. Come on. Follow me and stay quiet."

No part of me wanted Emily there for this part of the fight, but there we both were just like my dream had predicted. Emily and I slowly made our way around the right side of the house—the side Jordan, Emily, and Quinn initially took. The basement door was on the other side of a hedge maze of rosebushes. We both dodged into the maze when we saw another pair of coven members heading our way. Luckily, they didn't seem to be looking for us. They must have assumed whoever invaded was long gone.

We finally reached a small set of stone steps that led down to the basement door. Emily and I hurried down, and I was relieved to find Blaine left it unlocked as he promised he would. We slipped in easily, and I was quickly overcome with the familiar scents of damp earth, fresh-cut wood, and salt. We were in the right place.

"We're here. Can I help you now?" Emily demanded.

I nodded. "Yes, please. It stings pretty bad."

"Well, they shot you with an arrow. Sit down here," Emily instructed. "I've got some bandages packed in here somewhere."

"Don't you have the 'You Won't Feel a Thing?' That would be helpful."

"I forgot which one that was," Emily admitted.

"Green," I told her. "I think it was green."

She handed me the vial, and I plopped down onto the cold stone floor. With nothing attacking me, I finally realized how painful my injury was. My back ached from being thrown into the wall, and the right half of my body felt useless. I wondered how I would fight Maeve. Magical abilities or not, my body was still human. It was amazing what a little green potion could do, though. Almost instantly after drinking it, I felt better. My shoulder blade felt healed, my body rested.

"I've never been shot by an arrow before. Cross that off the bucket list," I told Emily, trying to lighten things up.

Emily didn't take the bait. "I can't believe you got shot." She took out a piece of gauze and gently blotted the wound. "It doesn't look too deep, but it's bleeding a lot. Maybe we should go back." She sounded pretty freaked out.

I shook my head. "No. Just help me wrap it."

"Emlyn, I—"

"Nope. We just have to wrap it."

She followed my instructions in silence. I really could've used a goofy Emily comment to lighten the mood, but Emily wasn't there. I couldn't blame her. Look at what she was dealing with. I owed her dinners, flowers, and at least 3 months of therapy sessions after this.

As we finished up wrapping my back and shoulder in bandages, we heard footsteps above us. They were right on time. I had expected them, but Emily grabbed the back of my shirt in fear.

"I don't want to hear your excuses, Stephen," Maeve spat. She was angry. All she knew was that someone was attacking the mansion. It could've been me or another coven. Maeve still had no idea where I was. "Let me spell this out for you. You find her, or you can explain to headquarters why you couldn't. They aren't as understanding as I am, Steve."

I almost felt sorry for Steve. Almost.

"I'll find them, I will," Steve responded. "I'll notify all our contacts in the southeast, ma'am."

"Yes, you will. Now get out of here, and cut the ma'am crap." A door slammed, and I knew Maeve was alone. It would only be a minute or so before Blaine was in the room with her. We'd be alone with her. It was time to move. I crept forward in the darkness, finally understanding the overwhelming urge to get upstairs. I used the wall as support in the dark, trying to compensate for my injured side.

I would've jumped if I wasn't expecting Emily's hand pulling at me suddenly. She grabbed me to keep me from moving forward. "Don't," she begged.

I squeezed Emily's hand and gently removed it from my arm. "I've got to do this," I told her before rubbing her shoulder. I meant it to comfort her, but I wasn't sure if it did any good.

When I reached the small staircase, adrenaline was pumping hard through my system. This was the moment I'd been waiting for. I took my first step, which made a small creaking noise, but I ignored it and kept going. This time, I knew the door opening was Blaine entering the room. I didn't fall backward in fear and roll my ankle. I was thankful that part of the dream had changed; I didn't think I could manage another injury right now.

"I'm surprised you let Stephen live," I heard Blaine joke from above. Emily crept over to stand beside me, grabbing my hand for comfort.

"He's an idiot, but he's our best psychic," Maeve exclaimed, frustrated. "If I killed him, headquarters wouldn't be happy."

"If he's our best, we have a problem," Blaine said with mocking undertones. "It was a fib, though, right? You haven't alerted headquarters that we failed a second time? They still think we're waiting for the right moment to attack?"

"Of course, Blaine. Can you imagine what they'd say? We'd be cut in an instant if they knew that girl outsmarted both of us."

"She's proving to be more and more intriguing, isn't she?" Blaine was practically telling Maeve he was on my side. His audacity was really something else. I hoped she didn't catch on before we had a chance to make our move.

"If I didn't know any better, Blaine, I might think you like this girl." Maeve didn't seem to like his tone. "Maybe last year wasn't just an act? Maybe you really have a thing for red-haired, light witches?"

"Someone's jealous," Blaine chuckled, unable to hide his amusement.

"Someone needs to remember who he's dealing with. Don't forget, I put my name on the line to spare your life with HQ. If we don't deliver, you won't be the only one they punish. We're both gone. Not trapped in a trophy. Dead gone."

"Lighten up, babe. You're gold to this coven. They wouldn't risk an asset like you."

"I'm serious, Blaine. I saved you once. I won't be able to do it again."

"We're going to find her. I'm going to kill her. Then we'll both be in the coven's good graces. I'll officially be one of the team."

"Are you blind or just stupid?" Maeve yelled sharply. She slammed something down on a table or countertop. "This isn't about your initiation. It's about her. It's what she could become."

It was time; I was ready to attack, and Blaine was prepared for me. I darted up the rest of the stairs as quietly as I could and reached for the doorknob.

"Emlyn!" Emily screamed at the top of her lungs.

"Emily? What are you—"

The last thing I felt was something heavy knocking me over the back of the head.

Chapter Twenty-Two

"She was on our property, and you couldn't sense her? Aren't you supposed to be our best psychic? We demoted Harold and gave you the job, Steve. Do I need to bring Harold back in here?" Maeve was lecturing poor Steve again.

My head throbbed, my shoulder stung, and I imagined most of my body was black and blue. Tonight was filled with firsts. It was the first time I'd raided a manor filled with dark witches, the first time I'd been shot with an arrow, and it the first time I'd been knocked out with a wine bottle. I was sure there was a lump on the back of my head the size of a golf ball. There was also a ringing in my head that was disorienting.

"No, ma'am," Steve sputtered out. "The witch must've used a spell or counter. I couldn't see her."

"Well, aren't you lucky Jamal was here to capture her?" Maeve continued. "Otherwise, your neck would've been on the chopping block."

Jamal, I thought to myself. The name sounded familiar. Why was Jamal familiar? I couldn't remember. Everything was muddled and fuzzy. Knowing I'd been captured gave me more incentive not to open my eyes. Maeve didn't need to know I was conscious. I needed time to develop a new plan, especially if this headache continued.

I tried to silently take stock of my inventory. I could feel that my robe was still on, which meant Maeve's minions might not have stripped me of my potions yet. The bad news was my hands were tied behind my back with a thin, itchy rope. If I was only bound and not ransacked of my belongings, I'd probably only been out fifteen minutes. It was a guess. Then I remembered that Emily was the one who hit me. Why would she do that? Did Jamal curse her? It made little sense.

"It was my pleasure," Jamal responded.

"What about the other two? You spoke of two men. What happened to them?" Maeve demanded. She must've been speaking about Quinn and Jordan. A ball of anxiety bubbled up inside me. Had they been caught?

"They knocked out Brax with some flowery potion. Then they took off into the woods. We've got five of our night crew searching the place now," Jamal reported.

"Brax is our new necromancer, right?" Maeve asked.

"Yes, ma'am."

"Well, this is fine work, Jamal. It's good to know I have a witch I can trust around here," Maeve told him. I could only imagine the "trust" comment was directed at Steve. "You'll be rewarded."

"It's an honor, ma'am," Jamal answered.

"I'd hate for Emlyn's friends to miss her death. You think you could take to the skies? Get a bird's-eye view on her missing comrades?"

"Bat sonar could prove effective here, ma'am. Consider it done."

Bat sonar? Was that Jamal's ability? It wasn't one I'd heard of before. Then it hit me. It was worse than the pain of my shoulder and head combined. I couldn't pretend to be asleep anymore. Jamal had shape-shifted into Emily. She didn't hit me. It was Jamal. He must've killed Emily when Jordan and Quinn were focused on the telepath. Jamal took over her body to trick me. My panicked breaths escalated out of control as anxiety suffocated my system. I pulled myself up to a sitting position, attempting to get more oxygen.

"Oh, Goddess," Maeve complained at the sounds of my whimpering. "Get to it, Jamal. Stephen, go tend to Emlyn before she's awake enough to attack us."

"You trust this idiot to properly check her?" Blaine interjected.

"Ma'am, I'm perfectly capable of—"

"Please. If you miss one potion, we could all pay for it. Don't underestimate this girl, Stephen. Blaine's right. Why don't you tend to a simpler task?"

Blaine was helping me, buying me time, and I should've been planning my next move. Unfortunately, Emily's death was the only thing on my mind. I couldn't think about escape or attack.

"Blaine will search Emlyn," Maeve instructed. "Stephen, are there any members left in the mansion? You mentioned many of our numbers took off into the woods to subdue Emlyn's friends. How many are left here?"

Blaine headed toward me, ignoring the conversation behind him, and for the first time I noticed where we were. This was likely Maeve's personal wing of the house. The kitchen wasn't all marble countertops, extravagant decoration, and top-of-the-line appliances as

I imagined the majority of the estate would've been. This room was modest, featuring aged white appliances nestled among bright cherry counters and cabinets. The open-concept kitchen transitioned into a small sitting area, where I was currently sitting in front of a plump, white sofa. Two cushy white armchairs were on opposite sides of me. They were tastefully decorated with burgundy and black throw pillows. The décor wasn't what I expected for the lair of an evil wealthy coven leader. There were no personal touches, either—no mementos from trips, no souvenirs from kills.

"I think Daryl, Ishan, Marnie, and Aya are the only ones inside the estate still, ma'am," Steve told Maeve. Hearing Marnie's name gave me hope. Blaine hadn't lied. Marnie was still alive, and they believed she was one of theirs.

"Bring them here. And get the old woman from the cell. She'll want to see what happens to her granddaughter," Maeve smirked.

Marjorie was alive, too.

"What about the other girl? The best friend?" Blaine asked. Hope gathered in my chest again. Was Blaine telling me Emily was alive? Had the shapeshifter only stolen her identity?

"Oh yeah," Maeve responded. "Have Ishan fetch her. We'll want to do this party right. After all, it'll be Emlyn's last."
Steve nodded and quickly exited the room.

"Are you going to behave, or are you going to make this difficult?" Blaine questioned me, as if to remind me we were supposed to be enemies. He was right. I wasn't playing my part well.

"Leave my friends alone, please!" I played the part of a beaten witch. "You have your prize, Maeve. Kill me, and let everyone else go."

"Ugh, that's such a goodie-two-shoes thing to say," Maeve taunted. "There's no use begging, and there's no trading. You'll all die here. It's just a matter of who dies first." She brushed her silver hair behind her ear and smiled smugly at me.

"We've got a mess to clean up because of you." Blaine grabbed me by both shoulders, yanking me to my feet. He pulled the potions from my pockets one by one, setting them on the counter for Maeve to see. "We really thought you'd be cleverer than this. Aren't these the same potions you used on us before?"

I struggled against Blaine's hands. "They worked against you, didn't they?" I blurted back at him. "Remember all the vomiting?"

"Shut up, Emlyn. I don't want to hear any more from you," Maeve spat. "You're disgusting."

"At least we gave it our all. My coven is honorable, which is more than I can say for yours."

Maeve scowled at me. "Blaine, I don't want her wearing our colors while we kill her. Remove them from her immediately."

"I can't take the robe off with her wrists bound," Blaine argued.

Maeve glared at him. "I said I don't want her wearing our colors. Cut her out of it."

"I don't have my pocket knife. Can you grab me one from the kitchen?" Blaine pointed toward the wall opposite from where I was positioned. As Maeve spun around toward the kitchen, Blaine slipped something into the back pocket of my jeans. Then I felt a sudden burst of confidence. I felt powerful and prepared. It must've been Blaine's magic.

"Here," Maeve walked over and handed Blaine the knife, giving me a once over. "Hard to believe you were worth all this trouble."

"Hold still," Blaine warned. "I'd hate to slip and start the big event before your friends get here." Blaine cut into the back of the robe so he could easily pull it from my body. In the same cut, I felt the ropes around my wrists loosen.

"I told you, they have nothing to do with this. Spare my friends."

"Not a chance," Maeve spat at me.

"I should've killed you when you could barely use your powers," Blaine remarked.

"Yes, you should've," Maeve jeered back at him.

"Why didn't you?" I asked. "You had every opportunity."

"He wanted glory," Maeve rolled her eyes and plopped onto her white sofa. "Now look at us, Blaine. We're barely holding onto our coven."

"She dies, and this all goes back to normal, babe," Blaine quickly jumped up and joined Maeve on the couch. He grabbed her hand and kissed her. "We're home free."

"Um, ma'am," Steve had reappeared in the entrance to the suite, looking very nervous.

"Stephen! Can't you see I'm sharing a moment?" Maeve's emotions seemed incredibly erratic. In the last ten minutes I had seen her go from anger to glee to sadness, then back to anger, at the drop of a hat.

"Well, ma'am. I—."

"Cut the ma'am crap. Where is everyone?" Maeve leaped to her feet.

"I—I found Ishan and Aya in their rooms," Steve stammered. "I can't wake either of them. Something—something has affected them. I couldn't find Marnie or Daryl. And... and Marjorie is missing from her cell."

Every sentence coming out of Steve's mouth was as equally good for me as it was terrible for Maeve, and he looked terrified to be the bearer of bad news. Our plan was working after all.

"WHAT?" Maeve's jaw locked, her body gone rigid with fury. Her eyes looked pitch black. She turned to me, her eyes wide, and created a ball of fire in her hands. "What did you do?"

"I honestly don't know, Maeve. Maybe you have a rat on the inside?" I offered her a smirk of my own. On the inside, though, I immediately berated myself for being so bold. Blaine must've given me too much confidence. It wasn't typically a good idea to taunt a woman holding a fireball.

"ENOUGH!" Maeve roared. She wound up the fireball, about to burn me alive, when Blaine struck her arm, throwing off her aim. The fireball hit Steve directly in the chest, sending him flying out of the room. Maeve spun around in shock, locking accusatory eyes on Blaine.

"You?" Maeve sounded as hurt as she was angry. I immediately recognized the hand motion she used on Blaine as he fell to his knees. Maeve was drowning him. Blaine's betrayal was miserable for her—enough to distract her from me. Weirdly, my instinct wasn't to freeze her. I jumped onto her back, grabbed a fist full of her ashen, grey hair, and pulled hard.

"You deserve everything you get," I screamed.

Maeve released Blaine from her hold and threw me off her back. She conjured another fireball, and I knew nothing would make her happier than to blaze me into oblivion. She threw it at me about a second before Blaine wrapped his arms around hers, constricting her motion and power. I froze the fireball in mid-air as Maeve struggled against Blaine's hold.

I instinctively reached for my neck and realized that the medallion wasn't there anymore.

"Jamal…" I whispered.

"Emlyn, look out!" a much-needed familiar voice rang out. I quickly dodged an incoming fireball, throwing myself to the ground. The throbbing pain in my shoulder returned, but it was nothing compared to the knot on my head. I was likely concussed—I felt woozy and unable to comprehend my surroundings quickly.

Suddenly, Marjorie was standing between me and Maeve with her hands above her head. She must've summoned a force-field to protect us, just like she did that day in the shop. Marnie slid onto the ground beside me, using one arm to support my head and shoulders.

"Marnie! Marjorie!" I cried out in relief.

"Celebrate later, girl," Marjorie ordered.

"Drink this." Marnie didn't wait. She poured a mixture into my mouth that tasted like tar. In seconds, the pain from my shoulder and head faded to a dull ache. It worked even better than the "You Won't Feel A Thing." With my wits about me again, I jumped to my feet to assess the situation.

Marjorie was holding off fireballs from Maeve, who was getting angrier by the second. The force-field Marjorie created wouldn't hold forever, but luckily it seemed like Maeve didn't want to take down her own house with her crushing earthquake power.

"You're all so dead," Maeve screamed.

"What potions do you have?" I asked Marnie.

"Nothing that will work against her," Marnie told me. I suddenly noticed the large laceration on Marnie's arm, along with a few cuts on her cheek. I looked at Marjorie. One eye was black. There was a gash down her cheek, and from what I could see, her arms were bruised. It looked like they had tortured her from the minute she arrived here. Guilt flooded my system.

I'd make it right.

"'Fire-Power?'" I asked Marnie.

"Um," Marnie reached through her robes and produced a vial. "Yes, but like I said, it won't work on Maeve."

"I know. Listen, Maeve will follow me. Find Emily."

With Maeve distracted by Marjorie's force field, I unfroze Blaine without her noticing. Then, I took off in a dash across the room. My plan was to hold her attention.

"What do you think you're doing?" Maeve demanded with a scowl.

I turned and barreled toward her, and at the same time, Blaine grabbed a lamp off the side table by the sofa. He swung it at Maeve, connecting solidly with the side of her head. She went down with a thud, and I grabbed Blaine by the arm. We darted toward the exterior wall, and I threw the "Fire Power" potion at the window, causing it to explode an instant. As the glass and wood paneling shattered, Blaine and I rolled out through it into the backyard.

I allowed myself a brief look behind us. Maeve was still moving, albeit slowly. She was rubbing her head, but I guessed she'd be up in a matter of seconds. Marjorie and Marnie had disappeared from the room, which was good. I told myself they'd find Emily.

"Come on." Blaine pulled me up from the rubble of the window. Fresh cuts on the left side of my body were painful now. It felt like I'd also rolled my ankle, but I ignored the pain. We limped our way to the back patio as fast as we could, trying to put distance between ourselves and Maeve. There wasn't a plan anymore. We were working with what we had.

"I can't freeze her," I told him. "Jamal must've taken the medallion."

"Go back," Blaine demanded. "Go back in time before Jamal knocked you out."

"I can't. Even at full strength, turning back time that far is tough. I don't have enough power right now. I can't even count all my injuries."

"Then we need to find Jamal."

"Can you take him down by yourself? Between the arrow, the wine bottle, and the window, I'm not feeling capable of much at the moment."

"Let's just keep moving. If we go in through the front, we can go to Maeve's vault. She keeps all her most powerful potions there. We'll use one to get rid of Jamal."

Blaine and I hobbled around the swimming pool where I'd left Alexander and Lillian. They were still lying on the concrete asleep.

"Your handiwork?" Blaine asked.

I nodded.

"Thanks for not killing him. I know he killed your mom."

"I couldn't do that." I would never admit how close I'd come. I was ashamed of it.

We were almost there when three figures moved toward us.

"Blaine, stop," I motioned toward the figures. "Three witches took off from the estate earlier after Jordan and Quinn. It has to be them."

We didn't move, hoping stillness in the dark would keep us hidden. I readied my powers, and Blaine looked around for something substantial. He picked up a small potted plant from a stone window ledge.

"When I give the signal, you freeze, and I'll go in swinging," Blaine ordered.

I nodded.

"Three... two... ONE!" Blaine yelled.

I threw my hands up to freeze the group, only to realize who I was freezing in the very last second. "Jordan! Quinn! Emily!" I shouted, throwing my arms around their necks. I could've kissed each one on the lips.

"Whoa, girl. You look rough," Jordan said.

"I don't care. I'm just so happy to see you!" I told them. Then I remembered the imposter, Emily. "Get away from Emily, guys."

"What?" Emily looked confused.

"Wait, because of that shapeshifter guy?" Quinn asked. "Nah, this is really Emily."

"Weird dude found us after we sent the other three witches to sleepy time," Jordan explained. "He tried to pass himself off as Emily, but we figured Emily wouldn't leave you without knowing if you were okay. That's when we knew something was fishy. So, we knocked the dude out with the poppy stuff. We ran into Emily on our way back here."

"Yeah, gurl, it's me. The one and only!" Emily beamed at me.

I almost tackled her in my enthusiasm. "I'm so happy you're alive!"

Blaine didn't share my excitement. "Where did you leave the shifter?" he asked.

"He's back by the car," Quinn told me.

I looked at Blaine. "The car is more than a mile away."

"What's the problem, girl?" Jordan wanted to know.

"He stole the medallion. I can't fight Maeve without it," I told them. "Wait… where is Maeve?" My eyes bugged out of my head. "Maeve didn't follow Blaine and me out here. I have to find Marjorie!"

I took off, running toward the front door. It was a few hundred yards away. My wounds felt like nothing—the adrenaline must've overpowered my pain receptors. Behind me, I could hear the voices of my friends. They wanted me to stop, think things through, and develop a plan. I couldn't. The only thought in my head was finding Marjorie and Marnie.

I came to a grand entrance with stone stags standing on either side of the dark wood door. It was unlocked, so I barreled in. I didn't even think before moving forward. The door opened to a familiar room. I'd seen Blaine meet Maeve in this hall. It was the entrance hall, complete with the painting of Fáelán Ainbertach. I darted past it, heading for the sound of people yelling somewhere nearby.

"Leave her alone, Maeve," Marnie's voice rang out.

"I'll deal with you later, traitor," Maeve spat at her. "A house full of traitors. How did I get so lucky, Múireann?"

I dashed towards the noise, past the grand staircase in the hall. They had to be in one of the rooms nearby. I looked for open doors, finding a parlor, a dining room, a professional-looking kitchen. In the kitchen I helped myself to one of the sharp-looking knives, tucking it into my waistband. It couldn't hurt to be armed. Finally, I found what looked like the drawing-room.

Daryl was posted by the wall to my left, with Marnie zip-tied at his feet. Marjorie was bound and gagged in an antique armchair across the room from them. She was sporting a fresh cut on her lower lip.

In the center of it all was Maeve, perched on a large, ornately carved loveseat. She seemed at ease as she soaked in warmth from the mahogany fireplace in front of her.

Maeve stood to face me as I entered the room. "What a pain in my butt you've been." She met my eyes with hers and continued. "I've faced countless witches—most of them a great deal more powerful than you. Somehow, you're the only one that's destroyed my reputation."

She snapped her fingers, and Daryl was striding forward, ready to subdue me. I froze him in place.

"He'll be done with that in point two seconds. Haven't you seen him before? Power of adaption. Good job wasting your powers." Maeve laughed as she conjured another fireball.

"She didn't waste them," Jordan yelled out. He threw a potion at Daryl's feet, and as Daryl reanimated, he started vomiting.

"Vomiting again? Isn't that getting old, Emlyn?" Maeve snarled as Quinn, Emily, Blaine, and Jordan ran into the room, throwing "Fire Power" potions. Small explosions started bursting throughout the room. In response, Maeve started hurling fireballs at the group, but she wasn't expecting Jordan's power of deflection. He could lob them right back at her. None of this harmed Maeve in the slightest, but it made for a good distraction.

Emily immediately ran to Marnie's aid, working to free her from the zip ties around her wrists. I motioned for them to find cover then ran to Marjorie's side. For now, it seemed Blaine was drawing Maeve's fire, playing with her emotions to cause some chaos.

"Baby, it was nothing personal," Blaine said in a hideously cold voice.

"How is this not personal!" Maeve shot back, sending another fireball at his head.

"I just want to succeed. How am I supposed to do that if you're holding me back?"

Maeve didn't respond. She just screamed, sending an earthquake-like reverberation through the room.

Fortunately, no one was paying me and Marjorie any attention. "I'm so sorry," I told her, bursting into tears. I wrapped my arms around her, breathing in the faint lavender scent that still clung to her hair and clothes despite her being a prisoner for days. I didn't want to let go in case she turned out to be a figment of my imagination. "I'll get us out of this. I will." I tried to pull myself together and started tugging at her restraints.

"Stop," she demanded. She took both sides of my face in her zip-tied hands. "No matter what happens, Celtic girl, this isn't your fault. I made this choice, and you've done better than any other witch could have. I am so proud of you."

"Don't talk like that. We're going to be fine," I told Marjorie as I cut through her restraints. I pulled her up from the armchair, trying my best to support her weight with my injuries. I wrapped my left arm around her waist.

"Emlyn!" I heard Quinn franticly yell. I knew Maeve had turned her attention back to me. I wasn't fast enough. Marjorie and I pushed away from each other to avoid getting hit by the flames of another fireball. We both toppled to the floor.

"You stupid, stupid good witches. When are you going to learn?" Maeve was full-on psychotic now. Her rage was more intense than I'd ever seen before. "Look at this." She strutted toward Marjorie, grabbing her by the hair.

"Maeve, no!" I ran out to meet her, but she immediately threw me to the ground, drowning me. "Please, take me," I choked out. I couldn't breathe, but I still fought.

Marnie and Emily were throwing potions at Maeve with no effect. Blaine, Quinn, and Jordan tried tackling her. There was no fighting it. With one swoop, Maeve had them all under the same spell, drowning all of us slowly as we helplessly watched her cruelest act.

"Let this be a lesson to all of you. This is what happens when you mess with the Ainbertach Coven." Maeve took an athame from her belt. Then she stabbed Marjorie through the back and straight into her heart.

"No! Please, no!" I choked out with my last bit of air. Because it was more fun to see me suffer, Maeve released me from her spell before I passed out from lack of air. Gasping, I crawled toward Marjorie as she slumped over on the floor. "No, no, no."

I pulled her into my lap and tried to use my hands to stop the bleeding. "You'll be okay, Marjorie," I told her as the tears flooded from my face, dripping onto her grey dress. "You'll be okay. You'll be okay." I clutched her body, gripping her tight, trying to cling onto the shred of life she had left.

"I love you, Celtic girl," Marjorie said. I watched her take her last breath and sobbed.

"No! No, no, no," I screamed.

"That's what happens when you go to war, Emlyn. People die," Maeve said. She walked over and bent down to condescendingly pat my back, but I didn't move. My body didn't feel real.

I heard deep sighs of relief behind me as Maeve released her drowning spell for everyone in the room. She wanted to kill us one by one, to torture me with the death of each person.

"I'll do you a favor this time. Who do you want to die next?" Maeve asked me. "You can choose the order. That's a nice gift, right?"

"Maeve, let's talk about this," Blaine tried. He was ready to bargain for his life. He didn't believe we could win anymore.

"Shut it, you. You're lucky I don't string you up and roast you like a hog on a spit," Maeve growled at him.

I couldn't express the amount of loss I'd felt in the last year and a half. First my mother, and now Marjorie. It was grief. Longing and mourning that I'd never felt before. There was also rage. I was angry. One coven had taken two of the people I loved most in this world.

Then I remembered the potion Blaine had slipped me in the other room. I reached for it quietly and found that it was the power-boosting potion Maeve herself had created—the one with her blood.

"I think it's your turn this time, Maeve," I told her.

Maeve laughed. "That's confident coming from a beaten-up goodie-two-shoes who just got her grandmother killed."

I popped the cork off the vial and downed the potion. It tasted coppery, like blood—just as I thought it would. But a shock of power accompanied the metallic flavor. There was a sudden course of strength pulsing through my body. It felt like when Blaine had altered my mood in Maeve's apartment, but this time it came from me. All weakness left my body. My cuts and scrapes and bruises evaporated from existence.

I turned to face Maeve with no doubt in my mind that I'd win.

"They don't learn, do they," Maeve said to no one in particular. She scanned the room and found Emily, hiding behind the sofa. "Emily, you want to speak some sense into your friend?"

I looked at Emily, who appeared both shocked and scared out of her mind.

"Leave my friends alone, Maeve. I'm warning you," I told her.

"Blaine? Quinn? Whoever this third guy is? You want to talk some sense into your girlfriend here?" Maeve scoffed. "She's about to get into a fight she can't handle."

"Don't hold back," I told her.

"Back at you, 'Celtic witch,'" she mocked me.

Maeve threw a fireball at me, and I waved my hand to extinguish the flame with ice. The potion was taking effect, and the power felt exhilarating—almost electric.

"What's happening? Does she have a frost ability now?" I heard Emily whisper to Marnie.

They were afraid and mourning our loss. Fright, sorrow, and fury—I would channel them all against Maeve. I pulled from every shred of force I had left in my body, fueled by memories with Mom, lessons with Marjorie, and the support of my friends.

I screamed at Maeve, "You're done hurting people I love!" I pointed both hands at her, and I felt a surge of energy leave my body and shoot into hers. Maeve's doubtful smirk soon turned to terror as she realized the power of wind couldn't block me. Not this time. Blue frost quickly covered her body in a thick layer of ice where she stood. I literally froze her.

It took me a minute to realize the gravity of what had happened. I stared at Maeve's motionless body as mine trembled with anger. It didn't feel final. There was no rush of relief like I had expected.

"Emlyn?" Emily squeaked out. I looked around the room. Everyone looked scared of me. I didn't have time to deal with their emotions, though. I ran to Emily's side, where she was holding Marjorie's head in her lap. I grabbed Marjorie's hand, and I could feel the life was gone from her.

"Oh, Marjorie," I whimpered with tears flowing down my face. "I can fix it, don't worry. We'll go back. You'll see."

"That's right. Undo it!" Emily smiled, suddenly remembering my ability to rewind time.

"You can't," Marnie interrupted. She was crying too.

"What do you mean I can't? Didn't you see what I just did? This potion made me massively powerful. I have more than enough strength to fix this," I assured her.

Quinn, Jordan, and Blaine approached quietly.

"Marjorie knew this would happen," Marnie explained. "She knew she would die tonight, and it's what she wanted."

"How did she know?" Emily blurted out.

"She had the gift of foresight," I reminded her. "So, she knew? Why does that matter?"

"Marjorie worked through several scenarios for how tonight would end. In all of them, we were victorious against Maeve—but at a cost. Several of us will die if tonight's events play out differently. Marjorie was positive about that."

"But, maybe there's a way," I begged. "This can't be what happens."

Marnie shook her head. "It has to be. I'm sorry. She made me promise not to tell you."

"It's my fault." The words spilled out of my mouth as hot tears dropped onto Marjorie's side. I couldn't explain the combination of guilt and grief. The only person who could understand was Blaine, and only because he could literally feel it. I wasn't about to accept comfort from him, either.

"It wasn't your fault," Quinn said from behind me. He knelt behind me on the floor, wrapped his arms around me, and let me sob for a few minutes. It felt like hours. I couldn't bring myself to let go of Marjorie's hand.

"I hate to break up this moment. I know this is a sad time, and my condolences, Emlyn, but we've still got work to do," Blaine interjected. "While Maeve looks pretty solidly frozen, we can't act like she'll stay that way forever."

"Can't you give her a minute?" Quinn snapped back.

"No." Blaine shook his head. "We need to get this done."

I heard Quinn mutter something under his breath. Words made little sense to me now, though. I didn't comprehend what he said. I wiped my face on my sleeve.

"She might stay frozen forever," I told Blaine.

"How did you do that, Emlyn?" Emily asked. "That's not one of your powers, right?"

"Blaine gave me a potion. It heightened my freezing ability, so I could create real ice. I didn't know it would happen." I heard the words come out of my mouth, but it didn't feel real. It was like this wasn't happening at all.

"We need to strip her powers and send her to another dimension while we still can," Blaine pushed. "Marnie, did you collect the crystals for the spell?"

Marnie nodded. "I'll go get them."

"Another dimension," I said in a monotone.

"Isn't that the plan?" Marnie asked me. She paused, not sure if I was ready.

A tiny fire ignited in the very center of my being. I let go of Marjorie's hand, stood up, and stepped away from Quinn's embrace. "Maeve's evil. It's her fault Marjorie is dead," I said through gritted teeth.

"It is. You need to remember that," Emily told me. "Keep the blame where it belongs. This isn't on you."

"I'm sorry, girl," Jordan added. He looked to Marnie, who still hadn't left to collect the crystals. "How can I help with the dimension spell?"

I shook my head. "No... no. This is wrong. IT'S HER FAULT!" I screeched. Without another thought, I darted to the fireplace across from us and grabbed the iron fire poker.

"Wait, Emlyn!" Quinn called out.

"Emlyn, don't let her do this to you. It's not worth it," Emily echoed.

All my friends were on their feet, spouting objections as if reading my mind. I ignored them, not allowing their voices to disrupt my rage.

"IT'S HER FAULT!" I repeated. With one intentional swing, I thrust the iron rod through Maeve's chest, shattering her frozen body into a million tiny pieces. As the glass-like shards tumbled to the ground, I tossed the fire poker on top of them.

That felt final. It was over. My anxieties, fear, and the pressure of holding the weight of the world fell. There was only one emotion left. I dropped to my knees, overcome with grief.

"Marjorie's gone," I sobbed. "She's really gone."

Chapter Twenty-Three

I hoisted a green cast-iron teapot onto the small stove, lit the burner, and then pulled two cups and saucers from the black cabinet above it. Our original antique stove hadn't survived the battle with Maeve two-and-a-half months ago, but I replaced it with a similar model I found on eBay. The teapot was the same one Marjorie had always used, though. I'd found it in the debris.

I'd done my best to replicate the shop as Marjorie herself had decorated it. I'd painted the back room's new walls navy blue, complete with gold trim around the baseboards. I found new maps to plaster over the walls—places in Ireland mostly—along with a fresh tapestry. There were new bookshelves and trunks filled with what was left of our collection. I was lucky that Marjorie had stashed away the valuable volumes and artifacts before our first fight with Maeve. Some tomes were first editions, and others were the only copies ever created, including our family Book of Shadows.

As the water boiled, I shuffled to the middle of the room and settled into one of the dark brown armchairs. These were finds on Facebook Marketplace. I had the wing-backed chairs reupholstered with the same design as the old ones, featuring golden starbursts. A Tiffany-style lamp and Marjorie's scrying mirror sat on the table between the two chairs.

The quiet was nice. I'd sent everyone out for the day, which was a welcome reprieve from the concerned glances and timid treatment. Jeb and Tephi were snoozing in their favorite corner as if nothing had changed. Of course, everything had.

Then, the moment I was waiting for arrived. The bell on the front door interrupted the silence. Jeb lifted his head, acknowledging the noise, but since I remained calm he deemed it unnecessary to investigate in the other room.

"In the back," I called out.

"Wow, you've done a great job on this place." Blaine stepped through the doorway. "You'd never know what it's been through."

"I wish I could say the same about all of us, but, yes. Jordan's been a big help in the renovations." I motioned toward the empty armchair opposite mine.

"How's the shoulder?" Blaine asked before plopping down.

"It aches from time to time, but I have a full range of motion. It doesn't affect the day to day, which is good. I'm just lucky Lillian didn't hit anything important."

"She never was a good shot," Blaine admitted. "So, Jordan's here still?"

"Yep. When we dropped off Nia's car and picked up Jeb and Tephi, Jordan came back with us. He feels like part of our coven now. I let him take over the apartment upstairs in exchange for helping restore the place."

"He does good work. Everything looks exactly the same."

"No, there's definitely a difference," I told him as I stood up and walked to the stove. I filled two loose-leaf tea bags, poured scorching water over them, dropped a sugar cube in each cup, and turned to Blaine again. "Tea?" I asked him.

He nodded.

"I'm surprised you remembered this meeting." I handed him the cup and saucer. "Two months of no communication is a long time, considering."

"Come on, lover. I wouldn't forget you. But, can we get down to business? I have an evil headquarters to run." He winked.

"There are some follow-up things I need to know. Can you recap everything that's happened? My end of things is same-old-same-old, but what's going on with the Ainbertachs?"

"The death of his daughter was not pleasing to Fionn Ainbertach, especially when I explained how she died. Laying Maeve to rest in pieces was not Fionn's ideal scenario. You threw me a curveball, not sticking with the dimensional shift plan. It probably would've gone over better with the family, but I spun it well."

I settled into my chair and took a sip of tea. I let the comment about Maeve's death roll off me. "The cadavers you used were successful? They know Marjorie is dead and think I am too?"

Blaine nodded. "Fionn sent a few of his 'true Irish' minions to assess both bodies. It probably would've been easier if you let me keep Marjorie's body, but I made due."

"Good."

"This is excellent tea, by the way." Blaine made a playful slurping sound.

"One of Marnie's blends"

"St. John's Wort?"

I nodded.

"Is the depression that bad, Em?"

I ignored his question. "How are things looking on your end? They put you in charge, right? Any lingering suspicions?"

"It's good to be at the top. You thinned the ranks well, if I'm honest. New recruits are scared to join us after what you did. They know most of the previous coven members had their powers stripped. Not a good selling point."

"Less evil in the world is fine by me," I told him flatly.

"I've still got Daryl. His mind had to be wiped for obvious reasons, but he's a fighter. I'm just hoping this interim leader position turns to a permanent one."

"You think they'd pick someone else to take over? Maybe send someone from Ireland?"

"Maybe. The leaders don't have the utmost faith in me. Technically, it's my fault you weren't killed the first time, which makes it my fault Maeve died."

"Well, you also plotted to kill her."

"True, but they don't know that. Power means a lot to this family, and killing you earned me the benefit of the doubt in this case."

"So, I'm dead? I killed Maeve in a rage for murdering Marjorie," I choked over her name, "and you supposedly gutted me after I took out Maeve?"

"Exactly."

"Don't take this the wrong way, but why would they believe you could kill me when Maeve couldn't? Your powers aren't extraordinary. I killed Maeve in two moves." The words came out more harshly than I meant them to.

"Need I remind you, Emlyn, you needed that potion to annihilate Maeve so easily. According to my story, I used the same potion to murder you."

"I took a potion, and I killed her. I didn't even need the medallion." I said to myself. There was a moment of silence, and then I realized how weird I was acting. I took another sip of tea.

"Are you okay, Em? You took a life. Are you dealing with that?"

It was a loaded question from an empath. Blaine could likely feel everything going on inside me. It would've been easy to admit that part of me was struggling. I felt guilt and shame, knowing I broke the cardinal rule of our coven. "Harm None" was taken seriously in our magic, and I hadn't followed the old ways.

I also could've confessed that killing Maeve felt like the right decision, and I'd do it one hundred times over. Everyone I loved slept more peacefully, knowing Maeve would never show up in our lives again. Had we stripped her powers, she could've come back and found a way to make us pay for that mercy.

The thing I was struggling with most, though, was the loss of Marjorie. It was hard not to blame myself or question whether I could've been smarter or stronger. What if I had known how powerful I'd be with that potion? We could've stolen the potion from Blaine before we ever left for New Orleans. Marjorie told Marnie this was the way things were meant to work out, but I didn't believe that. There was always another way.

Despite Marnie's objections, I tried traveling back to the first fight with Maeve dozens of times. It didn't matter, though. No matter how hard I tried, my powers only allowed me to observe the events of that day. I couldn't change the past. It was too far in the past to rewind. I had to accept the loss of Marjorie as a permanent one.

"I'm fine."

"Convincing," Blaine smiled at me.

"When do you find out if you got the promotion permanently?" I changed the subject.

"I'm flying out to Ireland tomorrow to meet Fionn in person."

"Are you sure he isn't going to kill you?"

"Tickets are first class. I kind of think Fionn would've stuck me in coach if he wanted me dead."

"You never know."

"I'll keep my eyes open."

I nodded.

"You know, you seem like you could use a little cheering up. You want to go out tonight and grab some dinner? It'd be like old times, before you knew I was ordered to kill you." Blaine seemed amused at his comment.

"It's a tempting offer, but I've got plans already."

"I'll see myself out then. You know how to reach me?" He pulled my old scrying mirror, the one connected to Marjorie's, out of his chest pocket. I had given it to him before we left the mansion, in case an emergency presented itself as he was tying up loose ends. There didn't seem to be a reason to take it back now.

"Thanks, Blaine. For everything."

He nodded and then walked out the way he'd come. A few seconds later, the chime on the shop's front door rang, letting me know Blaine was gone. I took a few minutes to mull everything over in my head. According to Blaine, I was a free witch. Before our deal, I didn't think this was possible.

I looked at the clock and sighed as I turned to Jeb. "I guess it's that time, isn't it?"

I walked over to a floor-length mirror on the far side of the room, checking my appearance briefly. My forest-green velvet dress was knee-length over a pair of brown tights. Being January, it was actually cold in Savannah. I'd debated wearing pants or something warmer, but I wanted to look nice. I bundled up with a hat, scarf, and gloves before applying a final swipe of mascara.

Around the time I finished primping, I heard the chime on the door for the third time. Now was the moment. I took a deep breath before clipping leashes on Jeb and Tephi. We walked out to the front room, which had also been beautifully restored by Jordan, to meet Emily, Jordan, Marnie, and Quinn. Like me, they all wore cozy winter gear over fancy clothes.

"Are you ready, Emlyn?" Emily asked me softly.

I nodded, fighting the urge to cry. It felt like I was always battling tears. I grabbed my messenger bag off the glass display case and followed them out the door to Marjorie's SUV, which was now my SUV. Marnie picked up Tephi so she could ride on Marnie's lap. Jeb jumped into the back cargo area, placing his head on my shoulder after I climbed into the backseat. I let Quinn drive. Bonaventure Cemetery was 15 minutes away, and we rode there in silence.

When we arrived, we kept Jeb and Tephi on leashes, allowing them to walk beside us as we made our way to the correct plot. It was comforting to have my friends with me, but I still felt lonely. Dad was already there when we reached our destination. He leaned down to pet Jeb and then wrapped me in a hug.

"I'm so sorry, Emlyn." He held me briefly and then released me so I could wipe my eyes.

"Thanks for coming, Dad," I told him.

He hugged Emily as well and nodded to Quinn. Jordan and Marnie introduced themselves and offered their sympathies, as people usually did in graveyards. I tuned it out mostly.

Múireann "Marjorie" Finnerty was buried next to her husband, my grandfather, Daniel Finnerty. It wasn't too far from where my mother, Rhiannon, was buried. Tephi immediately darted over to Marjorie's grave and curled up into a ball on the plot. There were fresh flowers—lilies—placed around the headstone. I'd visited frequently in the last two months.

This was a more special occasion, though. With my friends and father behind me, I walked up to Marjorie's grave, pulled her ritual goblet from my messenger bag, and placed it on the ground beside the marble stone. I uncorked a bottle of ceremonial wine and poured Marjorie a glass before taking a sip from the bottle. Jeb whined in response as he moved closer to sit by my side.

"Lá breithe shona duit, Múireann," I whispered before passing the bottle to Emily at my right.

"Happy Birthday, Marjorie," Emily and Marnie said together. They both took sips from the bottle and passed it down the line.

"Thank you for your sacrifice," Quinn nodded at Marjorie's grave.

"Respect, Marjorie," Jordan echoed.

My father spoke last. When he took the bottle, he looked at each of us, only able to imagine what we'd gone through together. He hadn't asked a lot of questions when we returned. He just seemed happy to have us back safe. I didn't show him the wound in my shoulder, but there was no hiding Marjorie's death. Maybe keeping him in the dark was worse. I doubted any explanation he might have come up with would be any worse than the truth. Maybe my father would never accept magic, but now I knew he would support me. He was at the grave with us.

"I'm not great with words. Marjorie, you and Daniel gave me the best gift I could ever have asked for in Rhiannon. Then we had Emlyn. We love her more than anything. You protected her, and I thank you for that. Happy Birthday. Celebrate with Rhiannon."

Dad took a sip of wine and looked at me for approval, hoping his words were enough. They were more than I expected. I nodded, and he handed me the bottle back.

I poured the rest of the bottle out over her grave as I sang the traditional Irish song, "The Parting Glass."

"O, all the money e'er I had,
I spent it in good company.
And all the harm that ever I've done,
Alas it was to none but me.
And all I've done for want of wit
To mem'ry now I can't recall;
So fill to me the parting glass,
Good night and joy be with you all."

I looked around to my friends as I sat near the grave with tears flowing freely from my eyes. Marnie and Dad chimed in, since they also knew the song.

"O, all the comrades e'er I had,
They're sorry for my going away.
And all the sweethearts e'er I had,
They'd wished me one more day to stay.
But since it falls unto my lot,
That I should rise and you should not,
I gently rise and softly call,
Goodnight and joy be with you all.

If I had money enough to spend,
And leisure time to sit awhile.
There is a fair maid in this town,
That sorely has my heart beguiled.
Her rosy cheeks and ruby lips,
I own, she has my heart in thrall;
Then fill to me the parting glass,
Good night and joy be with you all."

Emily knelt down beside me on one side. My father did the same opposite her. They both embraced me and then stepped away.

I wasn't sure how long I sat there staring at Marjorie's grave. Jeb remained by my side the entire time, along with Tephi, who wouldn't leave the plot. When we arrived, the sun was high in the sky. Now it was low, the remaining light turned orange and red.

Dad was the first to leave. He nodded at everyone and kissed me on the head before departing. Finally, Marnie, Jordan, and Emily gathered Tephi and Jeb, and they left too. Quinn stayed behind with me. We sat in silence for a while. I'd already been through Marjorie's wake and the burial, so I wasn't sure why her birthday was so difficult for me.

"You know, it's not your fault, Emlyn," Quinn assured me. "You can't go on like this anymore. I know you're grieving, but we're all worried about you."

"She was my connection," I told him. "She was all I had left."

"Your connection to the magic?"

"To Mom." I used the sleeve of my dress to wipe tears from my face. "And I let her down. She would've been disappointed in me."

"No, Emlyn. She was so proud of you. Everyone could see that. She even told you right before she died."

"That was before I broke the rule," I told him.

"It was self-defense. Maeve would've come after us again, and you have the right to defend yourself. It's a judicial law for a reason."

"It's not the law of the coven. Marjorie wouldn't have killed."

"You don't know that."

I shook my head. It wasn't worth the discussion. I took one final look at Marjorie's grave and then stood up. As I brushed the debris off my dress, Quinn grabbed my hands in his and looked into my eyes.

"I can't imagine what you're going through, but I'm here for you. We've been through so much together. We've got a bond that doesn't seem willing to break. It's fate, you and me."

I smiled at him before pulling my hands from his. I didn't respond. I wasn't sure what to say.

"Are you okay? You're acting so strangely. Did Blaine have bad news when he came by today? Do they know you're alive?"

"No. The coven believed the entire story. They won't come searching for us anymore," I told Quinn flatly.

"Are you serious? That's fantastic news!" Quinn cheered. "Why aren't you happy? Don't you understand? We can be together now. It's over!"

I shook my head. "No, Quinn. It's not even close to over."

Epilogue

Blaine's heart raced as he entered the throne room. It was times like these when Blaine wished he could use his empathic abilities on himself. His emotions were mixed. On the one hand, he was thrilled at the idea of being appointed as the Ainbertach Coven's first empath leader. Still, he was nervous about meeting with the Ainbertach patriarch in person. Blaine knew the plan had worked perfectly, and there was no reason for him to worry.

"Blaine Corwin?" A thick West Cork, Irish accent greeted him as he entered the stone chamber.

"My lords, Fionn and Fintan," Blaine replied as he approached the two men, who were regally seated on massive and intricately carved oaken thrones.

The room was magnificent, with chandeliers comprised of antlers hanging from the rafters. Banners of green and yellow hung from the walls, embellished with Celtic knots. A matching rug stretched 100 feet from the entrance all the way to the dais supporting the two men's thrones. Rustic benches lined both sides of the room near the dais, where a council of elders would sit during important meetings. Blaine noted they were empty as he approached. This was a closed conference.

Fionn and Fintan were both dressed in traditional robes. They stared down at Blaine with neutral faces, which made him more anxious. He couldn't read their emotions. Both men had silver hair, but Fionn was aged. His wrinkled skin was apparent even from a distance. Blaine knew magic was hard on the body, and Fionn had used a lot in his years leading the coven. Fionn wore his hair flowing down to his shoulders with a golden circlet around his head. In his youth he had been broader, with big shoulders and massive biceps, but he'd shrunk with age. What Fionn had lost, Fintan more than made up for. Fintan's body was all muscle. His hair was cut short, military style, and he'd opted out of the circlet.

"Was your task successful?" Fintan demanded.

"Yes, sir," Blaine nodded. "Emlyn feels no remorse for killing Maeve. Her depressed state is caused entirely by the loss of her grandmother."

"Then my daughter's death was a valuable sacrifice," Fionn stated. "The time manipulator is a worthy asset."

"And you're certain your plan will work?" Fintan questioned.

"Emlyn will be yours," Blaine promised.

"She'd better."

CPSIA information can be obtained
at www.ICGtesting.com
Printed in the USA
BVHW071445240720
584414BV00001B/53